'The most evocative parts of *The Marriage of Souls*, set in the Hampshire port of Lymington in 1798, describe the ominous rhythms of the salt-furnaces that dominate the surrounding landscape . . . The resulting atmosphere of smoke and gloom, periodically ignited by violent fires, is keyed to the novel's primary concern: the obscure motivations, repressed desires and sporadic passionate eruptions of its secretive cast . . . 'I perceive the nimbus of light, the faint emanations of sound,' as Hargood puts it, 'and try to deduce the shadowy structures and form of the world beneath.' . . . Collins pursues this goal with poise and skill. His ability to sustain interest in an outwardly uneventful plot, or in the merely internal trajectories of his protagonists' ongoing discoveries and resolutions, is striking' *Times Literary Supplement*

'Warwick Collins' descriptive powers are wonderfully evocative' *Daily Mail*

Warwick Collins is the author of six previous novels. One of them, *Gents*, portrays the lives of three Jamaican immigrants who work in a London lavatory; internationally acclaimed, *The Times* described it as 'profound, funny and tender'. Another novel, *Computer One*, elucidates the arcane world of artificial intelligence and the insidious threat it poses to humanity's future. Praising its eerie power, Arthur C. Clarke wrote, 'This novel really frightened me. I thought the last word had been said on artificial intelligence, but I was wrong . . . Move over, HAL.'

Increasingly recognised as a writer of international standing, Collins' Lymington trilogy, which began with *The Rationalist* and continues with *The Marriage of Souls*, promises to become one of modern literature's most ambitious fictional sequences.

The Marriage of Souls

WARWICK COLLINS

PHŒNIX

A PHOENIX PAPERBACK

First published in Great Britain
by Weidenfeld & Nicolson in 1999
This paperback edition published in 2000 by Phoenix,
an imprint of Orion Books Ltd,
Orion House, 5 Upper St Martin's Lane,
London WC2H 9EA

A CIP catalogue record for this book
is available from the British Library.

ISBN: 0 75380 988 5

Printed and bound in Great Britain by
Clays Ltd, St Ives plc

TO *Georgina Capel*

ACKNOWLEDGEMENTS

My deepest thanks are due to Fiona Stansbury, for her help and encouragement during the writing of the early drafts, to my editor Maggie McKernan and to Jude James for his historical advice. Any remaining errors or divergences from history are entirely my own.

Liberty, far from putting man in possession of himself, ceaselessly alienates him from his essence and his world.

MICHEL FOUCAULT *Madness and Civilisation*

'Art thou a silk-worm? Dost thou spin thy own shroud out of thyself?'

HERMAN MELVILLE *Moby Dick*

CHAPTER 1

From his study window, Dr Silas Grange stared out across the mouth of the Lymington river towards the Isle of Wight. Clouds were building there, presaging one of the late summer storms that seemed to be blown in on the south-west wind. Cloud shadows drifted across the white cliffs, where occasional flashes of sunlight turned the sheer faces a light gold. Towards Yarmouth, where the outgoing Solent tide was strongest, white water had begun to foam as wind met tide. A small lighter, reefed against the rising wind, had entered the foaming water and seemed suddenly affected by a perturbation, pitching and rolling sharply.

Grange shifted his position to ease a cramp in his left leg and glanced down at the scatter of red-roofed houses that formed the southern half of the town. At the quay a tangled mass of masts denoted the fishing fleet, port-bound against the rising storm. He could see a gang of men unloading rough hemp sacks of coal from a barge and another loading the coal onto a train of ox-carts that would transport it to the salt furnaces which lined the mainland coast from Milford to Beaulieu. Staring down from his advantage, he considered the provenance of the town.

Set on an inlet from the Solent, between Southampton and Christchurch, Lymington had been one of the earliest of those independent boroughs which seemed to spring up at the periphery of the great estates that dominated the local area of Hampshire. A small haven outside the feudal system, its own burgesses administered peremptory law and were jealous of its power. A precarious living was obtained from the manufacture of salt, which had begun in the locality as early as Roman times, and by barter and trade through the port on the Lymington river. In its somewhat chequered past the borough had defended its independence against numerous lawsuits, which were brought against it both by the surrounding landowners and the state, and in return it did not hesitate to sue in its own interests. Perhaps because of this, there had always been present, in its behaviour, the trace of a radical disposition, a certain nonconformity which set it at odds with the administration of the kingdom and the central authority of London. During the Civil War the borough had been a Parliamentarian stronghold and had suffered for its anti-royalism. After that, almost as if from instinct, it had supported the pretender Monmouth and his rebellion, though this time it escaped more lightly the depredations of state justice. So it continued into Grange's own time, pursuing its own interests, often at variance with its neighbours and rivals such as Southampton.

Ports are notorious for the free flow of ideas, transported on the backs of goods like fleas on a rat. In Lymington, the export of salt to the New World maintained the flow of travellers and radical ideas to and from distant shores. Refugees from Europe, most recently from the Revolution in France, provided a further yeast of opinions. Such refugees were largely welcomed in Lymington. A number of these birds of passage had settled in the locality and a smaller number had taken up their lives in new occupations or professions. The refugees of the French Revolution, in particular, had gathered so thickly that a regiment had been formed. As part of this Gallic influx, perhaps a century later, the exotic poet Paul Verlaine, notorious indigent and lover of Rimbaud, would teach for a time at a respectable girls' school, Murdoch's, on the High Street.

In 1798, though Dr Silas Grange had left the capital city some fourteen years before for a country practice, he was nevertheless sometimes reminded of London by the industrial environs of Lymington. The industry of extracting salt from sea water by means of evaporation and boiling was still thriving. It had been reported to the Crown as early as 1660, for example, that the Lymington salt furnaces burned more coal in the course of that year than all of London. By the late eighteenth century the industry had not yet suffered the decline which would later be caused by the mining of crystallised salt in Cheshire and its cheap shipment by railroads to coastal cities such as Liverpool. Now, in the heat of the summer months, between Pylewell and Pennington, out towards Oxey, all the salt furnaces were at full blast. High plumes of smoke were printed on the air, turning into a grey cloud of ash, which was carried on the prevailing south-west wind, depositing cinders and brine over the town and the surrounding New Forest. In the lee of the furnaces, for several miles inland towards Brockenhurst and Beaulieu, the tree trunks were grey or black with the deposits that had drifted with the wind.

At some deeper level Grange associated this burning with Lymington's past, with the soul or spirit of the place, which appeared to hang like smoke in the atmosphere, sustained and pervasive. Several times in earlier centuries the town had been burnt by the French, the last time in 1545. Yet it grew again, as a spirit might put on flesh. Its history of death and resurrection seemed to hover in the permanent dark horizon to seaward.

The summer cloud of industry could be observed even from a distance. As part of his duties he had sometimes visited Winchester to consult colleagues and once or twice had been summoned to offer medical evidence at the Salisbury assizes. Returning to Lymington from the landward side, through Burley or Sway, he observed the Lymington church tower of St Thomas and its surrounding buildings against a background of smoke and steam. It looked once again like a town that had been sacked, that was in the process of being permanently sacked and constantly rising out of its own flames. To Grange such smoke was an evanescence, evidence of the rumbustious life of the borough. He had grown used to the strange combination of New Forest and smoke-belching furnace. That it might hover between rural idyll and hellish industry no longer struck him as incongruous.

As he surveyed this small scene through his study window, the rising sea breeze removed the cloud of smoke to windward, though it left threads of smoke, fine as skeletons, from the salt furnaces. He came to the end of his reverie and, turning back from the window, returned to his desk.

CHAPTER 2

To Mr Henry Leman, Surgeon, Grant Way, Winchester, from Dr James Hargood, Physician, Court Lodge, Lymington.

7 July 1798

My dear Leman,

It did my heart good to see you again, my old friend, and in such good health. I dare believe you may have lost a little thatch on your roof over the last few years, but the ruddiness of your complexion and your good spirits are both, I should add, testimony to the power of your constitution.

I cannot count the months since we shared a measure of Bordeaux wine and discussed our Mr Fox, or the excess of French refugees in these parts after the troubles in France – or (since we speak of the French) the disastrous effects of the Quiberon expedition which has depleted us of a number of our former acquaintances in Lymington. I do recall that before our royalist allies were massacred on French shores in that ill-fated landing, the town seemed to hold as many French refugees as native English in its environs. At the height of their amiable occupation there were at the last count upwards of some 4000 foreign soldiers in Lymington, supported and sustained by a local population of hardly more than 2000. Even after the destruction of the French there remain large contingents of Dutch and Germans, and a sufficient motley of others, so that on certain days one may still walk from Gosport Street to Church Lane and hear nothing but foreign tongues.

Part of my solace during this occupation has been an acquaintance with certain of those refugees from France, whose character I have begun increasingly to admire. I had become as · used to the elaborate manners of their noblemen as to the genial roguery of their infantry. Yet after their brave attempted landing on the Normandy coast, and the massacre which followed their defeat by the Revolutionary forces, our town is rendered ghostly by their absence. Even so, the traces remain. I

4

observe certain young women who consorted with them and have myself assisted on several occasions in bringing into this world a number of their offspring. A generation of children will never see their fathers. I had not thought the terrible hand of the Revolution would reach into Lymington.

For the time being I leave aside that other subject which I raised, and which has to do with a difficult and personal matter of the heart. We spoke of it briefly when last we met, and perhaps, fate willing, you may permit me to raise it again in due course. I shall desist from mentioning it further in this letter for no other reason than that those things among which it began have not yet run their course, even though they may rumble in the distance, like those autumn storms that will soon begin to affect us.

My good friend, I believe that any retrospect of my inward life is difficult and perhaps a little obscure, even to my own view. Having reached three score years, it befits a man in my position to seek something of detachment. In some things I may seem to improve a little, but the flesh and the world still have a fearful hold upon me. My only consolation is that the thoughts which accompany me in my introspections may be darker than the actions which give rise to them. Yet the actions themselves continue to occupy me and to throw off some heat. I keep a mistress in London, though when have I not? And thus, though I may be tempted in certain things, at the same time certain other temptations begin to lessen with age. It is not my physical state which perplexes – in that, at least, I remain surprisingly robust. It is, instead, a particular humour which overlays my life. I begin to arrive at a condition of increasing morbidity or inactivity, where I may be mercifully free of any guilt regarding the temptations themselves, but not the thoughts that surround them. As a widower of some eighteen years, much used by now to my own devices, I believe I am not obliged to account for my behaviour to any other. Yet I feel that some part of me is missing or perhaps empty, and that, if I am not constrained to account for it to another, I am at least obliged to explain my behaviour to myself. In this final matter, perhaps all that is left is to accuse myself of committing 'adultery in the heart', and also that sin which I believe is well called *delectatio morosa* (the enjoyment of evil without the intention of action).

In another respect, though it be only loosely connected with the above, I have need of your counsel – or rather, your sympathetic witness – if you could spare me but a little time and your most esteemed attention. For I know that I am reaching an age in my life in which the sands are shifting once again and, despite a good living and some measure of social acceptability, I am subject to a kind of upheaval, whose dimensions and extent I do not fully understand. We may prepare ourselves for what we know, but against the unpredictable there are no adequate defences, except perhaps to trust in the temperance of fate and our own fortitude. I am apprehensive, nevertheless, of this interval between the stations of my life. Before the intimation of one's fate and its arrival there is an uneasy interregnum which must simply be endured.

In the meantime I must grow used again to writing as if to a friend. For the mere act of it, I find, is a consolation, perhaps even what the ancient Greeks called a *katharsis*. Committing these thoughts to paper in the quiet of the day is perhaps not unlike prayer – at least in its outward aspect. It concentrates the mind, though in other respects I believe I have lost most if not all of the religious disposition I once felt so naturally.

Perhaps the best that I may do with this strange business is to begin by opening an account in your sympathies, and to start as I mean to continue. For, if you will permit me, I mean to write to you regularly, for the good of my soul and the comfort of my conscience. During the course of these missives, I will attempt to convey that which concerns me, and which exercises my mind, as best as I am able.

And now, my dear Leman, I must add one final thought, which I believe is necessary both to the founding and the continuation of our present correspondence. I shall write to you about these matters on one condition only, which will seem strange to you in the first instance, though I trust you will perceive the circumstances in which the undertaking must be given. My condition shall be as follows. Much though I desire your views and opinions, I beg of you on no account should you reply to my letters. For if you respond, I will feel that I am placing upon you too onerous a burden of friendship and goodwill, and will cease to communicate my thoughts to paper. It would suffice, indeed more than suffice, if you would be kind enough to read what I shall write and, having perused these indeterminate and inchoate scratchings, take no further action.

If, sir, as I most humbly propose, you will be kind enough to follow these principles, for my part I shall take your silence as agreement that my correspondence may continue and thus, every day that passes without a letter from you will be an encouragement to me, that you are keeping to the bargain we have struck. My most earnest wish is merely that your kindly and beneficent eye has considered such thoughts as I may set down, however ill-informed and random they may be.

Thus, my dear friend, each day that you do not reply you will be affecting a kind permission for me to write further, and so I hope we may proceed, from day to day, by tacit agreement, until these matters are perhaps resolved.

I trust that you are as well as when we last met, and that your good wife and two daughters enjoy a similar health.

In the meanwhile, I remain, as ever,

Yours sincerely,

Hargood

CHAPTER 3

A wind in August, after a season of burning, would raise so many ashes and grits in Lymington that it was wise to shield one's eyes when climbing the High Street against the wind.

Mrs Thompson, Dr Grange's housekeeper, raised her arm to hold on her shawl as she made her way up the hill from the market at the lower end of the High Street. Carrying a half-dozen mackerel from Flushards, she halted briefly so that she could shift her heavy basket from one arm to the other, placing the handle in the crook of her elbow, which freed her hand to pull up her heavy skirts an inch or two, raising the outer hem of her dress against the dust of the road. As she advanced upwards, a little out of breath from the exercise of these various precautions, she kept a cautious eye on the terrain ahead of her, careful to protect her shoes from the piles of cattle dung, sheep and pig droppings that lay, a little too generously for her liking, about the roadway. Her progress up the High Street thus seemed to her like a ship navigating between islands, upon which the unwary could founder.

Reaching Dr Grange's house, she raised the latch of the spruce side gate and swung it open, passing through so that she could close it and lean against it in respite from the wind. Her eyes still smarted from the blown dust. There were sometimes gales in late summer and cold northerly winds that swept down the High Street from the Church at St Thomas, whistling in the gutters, causing the shop signs to sway and creak, and the casement windows to shudder. Ensconced in her temporary haven, she felt the brief shiver of the gate against her back as several gusts struck it and then rebounded down the street. Having rested for a few moments in the lee of the gate, she proceeded to the side door.

She hung her shawl and coat on the iron hooks on the inside of the door, then walked through the scullery into the kitchen itself. In the quietness of the kitchen she began to unload her basket, placing two fresh cod and the shining corpses of six mackerel on the oak sideboard. She poured water from a pitcher into a bowl and rinsed each of the fish in fresh water, wiping off the loose scales and effluvia that had collected on the fish stall. When the fish were cleaned to her satisfaction, she laid them out neatly on the scrubbed oak boards and poured a bowl of fresh water. Opening a wooden drawer, she removed a short, sharp knife and set it down beside the bowl. She was about to begin the evisceration, when something caused her to pause.

It was a sound like a sigh, of exasperation or perhaps resignation, the faint creak as a body shifted in a chair, then the whisper of a page being turned. The sounds seemed to impress themselves softly on the air. In the quietness of the kitchen Mrs Thompson waited.

The interior of the house was silent, except for the odd crackling of the flames of a fire in the sitting-room. She listened, but no further sound came. Taking up the knife, she began to gut the fish, slitting open the belly, scraping the liver and kidneys and alimentary canal into the nearby bucket. She sliced off the head and tail, and slipped the remaining body into the bowl of fresh water. Blood spread in a faint pink halo around the gutted and cleaned torsos.

When she was finished, Mrs Thompson set down the kitchen knife and wiped her hands on a cloth.

Dr Silas Grange, seated in front of the fire in the sitting-room, had heard her enter the scullery and the sounds of a meal being prepared. After a little while she halted. He waited while she paused in the kitchen, as if listening to him, then he heard her footsteps as she proceeded through to the dining-room to set the table.

As she passed the door she could see that he was seated in the taller of the two drawing-room chairs, facing the fire. Carefully she set the table for two courses, although she assumed that he would only accept the fish broth.

She knew that her master had walked that day and that the effort had brought on the shaking of his hands. When she entered the drawing-room he was still seated in the tall chair, resting a book on his thin legs, his long spine crouched over the opened volume. She could see the faint tremor of his hands as he turned a page. He seemed oblivious to her entrance.

Mrs Thompson stood still in the doorway, an impressive and buxom figure. She regarded him with a passionate objectivity.

Perhaps he sensed her presence by a slight occlusion of the light, or possibly the very intensity of her concentration somehow entered his thoughts. Whatever the reason, Grange stirred now from his book to look up at her, as though from some deep well. 'Good morning, Mrs Thompson. You have returned from the market?'

'Yes, sir.' Mrs Thompson considered the pallor of his face. 'I have bought and prepared fish for your broth.'

'Thank you.'

She considered him again, then said, 'I shall be serving in an hour.'

'Good.' He nodded, turned a page, bent his head towards the page and began once more to read.

9

Mrs Thompson paused. 'There is nothing more substantial that you would like to eat ... ?'

His head came up again, slowly, though he did not look directly at her this time. 'No, thank you.'

There was an implacable firmness in his decision that rendered any further discussion of the topic difficult. He looked at the wall for several seconds as though in contemplation. She in turn considered the line of his forehead, the almost vertical bridge of his nose, the mouth like a firm cut. There was no softness there that she could see, and precious little pliability.

Mrs Thompson was persistent, persistent beyond the call of duty. But persistence is nine-tenths patience and she knew she must wait. From her position in the doorway she watched him return once again to his reading.

She took advantage of the brief impasse to look around the room. There was a fine layer of dark soot on the window-sills, the accumulation of black grime from the salt furnaces that lined the windward shores of Woodside, Oxey and Pennington. She viewed the activities of the salt furnaces with unmitigated disapproval. It was the last of the summer's burning and the furnaces seemed to have redoubled their efforts. At night the shore was like the devil's industry, a network of small roofed structures with open doors and great fires burning inside. Discernible through the open doors were human figures, which appeared to move in a trance of concentration. The furnaces' dark powder, blown by the wind towards Lymington, seemed to her like the faint evidence of hell. Every few days during the summer months she set about with clean rags to obliterate the traces of the soot on the window-sills and upper surfaces of furniture.

Soon, in a matter of a few weeks, she knew the burning of the furnaces would halt and she could return to her normal regime. It was her conviction that the state of the house was too much of an affront on the eye to allow further time to elapse. There was a little interval before she would begin to prepare the meal in earnest. Standing behind Grange's chair, she decided she would clean the surfaces first and return afterwards to the cooking of the fish.

She was in the middle of these considerations when Grange,

turning a page, looked up at her, standing thoughtfully in the doorway. Caught unawares, Mrs Thompson said, 'I think I should clean the furniture again.'

Grange looked around him at the room and smiled. 'I believe your eyes are sharper than mine, Mrs Thompson.'

'It is a habit with women', Mrs Thompson said, 'to have an eye for such matters.'

She nodded to him and returned to the kitchen. In a drawer she found some rags and strips of old bedsheets. Gathering several pieces of cloth, she set about her work in the dining-room, taking particular care with the lintels and surfaces nearest the windows, where the soot seemed thickest.

CHAPTER 4

After perhaps half an hour of reading, Grange put the book aside, stood up and walked towards the window. He glanced down at the marshes. Then he moved through the sitting-room to the hallway.

She heard him walking up the stairs, his footsteps interrupted only by the occasional soft thump as the heel of his hand struck the banisters. He was still weak enough to have to use his hand for support. When he reached the landing he paused for breath, then she heard the creaking swing of his study door. In the brief ensuing silence Mrs Thompson stopped wiping the furniture, the rag paused in her hand, as she waited patiently to pick up the next trace of his movements.

She heard the drift and slide of a piece of furniture being moved, then a pause as he seemed to gather his breath.

Mrs Thompson considered Grange with an undisclosed mixture of emotions. When she did not hold him directly in sight, she listened to the sound of his footsteps on the oak boards above, invoking in the restlessness of his boots the perplexities of his mind. His indifference and his stray motions seemed to infect the fabric of the house. Sometimes one of the joists would emit a low moan or an internal sigh as he shifted weight in his chair. Sometimes he

paced slowly backwards and forwards, or crossed the floor to bring
down a book. She waited for the irregular heartbeat of his footsteps
across the boards, or the murmur of complaint in a settling timber.

A chair leg scraped the floor above, followed by the faint slump
of his body into the chair. She guessed that he had begun to read
again, though she observed that these days he no longer read
Hume. Perhaps he associated Hume too much with the circumstances of his badly reduced physical state and with the loss of Mrs
Quill from Lymington. Mrs Thompson had hoped that her caring
for him had established a base for greater expression of the
emotions, at least in the communication of his fears and apprehen-
sions. But, like an animal which retreats to its own lair, in the
process of recovery he had become more private still.

She finished wiping the furniture and, putting the rag in a metal
trunk in which she stored odds and ends, she moved through to the
kitchen. Taking a sharp knife from the drawer, she prepared to slice
the mackerel for the soup. She could hear no further movement
from upstairs. Standing on the stone flags in front of the scrubbed
teak boards, she began to make his meal, her mind still attentive to
the plenitude of silence that had now descended on the house.

CHAPTER 5

My dear Leman,
You have begun our correspondence as I had hoped, by not
replying to my letter, even though a week has passed since I
wrote to you. I thank you for your abstinence, kind friend.
Taking your lack of response as permission to write further, I
will therefore begin those missives which I mentioned.

On account of your clemency, I will make a start by raising
that which concerns me and proceed from it to those matters
which actively perturb me, though I do not yet fully understand
their import.

You will know that my young colleague Silas Grange, who

has a nature both more studious and more serious than my own, has established a firm reputation in Lymington as a physician. He is educated, you may recall, in Scottish academies, which may partially account for the oddness of some of his opinions and also, perhaps, for a vein of radicalism in his thought. No soul can be entirely perfect. These matters aside, and though I may disagree with him on virtually every subject which we raise, I have found him a most engaging companion. We collaborate in many matters and, when I have had occasion to visit my mistress in London, he has been kind enough to accept, during the time of my absence, the added burden of my own patients. In the past I have had the chance to reciprocate in my turn by relieving him of his own duties on those occasions when he is taken low, or when he wishes to walk the marshes for a day (for he is something of a student of nature and collects specimens of local flora). More recently, however, I have had more opportunity to repay in some degree that debt I owe him for my regular sojourns in London. It happens that – somewhat unexpectedly for one who had committed himself so punctiliously and profoundly to the celibate life – he has pursued his own matter of the heart. With this *extempore*, I shall now proceed to relate that which concerns me.

There arrived in our community, some three years ago, a widow called Mrs Celia Quill. She took residence in a house called The Gaskills, set upon Walhampton Hill, and proceeded by slow degrees, but with a calm confidence, to establish herself as an influence in local society. She is a singularly handsome woman, with easy manners and a mind which, though it has its serious side, charms others by its good nature and lack of affectation. It is her very ease, and the confidence she spreads about her, which have caused her to win numerous friends among the female sex and some admirers among the male. She is unusual in her independence, for just as Silas Grange seems to make earnest bachelorhood a profession, so she has striven to make her widowhood a thing of grace. I cannot easily describe her character to you, except to say that she is sympathetic and at the same time detached. Her companionship is genuine, yet she appears to make no claim on the attention or loyalties of others. On those occasions where a person has had cause to rely on her, by such accounts as we may trust, she has proved a most sympathetic and discreet *confidante*.

Above all, she is charitable. There is no one in our local society who has been so consistent in her devotions towards the less fortunate. Among her various activities aimed at alleviation in the parish, she has established a committee to fund some improvements to the Poor House, in the form of several small additional workhouses which our rates would not of themselves support. But these are more than good intentions, or the proceedings of cold virtue. For, like a good commander, she leads from a forward position, and no one works more determinedly in the execution of her own good works. Whether it is knitting or sewing, or collecting clothes from gentlefolk which, though they are no longer the fashion, will serve to clothe some poor body against the cold, she is always the most assiduous of her company in supplying the needy. In these activities she has proceeded with a singular determination, as if her life has no greater cause than to fulfil those charitable obligations she has placed upon herself.

So you may see, my dear Leman, it was something of a surprise, and perhaps even a consternation, when these two paragons of the independent life, my younger colleague and Mrs Celia Quill, should begin to form a bond of sympathy, an alliance of minds at first and, in due course it would seem, even some intimacy of the heart. I noticed them at certain social gatherings, with their heads together in confabulation, and I observed further that if I should decide to join with them in some discussion of events, more often than not I experienced that strange but direct sense of intrusion – never expressed but somehow implicit – which served as witness to their increasing union of minds.

You may perceive in due course, sir, that the relation of these two has had a certain effect on my own existence. I apply the saying that whatever affects my life or circumstances, no matter how distantly, is, by virtue of it, also my concern. The rest I shall relate, what I know of it, in order to place some knowledge of events with you. My account is set out so that we may proceed further with this matter, for its echoes and reverberations are still with me now and, even as I write, certain aspects of it continue to unfold, as if I were both living my life and observing it from a position of detachment. In view of this, if what I shall relate appears incongruous, I pray that you will forgive me. For my part I shall hope that, though certain of my actions may not easily be defended, they have had what the French are inclined to call a *rationale*. But let us return to the matters in hand.

Since my younger colleague's arrival in Lymington a dozen or more years ago, I have done my best to provide him with what I hope is reasonable advice and sound report. I have done so not least out of a sense of gratitude, for (as I wrote earlier) he has responded in like manner by taking up my burdens when I am departed to London. Thus, in the same spirit of good advice, when I observed him begin to exhibit that enthusiasm for the company of Mrs Celia Quill which borders on infatuation, I felt duty bound, as his adviser and senior physician, to offer some observations which might help him to a more objective view. In particular, I expressed my suspicion that, much though I admired her, certain aspects of Mrs Quill's background did not entirely fit the circumstances of her appearance in Lymington. My dear friend, if you will believe me, or perhaps take my word in lieu of further evidence, I intended no mischief, for just as I wished to appraise him of circumstances, so my respect for her was such that I wished her no harm. Even now, after certain events, I cannot remove from my mind the impression that it was I – I and perhaps my infernal curiosity – who have brought certain aspects of the matter to their present pass. But I shall continue with the events in question.

When I began to notice some initial signs of attachment between these two solitaries, I took it upon myself to raise with my younger colleague certain matters which it seemed to me should be placed in account. For example, in citing the material fact of Mrs Quill's widowhood, I also suggested that, in her conversation and circumstances, it seemed that she was remarkably free of any trace of her former husband. This, I do believe, required some comment. For just as religion becomes for most of us a ritual in which we invoke the name of the Lord in our minds, though not necessarily in our hearts, so it is my experience that widows, however independent they may become, invoke their husbands' names at certain times, though the period of their physical dependence may be long past. It is, after all, no more than the natural impress of one person's life upon another. Yet Mrs Quill appeared remarkably free of any such traces of her late husband. Indeed, she exhibited a degree of independence which indicated little external sign at least of ever having been in that state of dependence called matrimony. I raised these and other matters with my younger colleague, not to cast doubt on her honour, but to apply a sense of caution in his relations with her and some perspective to his championship of her.

Wiser in the ways of the world than I, my dear Leman, you may guess that his infatuation was sufficiently advanced for my words to have little effect on him, except perhaps to induce in him the opposite of what I had intended and to fortify him in his advocacy of her. For just as bones may often knit more strongly at the join than their original disposition, so he began to construct his defences against my comments. I was concerned that we would soon reach a position where, if I were to make any further suggestion of caution in his behaviour towards her, it would be dismissed as a sign of prejudice on my part.

Yet if I were to ask myself, in the light of what has happened, would I attempt, in the same circumstances, to warn him again, the answer must be reaffirmed. Thus we may live in the cycle of our own character and are bound to repeat our actions, though we may be aware of our deficiencies even as we enact them. But I shall proceed now from this melancholy observation to the next stage in my account.

It seemed that as they drew together, so some particular understanding was reached between them, the nature of which I cannot truly tell, except that it caused my colleague much deliberation, even to fall into what sometimes seemed a state of mind close to doubt or perplexity. At certain times I sensed an agitation so profound that I began to feel nervous that he would succumb to desperation, or even despair. I will not speculate on the nature of the cause of these changes to his accustomed equanimity, except to say that the events in question had a profound effect on his emotions and even his constitution. Since I shall not speculate on their origin, I will limit myself, for the time being at least, only to describing the exterior, the observable consequences, so to speak, of the events I am about to relate.

Just as we may only start to understand changed circumstances if we hold in our mind an idea of matters before the change in question took effect, so I shall take it upon myself to describe in the most precise terms what it is that has altered in my younger colleague, in order that you may more fully appreciate the strangeness of his subsequent behaviour.

I have mentioned that, until the time of which I speak, he appeared to have settled into the life of a studious bachelor. I do not pretend to any special knowledge of the *species celibate*, except that I may incline to the view that there are among us certain rare individuals who are suited by temperament to become monks, or scholars, or even saints. Though I may aver that he belonged, in spirit at least, to the two former categories, I shall not compound these assertions by accusing him of saintliness, for certain aspects of his character are both robust and direct. What I mean to convey, rather, is some initial impression of his own sensibility. His dedication to his profession seemed to take precedence above all else, even – until the advent of Mrs Quill – the tender aspects of the heart. Thus I perceived him as like some scholar whose withdrawal from the world is proof and perhaps guarantee of his integrity.

It is not in my nature to pry too deeply into the lives of others, particularly those possessed of a character so dissimilar to my own. I prefer to accept them as they are and proceed thus to whatever arrangement we mutually agree. But in the interests of what follows, I should perhaps add another comment to this aspect of his character, which may bring a fresh perspective to our considerations.

Not long ago, by chance, I happened to meet, in my secretarial duties as a member of the College of Physicians, a

17

Dr James Granthill, who for several years was trained in the same Scottish academy as my colleague; that is to say, the University of Edinburgh. In the course of our discussions this same Dr Granthill recorded that my younger colleague had been something of a rake in his youth, with a reputation as a man for the ladies. At first this assertion surprised me and I wondered if it were the product of a casual and well-meant exaggeration, for in conditions of informality we may be inclined to dwell in pleasant consternation upon the intemperance of our own youth and that of our acquaintances. But Dr Granthill is a Calvinist and a most sober individual, not given to exaggerating any matter – indeed the opposite – so that if he called the younger Grange a rake, I should perhaps hold myself impressed by the scale of the latter's depredations. And I even began to consider that if my younger colleague pursued any matter with the singleness of purpose which he brings to his profession of physician, then his youthful reputation may have been deserved. Thus I have heard of celibates who, in their early days, were inclined towards the life of the senses, perhaps so strongly that in their later years they reacted against their early excesses. I believe our own great Thomas More was such, and I have heard of other examples, such as the plaint of St Augustine, who cried out, I do believe, 'Make me chaste, but not yet.' These examples do incline me to a similar view regarding my younger colleague. I believe he is a man of strong passions, though tightly controlled. I mention this because, as you will see, it seems to bear upon what follows.

For the moment, then, I merely notify you of a certain cast of character in my colleague. It would seem that there is a type of celibate, or celibate in waiting, who does not lack the physical passions but, on the contrary, uses his own passionate nature as a spur to drive him in his chosen field of study. He thus directs himself more fiercely into his work, or profession, with a dedication which draws its strength from precisely those passions which, in others, may lead to the physical life.

Leman, you know my predilection for the table, for horses and the company of women. In the matter of my colleague, permit me to say that in these propensities I found, if not an answering voice, at least a conviction in my own heart that I shared my thoughts with another being who was not entirely insensible of them, though he had yet chosen another path. It was precisely this, that he was sensible of these temptations and at the same time detached, that has given me such good sport at table and has allowed to flow between us such a currency of good opinion, despite our differences of outlook. For I do believe that I observe in him the man I might have been if I had taken a more studious course in my life. And by the same token I consider that perhaps he observes in me the man he might have become if he had relinquished that fierce and subtle discipline of the soul which marks his own behaviour.

Now I turn to one final aspect of his character, which follows from the above. If I were to describe the life of a monk or a nun in the abstract, I believe the attempted task would perplex me. Yet which of us has not walked past a member of a religious order and seen, in a face partially hooded by cloth, a trace of some sanctity, a gleam or indication of fulfilment or happiness? And who among us, in similar circumstances, has not assumed, at the evidence of the eyes, the presence in such a life of certain quiet and perhaps spiritual joys of which we yet remain innocent? I digress merely to emphasise that my colleague seemed contented with his lot, even happy. And perhaps precisely because of his commitment, much though I might presume to tease him on occasion, he was a good companion at table, and on occasions would drink with me and parry my arguments with good grace, so that I came to rely upon his company once or twice a week for entertainment.

I have laboured, my dear Leman, for a little while in the composition of these few lines, in the course of a morning in which I have been spared immediate or pressing duties. I usually devote such welcome intervals of time to riding or perhaps shooting, but I have preferred this day to sit myself down and struggle to set forth my poor thoughts. It is something of a surprise, and no great consolation, to find myself writing in serious vein of dedicated nuns and celibates. At the same time in my ear I hear the bell for lunch being rung by my housekeeper Mrs Simmonds, which commands my more earthly appetites and invites me to a most unspiritual repast. Since I must take to the table shortly, and since the afternoon is now almost upon us, I must soon afterwards perform my duties in respect of several patients. Thus it may be a day or two before I am able once more to continue these disquisitions.

Since, by the grace of God, I am not of an ascetic or scholarly disposition, such concentrations are tiring to my brain. I shall go forth to table and there reflect a little on what has been written, though not so much as to prejudice the enjoyment of my meal.

In the meantime, sir, I shall leave you with these brief and uncompleted thoughts, such as they are. And I shall trust that the interval of rest I shall now afford myself will improve my mind for their continuation.

Until such time, sir, I remain, in true gratitude of your patience,

Yours most sincerely,

Hargood

CHAPTER 6

Each day, when Grange took his exercise by walking along the deserted sea-shore, he was careful to harbour his energy. Taking frequent rests, he observed the thoroughfare of the Solent, the single shining pathway of water between the mainland and the Isle of Wight.

He had always been tall, but his recent illness gave him the appearance of a skeleton, or of some elongated bird such as a stork or crane. Now he halted for perhaps the third or fourth time that morning, gathering his breath in short gasps, staring out across the marshes to the open water.

The day was filled with sunlight, but the breeze dissipated the heat. He was wrapped against the cold as if against a winter chill, his cravat tight, his overcoat collar pulled up around his neck to ward off the sea wind. His clothes were adequate protection against the chill day, but not against the coldness which seemed to have taken up permanent residence inside him. Sometimes, leaning on his Malacca cane after the effort of walking, he could feel himself shaking slightly; the tremors passed through him like those small seismographic changes that hint at some deeper activities in the earth's core.

He raised his free hand to shade his eyes against the sun. A few hundred yards away a pinnace swung briskly out of the Lymington river, caught a gust of wind and heeled almost to the gunwales while the midshipman in the stern paid out mainsheet to ease the sail. Ahead of her, out beyond Jack-in-the-basket, whitecaps dotted the Solent. Perhaps half a mile away, a heavy, flat barge was running westward, holding to the mainland shore to reduce the effect of the tide; her high mainsail bellied, her blunt bows punched through the crests that seem to spring up so swiftly when wind is set against current.

Grange scanned the water for other signs of traffic. To the west, a frigate was entering the Hurst Narrows, using the incoming tide to offset the easterly wind against which it tacked. By the sleekness of its bows and the elegance of its lines, he gained the impression of a French design – perhaps some prize that had been taken and converted.

A coughing fit caused him to double up. It served to remove for a few moments his concentration on the water traffic. When he had recovered, he raised his head again and stared in rapt attention at the evidence of human endeavour, observing the cross-currents of wind, tide and human vessels.

After a few minutes he regained his breath sufficiently to walk the few hundred yards to Oxey. There he intended to turn inland and walk back to his house in Lymington High Street.

He had braced himself for further activity when a voice, arising out of the silent marshes, accosted him: 'Your pardon, sir.'

Grange heard the rasping sound as though behind him, but it was carried away briskly by the wind. Distracted by its nearness, Grange looked around him. The voice said again, closer than he had at first expected, 'Sir.'

He looked down. Swann was below him, looking upwards. He had a sack on his back and was leaning forward against its weight.

At the first sound of Swann's voice behind him, Grange had swung his gaze across the top of Swann's head, such was the difference in height between them. Out of embarrassment Grange almost bowed in greeting. 'Good-day, Mr Swann.'

'Fine morning, sir.'

Swann had approached him entirely unobserved. It appeared to be Swann's privilege to move across the landscape like a crab, concerned on his own errands, appearing occasionally and usually unexpectedly. He was a scavenger by trade, albeit a somewhat inspired one. His preferred terrain was the sea-shore, from Woodside to the Oxey and Pennington marshes. The bag over his shoulder was half full of salvaged driftwood. What Swann lacked in height he compensated in bulk, standing with his head slightly lowered like a bull.

Grange considered whether one final glance at the frigate in the Hurst Narrows would breach the propriety of greeting. Since Swann was as at least as knowledgeable as he on the traffic in the narrows, if not more so, he decided to risk directing one last searching look towards the incoming ship, whose sails now clearly etched against the cream cliffs of the Island. It was moving fast and effortlessly, with occasional graceful lifts of the bow over incoming swells.

His curiosity temporarily satisfied, Grange lowered his gaze again to the former mariner. 'You surprised me, Swann.'

'You were occupied, I believe.'

'I was observing the traffic.'

'The frigate, sir?'

Grange nodded. He murmured softly, almost to himself, 'I wondered about her origins.'

For several moments they both stared out at her, attempting to place the shape of her stern, the poop lower than usual. She bore no figurehead, rather a blank space at the bows where once the figurehead had been. It was another sign that the ship had changed her name.

'French ships are more slender than ours,' Swann said.

'You think so?'

'Finer bows, usually. Narrower on the waterline.'

'You are a student of form, I see.'

22

'A little more tender, perhaps, but they can be fast as a witch in light weather.'

'You advance your case, Mr Swann. You are certain she's French?'

'I trust my senses, sir. French ships are like French women, sir, handsome to the eye and by reputation perhaps a little faster than our own.'

In the wake of Mrs Quill's departure, Grange was disinclined to be drawn about women. 'With what crew?'

'English, I'd say.'

'And how do you surmise that?'

'The set of her sails. English cut tends to be fuller.'

'Why?' Grange asked, intrigued.

'French vessels must sail more often off a windward shore, into Biscay, as often as not, against prevailing westerlies. Their jibs and squaresails are cut flatter for windward work.'

'An eloquent theory.'

'A good combination, it is generally thought,' Swann suggested, 'is a French vessel with an English crew aboard her.'

Grange considered her lines again. He decided to run a little with Swann's implications.

'Do you speak from experience, Mr Swann?' Grange asked quietly, without diverting his eye from the procedures that were now taking place on board the ship's deck. Gangs of men were running to the forward and amidships stations preparatory to hauling sheets.

'I do, sir. The *Harland*, on which I once sailed, was a French ship. The *Sauvage*, I think she was once called. Hard in the mouth to windward when we first trialled her, but we extended the bowsprit to balance her and added an extra foresail. She could pick up her skirts in a breeze, with hardly a change on the wheel.'

The frigate was tacking now, using her momentum to come through the wind. Most of the crew were set to handling the sails. The two jibs fluttered as she came head up. On the deck, two parties of half a dozen men each were hauling on the sheets as she passed through onto the new tack, taking in as much rope as possible before the sails filled. Grange observed their sudden fervent activity and imagined the shouted instructions from the sailing

23

master. As more rope was hauled in, the man furthest aft in the hauling gang rotated forward to take up the strain again.

'In irons, do you think?' Grange whispered in calm suspension.

They watched to see whether the helmsman would be forced, ignominiously, to reverse helm for a backward leg. But the frigate's bow was still paying off, and the sails were now beginning to belly and fill on the new tack.

A palpable sense of relief, of sympathy, filled Grange. 'A manoeuvre well executed, I think.'

'A good crew, sir, certainly.'

Whitecaps dotted the surface of the water, small white flames. The ship increased its way, heeling now, and a wake like a pale path began to stretch out astern.

'You hanker after the sea, Swann?'

'Sometimes,' Swann admitted. 'Sometimes I do.'

The frigate was still increasing speed. Her slender bow carved a swell; two white flutes rose and fell.

Grange lowered his gaze again. 'To my eye at least, Mr Swann, you seem in good heart.'

It was an oblique reference to the stump of Swann's left arm, the empty shirt-sleeve folded like a bird's wing and secured by an iron pin. Grange's glance fell briefly on the untenanted sleeve.

'Well as I could hope for.'

'I sometimes feel that it was I who severed you from your profession.'

'You should save your conscience, sir, for a better day,' Swann said. 'My arm was gone and I would have gone with it, but for your kind attentions.'

It was genuinely meant and perhaps even true. Yet a feeling rose inside Grange of discomfiture. He felt subtly ashamed. Swann stood before him, minus a limb, but instinct with health, his face full of shining power. Before the loss of his arm, in his prime, he had served on the packet ship *Feather* as second mate. Yet even now, forced to live on the thin pickings of the foreshore, he seemed as certain of his role as any animal in its natural terrain.

By contrast, Grange stood beside him, hale of limb, but suffering from some internal malaise which he could not easily describe.

In his unease, Grange was overtaken by another fit of trembling.

24

It seemed as if the coldness emerged from deep within him, from the hollows of his spine, and spread through his body into the viscera, then outwards into the skin. He smiled to reassure Swann, but his smile was a little awkward.

Swann said, 'And you, sir? Are you recovering?'

'Slowly.' Grange tried to control his tremors, which now had moved out from the core of his body into his limbs, and whose manifestations were increasingly visible. He put both hands on the head of his Malacca cane, in order to stop them trembling. In his own view, the regular bleedings administered by his older colleague Hargood protracted the process of recovery. But, out of deference to the senior physician, he submitted to the procedures.

'Slow is sure,' Swann stated. His eyes turned diplomatically towards the frigate.

Grange smiled again out of defiance, feeling faint inside. While the shaking lasted, he was inclined to engage his mind elsewhere. He looked steadfastly out to the Solent. Having gained full way again, the frigate now turned closer upwind; with her beautiful lines, her sails hauled in tight, she began beating up the Solent towards Southampton or Portsmouth. Behind her, sunlight picked out the cream cliffs of the Isle of Wight. Grange drew a measure of courage from the sight of natural and man-made beauty in such brief and evanescent harmony.

Inside him, the tremors that had caused his body to shake now seemed to dissipate themselves. He thought he heard Swann murmur, 'Your work must be a consolation.' But Grange was so rapt in the scene in front of him that it was several seconds before he registered the statement.

Turning back towards Swann, Grange said, 'I am forbidden, while I recover, from attending patients.'

'Another doctor instructs you, sir?'

'That is right. My colleague Dr Hargood.' He felt obliged to defend Hargood, as if against his own doubts. 'A most eminent physician.'

Swann nodded. He would accept Grange's authority in the matter of fellow physicians.

Grange continued, 'Since I am not able to meet you in my study

25

as a patient, perhaps you would kindly consider joining me as a guest for supper one of these evenings.'

Swann seemed to hesitate at the proffered invitation, however vague. It was a matter of social nicety. There was a gulf between their stations.

Sensing Swann's reluctance, Grange went on, 'I wish to tax your mind on a subject.'

Swann seemed to relax a little. This was at least a reason for visiting. 'Ships, or boats, perhaps?'

'No.' Grange turned towards the shore and, bracing himself for the effort of raising his arm, indicated the line of salt furnaces on the foreshore with his thin hand. 'Our industry.'

Swann said, 'I'm sure there are others who could advise you better . . .'

'Perhaps there are. But they are not so convenient to my purposes.'

Grange wondered, nevertheless, of whom Swann thought. Perhaps St Just, the banker, who owned an increasing number of the furnaces, buying one after another as their original owners fell into loss or bankruptcy. He felt obliged to elaborate on his original statement. 'Unfortunately, they also have financial interests, in one form or another. I should prefer a point of detachment.'

'Well, sir, if you think I am able to assist you.'

'In a week or so, perhaps.' Grange braced himself again to walk. 'I would be greatly obliged if you would visit me.'

His shivering had almost halted. Now he touched his hat to Swann, who raised his hand to his own forehead in acknowledgement.

'Good-day, sir.'

'Good-day, Mr Swann.'

Swann watched him go. Thin as a candle flame, Grange picked his way against the wind.

CHAPTER 7

My dear Leman,

I return several days after last addressing you to take up the pen and so continue my missive, having found much to occupy my attention in the intervening period. I have considered again what I wrote and hope I shall not bore you too much with these further accounts of my younger colleague's character.

Accordingly, my dear friend, if you will kindly permit me the privilege of your further consideration, let us return to our subject directly.

There remains, in the difference between my colleague and myself, one strange aspect, which I have not hitherto touched upon, but which may bear a closer inspection. I noted before that he had been educated in Scottish academies, and that this unfortunate fact may account for the unusual nature of certain opinions and attitudes which he holds. Although these attitudes are various, they return to a single aspect, which seems to me to act as a kind of point or *fulcrum* for all the differences between us. Stated most simply, he is without belief in God. But that is perhaps too weak an expression to describe what separates us. For, if I may be so bold as to describe the views of another, it appears not so much that he does not believe in God, but that he actively believes God does not exist. I know that there is a great deal of Godlessness abroad in these times, but he assumes his own belief (for a conviction that there is no God is surely another form of belief?) with a positive zeal. In conversation between us, he is not only direct in owning to the fact, but is prepared to defend his intransigence as though it were an asset. To which I am inclined to respond that, since he is not even prepared to admit of God's existence, his views may not be dignified with the word heresy. Thus his bachelorhood, and the unswerving nature of his dedication to his profession, which in other men may be put down to a religious cast of mind, require in his own case some alternative form of explanation than piety. Which very fact I am obliged to address, for no other reason than that I have promised I would attempt to outline his cast of mind to you.

I approach it thus. I believe such dedication in his case to be an expression of his own inner character, which is both fierce and austere. And if I pause deliberately at this stage in our proceedings, it is only to point out the difference between us, by attempting to distinguish my own views on the matter. For I do believe most fervently that there is some potent force whom we call God, who surveys us and judges us, and whose mercy we may sometimes feel upon us, like sunlight.

And yet, how strange it is that this perception of the Deity should have the opposite effect upon me from that which his Godlessness has upon him. For, believing in God's creation, I also feel that sin is part of the world, part of His great and varied work and, though I may occasion His displeasure in subscribing to such sin, yet to give in occasionally to what He has created is also to participate, to some degree, in His greater offices. Thus I do believe that, if the balance of my activities are benevolent, though not every detail of it, perhaps He will forgive occasional excesses.

My colleague, on the other hand, has recourse to no such forgiving Lord. In all his behaviour he is subjected to the full discipline of his own stern character, on account of which his only judge is himself. And what a terrible resolution that would seem to be! For if I may trust in the mercy and greater understanding of Our Lord, my younger colleague knows that he can hide nothing from himself, and that therefore nothing may be forgiven. No larger Mind, kindlier than his, may intercede on his behalf. Yet if what I say has some truth, how strange are these effects, that the religious in my own nature should permit me a little *latitude* in my traffic with the world and, in his own, should allow him none.

Such digressions upon his character may serve in due course to explain that process by which one such as I may find, owing to that larger forgiveness, some freedom in which to move. Yet that lack of latitude in his character is something which I might otherwise call fixity. For if my notion of sin allows me to bend a little in the breeze, in my colleague the lack of it permits no such flexibility. There may be present, then, in his mind and character, a certain *brittleness* of disposition, which I believe may have brought him to the pass which I will now describe.

If I have digressed from the first subject, which is the relation between him and the widow, Mrs Celia Quill, I make my apologies and do now return.

After the first attraction between these two souls had cemented itself, by which I submit an understanding had been reached between them, it seemed to me that in the initial stages of their intimacy my colleague began to change for the better. He gave all the signs of having reached a certain calm in his general affairs, which I dare say I put down to the fact of his companionship with this unusual and perhaps remarkable woman. For myself, seeing him increasingly thus disposed and believing his happiness to be the true judge of their relations, for the time being, at least, I raised no further cautions against his increased acquaintance. It was only later, when the attachment deepened and he began to show those signs of being insensible of evidence which I have outlined above, that I started actively to exercise my doubts, and thus to believe I should help him to consider more carefully the course he was pursuing.

For several months the same continued. I had become lulled by my own assumptions and by the goodwill which existed between them, surmounted as it was by the beneficial effects of Mrs Quill's influence upon his disposition and character.

It was during the middle summer that my colleague began to act in a manner that appeared unusual. His behaviour coincided with another event, which being in close conjunction I am inclined to believe was perhaps one of the causes of the effect I observed. It happened that after a time of increasing intimacy been the two solitaries there came upon the scene, as though by accident, Mrs Quill's daughter, Jane. She arrived to pay her mother a visit in the middle of summer and stayed for several weeks in Lymington. I deduced, and it was later confirmed by Mrs Thompson, that my younger colleague was asked to dinner on several occasions at Mrs Quill's house in celebration of her daughter's visit, and so in the course of such visits he enjoyed the amiable companionship at dinner of both mother and daughter.

And thus we may begin to advance into an area of which I know precious little, though to know something of it might have explained much that ensued.

Sir, I must reserve this disquisition for a later time. I am called out again upon my rounds, and shall obey with immediacy as a good physician should. I hear, even now, the sounds of my fly being brought to the front door by my stable-boy.

I will take up this matter again, sir, as soon as time permits.

In the meanwhile, I remain,

> Yours most sincerely,
> Hargood

CHAPTER 8

Mrs Thompson was an expert on fire.

Since it warmed the house, cooked food, brought comfort to her in her rest and in other ways was an adjunct to her needs, she decided at an early stage to render herself self-reliant in its maintenance and manufacture. She nourished it carefully. In the early morning she used tongs to carry a grey, almost lifeless ember from the remnants of the main fire into her kitchen, trailing a stream of smoke as thin as an elver. There she would place it upon a slate and, bending her face to it, blow upon its grey scales, holding aside the pendants of her lace cap with her free hand. She would continue to blow patiently until it glowed red. Once life had been re-awakened, she would apply the edge of a piece of paper to the glinting red surface of the wood, breathing upon it until it caught a little yellow flame. As tenderly as a mother, she would nurse this into a more active life. If paper was not available to set alight, she used a dry leaf of which she kept a small supply in a metal box.

When the paper or leaf was alight, she carefully touched the flame to the tinder she had gathered in the stove and watched the fire creep slowly through the dry wooden pyre of kindling, as furtive and fluent as a snake. Once the flames had taken hold in the belly of the stove, she closed the door, set the nozzle of the bellows to the vent, and applied half a dozen brisk expansions and contractions of its leather lungs.

It often happened, at this point in her ritual, that smoke drifted into the interior of the kitchen until a sufficient draught had been created by the warmth of fire to drive it up the chimney. Mrs Thompson coughed. This was the first sound that Grange would hear in the house each morning – Mrs Thompson's brisk, satisfied cough as she waved the smoke of her spreading fire away from her and started to gather the pots.

Grange slept lightly, hovering on consciousness. He usually lay on his side, his long legs drawn upwards against the cold. At her cough or the sound of her stirring he would turn on his back and open his eyes, staring into the early morning darkness while she heated a pot of water on the stove. He woke often with a quickly beating heart, the result of some dream he could only vaguely recall.

After a few moments he heard her footsteps on the stair; he observed the faint penumbra of light around the edges of the door from her candle, the sound of the pot of water being placed on the landing, her perfunctory knock; the latch being raised, the sudden influx of light into the room as the door was pressed open, her faint sigh of effort as she reached down to pick up the pot of heated water once again.

Mrs Thompson traversed the room softly, like a cloud. He observed the candle-light on the flesh of her forearms as her buxom form crossed the floorboards to the side table where his wash-bowl stood. Placing the candle holder on the side table, she took the pot in both hands and filled the bowl. Steam rose in the faint light.

She removed from the recesses of one of her deep pockets another candle and placed it on the spike of another candle holder which stood ready on the side table in a small iron holding dish. She raised her own candle and applied the flame to the unlit candle, watching the wick catch light, then separated the mated flames.

31

Grange, out of deference to her concentration, usually feigned sleep, but this morning he shifted carefully in his bed until he lay on his side and said, 'Thank you, Mrs Thompson.'

Mrs Thompson seemed to pause at his voice, as though it were an unexpected intrusion.

'Sir.' She crossed the floor and drew the door to behind her. He heard her descending the stairs and observed the faint luminescence of the departing flame around the edges of the closed door.

A few moments later he rose from the sheets, shivering from the cold, and placed his coat over his night-shirt against the early autumn chill. She had set out his shaving brush and soap beside the shaver and strop. He reached for the brush and began to apply the soap.

So he commenced that curious and peaceful ceremony with which men enter the world after sleep, standing in front of their own images, accumulating their senses for the day. Shaving, he seemed to be reborn afresh. Accordingly, he sometimes looked sternly into the mirror, as if assuming the role of patriarch, drawing the mouth down and hardening the muscles of his jaw. Or perhaps he assumed the wicked smile of the gleeful child. Being of an inquisitive disposition, Grange was more inclined to study his apparition with a certain detachment, returning his own stare cautiously, as if he considered another person. He was largely without vanity, viewing his physical image as no more than a reflection on water.

The ritual calmed him, but it also raised various thoughts to the surface. His mind pursued the vanishing tails of certain dreams. It was curious how, to his own mind at least, there was a mysterious centre to those dreams. He knew what that centre was. Sometimes he saw Mrs Celia Quill seated at the head of a table, detached, unassailable. At other times he caught sight of her familiar figure at the end of the street. In his dreams, at least, he seemed powerless to approach her. At some level he knew or suspected that his mind rehearsed the impotence of his position, as though inciting him to act.

CHAPTER 9

My dear Leman,

I have expressed my surprise that my younger colleague could form so close an association with Mrs Quill. Yet once that association had formed, I began to observe the happiness that it brought to him and the benign nature of her influence upon him. It is difficult to be precise in the description of happiness, but I perceived in him some curious sense of ease, that I had not noticed before, as though the ferocity of his mind had been satiated, or as if he had received some answer, perhaps a satisfactory one, to the resolute questions he had placed upon his life. Yet I must caution my memory and my deductions. For I am determined to explain to you why I assumed more than merely a friendship, but some intimacy between him and Mrs Quill.

My good friend, how may we detect in our fellow man the sense of physical happiness? At those times in our lives when we ourselves are physically contented, we are so engrossed in our good fortune that I do not believe we analyse our improved being with any rigour, but merely enjoy our enhanced state. If we are unaware of any change in ourselves, except the happiness we feel, how may we describe that state in others? In the absence of direct evidence, perhaps you will forgive me if I say that I believe there was something in the very ease with which he carried himself that was both the same and yet different. I cannot describe a state of mind, yet certain external matters gave an indication of changed circumstances. He seemed – if I may speak directly of his physical state – less angular in his dispositions. I remember him sitting in his habitual chair at the end of my dining-table, and in surveying him I attempted to locate what it was that was no longer singular and odd about him. Until then, I had never seen him settle back in a seat with any degree of contentment or comfort – without, that is, at the same time seeming about to spring out of it. Yet in the course of an evening's meal, I observed him absolve himself into that chair as calmly as a cat, and noted to myself that his face took on an expression of peculiar calm. He seemed, in short, at one with his surroundings. Though he remained watchful, he appeared disposed about a centre that no longer seemed restless. If intimacy is a commingling of souls, I believe he had found in his own being some kind of rest. I have laboured the point, sir, because it brings us to that strange turn of events which followed.

Perhaps a few months passed in this curious but welcome state of grace. When I had come to accept his changed disposition and assumed it for the best, her daughter came to visit, as I have reported, and another cycle of events began, that seemed subtly to change the first. The initial, and perhaps the oddest of these, was that almost as soon as some level of understanding had been reached between them as regards companionship, my younger colleague appeared to turn his attention from his companion and confidante, Mrs Quill, and to direct himself to some degree towards her daughter.

This was a strange manner of behaviour indeed for a man who, before Mrs Celia Quill made her appearance, appeared to harbour no need for love or intimacy in his character. Perhaps a man starved of affection for so long a period, once the barriers are breached, may show it to excess, and thus may turn naturally from one recipient to another. Perhaps, in some strange manner, Mrs Quill had showed him another perspective upon life, that the intimacy of souls is greater than a singular isolation, which before he had not fully comprehended. I do not know, but attempt to confine myself to the case in point.

Was he truly deflected? Did he perceive in her daughter some hint of her mother – a branch, so to speak, from the same tree? Her daughter is certainly of a most comely disposition. And we may surmise, too, that there is a certain resemblance between mother and offspring. I have seen them once or twice together and they are like sisters. Any man would be forgiven for finding her daughter attractive. But we are not discussing any man, but one whose devotion to his bachelorhood has caused him to resist all previous temptations for the duration which I have known him. Yet, in the course of a few months, he breaks the habits of his previous existence by paying attention not to one woman, but two. You will see from this that that there was much to perplex the innocent observer.

And then there was further strangeness. Though Mrs Quill and he had become intimate, at least to external appearances, she apparently held no objection to his deflecting his attentions to her daughter. Perhaps she was too much wedded to the freedoms of widowhood to consider marriage herself, and thus, despite her evident affection for my younger colleague, she may have been pleased that his attentions were directed at another object.

Whatever the explanation, these new dispositions did not give the impression of unsettling him. If a man changes the direction of his intimacy from a mother to a daughter, you may expect some disturbance. Yet, while her daughter was here, it seemed that his new state of grace was unaltered. I was aware of his comportment during her daughter's visit, and he continued to show that sense of ease or perhaps happiness with which I had become acquainted and which I was willing to grant to Mrs Quill's influence over him.

My dear Leman, I struggle again to express myself, to convey an intuition, to explain some aspect which, if it does not resolve the series of events I witnessed, at least moves them a little distance from incomprehensibility. It almost seemed as if Mrs Quill was his teacher and, having taught him a lesson concerning intimacy, was not averse to encouraging him to express himself in other spheres.

So much is speculation. Although these events seem strange, they had no effect on society, since whatever occurred in the changed relations between the parties took place outside the purview of others. Certain details relating to my younger colleague's pursuit of Mrs Quill's daughter have only emerged following some careful questioning of both him and Mrs Thompson, his housekeeper, and some deductions on my own part as to the course of events.

Much of what I describe is proposed with the benefit of hindsight, for although I did observe some turns of events and certain moods in my colleague which, in the latter stages of his courtship, gave cause for concern, yet the circumstances which I have described appear to be confirmed by such investigations as I have been able to undertake. It is true that a number of aspects may be embellished by virtue of deduction, and that some of the details that were missing have been filled by discussion with my colleague after the event, but with their help I attempt to write as accurate an account of the events of the time as I am capable.

In all this, I feel like a man who is missing some vital component. He observes what is before his eyes, but at the same time the picture is askew. Some aspect is lacking. Without that same missing element there is little that makes sense. Everything floats, or is strangely weighted, as if there is some magnet which he cannot see.

Sometimes the obvious obscures; sometimes what is vague or hidden provides unexpected clarity. This would not be any the less so if the protagonists of my account were themselves not so remarkable in their own right. I have written above that we may perceive too easily how any man might be taken with Mrs Quill's daughter. For she seems like an angel. Her mother's fine figure is, on her daughter, still slender with youth. Her looks are delicate. Yet there is a strength beneath them that promises the character of her mother. In certain glances, and in the quickness of her intelligence, we may perceive something of her mother's temperament, some equal firmness of resolve. Such infatuation may be understandable in any man, I say, but yet it sits oddly with another fact, which I will now relate.

Here, sir, we find a further and final complication, for so much surprises that each new fact or strangeness seems like a fresh outrage upon the senses, or at least upon the equanimity of the observer. I record what follows merely as a matter of truth, and because it adds a final component which, though it stretches the credulity, in due course may yet perhaps offer us a clue as to the procession of events.

I have recently discovered that Mrs Quill's daughter Jane was herself married. Perhaps her marriage had been merely in name, one of those cold alliances that are more common than we care to believe. But even so, to one outside the charmed circle of their companionship, Mrs Quill's toleration of Grange's interest in her daughter seemed tantamount to a consent. Since Mrs Quill herself was so much respected by society, her behaviour in relation to a man's pursuit of her married daughter causes further reason for consideration.

We have observed, then, that Mrs Quill showed no inclination to discourage him in expressing his interest in her daughter, despite her being married. I have implied above that Mrs Celia Quill's attitude to her own former marriage, which appears not to have affected her, verges on the *galante*. Here now is another example of a somewhat unusual attitude to her own daughter's matrimonial affairs. Her great companion and intimate, Silas Grange, whose friendship and trust she has cultivated and who seems close to her in all matters of companionship, expresses an interest in her own married daughter. And she, for her part, does nothing to halt him, but on the contrary, appears to approve his attentions! What dance is this, whose footsteps appear so delicate and yet, to the outside eye, so unorthodox?

And now, Leman, since I have already reached a certain point in this my missive, I am bound to continue a little further, if only to set a temporary and providential cap on my account. Since I have already taxed your powers of patience, I pray you will bear with me a little longer.

My younger colleague is nothing if not honourable, and honest. Having exhibited his interest in Mrs Quill's daughter, with the full approval of her mother, it seems he then notified Mrs Celia Quill that in the fullness of time he wished to cement these relations in marriage, giving the young woman as much time as was necessary and prudent to annul the first. Following Mrs Quill's encouragement of the relations between them, this may appear reasonable, even though the suggestion of marriage towards one who is already married may seem somewhat impolitic, given the permanence and venerability of the institution. That being said, it is also true, surely, that our own English Church was founded in divorce, and therefore that fact alone may not induce in me the greatest disapproval. I merely continue with my account, in the trust that my efforts will reveal a rationale, or motive, by which we will hope to explain these odd events.

I have spent much effort in attempting to describe these strange matters. My mind is not such that it is easily able to disentangle the soul's complexities. There is much, I freely admit, that I cannot explain. I merely record the facts in terms of my limited understanding and attempt a tentative explanation of their outer aspects. But at the heart of my colleague's behaviour towards Mrs Quill and her daughter I perceive nothing more than a kind of darkness, which defeats my scrutiny and which remains with me, so to speak, as a reminder of my failure.

With these thoughts I must leave you, sir, and return to my daily existence.

I thank you again for your patience, and remain,

    Yours sincerely,

     Hargood

CHAPTER 10

Downstairs a fire crackled in the hearth.

Before he had succumbed to illness, Grange himself would start a fire using Hender's Device, a patented hammer spring which brought a flint down upon a steel anvil, generating a handsome spark of gold and white. Several applications of it were usually sufficient to start dry paper, leaves or white shavings. Now, during his illness and convalescence, Mrs Thompson, with her older methods, had begun to rule the household fires. It was a measure of the ground that he had lost to her.

Once Mrs Thompson had gained a certain holding she was unlikely to give it up without resistance. If, before his illness, she had been the unseen presence of the house, now she moved into the foreground, organising the household in lieu of her ailing master. It seemed to Grange sometimes that she had almost taken over the duties of wife and mistress of the house – a discreet but very assertive wife to be sure.

Her certainty about her own role was such that, during breakfast that morning, he found her incorrigibly curious about the guest he intended that evening.

Finishing his fish broth, Grange had called, 'Mrs Thompson?'

'Sir?' Mrs Thompson stood off when summoned, as though suspicious of a sudden intrusion into her administration of the house.

'Would you make the table for a guest tonight?'

'Dr Hargood, sir?'

He was surprised at the swiftness of her deduction. It had become clear, during the course of his illness, that she and Dr Hargood shared a number of views and assumptions, not least on diet, which were at odds with his own. Inviting Hargood to dine would have met with her approval.

'No. I am speaking of Mr Swann.'

Mrs Thompson hovered at the edge of incredulity. 'Mr Swann?' She stood at the foot of the table, waiting for his attention.

'Mr Swann', Grange said, 'has recovered well, remarkably well, from his amputation.'

He noticed that she had not moved, so deeply was her mind concerned with the information. At length Mrs Thompson said, 'In that case, sir, should you not ask him to visit you in the surgery?'

'I would if it were a medical visit, Mrs Thompson. But it is not. His visit this evening is more in the manner of a social occasion.'

'I see.'

'I have invited him to dine with me because we have a number of matters of mutual interest to discuss. He will arrive at seven.'

It was precisely their mutual interests, Grange suspected, that caused Mrs Thompson to be so suspicious towards Swann. She had taken a view that her master spent too much time unsupervised and alone on the marsh, subject to the chill winds on the open foreshore, and when she heard subsequently that some considerable part of his time was passed in the company of Swann, she deduced that Swann was in part responsible for that behaviour. It seemed to Grange that human minds had a tendency to associate one evil with another.

Mrs Thompson emerged from her surprise at Swann's invitation. She asked, 'And what would you like to eat tonight, sir?'

'Since I do not expect him to share my taste for a fish diet, I believe it is an occasion for lamb.'

Mrs Thompson saw her opportunity. 'And lamb for you, too, sir?'

'I believe it would be inconsiderate for me to eat one thing, while my guest ate another.'

This concession was at least a partial compensation for inviting a guest of whom she so clearly disapproved. Mrs Thompson nodded again and without further hesitation turned on her heel. Her expression was impervious and impartial. Grange knew she had the intelligence never to show triumph, though her satisfaction some-times translated itself into a certain briskness which was observable in her actions. He watched for a moment her fine, though perhaps somewhat disdainful, figure disappear through the doorway into the kitchen.

CHAPTER 11

My dear Leman,

Hard though I may try to outline the salient facts of my younger colleague's infatuation with Mrs Quill, and the subsequent complications of the arrival of her daughter upon the scene, I remain aware that my attempts to provide an account are based upon mere outward impression. The engine of these events is hidden, so to speak, within the case, out of view. Thus, sir, I am aware that in outlining these events to you I am also describing the shape of my own ignorance.

This brings me to the final aspect of this strange affair, at least as regards my colleague's relations with Mrs Quill's daughter – an aspect which I attest is perhaps as odd and remarkable as any other that I have recounted above. I understand, having the benefit of later investigations, that precisely when my colleague gave notice of his interest in her daughter as a subject for marriage – that is to say, when he made his intentions honourable – why then, Mrs Celia Quill, his *confidante* and intimate, objected so strongly to this idea that he felt no longer welcome in her company.

I repeat, sir, that I can only describe the train of events in its external sense. A coldness developed between them which, by all accounts, seemed unbridgeable. Thus, his relationship with Mrs Quill, which until these events had been close, did not suffer from his infatuation with her daughter. But when he clarified his intentions, showed himself consistent and proposed marriage, why then the strain on the relations between my younger colleague and Mrs Quill became such that the two of them appeared to break apart, and to outside appearances their difference over this matter became irreconcilable.

Having observed the beauty of the daughter and guessed at my younger colleague's infatuation, I did not know for certain at the time what might have happened between them, for he was concerned to ensure the privacy of his relations with both ladies from outside eyes.

Since I consider myself impervious to the demands of the higher life of learning, except as it directly affects the practice of medicine, I do not profess to understand the deeper workings of his motivation. Yet there is in the dedication of my younger colleague, in the setting aside of life's other pleasures, another outline, of a more distant and oblique nature. I do not know what the word 'heroic' means to you, or even whether you should hold the word in any esteem, since those who are truly heroic are perhaps unaware of its nature. But in my own mind at least the term has something to do with this lack of conscious aggrandisement. Thus, though I may take every opportunity to question my younger colleague's loyalties and to pour customary scorn upon his notions, I do concede some small trace or flavour of admiration. In the course of pursuing what he held dear, or valuable, I believe that in some strange manner he placed himself at risk. And though the risk was of a nature that has more to do with the inner workings of his mind, or (if he would permit me!) the soul, than any external endeavour, I am sure that in some part of him he took such risks knowingly. For I have no doubt that he hazarded his own well-being in his relations with these two formidable women, despite my initial warnings and admonishments concerning the independence of Mrs Quill. And when he was struck down by subsequent events and subsided into the apathy of defeat, he showed no bitterness towards either the lady or her daughter, and would listen to no criticism of either.

Thus I perceive in my younger colleague, the faint workings and embellishments of a tragic outline. And my curiosity is further engaged because, like a bystander or gawping witness to some tragic event, I do wish to know more of what this mysterious entity consists, and whether it will concede itself in due course to my curiosity.

There is one last aspect of this matter that I have learned and will impart in greater detail in my next letter. For it concerns an aspect of Mrs Quill's background which, though it does not begin to explain the full workings of the play I have attempted to outline above, yet offers a clue upon which we may at least consider the thing further. If I am able to console myself over my own, perhaps ignominious, role in what has happened, it is only that, in warning my younger colleague of the complexities of her background, I had to some extent been justified in my suspicions. Even so, it is a poor consolation for the ruin that I may have brought upon two lives.

I read these writings again, as if to find some path in my investigations, and instead observe in my actions little but my own perplexity. My mind lacks both the force and the penetration of my younger colleague's. That is my burden. Yet perhaps in compensation for my lack of profundity, I am a veritable terrier for the truth. I will work at what I know, until I have dislodged some scrap of meaning from that pile of bones which once was a living relation between two of the most remarkable characters I have met.

With these thoughts, sir, I must return to the world of my own responsibilities and obligations.

In the meanwhile, I remain,
    Sincerely yours
        Hargood

CHAPTER 12

That evening, when the knock came, Mrs Thompson was surprisingly swift to reach the door.

Seated in front of the fire in the drawing-room, Grange heard her long pause, as though she considered her guest. He heard Swann say, almost defensively, 'I've come to visit Dr Grange.'

Having extracted this introduction from his guest, Mrs Thompson opened the door further and stood aside. Swann entered the front door, nodding to her, raising his hand briefly to his forehead. He stood short and bulky in the hallway, the empty sleeve of his amputated arm hanging in the light.

Inside the house, Swann was like an animal at bay, moving to the empty spaces, as though judging with his quick eye the avenues of escape. Mrs Thompson led him across the hallway into the inner hall and halted at the entrance to the drawing-room, so that Swann might enter and be introduced. He nodded again, nervously, at Mrs Thompson, who took his further salute as a sign of confusion and, in lieu of his own entrance, turned and walked ahead of him until Grange, hearing her approaching footsteps, rose, tall and pale, from a high-backed chair in front of the fire.

For a moment the three were in an odd confrontation: Grange with a volume of Seneca in his hand, which he had been reading, Mrs Thompson still upright. Behind her Swann stood, nervous in his best dark clothes, arrested in the doorway. Grange set aside the book on the mantel, nodded at his housekeeper and stepped past Mrs Thompson towards his nervously hovering guest.

When he reached out to shake Swann's hand, Swann's expression seemed to compose itself.

Half turning, Grange said, 'Thank you, Mrs Thompson.'

She moved silently towards the kitchen, in the direction of her domain. The atmosphere seemed to lighten a little.

'Mr Swann,' Grange said. 'You seem in good health. Would you care for some refreshment?'

'Thank you, sir.'

Grange indicated a second chair, which Swann took tentatively.

'Your wife, Mr Swann? In good health?'

'My woman? She's well . . .'

'And your two daughters?'

'Three. All well, sir.'

If, on the foreshore, Swann was like a bull or perhaps a minotaur, here he looked displaced. He sat on the edge of his chair, regarding Grange cautiously. A clutter of plates from Mrs Thompson in the kitchen caused him to pause suddenly.

Noticing his apprehension, Grange said, 'You have no objection to a quarter of lamb for our dinner?'

Swann shook his head, but he remained upright and alert.

'Would you perhaps care for some wine?'

Swann hesitated. 'I would, sir, if you have it.'

'My colleague Dr Hargood keeps a cellar. French and Spanish, mostly. He also holds in reserve a number of casks of Italian, from which he kindly dispenses upon me one or two.'

Grange would have continued to banter about the availability of wine if he had not noticed the look of polite incomprehension in Swann's eyes. It occurred to him that the nature of wine was as remote to his guest as the darker side of the moon. Swann drank beer and spirits. Perhaps his only acquaintance with wine would have been on a prize ship, when the crew were permitted to help themselves on some captured Spanish or French vessel. It would be a time of drunkenness and orgy, not of appreciation. There would be something of the contraband in his notion of wine, even something of licence. Noticing his unease, Grange checked himself.

'Mrs Thompson!'

In the doorway Mrs Thompson appeared. 'Sir?'

'Would you pour us some wine?'

Mrs Thompson glanced at Swann deliberately, then turned her gaze to Grange. 'Which wine, sir?'

'The Italian, Mrs Thompson.'

'Which Italian, sir?'

He had discussed the wine with her that afternoon, and it was

44

unlike her to forget details. At the same time, while he had mentioned the Italian wine, he had not specifically asked her to supply it that evening. Instead, he had assumed that since the conversation had settled upon one particular wine, she would understand that it would be served. It was this odd manoeuvring within the letter of their usual understanding that caused him some concern, though he could not directly blame her for ignoring an instruction that he had not issued.

'The Cagliari.'

'Sir.' Mrs Thompson nodded, as though the name itself were new to her, and remarkably strange. She left the room several degrees colder than when she had entered.

'We have had clear weather recently,' Grange said, 'despite the breezes.'

Swann nodded. In truth, it was unexpectedly cold that night for late summer and, though the fire added a layer of heat, there was a background chill. Grange smiled at Swann, but Swann was listening to Mrs Thompson's footsteps descend into the cellar.

'I believe Mrs Thompson is under the impression that you lead me astray,' Grange offered.

He observed Swann's expression move back from its concentration, as though disturbed from some deep intimacy of thought.

'Astray?' Swann asked.

'She disapproves of my long and solitary walks. She has gained the impression that you encourage me in them.'

'Why should she?' Swann enquired, his curiosity direct, half of him still listening to the sounds in the cellar. They could hear the faint squeak of the lid of a cask being removed, and Grange guessed Mrs Thompson was dipping a ladle to fill a carafe.

'I believe I make occasional mention of our conversations – since I find much of what you say to be of interest. She disapproves of my being subject to the sea breezes. I can only suppose that she damns you by association.'

Swann nodded. 'When a woman forms a view of a man, it does not easily change.'

'I believe you are damned, then – perhaps for eternity.'

They heard Mrs Thompson's footsteps again on the stones of the cellar and they might have been listening to a panther in a cage beneath.

'Of course, I find that on clear nights it grows colder,' Grange said.

At mention of the weather, Swann's composure visibly returned. 'Particularly when the nights are still,' he agreed.

Mrs Thompson closed the door to the cellar. Her footsteps crossed the pantry into the kitchen.

'We have had more thunderstorms this summer,' Grange said.

Swann nodded, though he would not be drawn immediately.

'You have had good weather this year for your own occupations?' Grange asked.

'There's more easting in the storms than last year.'

'Easting?'

'Northerlies too. Those are the worst for me.'

Grange struggled to grasp something. 'Because they are offshore?'

'That's right, sir. The offshore breezes bring no driftwood, nothing to salvage, not even firewood.'

It was true that the weather had been curiously irregular. When the wind turned from its customary south-westerly direction to the east, it usually heralded inconstancy, odd squalls, unexpected rain.

At Grange's suggestion they moved to the dining-room and sat down at the table. Mrs Thompson had set a fire in the grate behind Grange, to warm his back. The discussion moved forward in stops and halts. On the marsh, on his preferred terrain, Swann would speak eloquently and at length, choosing whatever subject came to mind, a natural orator. Now Grange's entire concentration was required to start the engine of his conversation.

When Mrs Thompson appeared once again with the wine, Grange nodded her in Swann's direction at the other end of the table. But she deliberately ignored the implication and approached her master, setting down a glass on the side table beside him, and poured his wine.

'If you will forgive me, Mr Swann, I shall taste the wine first.'

He drank, paused and nodded to Mrs Thompson.

She moved to Swann's end to pour wine into the glass on the table to the side of him, though without directly acknowledging him. Then she nodded to Grange, as though he were the only person in the room whom she recognised, and left. The partiality of her behaviour so astonished Grange that for several seconds he lost himself in contemplation of it.

Having watched her departure, he turned towards Swann, not knowing precisely what to expect by way of reaction to this display, when Swann's own behaviour caught his eye. To Grange's further surprise he was smiling to himself now, shaking his head softly; there was an expression of quiet consternation there; his eyes were lit by some form of internal contemplation. It seemed to Grange that Swann's behaviour could only have been in response to Mrs Thompson. It appeared – though Grange could not be entirely certain – as though Swann himself could not help but admire the magnificent and lofty consistency of her demeanour. Momentarily lost in his own thoughts, Grange wondered what form this appreciation might take. His only explanation, tentative though it might be, was that it was the type of admiration Swann would reserve for a large bull or truculent ram which consistently charged trespassers – the respect which a countryman normally and easily accorded a force of nature.

Somewhat perplexed by his own thoughts, Grange raised his glass. 'To your continued good health, Mr Swann.'

'To yours, sir.'

They set down their glasses. The expression of contemplation left Swann's face. Allowing a pause for these diversions to settle, Grange said, 'I wished to raise a matter with you.'

'A matter?'

'This time last year there were no salt furnaces in operation. I believe the normal season of burning is from May through to August. Now we are at the beginning of September, yet I perceive three furnaces are still in use.'

Swann nodded a trifle cautiously.

'You have an explanation? I am used to profiting by your knowledge.'

Swann considered his words. 'I understand they all belong to Mr St Just.'

'Why do they continue?'

'It is a notion of their owner, I believe.'

47

'But what is his reason, do you think?'

There was a rattle of plates as Mrs Thompson made her preparations for the main meal.

Swann glanced towards the kitchen, but now, apparently having ascertained the deeper nature of Mrs Thompson's character to his own satisfaction, he began to speak more easily. 'It was previously assumed that when August came, the sun was no longer hot enough to evaporate the salt-pans at sufficient speed to make brine, sir.'

'And what has changed?'

'As various furnaces have closed, so Mr St Just has purchased the additional pans.'

'I do not catch your import. Why should this affect the late-season burnings?'

'I think it is the changed ratio, sir, of storage pans to furnaces under his ownership. He has closed down certain furnaces, though he has kept the storage pans that came with them. With more pans holding brine relative to furnaces, he has enough stored brine to continue through the season with at least three furnaces burning.'

'I see. Why have certain other furnaces closed down?'

'There is pressure from the salt mines in the north country, particularly in Cheshire, I believe. A number of the smaller owners of the salt furnaces in Lymington have made a loss and one or two have been forced to sell.'

'Cheshire?' Grange asked. 'Cheshire has a flat coastline suitable for salt-pans?'

'They have found salt seams directly in the earth inland. There is no need to burn sea water. So they are not forced to suffer the cost of using coal.'

'If that is the general predicament, you think our industry is in its final stages?'

Swann nodded carefully.

Grange said, 'Yet one owner at least is confident enough to burn through the winter.'

'Sometimes, when a tree is ill,' Swann suggested, 'it puts on its finest show of flowers.'

'But if the Cheshire salt is less costly, because it requires no coal for evaporation, why do we survive at all?'

'The exorbitance of the Salt Tax is a help, sir, strange though it

48

may seem at first. It puts such a high price on the salt that the cost of coal burning is a much smaller proportion of the total. That allows some competition, at least.'

'You are a veritable mine of information, if I may say so.'

'I observe from a distance.'

'This is the explanation of our difficulties, then – competition from the Cheshire mines?'

'There is another thing that helps us to bear the load. The mines in Cheshire have no immediate ports and the cost of transportation to the port of Liverpool by ox-cart adds a price which is almost comparable with that of coal burning for evaporation.'

'There is a logic to our situation, then.'

'They supply middle and upper England, sir. But we still have retained a good market here in the south, where their transport costs are high. And we supply the demand from abroad, with ships able to ply to foreign places like Newfoundland directly from Lymington.'

'Our sea routes are safe, then?'

'God help us', Swann said, 'if the Cheshire mines should find some cheaper method of transportation to the coast.'

'Presumably they are not as seasonal as we are. Without the need for the sun's evaporation, I mean.'

'That is true, sir. That is another factor which Mr St Just attempts to change by burning through the year. Our rivals may mine their salt throughout the year. Their competition may incline us to change our own nature in response.'

Mrs Thompson appeared in the room and moved on the periphery of the conversation, setting down plates. Swann was occasionally distracted, but he seemed, finally, to have lost his overall apprehension.

To continue the conversation, and satisfy his curiosity further, Grange asked, 'This St Just. He sounds a man of independent thought.'

'He is clever, sir. Exceptionally clever, by some accounts.'

'Yet –' Grange attempted to pick up a tone he believed he detected '– you do not necessarily admire him?'

Mrs Thompson left and Grange noticed the change that came over Swann's face. It was the first time that he had truly smiled that evening and, observing it, Grange felt an obscure sense of satisfaction that perhaps Swann had finally found a sense of ease as a guest in his household. It was a reflective smile, and it spread slowly across Swann's features and then as slowly disappeared, replaced by an expression of sobriety.

'You do not answer my question, Mr Swann?'

There was caution in his guest's reply. Perhaps he was nervous of some association, even that St Just might be a patient of the physician in whose house he was a guest. 'You've met him?' Swann asked.

'Never in person. Perhaps now', Grange suggested, 'you may be inclined to consider my question. You admire Mr St Just?'

'No, sir,' Swann said carefully. 'I do not admire him greatly.'

'Then allow me, if you will, to be the devil's advocate and press you a little as to why that is so.'

He waited for several seconds.

Swann said, 'I do not know what are his motivations, but there are dangers in the course he is pursuing.'

'Dangers?'

'Physical dangers, mostly.'

'And what might they be?'

'It is better explained on the marsh.'

'What is there on the marsh,' Grange persisted, 'which cannot be mentioned here?'

'I believe that on the marsh we may witness directly some of the things about which I could speak.'

'Physical dangers, you say? Could you perhaps go so far as to give me the outline so that I may be apprised of what to look for in due course?'

Swann considered his host. 'The first thing is, air feeds the furnaces and the flow of air to the fire is controlled by the doors.' He paused. 'After September, the pattern of the winds is different from in summer. The winds themselves are stronger and more irregular in their direction. There's some danger in what they are doing now.'

'That is all you are prepared to tell me?'

Swann smiled. 'It is all I could easily explain at present.'

They continued the meal, speaking of this and that. Mrs

Thompson brought in the food, setting the plates down with a fearsome detachment. Swann ate reasonably well, though he was never entirely at ease while Mrs Thompson patrolled the neighbourhood, and such was his relief at her departure that more than once he broke into a shy smile when she left.

Afterwards, Grange offered his guest Madeira, and they went through to the sitting-room and talked by the fireside for perhaps an hour. But their conversation was discursive and fragmented, merely an exchange of pleasantries.

As the evening drew on, Grange stood up, excused himself and walked into the kitchen. 'Mrs Thompson, I shall see my guest out in due course. There is no need for you to stay up further.'

'Thank you, sir.'

Grange returned to Swann in the sitting-room. A short while afterwards they both listened to the inner door being closed as Mrs Thompson retired for the night to her rooms beyond the kitchen and pantry. A certain relief came over Swann and the possibility opened once again of a more lively discussion, but by then Grange had used up the small remains of his energy and felt a little too tired to question Swann further on the dangers of the late-burning furnaces.

When Swann left, shortly before midnight, Grange stood at the door and observed his short, heavy figure depart down the street.

In the role of host, Grange had taxed himself in the amount he usually ate or drank. Now he moved towards the stairs, laden with heavy food. It seemed to him that Hargood's regular bleedings had removed the energy to digest such a meal. In his normal routine he was able to counteract this by keeping to a lighter diet of fish and broth. But the extra movement of blood to his stomach to digest the heavy meal made him feel faint. He walked up the stairs carefully. At the landing he found himself swallowing heavily and involuntarily, with a trace of salt in his saliva. After he had closed the door to his room he crossed over to the basin and threw up, silently and copiously, the entire contents of the evening's meal.

CHAPTER 13

Dear Leman,

I come now to a crucial matter in this strange account, in whose development I may have played a sad and perhaps a terrible role. It happened that for some time I had remained curious about Mrs Celia Quill's background. I could not believe that one who had made so profound an impression in local society would have passed entirely unnoticed in London – that one so learned, so kind, so deserving of the companionship of others, could have left behind her a vacuum in her previous milieu. As I have recorded in my earlier correspondence, I ceased to chide my younger colleague on his impetuous flight to the intimacy of a handsome widow whose origins were obscure.

Thus there passed several further months. My concern returned to me when I discovered how withdrawn my colleague had become, how struck by his own thoughts regarding her. But I had known from previous experience that remonstration with him of any kind was unlikely to achieve the desired effect. Thus, having counselled caution to him in his affair with Mrs Celia Quill, I now did the same to myself in the exercise of further criticism.

As the days proceeded I did merely observe his condition. I watched him cast down into his own thoughts. I considered the strange power of his arrest by her, and the effect upon his life.

My caution extended to making discreet enquiries about Mrs Quill in other directions. I mentioned my curiosity about her past to my mistress in London, who corresponded with me regularly. To satisfy my curiosity, she was willing to take up the matter and explore some aspects further, and even to raise a question or two with several of her acquaintances in the capital. My mistress is naturally affable and avid to please, yet even so she set about her business with a thoroughness which surprised me. After perhaps a fortnight she wrote to me that she had heard of a story of a woman by the same name, though it seemed to her merely coincidence and she recorded the fact only to amuse me. It appeared from her investigation that there had been a certain Mrs Celia Quill who had a reputation in society, though of a kind so far removed from the Mrs Quill of Lymington that it seemed absurd to reproduce it. My mistress could not be sure whether she had gathered the story correctly and perhaps had misplaced certain parts of it. She wrote to me subsequently that she wished to make further enquiries before committing the account to paper. For a number of weeks I heard nothing further, and began to think she had discovered no evidence or additional confirmation. But a letter arrived in due course in which she recorded the following summary of it.

It appeared, from her sources, that there had been a notorious madam of the name of Celia Quill, who owned one of those establishments which are set aside for the entertainment of rich men. According to her information, the site of this place had been in Chelsea, in Cheyne Walk, but further corroboration had been difficult because some years previously the establishment had closed in mysterious circumstances, the house had been sold to a prosperous merchant and nothing further had been heard of its owner since. My mistress added that it could not possibly be the same woman, even though the name 'Quill' was distinct and unusual and, in combination with the Christian name Celia, a further odd coincidence.

Merely out of curiosity, in the course of writing my return letter to her, I asked my mistress to assemble what further evidence she could regarding the affair of that other Mrs Quill, who seemed so far removed from any notion of our paragon of Lymington. The information she subsequently imparted to me was so strange, so peculiarly disturbing, that I began to feel almost an obligation upon me to pass at least the outline of it on to my colleague. For certain aspects of the story rang oddly, almost in a different world, like one of those bells that sailors sometimes are thought to hear underwater, or those singing voices which they may detect in the clear air and, finding no source, ascribe to such mythical beings as mermaids.

I did not take the matter seriously at first, as I have reported. But some aspects of her account remained with me. For several weeks I ignored the message it contained; yet, far from receding, slowly the story seemed to perturbate my sensibility and to find some home in me, as if the disquiet I felt about her past had found an echo, albeit an absurd one.

I found myself, in certain moments of privacy, considering the matter, as if it held some deeper meaning. Once or twice, indeed, I discovered myself staring out of the window, in contemplation of my mistress's account, as though the shore and water which lie beneath my purview could supply some explanation.

My dear Leman, you will forgive me if I digress briefly, if only to establish a metaphor, whose purpose is nothing so humble as to convey a sense of oddness, suggestive at the very least of the strange light which hung about these proceedings. It sometimes happens, if the mist is thick about the mouth of the Lymington river and the sounds are muffled, that one may see, burning through the outer reaches of the fog, the recognition lights of a vessel – a faint halo of a lamp swinging in the rigging at the bow and at the stern. One may deduce that beneath the faint light is the body of a ship – its timbers solid, its master walking the deck, its crew swinging the line for depth, perhaps a jolly-boat under the bows attempting to pull the vessel slowly forward. One may infer further, from such tiny emanations of sound, from such faint tapers and ghosts of light, a solid and complex physical presence, the true dimensions of which may yet be hidden from the senses. So it is with much of what I shall write. I perceive the nimbus of light, the faint emanations of sound, and try to deduce the shadowy structure and form of the floating world beneath.

These considerations may justify my interest, but they do not protect me from the consequences of my own actions. For if I believed there was substance to the story – more substance than mere far-off noise and lights – then it became my duty to impart such information to my colleague, not so that it could dissuade him from his course, but so that he might have the opportunity, in hearing of it, to refute it entirely. Thus, I hoped and trusted, his superior knowledge of Mrs Quill would provide him with all the evidence for rendering the story inert and excluding the account from further consideration.

In the meantime, I conscientiously gathered what further evidence I could from my mistress, and chose a time to invite my colleague to my house, where I could apprise him of the story. Again, my dear Leman, I am invaded by doubt as to my motives, for I shall admit to you now that a part of me was curious to see what he would make of my mistress's report. I wondered whether some pieces of the account might ring true, sufficient at least that he might betray some concern or consternation which would arrest his defence of her. In short, I own that my motives, my curiosity, played a role in bringing the evidence before him, such as it was, and that in the pursuit of my own aims I may be accused of being less than sensible of his feelings and constitution.

Whatever reasons I may ascribe to myself, or you may in your wisdom impute to me, I do maintain that I myself would never have believed the strength of my colleague's reaction. For it seemed that, loyal though he was to her, the report fitted certain doubts and sentiments which he himself entertained regarding her. When he heard my first report his countenance drained of its colour and I thought that he would faint. At a certain point in my account he cried out, like an animal in pain, then buried his face in his hands. When he looked up I saw, after an interval, an expression which I do not particularly wish to see again. It was calm on the surface, but there was something beneath, some hidden resolve or despair, like a kind of madness, as if some aspect of his life had been unutterably altered.

I myself was shaken by the experience, as if I had released who knows what dark forces or suspicions in his mind. I offered to accompany him home, fearing some terrible inclination on his part might drive him to an extreme which I did not wish to contemplate, but he assured me that he was in sufficient equanimity to reach his house safely. Having reluctantly accepted his assurances, I allowed him to depart by foot. Short of countermanding his own wishes, I believe I could not have done otherwise.

I understand from Mrs Thompson, whom I had cause to

question the following morning, that he returned home safely, then went directly to his study, closing the door; after which she heard nothing. She believes he attempted to read (for she found a volume of Hume open on his desk that she had not seen before while tidying the room earlier that day). She thought that his outward calm lasted until he went to sleep, but that in the course of the night he entered a high fever.

The following morning, having been summoned by her to attend to him, I found his fever so advanced and his pulse so fast that I decided to take drastic measures and bleed him, if only to draw forth some of the terrible energy of his humour. Once I had absolved him of much blood, his fever seemed to calm a little, and I felt after some hours of sitting by his bed that I could leave him to the kind and expert attendance of Mrs Thompson, who had gathered much experience in supervising his patients.

It is from this that he now recovers, albeit slowly. And I, for my own part, must come to terms with the fact that it was I who imparted the information to him, I who perhaps was the cause of his malaise.

My own guilt haunts me. If he was struck down so far, it was in part because I did not know in what simple and direct domain he had placed his soul. Perhaps I should have guessed that his infatuation with Mrs Quill and her daughter had progressed to a point beyond that of easy recall. I have said before that there is something in him that is fearless, almost heroic. He had placed himself at risk without a thought of the consequences to himself. In the turmoil of my own guilt, sometimes I consider that perhaps what he has demonstrated is greater than fearlessness, or simple foolhardiness. Perhaps it is courage itself. Though there is much in this affair that perplexes me, I feel it is incumbent upon me to do all I can to help him to recover his equanimity.

On the surface of things at least we are cheerful, he and I. We exchange good humour, albeit a little uneasily. But beneath our conversation our thoughts run to our own particular considerations and, I dare say, to our own demons. In the meantime he appears to listen to what I say. For my part, I am determined to understand something more of what has happened, not least because certain aspects of it affect me directly, and not only to the degree, that he is my colleague and I consider his well-being a part of my responsibility. To this end I will attempt to piece together those fragments which arise from our conversation.

I must end my missive here. Perhaps you will forgive me for an account which, in the telling of it, appears so strange not only in its outline, but also in its details.

In the interim, sir, I remain,

Sincerely yours,

Hargood

CHAPTER 14

'Silas, my dear fellow.'

Kneeling down, making a shuffling sound, Hargood emerged from the chicken run, his face clouded and soiled, but indefatigably handsome. Two lines proceeded upwards from the ridge of his nose, emphasising the vertical and hieratic force of his face, which was broad, the cheeks almost pointed. The silver in his hair was like a limn of light. Only the boar-like strength of his neck subverted final elegance.

Earlier that morning he had been cleaning his guns and traces of oil covered his hands. A further touch of gun oil lay on his cheekbone, where he had wiped it inadvertently. Then, while the urge of maintenance was upon him, he had set to at repairing one of the large chicken runs at the back of his property. He had considered asking his manservant Simmonds to attend to it, but Simmonds was infirm and, if the truth were told, Hargood enjoyed the use of his hands in simple woodwork. He stood back from the construction, which had been hammered together with great force using large iron nails. It was not refined, but it seemed crude and strong, and Hargood was pleased enough to admire it. With a degree of satisfaction, then, he turned to observe Grange from under his leonine eyebrows.

'Do we walk, sir?' Hargood asked.

'We do.'

'Let me rinse this grime and fetch my coat.' They moved together through the apple orchard at the back of the house to the rear door.

'I will not be long, sir.'

Grange heard the swill of liquid from a pitcher into a basin, the splash of soap and water, the brisk rubbing of a drying cloth. Then Hargood appeared again, was arrested by a thought and swung to face the interior of the house. He shouted into the darkened passage that led into the kitchens, 'Mr Simmonds! I go now.'

'Sir.' Simmonds shuffled to the doorway, observing his master through his spectacles, perhaps awaiting some further order. But Hargood had already taken Grange by the shoulder and guided him forward along the passageway to the main hall, where they paused briefly in the gloom beneath the row of guns of various kinds – from single-barrelled muskets to double-barrelled fowling pieces – that constituted Hargood's forward lines of sporting artillery.

Hargood, having lifted his coat off its peg, drew it on as they walked towards the door and gave a final brief but assertive tug with both hands at a point below the collars. The catch was lifted and Grange was suddenly outside, driven by the onrush of Hargood's enthusiasm, blinking in febrile sunlight. Hargood glanced down and saw that his dress was in disorder, that a piece of shirt protruded from his fly. Without losing speed, he tucked the offending corner back into his breeches, and proceeded to hook the catches together and repair the damage. For several moments he was closely engaged while walking. Grange, aware of his concentration, entertained the faint hope that Hargood would collide with a wooden corner post, and so he might begin the journey with some advantage over his winded companion. But his mentor successfully navigated the obstruction.

With his dress in reasonable order, Hargood began to stride out and look about him. 'I am not sure this walking exercise is suitable to my own constitution. I believe I should prefer to take to horse and drive you before me like a sheep or cow.'

'I believe you would enjoy that, Hargood.'

'I believe you are right, sir.'

'Yet', Grange said, determined to move onto the attack, 'it seems to me that, in the spiritual sense at least, it is you who prefer to be driven like a sheep or cow.'

'Explain yourself, sir.'

'The Lord is your shepherd, Hargood, so you tell me.'

'Unfortunately, the Lord is manifestly not *your* shepherd. That is your problem, sir. You will accept no guidance from higher sources.'

'In the absence of my belief, you see yourself as a higher source?'

'Of course. That is only natural. In the absence of divine influence, I believe I am the best alternative in the matter of authority.'

Hargood increased his pace further, determined to make his disapproval felt. He had always been surprised by the physical resilience of Grange, now more than two months into the rest into which he had been induced by the departure of Mrs Quill. Having turned from Hargood's colleague into his patient, Grange reluctantly accepted the tutelage of the older man. Hargood, a benign uncle or father, had asserted his role with a sure command. Grange, more contemplative, seemed to withdraw further into himself, drifting to that outer periphery where privacy meets silence. He was like a shadow to Hargood, as though he accepted the mild indignity of Hargood's supervision as the price of internal calm.

'Since you are silent, I will speak for us both.' Hargood knew that it was abstraction, or the prospect of it, that could draw Grange from his reverie. Most men regarded abstraction as a superficial aspect, but to Grange it seemed the heart of the matter. So, in his role as Grange's guardian and adviser, Hargood approached his subject obliquely. 'I wonder in your case whether I should discuss with you your illness.'

'Why should you not?' came the calm reply.

Hargood ignored this response, but proceeded nevertheless. 'As you are aware, I am of the opinion that the patient should know as little as possible about his inner workings.'

'In order that the physician may give full voice to his own position?'

'One of the singular duties of the physician', Hargood said, 'should be to obscure and mystify the cause as much as possible so that the patient's system, freed of the fretful supervision and intervention by its owner, is allowed sufficient latitude to cure itself.'

'Admirably put, if I may say so.'

'Then kindly do not interrupt me, sir. The more complex the explanations, the more prolix the reasoning, the more replete with Latin names, the better for both physician and patient. All serve their due and justifiable purpose in obscuring and solemnifying the illness.'

There was perhaps a trace of a smile on Grange's face, as he listened to his older colleague's strictures, which only made Hargood more determined to drive the matter further. 'The point is surely this, sir. Though we physicians know little, we may yet bask in one absolute certainty – that the patient knows even less. That is, if you like, the solid and final foundation of our ancient practice.'

'Agreed.'

Hargood paused briefly, if for no other reason than to consider how he might advance. 'Then you will also agree, since the departure of Mrs Quill has brought about the gradual return of your faculties, it would run against the notions of our profession to enlighten you on her circumstances, or to convey any recent news of her whereabouts.'

They reached the brow of a shallow hill and gazed down the Solent towards Lepe. Grange felt his heart shudder and a sensation like a shadow passing across him, but he was determined to give Hargood no grounds for increasing his dependency.

'I believe,' Grange said, 'as a principle it is perfectly logical.'

'What reason would there be for my conveying a message I received from my mistress this morning, for example, regarding Mrs Quill?'

'No reason whatsoever.'

'You are not prepared to fight for the privilege?'

'I believe not.'

'Not even to tug at the other end of the bone? You will not attempt, using your sophistical and damnable intelligence, to provide a rationale for persuading me to convey the information to you?' Hargood was incensed. 'Not that I would take any notice of it, I hasten to add.'

'No.'

'No indeed?'

'No indeed, sir.'

'And you give no reason for this perversity?'

'None whatsoever.'

'Why not?'

'I know that you will convey such information not because I am able to persuade you, but because, for your own reasons, you wish to convey it. No effort on my part will alter that fact.'

'You agree with me, then, that there are no grounds for conveying the information other than my own personal wish and indulgence?'

'I agree.'

'It seems we have too much agreement in this world,' Hargood said. 'I had hoped for a little more stimulus.'

'You shall not find it in me, I am afraid.'

'Agreement or stimulus?'

'Neither.'

'You are not prepared even to encourage me?'

'No.'

'It seems to me, sir, you are taking an intolerable liberty with my authority.'

'You are, I believe, best able to judge your authority.'

'Beneath your usual diplomacy, I judge your attitude to be insurrectionary.'

'I believe you are entirely right.'

'I am tired of being told I am right. When we pass Hatchett Pond I shall be tempted to take you by the scruff of the neck and pitch you face forward into the brack. Before I do so, no doubt you will give me the satisfaction of agreeing with my sentiment, at least as regards the justice of my intention.'

'Entirely,' Grange confirmed.

After Hatchett Pond, where Hargood mercifully restrained himself from carrying out his threat, they turned south and west, and walked towards the shore, following footpaths through the fields. The grass was high and the sun had gained in heat. They walked for a good half-hour before they came to a meadow that sloped downwards to the marshes.

After a further several hundred paces, Grange paused again to allow the clamour of his heart to subside. Another spell of faintness, briefer than the first, caused him to close his eyes. They were on a slight incline and much of the Solent could be seen. He leaned on his cane, attempted to control his breathing in order to keep his distress from Hargood and stared out towards the water. In one respect at least, Hargood had been right about the message he had imparted to Grange regarding Mrs Quill. It had induced a state of excitation in his patient, a fluttering in his pulse. It was that, more than tiredness, which had caused him to halt.

Hargood was unexpectedly silent beside him, his hands clasped behind his back, staring out across the moving tides.

An event came to Grange's assistance, at least one which could distract them both from the vagaries of the present circumstances. Behind a line of elms an elderly merchantman emerged, driving against the tide as she closed with the Pennington shore, avoiding the faster flow in the deepest part of the channel towards Yarmouth. Her sails, which once were white, were now so distempered by use and sunlight they had become a patchwork of cream and yellow. He wondered whether she would enter the Lymington river mouth, or perhaps anchor offshore and ship her cargo upriver by longboat. But there was no sign of reducing sail and her slow progress suggested a further destination, Southampton or Portsmouth.

As if sensing his younger colleague's thoughts, Hargood said, 'Fifty years ago she would have docked in Lymington.'

Grange nodded. It was common knowledge that the causeway built across the river some sixty years before by a certain Captain Cross had caused the river to silt and slowly its former maritime functions had been strangled. Only the lighter ships and flat-bottomed barges could easily use the channel. Now Lymington was being overtaken as a port and so its reliance on the salt industry had grown, if anything, greater.

Beyond the elms the merchantman changed course to make the best use of the tide along the nearer shore. By general reckoning it was shallower along the mainland shore, but the contrary tidal current was less. The manoeuvre necessitated a gybe, and they heard the creak of the yard-arms as her sailing master adjusted the squaresails to the new tack. As they watched, the crew moved forward to the foredeck and began to thread ropes through tackles. Now, with the main forces realigned, the two jibs were hauled across to the new tack. The final flutter of the sails subsided.

Hargood said, 'Shall we continue, sir?'

'By all means.'

Their path took them towards the shore. Reaching the shoreline itself, they paused while two ox-carts pulled coal across the muddied path to the group of furnaces that lay out beyond Pylewell.

A curious change had overtaken them. They had emerged from rural peace to a segment of the shoreline close by a salt furnace. As they approached more closely, the faint roar of the flames inside the furnace house became louder and they had to raise their voices to speak.

A gang of ragged men followed the ox-carts, their overseer marching ahead of them. They were wretched, their clothes hardly more than rags. They left behind the desperate smell of unwashed bodies.

Grange felt a surge of anger at such misery. Hargood, as though anticipating him, said, 'They are paid sufficient to live by their labours. It is unfortunate that they spend it all on drink.'

'The heat of the furnaces evaporates their body fluids. They are forced to replenish.'

'They could drink water, sir.'

'They are encouraged to drink beer by their paymasters, who have a franchise. It is subtracted from their wages.'

Hargood, for a single, brief occasion, was silent.

Despite his determination not to provoke Hargood, Grange felt the flame of uprising in himself. 'They work, they sweat, they drink beer which consumes their money and in turn, to earn more wages, they are forced out on the marshes again to man the furnaces. It is an infernal machine. It is a wheel on which, as the years proceed, they are casually broken.'

'The industry is our common inheritance,' Hargood said.

There was at least some truth in this. Salt had been the staple manufacture of Lymington from the earliest times, even before the Romans. The settlement had grown with salt-workings. During the previous century it had become one of the most concentrated sites of industry in the world, perhaps the greatest. The level of burning had not reduced since then, but had, if anything, grown.

'Precedent', Grange said, 'does not make it right.'

'Precedent is no moral judge. What would they do otherwise? They would be beggars and worse. Or they would be press-ganged for the Navy.'

'Press-gangers no longer come to Lymington, I do believe, for the reason that the majority of our able-bodied men are being broken in the salt furnaces. And those that are spewed out are so depleted in body and spirit that they could not make sailors.'

'Then that is another virtue of the salt furnaces,' Hargood said. 'We are no longer plagued by press-gangers.'

'Just as, for example, the advantage of being drowned might be that we no longer carry any live fleas upon our person.'

'Sir,' Hargood announced, 'speaking as a Tory, I believe I am impervious to irony.'

They halted on a low hill and stared into the impassive morning silence. The great industry lay spread about the shore. The salterns were made on flat land divided into shallow pools about twenty feet square by low mudbanks a few inches high. Into these shallow basins water was scooped by large wooden balers from the ponds which had trapped it at high tides. Here it was allowed to evaporate under the sun's heat. Spread throughout the works were small windmills about twelve feet high, which continually pumped the water into different sets of pans. When evaporation had caused the salt water to reach the condition of brine, it was lifted up to large cisterns from which it ran direct to the boiler houses.

Hargood swung an arm through an arc that encompassed the shoreline, the waterway of the Solent, the boiling clouds that rose above the shore. 'This is our community. Those of us who settle here accept its workings, as we accept those of the sun and tides.'

'I believe you are a veritable Dr Pangloss, sir,' Grange commented. 'All things are good to you.'

'And you, on the other hand, are like Dr Pangloss's author, sir – cold, rational and no respecter of traditions.'

The boiler houses were brick sheds with low walls, surmounted by a large expanse of tiled roof to within a few feet of the ground. Under the angled roofs were the raised pans of water. Beneath them the furnaces constantly flamed, burning all day and through the night.

'Each furnace is a mechanism of disease,' Grange said, 'made for inducing chills, colds, pneumonia.'

'There is no activity on earth that is not without its risks. Even love, sir, has its poxes.'

From where they stood, they could see that clouds of steam filled the boiler house closest to them. Sometimes figures in sweat-drenched clothes moved outside to cool before they were overcome by steam, then returned. Others carried fresh brine from the waiting pools outside into the heat of the furnace houses and poured them into the great vats for boiling. A third group of workers, perhaps the most wretched, carried coal from heaps piled at the side of the furnace houses, shovelling it into the intense flames with long-handled staves.

The boiling of the brine was only the final process in the making of salt. The majority of water was removed by the action of the sun on the shallow evaporation pools. This limited the main season to perhaps four months in midsummer. During this period the industry was intensive, day and night, every day of the week without rest.

Now, after a season's burning, the roads around were black with ashes. Once, halting on the course of his walk to Oxey to stare out to sea, Grange glanced down at the dark paths, filled with ash and cinders. 'It is the end of the burning season. Now that only three furnaces continue, at least the majority of the workers will find some rest.'

'You see, my dear Silas,' Hargood said with evident satisfaction. 'In the end, nature regulates herself.'

CHAPTER 15

'I believe that you do good.' Hargood gathered himself for the sub-clause. 'But in a dark way.'

Grange laughed quietly. The sensation was strange to him, walking with his older colleague on the hillside. Beside him, Hargood moved with his head down, driving forward, perhaps considering how he might come at Grange again.

To forestall him, or perhaps to deflect him, Grange asked: 'How dark, then, is dark?'

'Let me see, now.' Hargood was concerned to extend the metaphor. 'Your darkness is not the darkness of mal-intention. Rather, it is the darkness of hiding your intention.'

'You mean, if my interpretation is correct, that since my intention is private, you feel annoyed.'

'As your physician and adviser, sir, I do believe I have a right to be annoyed.'

'As much as I have a right to keep my intention private?'

If the best means of defence against Hargood was attack, it was Hargood who now appeared immune to distraction. 'Your condition is of the mind as much as the body. Yet you keep your mind well hidden. I say this, sir, that if you had a leg which malingered you would allow me to examine it.'

'But as you yourself have said, it is not my leg which you wish to examine. It is my thoughts. I fail to see how I may expose my mind to your view. After all, I myself cannot be entirely sure about its contents.'

'Precisely,' Hargood said. 'The working of each man's mind is a mystery to himself.'

'You speak philosophically.'

'A man's thoughts, by their very nature, are part and parcel of what he is. That illustrates the point perfectly. He may no more perceive them than the eye may see itself. It is for others to consider them in objectivity.'

'For example, you.'

'For example, me.'

Grange smiled to himself at Hargood's beavering intensity. 'Then, since you are so much exercised, please proceed to examine my mind.'

Hargood, having won an initial round, was now concerned to move cautiously, consolidating his gains. 'There is much still that we do not understand. With each day that passes your physical disposition improves, despite your adherence to an impoverished diet. Yet concerning the true cause of your condition there is much that you retain.'

'What, would you say, is the true cause of my condition?'

'Well, sir, I believe you know as well as I. The true cause of your condition is a certain lady, whose participation in this matter you do not discuss and whose name, when I raise it, you studiously ignore.'

'I am silent about Mrs Quill simply because she is absent.'

'Absent in body, perhaps. But present in your thoughts.'

'In your thoughts, too?' Grange asked slyly.

'Indeed. And I have the temerity to assert, further, that she is what we should discuss, if we begin to examine the contents of your mind.'

They walked in silence for several seconds. Grange said, 'Then let us begin.'

'I used to believe you were innocent, Silas. But now I do not think so any more. I believe you are something far more dangerous . . .' Hargood paused, as though searching. 'I believe you are pure.'

Grange was silent for several seconds while he considered the accusation.

'Perhaps you would explain what you mean by "pure"?'

'It is an odd word, I agree. I will determine to address it.' Grange observed his solid walking gait, head pushed forward. Hargood raised his eyes, as if about to deliver to an audience. 'For example, one can use the word "pure" without a sense of contradiction in the phrase "pure evil" – though for the time being I should perhaps add that I happen to think that you are also largely, though not entirely, benevolent.'

'I am grateful for small mercies. Perhaps you would explain further.'

'As a believer in the Church of England,' Hargood went on, 'I do not consider the Pope is innocent, though I am prepared to concede he might be pure.'

'You intrigue me, Hargood.'

'Do I?'

'Since you have raised the matter of purity, please extend the metaphor.'

'By all means, sir. Purity seems to me an expression of wholeness, of what the Greeks called integrity. I believe, in practical terms, it means the art of living according to one's own lights and accepting the consequences.'

'What you say is interesting.'

Hargood seemed to gather himself. 'From my point of view Celia Quill is, in her own way, equally pure.'

The mention of her name again seemed to cause a kind of heaviness between them, but Grange was anxious to dispel the notion of too intense a confrontation. 'Please continue.'

'The difference between innocence and purity seems to be particularly highlighted by experience.'

'By what kinds of experience?'

'The effect of experience, let us say.'

'I am no closer to your meaning.'

'We are men of the world, sir. I mean, for example, experience of the flesh. People may lose their innocence – whatever "innocence" means – through sexual experience, but in the process they may also become purer, that is to say, more purely themselves.'

'These are interesting thoughts. Since I am – according to you – dangerously pure, how would you describe yourself?'

'Benevolently impure, I do believe,' Hargood said with a certain pride. 'But you have succeeded in deflecting me from my course, which is to arraign you for your purity.'

They had come to a promontory overlooking the Solent and the sudden view brought a halt to the proceedings of trial according to the notion of purity. Standing on the rim of a shallow hill, they overlooked the mudflats that spread around the Solent shore. Towards Hurst Castle, the horizontal meniscus of light on the horizon was bisected by the thin, vertical columns of smoke from the remaining salt furnaces, the patient and pitiful signs of man's

68

efforts. To Grange they seemed like a few straggling hairs on the bald dome of the earth.

They halted, as if by mutual agreement, to take in the view of earthworks and several small, man-made lakes. Grange said, 'Beside the furnace houses there are storing pools for the brine that has been evaporated by the sun.'

Hargood was suspicious of a further deflection. 'Indeed?'

Grange continued, 'I understand there is an organism, the Lymington brine shrimp, which is the only animal capable of living in such concentrations of salt. I seem to recall it was discovered by a physician, Dr Watley, some years ago.'

'You test my knowledge, sir. Though I do not know whether you intend to question me on Dr Watley, or the animal in question. Or do you make a point?'

'The point I attempt to make is that what may be a pure environment for one being may be poisonous to another.'

'These dissertations, which are interesting in themselves, serve no immediate purpose that I can see.'

'Perhaps Mrs Quill, whom you also describe as dangerously pure, inhabited an environment which others would not find congenial, but in which she herself felt free.'

'An interesting notion. There are, I believe, exotic beings who live in odd situations. What of it?'

'There is another aspect of the Lymington brine shrimp. I am informed that the salt-makers do swear that the organism purifies the brine ponds. They insist on spreading it from pool to pool, so that it may do its good works.'

'It purifies?'

'It feeds on weed, they say, and the salt products of the boiling are purer in consequence.'

'My dear Silas, when I next take a pinch of white salt for my soup, I will bless the shrimp for it. But let us not be carried away by the achievements of the animal. I have only to mention purity and you depart on a lecture on the Lymington brine shrimp. I believe, sir, I should now call this conversation to order.'

By a kind of mutual agreement, however, for several minutes they desisted from immediate further discussion of Mrs Quill and looked out across the marshes towards Hurst Castle, to the two lighthouses, one short and one tall, that guided ships through the deep channel between the shoal banks.

'Purity, then,' Grange reminded Hargood. 'You spoke of purity.'

But it seemed to Hargood that he had made sufficient progress that day not to tempt fate, and he was inclined towards silence. They walked the final distance to Hargood's house without speaking much further. Hargood invited Grange to take tea with him before he returned home. After tea, Hargood offered his guest the use of the fly home, but Grange insisted on walking. To Hargood's eye, at least, his younger colleague seemed undisturbed, though a little withdrawn and reflective. They bade goodbye at the door and Grange set out to walk the two miles back to his home.

CHAPTER 16

Hargood was surprised when, knocking on the door of Grange's house the following morning, the bolts were drawn open and Mrs Thompson appeared like a sudden angry angel in the doorway. 'He has fainted, sir.'

Hargood was taken aback. The words were delivered like an accusation.

'When?'

'After your walk yesterday.'

'And now?' Hargood enquired.

'Now he is in a fever.'

'Let me examine him.'

Hargood had almost to force his way past Mrs Thompson, who reluctantly acquiesced, as though he alone were responsible for her master's relapse, and at the very least should be restricted from further mischief. In the hallway for a moment they confronted one another like hostile witnesses, until Mrs Thompson drew back and Hargood threw his coat over the rails. He ascended the stairs, his large hand gliding on the railing, peering upwards into the gloom of the landing, as though driving his presentiment ahead of him.

Mrs Thompson hurried after him, talking as they rose. 'When he returned from his walk yesterday, he seemed distracted. He did not take supper and I heard him cross the floor. After a while I heard the sound of his body – a weight falling – collapsing on the floorboards. When I reached him he was lying in a sweat and fever. I could not rouse him sufficiently for him to stand but I managed to convey him to his bed.'

On the landing Hargood paused, then pulled open the door and entered the bedroom. The curtain had been drawn against the strong light. A slight breeze filtered through the half-open sash window. In his bed in the further corner, Grange lay breathing quietly, apparently peacefully asleep.

Hargood laid a hand on his brow and felt his pulse. He turned towards Mrs Thompson. 'The fever has subsided.'

'In the night he was agitated,' Mrs Thompson said, 'and called out.'

'Has he woken?'

'Briefly, sir. Then he seemed exhausted and fell into sleep again. He has not woken since.'

Hargood glanced down at the white face, with its shiny covering of moisture. 'Bring me a damp, cold cloth.'

Mrs Thompson walked to the sideboard, dipped a cloth in the pitcher of water and returned. Hargood drew up a chair, sat down, leaned forward and put the cold cloth on Grange's face. Almost immediately there was an intake of breath from the patient and his eyes opened.

Grange's eyes seemed to waver, then focused. 'Hargood?'

'Silas, my dear fellow. I understand you were struck down.'

Grange's eyes glanced around the room, at Mrs Thompson smiling behind Hargood's shoulder. Then he closed them again, as though gathering himself. He swallowed. 'I fainted.'

'Mrs Thompson found you lying on the floorboards in a fever. It was a good thing she heard you fall. You might have lain for several hours.'

Grange swallowed once more. His Adam's apple moved convulsively against his unshaven neck.

'Silas, my dear fellow. I believe that something in our discussion agitated you. I shall not ply you with it further. Rest now. I will

71

return this evening. In the meantime, I leave you in most capable hands.'

He was about to stand and leave when the cold, firm hand of the patient reached about his wrist. It was a casual encirclement, but when the grip tightened, as if to impart a message, Hargood had not experienced such icy and violent strength. 'Hargood, I would ask you. Do not withhold information.'

'Silas, if the subject causes such a profound reaction, I believe we should desist from it until . . .'

'It is not discussion of Mrs Quill which causes my consternation, but the withholding of information regarding her.'

The grip relaxed, as if the patient's strength had exhausted itself in the intensity of his communication.

Hargood withdrew his chastened wrist and, with his other hand, rubbed it thoughtfully. He nodded briefly at Mrs Thompson and repeated, 'I will visit you this evening, when I have finished my duties.'

But Grange had closed his eyes, and began breathing softly and deeply, as if from great relief.

Hargood raised himself and stood before the appraising eyes of Mrs Thompson. She smiled at him, as if in sympathy with his loss of composure, though perhaps she was satisfied now that he was sufficiently chastened by the turn of events.

In due course she followed him down the stairs, helped him on with his coat, and watched his fly depart with a certain detached speculation.

CHAPTER 17

When Hargood visited that evening, he found Grange seated in the chair next to the window, looking out at the light above the Solent. He sat down beside him. For several moments neither spoke. At length Hargood said, 'You wish me to speak of Mrs Quill?'

Grange did not move, staring out across the marshes towards the folding light, where blue graded into black.

Eventually Hargood spoke again: 'My mistress wrote to me a few days ago, to say that she heard, from a friend in Chiswick, that a certain woman had come to visit her boarding-house and she knew only that this woman had come from Lymington. She learned it because the ostler, lifting the traveller's luggage to the hall of the boarding-house, mentioned the point of embarkation. It was a wholly chance remark, except that her friend described her as having a certain presence and also mentioned that she seemed incongruous in that place.'

Hargood waited for some sign of response, but Grange did not move, staring out across the still water. Hargood continued, 'I wrote asking my mistress to pursue the matter, in the hope that she might uncover some further fragment of information. But it seemed that, by the time she looked into it further, the woman had moved on from the boarding-house and had given no forwarding address. She had left no name, either, and she merely paid in coin directly for her lodging. That, and the fact that she was unaccompanied, had caused her to be noticed.' He swallowed, once, heavily. 'My mistress says she left no trace.'

It seemed a strangely impoverished ending. Perhaps Hargood felt subject to a particular guilt in withholding something which gave so little succour. He breathed out deeply and spoke again: 'I will report one other matter, which I am nervous of and which I have withheld until such time as you might be able to receive it.' Hargood paused and composed himself. 'I know that I have never met a more formidable woman. Yet on one occasion only I saw her discountenanced. It occurred during my last visit to her, before she left Lymington, when I first informed her of the public reports of her past in the London *Courier*. I have told you that she showed no fear or anger, but observed me with a detachment and directness that I found uncomfortable. But I now add something else. After we had finished our conversation, we moved towards the doorway of the house. She said, suddenly and unexpectedly, "How is Dr Grange?"

'I mentioned you were ill, that you had been close at death's door. I noticed, in that moment, a freezing of her attitude. I shall not try to describe her expression, because it did not change in the course of the event. When I say she did not move, it is because I am at a loss to describe a negative which struck me so forcibly – you might say so positively.'

Hargood paused, appeared to gather himself once again, then continued, 'With another woman I would have reached out an arm and offered my support. But her outward composure was such that I was frozen in my sympathy. For several seconds both of us were still. The moment passed and she turned away. I have hidden this because I believe it was for your own good, perhaps from myself, but lately I have become wary of the things I do for others' sakes.' Hargood sighed suddenly. 'It is the details which haunt us, these details that one keeps.'

He glanced at Grange's unmoving face.

'I went outside and she closed the door. There were seagulls moving about the house in the late-afternoon sunlight, drifting and squabbling. Normally, I love their motley. Their voices are sweet, like children. Yet I myself was in some turmoil. As I glanced up towards the sky, through their mewing and falling I heard a sound like a cry of rage, or frustration, or perhaps even despair. I wondered for an instant if it had come from inside the house. I was unsure, my thoughts displaced a little by the gulls. My disturbance was such that I thought it might even have emerged from my own imaginings. For some time I have carried the sound of that cry inside myself.' Hargood paused. 'I am convinced, as time passes, that it came from Mrs Quill.'

He observed his patient opposite him. Grange shifted in his chair and appeared to be about to speak, but after a little while he relaxed. Whatever thoughts he might have intended to impart it seemed that he would keep to himself. In this acquiescence to silence, Hargood stood up, nodded to his colleague silently and left shortly afterwards.

The following evening Hargood returned, to offer company, or at least some complicit presence in the solitary vigil of his patient. He had now received another letter from London.

'Throughout your convalescence my mistress has continued to write to me about Mrs Quill, of her former reputation in London and occasionally she passes me stray pieces of information.' He expected no response from Grange, but proceeded now from habit.

'I will tell you what I believe of her background and what I have pieced together as best as I am able from my mistress's letters. I think at some young age she had a lover, that at this time she produced a child by him, a girl – whom you know as Jane. I do not know whether her gentleman promised to marry her, or whether he abandoned her, or whether out of some obscure pride she decided to pursue her own course.'

Hargood paused. 'I ask myself, in a world in which a woman has a secondary place, what course was available to her? Who knows the turns of the heart? Perhaps it was part of her revenge to exploit men's more basic instincts. Whatever the reason, I believe she ran a house. I understand that, as houses go, it was presided over with something like efficiency, even grace. She made a living. And so it might have continued. Her establishment came to light because of the embroilment of her daughter with a young man. It was he, when rejected by Mrs Quill as unsuitable, who decided to take revenge by exposing Mrs Quill in public and making a case of it.

'My mistress theorises. She has taken an interest in this affair and wishes to know more about it. She grows more sympathetic towards Mrs Quill. She says that perhaps Mrs Quill attempted in some way to deflect the attentions of the youth away from her daughter and towards other women. Perhaps she suspected the same fate that she herself experienced – a love affair with an unwanted consequence. We do not know and I admit that if we proceed to any examination of motive in so difficult an affair, these thoughts become as vaporous as one another. I do believe that the attraction of those accounts which we read in the news-sheets is not that they provide the truth, but that they simplify, they reduce the facts to acceptable fictions. The more facts we seek in this matter, it seems to me, the less we know . . .'

He was interrupted in this disquisition by a movement of Grange's shoulder, hardly more than a twitch, as though he were simply shaking away a fly. Thrown a little off course by this sign of agitation, however slight, Hargood came to the end of his speech, and added, 'That is all I have to impart.'

He studied Grange for further reaction. Seeing none, he was inclined to believe that he would not reply, that instead Grange would take his customary course and maintain his silence.

It seemed to Hargood there was now an attempt in the younger man to gather his strength by harbouring it. Yet at the same time perhaps something of what Hargood said seemed to catch fire in him. A movement in his cheeks suggested he would speak.

Despite his condition of apathy, Grange said suddenly, with a peculiar shiver of internal animation, 'Hargood, why do we fear women so?'

The sentence had emerged in such a monotone that it sounded almost as if Grange were speaking to himself. Nevertheless, Hargood was sufficiently taken by surprise that he himself paused for several seconds before replying. When the brief mist of his consternation had cleared, he said, 'I do not entirely know, but there is some truth in the observation.'

He perceived that Grange was making an effort to continue, that the muscles in his cheek twitched again. 'Perhaps our fear of them is based on our fear of ourselves, of showing ourselves . . . It is one of those terrible constructions we place upon women, that we expect them to despise us for showing our emotions . . .'

'Silas, my dear fellow . . .'

'Perhaps it is one of those constructions which we have placed upon Mrs Quill . . . We have persuaded ourselves that inside our great lady is a whore. Yet I at least begin to acknowledge the possibility of its opposite . . . that inside our whore is a great lady . . .'

'Silas . . .' Hargood was concerned at the febrile nature of his patient's animation. 'So be it.' Hargood placed a hand on his colleague's shoulder. 'Come to terms with the past as you wish.'

Whether as a result of his calming words, or merely because the outburst exhausted him, Grange's tension seemed to recede. His frame relaxed. He was no more communicative as the evening progressed, as if his effort had depleted him entirely. Hargood talked occasionally of other things, of the infernal heat of the summer sun, keeping largely away from medical matters, except a general complaint of an outbreak of fevers and rashes at Baddesley. It was raised in such a manner that it was of no more or less interest than that other perennial of Englishmen, the weather.

76

The room having become calm, Hargood proceeded in due course to the outside and, in sombre thought, took the fly before the last of the evening light disappeared.

CHAPTER 18

Dear Leman,

I witnessed recently the terrible force and power of longing, which inhabits the darker regions and basements of our souls.

My patient, of whose recovery I had high hopes, collapsed and fell to the floor of his house shortly after completing one of our customary walks. We had finished our tour of the countryside and I had left him in what I believed to be good spirits. In the course of that perambulation I had talked with him on information which I had received regarding Mrs Quill, with which I had hoped to entice a response from him. We joked, sir, on the surface of our discussion, yet underneath this same efficacious banter he was suffering the pains of an inexpressible emotion.

If I had meant my occasional sallies in any other spirit than innocence and a certain playful regard, I would be feeling the pangs of an even greater remorse than I feel now. Yet there is little virtue in a *post facto* despair, except as it may help us to proceed. We should attempt to learn from what we have inflicted, not least if we have inadvertently caused pain.

I do believe that for the time being he is comfortable and that in a few days he will return to his recovery. But he has unnerved me, and demonstrated the strange and multifarious levels at which we live our lives – for which there is far less accounting. If my discussion with him had been in the form of an experiment, then we might agree that it had drawn forth, beneath the panoply of daily activity and simple habit, a stranger and perhaps more profound sensibility than we had previously imagined.

77

His ministering angel, Mrs Thompson, whose instincts are purposeful and sure, confronted me on the doorstep of his house with the news of his collapse, as though she sensed I was in some measure responsible. She has always been co-operative with me and, I believe, sympathetic, but when matters reach a crisis we may perceive the emergence of her fierce protectiveness. Her head may support my attempts at effecting a cure, but her heart lies with her master. I demanded to see the patient and in the hall there was a moment when we confronted one another like beasts of prey that meet unexpectedly upon a path. She did not mean to prevent me from seeing him, but the brief confrontation was a warning. I was placed on my mettle. In normal circumstances I would politely ask a servant to leave the room while I administered medicine, but she has assumed a right to be present on such occasions – a right I believe she earned by nursing him through the first and deeper crisis.

When, through my discourse, I had tried to impart a little amiable comfort in the form of kind words and admonitions, he reached out a hand that encircled my wrist and asked me not to withhold information from him concerning Mrs Quill again. In the strength of his grip I felt the charge of those subterranean emotions. I hope I did not *blanch* too much with pain, for what lasted a few seconds drained me of much of my equilibrium and gave me some cause for thought regarding the manumission of my own sins.

Those sins are greater than you may at first believe or understand. For at each incident I find myself being drawn down, towards some reckoning of the soul.

In the meanwhile we have lived through another incident, whose reverberations echo through our lives and which in turn throws a little light on the relationship between us.

I write this in haste, as a small note of consequence in our correspondence, in between other duties.

In the meanwhile, I remain, sir,

    Yours sincerely,

      Hargood

CHAPTER 19

Hargood walked beside him, saturnine and inflexibly correct. It was a full week now since the incident and Grange had done his best to return to his programme of walks. He was forced to rest more often, though one of the saving graces of his current weakness was that Hargood, at least temporarily, had put aside the bleedings he had administered regularly before the incident. Grange suspected his fainting fits and the bleedings were related. Although he had been weaker since the most recent fever, he was less subject to fainting and he was sure that, for his own satisfaction, he had established a connection.

Hargood, walking beside him, said, 'It is a part of our uncertainty that we do not know how much of any illness is in the mind.'

Grange suppressed a cough and any words of overt disapproval he might feel.

'You have heard of the physician Anton Mesmer?' Hargood asked.

Grange paused. 'The Frenchman?'

'An Austrian by origin, I believe – though he settled in Paris.'

Grange was cautious. 'I think I remember reports of an investigation into his practices.'

'I visited Paris some years ago – before the troubles – to establish some beginnings of a common ground with our colleagues. The French authorities had by then ordered the investigation of Monsieur Mesmer's claims and activities of which you speak. My French colleagues informed me there were several thousand of his disciples in Paris alone.'

Grange nodded. They walked for some moments without speaking.

'You raise his name for a purpose?'

'His theories and prognostications,' Hargood said. 'You are aware of them?'

'I have an impression', Grange conceded cautiously, 'that he believes he has a healing power, which he calls "animal magnet-ism".'

'You are well-informed, my dear Silas. But we should separate the man from his influence. Mesmer himself insisted that he was merely a conduit for natural forces. In many respects his actions seemed no more than those of rustic shamans and faith-healers. The commission that investigated his claims and practices found that there were indeed many remarkable cures, though they were inclined to distrust his explanations. Mr Benjamin Franklin, for example, who was among the distinguished men who served on that commission, expressed his views that while many of the cures might be genuine, they were due to the "imagination" of his patients.'

'You agree with Mr Franklin's report?'

'It was my duty merely to summarise the findings, such as they were, of the investigation by the French authorities to the Royal College of Physicians.'

'Hargood, you constantly surprise me.'

'I was a humble messenger, no more, carrying out my official duties on behalf of the College. But let us not be distracted by my small role in this matter. Although Monsieur Mesmer's explana-tions of his powers appeared inadequate to describe his successes with certain hysterical patients, there were other explanations.'

'Others?'

'Certain of his disciples, I discovered, take a different view. The Marquis de Puysegur, for example, is of the view that the true explanation of Mesmer's cures consists in certain unknown properties of the mind.'

'He agrees, then, with Mr Franklin – it is in the imagination?'

'The Marquis, I believe, is more systematic. He has proposed an alternative explanation. His hypothesis advocates the presence of a second mind, lying beneath the first.'

Grange felt a stirring of interest, an odd shifting of the balances inside him, as though a new perspective had come into view. They were walking along the brow of a small hill covered in gorse.

Grange said, 'This second mind that he proposes? It is . . . accessible?'

'No, it is not easily accessible. That is his claim. According to his own account, this second mind not only exists, but is hidden from the first, though its presence may be deduced. Only by causing the patient to enter a trance may some communication with the patient's second mind be established.'

'Hargood, I did not believe you were vulnerable to these fashions.'

'I am not, sir.'

'Yet you raise the topic for a reason.'

'There is much that can be discussed to good effect, without being supported by our belief.'

Grange felt in himself again the trace or itch of curiosity. 'You believe perhaps that I should be subject to . . . one of these trances?'

'No, I do not.'

A brief consternation moved across Grange's thoughts, like the shadow of a cloud. He was determined to keep his curiosity in check. In the sudden plethora of questions which seemed to raise themselves, he chose instead to press Hargood on the subject of its introduction. 'Then what is your purpose in mentioning Mesmer?'

'I have no deeper purpose than to bring to your attention a matter of medical interest to both of us. A principle, in fact.'

'Which principle?'

'The principle of a second mind, lying beneath the first, as outlined by de Puysegur.'

'Indeed.'

'It is an interesting prospect, is it not? The concept of a hidden mind?'

'I believe so,' Grange said cautiously.

Hargood continued to walk. 'I merely outline a position, which may serve as a text.'

'A text to what?'

Yet Grange knew without asking to what Hargood referred, the subject that lay like a shadow across their discussion. They had reached Hatchett Pond and stood on its shallow bank. Several moorhens, disturbed by their presence, fluttered away across the dark lake, their trailing feet causing the black surface to turn white.

The water settled gradually until it had become still. Both gazed down for a moment as though taken by surprise at such perfection. The reflection of reeds lay upon the water, surrounded by sky and an occasional pure white cloud. After a while Hargood shifted uneasily, as if their amiable collusion in this simple act of witnessing the beauty of the day were a threat to his relation of physician to patient.

On the other side of the still water they could see that a small breeze was rising, causing the ferns and heather to move in light waves. They turned away, as if by common consent, and were once again in movement.

Across the path was a rutted road that led from Brockenhurst to Beaulieu. There was a sign of movement, hidden by a group of willows: two horses hauling a glossy black landau with Sellinge axles and purring, iron-sheathed wheels. A fine woman sat in the back seat, staring forward, and her figure and stance reminded Grange of another in his memory. He heard the dry drubbing of the horses' hooves and the faint sigh of the suspension C-springs as the body of the landau rose and fell.

Grange stared into a cold darkness. There was no comfort in this wind, which was like a breath of the past.

CHAPTER 20

My dear Leman,
I write to you as always, as one in whom I may confide.
I pray you now, whose silence is itself like an old comrade. You, my oldest friend, who shared my lodgings with me when we were both students in our differing medical fields; you who were party to the escapades and wickedness of my youth, if you did not inspire them directly; you who now read my words patiently, without inflicting upon me either the uncertainty or recrimination of your reply.

My chief concern, above my other duties, is my younger colleague's constitution and state of mind. I have taken personal responsibility for his return to health. He is, after all, my protégé. I watch over his progress like a father, ably supported in these endeavours by his most excellent housekeeper, Mrs Thompson.

He talks quite brightly about this and that, but beneath the surface of his discourse, it seems to me, one may detect there is a hidden side in his character, a vault or cellar which lies underneath his conversation. As he regains his strength and sense of purpose, my concern for him changes. There has occurred what seems in retrospect a strange transfiguration of our respective circumstances. I used to think of him as weaker than I, less decided in many purposes, but now I see that perhaps he embodies a different type of strength. He has what I may perhaps describe as a form of self-sufficiency, internal to his nature. It was always evident that he had a certainty about his life's work which perhaps in me was lacking. But if I say there is a vault or cellar beneath him, I do not mean by it that he lacks some aspect, rather that some part of him is hidden, at least from the exterior world. The most dedicated among us are those who do not advertise their dedication.

Slowly, as he returns to health, he overtakes his previous position, he continues to move forward, towards some destination of which I am not aware.

His conviction is such that his outward face is reticent, modest and entails little that is forward, or self-commending. When I walk beside him I become aware of the depth of his silence. I know that I must be patient. I know also, in some part of myself, with a perfect certitude, that his silence is focused upon me.

These are not matters about which it is easy to communicate, for they lie beneath the surface of our discussion. I believe, increasingly, that he waits for me to disclose something, though he does not know what precisely it might consist of. Meanwhile he is stoical, so that while we discourse on this or that matter, I am aware of the great depth of patience in him and the calm force of his surveillance.

I commit these brief thoughts to paper, in the knowledge that whatever will unfold between us will be revealed in the course of time.

In the meanwhile, I remain, sir,
    Yours sincerely,
        Hargood

CHAPTER 21

Meeting Swann on the marsh again, Grange questioned him a little
further on details of working practices in the salt industry. After
their usual brisk exchange of views, Swann said, 'It is one thing to
talk about the conditions inside a furnace. But it is another to see
them directly.'

'You think I should see one of these infernal machines at first
hand?'

'If you are ever to do good, sir, or to obtain the men a favour
with the powers that be, it is better to know exactly the conditions
in which they work.'

Grange regarded the former mariner, peering up at him with an
expression half concerned, half cynical. 'You could arrange for me
to view one of these furnaces?'

Swann became silent while he considered.

As it happened, Swann was acquainted with one of the foremen
on the furnaces, a certain Elijah Frome, because Frome had once
served aboard a ship as second mate. Frome had proved suspicious
at first – wary perhaps of spies from the Customs and Excise offices
– but there was some impulsion that drove Swann in pursuit; he
wanted Grange to see how the men worked, to observe at close
hand the precise conditions pertaining there. It was only perhaps
because Grange was known as a physician who had treated the
occasional casualties from the furnaces that Frome grudgingly
conceded to the physician's visit.

'Only one call, mind,' Frome said to Swann, 'because you're an
old shipmate and he's bandaged one or two of the men.'

As he talked, Frome looked out over the field to where the Solent
lay, white and calm.

'One visit it is,' Swann agreed.

'Make it at night, too,' Frome muttered, without looking directly
at him, gazing instead out across the long fields.

'At night?' Swann asked.

Frome replied, 'We don't want anyone else seeing him visit and thinking they can approach at their own leisure.'

'Night it is,' Swann affirmed.

'Close after eight would be best,' Frome suggested. 'I'd be outside, organising the coal loading at the start of the night shift.'

'Close after eight, then.'

'Best night would be Tuesday,' Frome insisted relentlessly.

By then it had become a formal visit, constrained within the tightest bounds to cause the least inconvenience to the foreman. That way, Swann also knew, nothing would be seen by an outsider that shouldn't be seen.

Afterwards Swann had recounted the conversation to Grange, as a favour won against significant odds.

At night, walking along the towpath behind Swann, Grange noticed the eyes of animals drifting in the darkness of the fields inland: fox, weasel, hare, deer.

The flame of the nearest furnace was like a fluke or flail in the darkness. He could walk along the foreshore, with the fires in the furnaces no more than a faint hiss or whisper. Then one of the fire mouths would open and the roar of the flames would choke in his ears. When the doors opened, it seemed to him that he stared into the white eye of the beast.

Out on the marshes the grey-green eyes of a hare drifted across the marsh grass in soft, gliding loops.

Across the water the great braziers on the harbour wall at Yarmouth sent a cloud of fine sparks like fireflies into the air. Somewhere, beneath the blaze, the harbour-master's assistant stirred the roots of the blaze with an iron rake. It reminded Grange of the furnaces towards which they now walked. Sometimes, in the deep hush of the evening, the doors of one of the boiler houses would open and the flames of the coal fires could be seen burning. He would stare into hell, a simple, bright hell that was like the eye of an animal. Occasionally Grange had seen the faces of rakers, their skin blackened with soot, eyes reddened like dervishes or devils. He had observed the swift slash of the iron rake into the intense heat of the coals.

The last of the dusk light was fading fast beyond Hurst. Following the heavy figure of Swann, in the deep silence sometimes the rose-white flame of an open furnace would appear on Swann's shoulder, or replicate itself on the oil-lit lagoons of water. This was his impression as he walked along the sea wall: the deep breath of the fires, the sudden crisis of flame, hooded darkness, then the slowly opened doors again releasing into the night their turbulent light and flame.

'A boiler house', Swann told him, 'is an engine for transforming water into salt. There are perhaps twenty-six such engines at work on a single evening between Milford and Beaulieu. Each requires its own constant supplies of coal. On summer nights, when the sea breezes come in and ventilate the fires, more coal is burned on our Lymington foreshore than anywhere else in the world, I do believe.'

They were standing in the dusk, resting a little to allow the final shading into night before moving on. Swann had sensed that Grange was suffering from one of his fits of exhaustion and had waited, out of deference, for him to catch up. He was patient while Grange, leaning on his Malacca cane, waited for the shaking fit to subside. When the final shudders had ceased, Grange could see, outlined in the final light of dusk against Hurst, slow trains of men pulling a coal barge across the marshes; other men with long poles held the barge off the shore of the dyke.

They were moving along a tongue or isthmus of land that stretched parallel with the shore, separated by a canal used for transport. The train of fires that lay along the marshes seemed like signal pyres.

Swann led him off the tow-path towards a cluster of three boiler houses. 'There it is now,' he said. They could hear the faint roar from the closest of the boiler houses. It was like a full barrel being rolled along the cobbles towards one of the public houses, one of the big heavy kegs that set up a low rumbling as though beneath the ground. Closer to, Grange could sense the force of the smoke and steam as it rose upwards in thick curls.

They were close enough to see through the open doors into the building itself. In that nascent fire, the figures of the rakers were like ghosts. Heat made them sweat. Water evaporated from the body at a terrible rate from the wind and the fire. Tending machines,

Grange knew, their human operators themselves became machines, mere repositories of fluid and energy, to be drained and replenished. He watched the faint outline of the men as they moved in a trance about their work. A loose outer door was swinging slowly backwards and forwards on its hinges from the draft generated by the fire.

They were still sufficiently far off to hear themselves speak. Grange said, 'I have sometimes noticed that the furnacers do not appear to work with any urgency.'

'Urgency?' Swann asked.

'With any outward sense of speed.' Grange tried to gather together something of what he had seen. 'They seem to move with an odd sort of deliberation, as if they are in a trance.'

'In the furnace houses –' Swann was forced to half-turn his head to speak '– you don't think. You don't dare think. Thinking makes you hot. You heat up, the fire becomes unbearable. The best way to face fire is if you are cold inside.'

Grange, walking behind him, was perplexed at the phrase. 'Cold inside?'

'They learn to leave their troubles behind at the door,' Swann said. 'They live like Hindoos in the presence of fire. They abandon themselves to it. It is when they return to the world that they face the consequences.'

That was, perhaps, the sense of depression Grange had sometimes perceived in the returning men. It was not mere physical exhaustion. If Swann was right, they learned to empty their minds. Afterwards, they put on their shirts and emerged from the trance of their work into the light of day. And as they did, their troubles returned, perhaps redoubled by absence. The misery of their lives closed in upon them. So they went back to their hovels at Pennington or Woodside. There they drank to replenish their fluids, and lay on the floors of their houses among the lice and fleas and rats. In the morning they dragged themselves to the next shift. As their local physician, he had come across their wretched existence, had ministered to their depleted bodies, had attempted, above all, to persuade them to take a day or two off from the infernal rigours of their occupation – offering, where necessary, to

87

speak to the foremen on their behalf. Needless to say, his efforts had been largely without effect.

The faint breeze had died and Grange could see that the doors were opened fully to increase the flow of air. He could see also, through these temporary embrasures, the great engine of fire. Now the men inside were more clearly visible, standing in attendance on the flames.

Outside, a group of men were transporting coal from one of the bunkers by the side of the building into the furnace house, standing several feet off from the fire and flinging the coal into the flames. Another group of men, so lacking in clothes that they seemed like savages or cannibals, stood close to the flames and raked in the fresh coals, distributing them into the intense and burning core.

Swann led Grange the final distance towards the flames, like a devil leading a sinner into hell. They were perhaps fifty yards from the boiler house now, approaching its open doors, and Grange could feel the wave of intense heat on his face.

In the darkness other shapes were moving. Voices could be heard, the grunts of men *in extremis*. Several were lifting coal into a bunker at the side of the furnace, carrying wheelbarrows from a nearby coal barge that lay moored against the canal bank. In pouring their loads into bunkers, thick coal-dust had risen and covered them, so that they looked like blackamoors, hardly visible in the dark.

A heavy-set man was standing off a little way from these efforts, calling directions. He stood square, with hands on hips, surveying the coal lifters. By now the sound of the fires was too loud to hail him easily, particularly against his own shouted orders. When Swann tapped him on the shoulder to attract his attention he turned, burly and angry, and surveyed them out of bloodshot eyes.

'Elijah Frome,' Swann said by way of introduction. 'The foreman of the furnace.'

Swann indicated his visitor, 'Dr Silas Grange.'

'Good-day, sir,' Grange said.

Elijah Frome stared at Grange without acknowledgement, as though at some unannounced interloper. Then, without speaking, he turned his attention once more to Swann.

'May we view the works?' Swann asked.

Frome cleared his throat and spat ostentatiously onto the parched earth. 'At your own risk.'

His action made Grange go cold. When angry he was inclined towards irony, a calculated economy of expression. He lowered his head a little towards Frome. 'I thank you for your courtesy.'

Frome glanced at Swann, turned and spat again, then looked at Grange with his heavy-lidded eyes, as though marking him down for the future. He nodded perfunctorily and perhaps unexpectedly.

Swann touched the foreman's arm in gratitude, but Frome took no notice of the gesture. He was still watching Grange.

'Follow me,' Swann said.

Inside the furnace house the fire roared with a relentless, deep energy. In all his life Grange had never experienced such heat. It seemed to reach out and seize him. Figures in hardly more than loincloths were working in the fierce steam and smoke. In the centre of the furnace house was a great iron tray of water, measuring perhaps twelve feet by eight. It was the most monstrous of open kettles Grange had ever witnessed. Beneath it the flames of the fires roared. Smoke poured around the periphery of the great iron tray like shadows. The smoke and steam united above it. Combined heat and smoke sent up a thick column, heavy and swirling, through the great aperture in the roof and into the black sky.

Grange paused to gather breath. The air was so hot it seemed to ignite his lungs. Once, during an earlier walk along the foreshore, he had asked Swann whether the furnace-men closed the roof aperture when it rained, so that the fires were not put out. Swann had smiled almost mirthlessly. 'Close it, sir? Any rain that falls through that roof will not so much as touch the pan. You could stand above that furnace with a fire-hose, and hand pump as much water as you like and the heat would beat back any flow of liquid you could rain upon it. It would come straight back into your face as steam. And as for the water touching the flames that burn beneath the pan . . .' Swann's voice had trailed off, as though out of pity for so abject a lack of understanding.

Close to its fierce and roaring heart, Grange began to perceive the dynamics of the place. Just as the radiant heat of the flames pressed on the front of the body, so the cold air that flowed in from the open doors on either side of the building was fierce on his back. Under the counterpoint of these fierce flows, Grange felt the steam and sweat uniting on his skin and drying on his back.

Swann, unable to talk or to instruct him, pushed Grange further forward towards the fire, as though to incinerate him, and Grange found himself blinking before the roaring white flames, until he was surrounded and enclosed by fire. The heat reached into his soul and he felt curiously lifeless, floating, a mere feather on the hot core of the world.

CHAPTER 22

When Grange returned home afterwards, Mrs Thompson, seeing him standing sweat-stained and soaked at the door, let out a cry of rage. She reached out and almost hauled him inside, like an urchin who had stayed out late against his mother's orders. Afterwards, when she had ushered him out of the cold into the sitting-room where the main fire burned, she insisted that Grange should remove his coat and soaked shirt immediately.

He remonstrated that he should wash and dry himself in his study. But she said with a firmer insistence that there was no fire upstairs, and it would take too long to make one. 'The damage would be done before the first logs caught light.' The nature of this 'damage' was unspecified, but perhaps it was all the more terrible for being so.

He did not tell her that such had been the intensity of the fire upon his body that afterwards, when he had been hauled backwards by Swann and into the cold air, gasping for breath, his eyes blinded by the heat, the singe of flames on his face, his body was still so heated he had found it necessary to walk to the canal side, reach down with cupped hands, and throw copious cold water over his face and neck and shoulders. No doubt his actions would have brought an extra shudder to Mrs Thompson's sensibilities. As it was, faced with her implacable wrath, he removed his shirt in front of the warmth of a more domestic fire.

It happened that before he had returned she had been boiling a pot of water for her own use. While he removed his clothes, she poured this heated water into a bowl, diluted it with a little cold, put on a fresh kettle and returned to the sitting-room, where she set down the bowl and soap and sponge. She returned to the kitchen for the hardy wooden stool that she sometimes used when sitting in front of the stove. She told him to sit down upon it and he did so. Standing behind him, she began to soap his neck and shoulders. 'Mr Swann?' she asked.

'He accompanied me,' Grange replied. He was determined to take the blame upon himself, though he knew when the mood took her Mrs Thompson ascribed no more responsibility to him than to an errant puppy.

'Accompanied.' She sounded as though she was gathering evidence. It was more a statement than a question.

While she washed him, she continued her calm, chiding imprecations at the state of him. Did Mr Swann 'accompany' him home, she asked, or did he leave Grange to make his own way through the darkness?

'He was my kind attendant and help throughout the evening.'

'Attendant and help,' Mrs Thompson said, as if the weight of evidence was now overwhelming in the direction she suspected and she needed little more to make a full case.

When she had rinsed him down with a fresh bowl of warm water and rubbed him dry with a towel, she found a clean woollen shirt and insisted that he complete his change of clothes by removing his breeches and stockings, which were also soaked, so that she could wash the rest of him in front of the sitting-room fire and complete the work.

Grange raised his eyebrows. The first sign of a smile touched Mrs Thompson's lips since his return. She said, 'You are like a child, sir. I think I know my way around a man's body without too many surprises.'

The quaintness of the expression amused him. He tried hard to keep a straight face. But his attempts at self-repression lost him the initiative. Before he had time to riposte, she was already off to change the bowl of water and, having refilled the kettle, in the process of adding fresh hot water to it.

She returned, left the bowl and sponge, and retired again with a brisk sweep of her hips. 'I shall go into the kitchen, sir,' Mrs Thompson called over her shoulder, 'if your modesty is so great. But your breeches must be off when I return.' She closed the door emphatically.

Grange, having been pressed forward into the fire by Swann and upbraided by his angry housekeeper for his acquiescence to such a scheme, at last found himself with a few seconds of peace to remove his breeches and stockings, and place them in a pile in the corner.

The intermission did not last long. Mrs Thompson returned, having fetched a clean pair of breeches and stockings from the linen cupboard in the pantry that lay off the kitchen. She set them down over the back of the high-backed chair and picked up the sponge and soap. Then she kneeled at his feet and started behind him, working from the ankles upwards, by way of the calves and the insides of his knees.

While she washed him Grange attempted to alleviate the mild indignity by considering more closely Swann's motives in insisting that he should see at first hand the inside of one of the furnaces. There was something in what Mrs Thompson had said about Swann, a hint of compulsion in what he did, pressing Grange firmly forward to the fire, almost into the flames themselves, as though towards some deeper understanding. He was reminded again of a devil pressing a sinner towards his penance, as though the very flames themselves would be his teacher. At the same time as the image was upon him, he attempted to see Swann's behaviour in its most favourable light. No doubt there were several mitigating circumstances.

Perhaps the most important of these was that Swann was a sailor, a being notoriously impregnable to climate, a man who had survived innumerable gales and showers, and sweltering tropical days. Yet in all other respects he was unusually sensitive to Grange's frailties, even solicitous. In walking beside him, if Grange showed the slightest hesitation, or an early indication of one of his shivering fits, Swann would halt and mark time with conversation. All the more reason for believing that if he had risked Grange's health in pressing him forward into the furnace fire, there would be reason underlying it. Grange considered what that reason might be and was left with the conclusion that Swann had thought it sufficiently important for him to witness the real state of the furnaces at first hand, and perhaps to understand through his own direct example that to be exposed for only a few seconds to the conditions in which the furnace-men worked day after day was to be at severe risk of lethal chills and fevers, and that it might be one thing to face it once and briefly, but another to work there every day without cease.

Kneeling behind him, Mrs Thompson was soaping Grange's thighs and buttocks. He looked down at himself and saw, to his embarrassment, signs of stirrage. The independence of the body was never so direct, he reflected, as the orientation of the most private parts. He contented himself with the thought that when Mrs Thompson came round to his front, with a little luck she might stub her forehead on it.

Even so, when Mrs Thompson had finally finished the ablution and dried him down, rising to stand directly in front of him, Grange felt a faint blush coming to his cheek.

Mrs Thompson had seen him close-to, or to use naval terminology, had run up alongside him athwartships and, so to speak, had practically put the telescope to her eye. She was still in the lee of him now, standing off a little but still hove-to and at close quarters. So it was that neither of them was quite able to look the other directly in the face. Instead, Mrs Thompson put the towel over her fine shoulder, and picked up the bowl and sponge. He believed he saw amusement in her expression, and the skin of her neck and cheeks seemed to him to be positively glowing with the effort of washing him. As she departed for the kitchen he fancied he heard her say to herself, calmly though quite distinctly enough for him to hear, 'No surprises at all.'

CHAPTER 23

Grange's study, above the drawing-room, benefited from the warmth beneath. The chimney, which abutted the inner wall, was another source of heat. Mrs Thompson had suggested that he move his desk closer to the breastwork so that he could enjoy, if but indirectly, her carefully nurtured fire. More out of a desire for peace than a consideration of her wishes, he acquiesced.

Even if he stayed in front of the drawing-room fire, he still felt cold, as though the blood that had been drained from him had not been fully recovered. Sometimes, even inside the house, without warning his body shook involuntarily for several minutes, however hot his position.

Mrs Thompson continued to be certain that this coldness was in part at least the result of his diet, which excluded red meat, and that it showed its consequences in the blood's depleted tides. Her disapproval manifested itself at certain times, not least when she put in front of him the fish broth which was his preferred diet, against both Hargood's instructions and her own preferences. She was concerned to emphasise that she felt the soup offered little or no replenishment.

'Your soup,' Mrs Thompson said.

'Thank you.'

Rather than leaving, Mrs Thompson appeared to hesitate a moment, then said, 'Sir.'

'Yes?'

Mrs Thompson went on, 'I know it is not my business. If Dr Hargood proceeds to bleed you again, would it not be wise to take some red meat?'

'Why, Mrs Thompson?'

'To build up the strength of the blood.'

Grange smiled, wiping his mouth on the table-cloth. 'At present, we have two conflicting physicians' cures. Now, it seems to me, you wish to add the diagnosis of a third.'

'I am not a physician, sir. I merely cook your food.'

Grange nodded. 'Indeed, Mrs Thompson.'

She stiffened a little, and stared ahead.

'Thank you, sir.' She turned and departed.

Grange experienced a sudden guilt at his attack. She had challenged him in the one domain in which he continued to hold sway, and he felt perhaps he had responded in a manner both instinctive and irrational. 'Mrs Thompson?' he called out after her.

'Sir?' She turned at the doorway.

'I agree with you that we seem to have the worst of two cures. A regimen of bleeding may be combined efficaciously with a diet of rich food. On the other hand, a diet of fish and thin gruel may function well enough on its own, without bleeding.'

She studied him from the doorway.

'I believe there is much in what you say. We cannot allow this state of affairs to continue *ad infinitum*. It is time a choice were made.'

'Sir?'

'I will inform Dr Hargood that we shall not continue with his regimen of bleeding.'

Mrs Thompson half nodded, sufficiently to acknowledge that she had heard him, insufficiently to denote any enthusiasm at his solution. 'Will there be anything else, sir?'

'Thank you, no.'

Mrs Thompson paused a moment longer, as though judging this latest expression, then departed for the kitchen, leaving him in control at least of a small aspect of his house.

Yet Mrs Thompson's presence continued to gain strength in the household, in the places not subject to his direct purview, much as darkness gathered inexorably behind the salt furnaces in the evening. In his weakness, she was the presiding spirit and her force had never been greater. It took certain reserves on his part to resist the temptation to fall back upon her management, as one might sink into a comfortable armchair.

In the afternoon she appeared in the doorway, carrying his tray. 'Tea, sir.'

He had resolved something else in which he must challenge Hargood. When she set down the tray, he said, 'I believe I must begin seeing my patients again.'

95

'You are not well enough.'

'It seems to me that you mix cause and effect, Mrs Thompson. I am not well enough to avoid it.'

'Sir?'

Grange felt faintness creeping around the edges of his thoughts. He blinked to clear his mind. At certain times of the day he felt susceptible to weakness or sleeping, at other times not. His physical state seemed to have rendered him more delicate to these daily rhythms. 'I require preoccupation. I need my work. That way I will recover faster.'

'But Dr Hargood said several months. It is hardly two months since . . .'

'Since?'

'Since you became ill.' Mrs Thompson was determined not to be intimidated in what she had to say. 'Sir,' she added, as though by afterthought.

'I believe we are speaking about the mind, Mrs Thompson, as much as the body. It is the mind which I wish to address through my work.'

'Since Dr Hargood bled you, sir –' Mrs Thompson insisted, '– you are still weak, in your physical self.'

Grange smiled. 'If I am physically strong enough to accompany Dr Hargood on walks, I believe I shall be able to cross my study floor to greet a patient.'

Mrs Thompson considered him. She suspected that a few minutes before he had casually passed and glibly survived another fainting fit. Without proof of it, however, it seemed to her this was not the best time to press a contrary view. She nodded, as if to register his statement, and turned towards the kitchen. Grange watched her disappearing back, the firmness of purpose in her walk, the lightness of her tread, despite a full figure. She used the kitchen, he sometimes felt, as a baron used his castle, not to change her opinion about his actions, but to gather fresh resources and return to the fray.

Later that afternoon Mrs Thompson came home from the market stalls with a leg of lamb and hung it in the cool basement on the north side of the house. He heard her closing the back door, the brisk sound of her footsteps across the wooden floors of the pantry and then the flatter, lighter tone of her heels on the stone flags of the kitchen. When she returned from the basement she closed the door to the cold-room. He heard her footsteps on the stone stairs and then the careful closing of the kitchen door.

She began to scour the pots. He listened to the movement of the scourer, like a kettledrum on the echoing insides of the larger pots. It seemed to him that she was stirring the sound like discontent. When she had finished, she started to prepare something to eat for herself, though he could not guess precisely what. She employed herbs to savour her meals and he surmised that she was pounding some herbal concoction with a pestle.

Grange left the sitting-room for his study. In the unabridged silence, she continued to pound with the pestle and mortar, the soft thumps of her agitation rising through the floor.

For the time being she had stored the lamb's leg in the cold-room, for her own purposes, like a predator which puts aside its prey. She would eat it herself if necessary, as an admonition to him, and her own magnificent health would be a further lesson to him, set against his own weak and feverish state. In the meantime, she dared him to contradict her, while she waited for an opportunity which she was certain would come.

CHAPTER 24

Dear Leman,

When I consider my younger colleague, I begin to perceive that it is not only that he withholds himself from the most direct and easy communication, but that on certain subjects he feels differently from other men. For example, I know now that when most men talk about the fairer sex, even with affection, it is more often than not to denigrate them in direct or subtle manner, to attribute irrationality, even if we disguise such comments with our amiability. I perceive in my colleague a lack of any such inclination to belittle our female companions. In his conversation there has never been any boasting about sexual conquests, even to an intimate such as me – nor any comments about the other sex, such as most of us men are prone to when we are in the company of other men. In the earlier days of our association I thought that this was another of those failings in his nature, a lack of what the French call *bonhomie*, a coldness in his disposition which has tempered his relations with his fellow man and perhaps inhibited his relations with women. But as I speak with him, and acquaint myself more fully with his position, so by strange degrees it would seem that my own changes. For I begin to perceive in him not a lack of feeling towards women, but something approaching a respect for them. And if I ask myself which of these things is the more important, the more valuable in a man – good-hearted *bonhomie* or a genuine regard for the female sex – I am increasingly inclined to give him the benefit of the doubt.

I struggle to express myself, regarding a character whom I have found elusive, retiring. I thought he was made of glass, that this transparency of his was an indication of a nature which was without guile, to be sure, but also without those depths which contradiction indicates. But now I increasingly perceive that his true nature is not transparent, but deeper than I had first thought and largely invisible. I begin, I say again, to give him the benefit of the doubt. For among the other things which I had held him guilty of, I believed he fostered certain untenable assumptions about the world, and those of us who inhabit his close environment. Now I begin to perceive that, although I had thought him invulnerable to the truth, yet he is strangely without illusions.

It is precisely because of this reticence – for it may be said of him that he keeps his powder dry – that I think of his character as a kind of projectile or missile, though I do not know much about the spring or propulsive force which in due course may send it into action. I only sense that, one day, whatever he holds inside himself will be turned into action or motivated. The flint will come down on the firing pan. We will observe the effects.

In writing to you of my own perplexities in these and related matters, it is strange how I wait on this occurrence, as if it will guide me in some intricate problem regarding my own character – as if, in illuminating his motive, I will begin to clarify my own. For it is true that I write these missives, and beg your patience, out of my own perplexity rather than his.

But I return to my central concern. It seemed to me that in some sense at least he distanced himself from women and that this was in part responsible for the particular nature of the difficulties that have arisen with Mrs Quill. Yet I see now that he does not set himself apart from women so much as men. I start to envisage that this very separateness was his protection from such as myself, who would enquire in bluff manner too closely into his deeper feelings. I begin even to consider the notion, strange as it may seem, that he protected these personal thoughts concerning women from other men not because they are illusions, or because they cannot bear the light, but because he believed such other men might find themselves uncomfortable with their truth.

I am closer to the conventional, of course, than my younger colleague, and this is enough to cause an odd sensation of difference when my own thoughts are set against so strange a beast. But I am sure you agree that to render him as entirely detached from this world would also be mistaken. There is much that is stubborn and intransigent, and much in him too that makes him determined upon his own path, whatever the consequences. If I do begin to absolve him from lack of connection with the world and its ways, even so, he remains a strange and inaccessible soul.

My dear Leman, in our past you have listened so often to my accounts of small triumphs and tribulations that I pray you will forgive these obscure and perhaps incoherent meditations. In your company I have always felt the freedom of true friendship and shamelessly exercised my conscience. You know or may suspect that I beg forgiveness from you when perhaps I hope for forgiveness from myself. Among these poor efforts, I shall brace myself in due course to tell you of one other aspect, which has a bearing on what will follow, so that you alone may know that when we speak of Mrs Celia Quill and her effect on my colleague, we move deeper into the past than I prefer to admit.

In the meantime I walk with him, for walking with its motion subdues the mind. We traverse the earth, the two of us, in active discourse or in animated silence, and I allow myself the odd privilege of considering his own thoughts or motivations. He has many attractive aspects, at least to me. But what a strange world it is, how oddly hidden are its meanings. I know that he observes me as carefully as I observe him, as if he too waits upon some event. It is a game between us, in which each holds a portion of the truth to himself in the hope that the other may reveal his true nature.

So it is and so it may continue. And so, sir, in prolonged respect of your silence and good offices, I remain,

Sincerely yours,

Hargood

CHAPTER 25

At his home that evening, Hargood carved venison, driving through the thick of the hindquarters with his firm blade, lifting peremptory slices on to his plate.

Grange watched him eye each approvingly as he speared it. 'Hargood, I believe it is time I began to take up my work again.'

'Nonsense, sir,' Hargood said, almost without thinking. He examined with approval a fine slice of meat upon the fork, beaded with blood. 'You are not yet well.' He raised it beneath Grange's eye, as though to tempt him.

Grange raised a hand in negation. He watched Hargood convey the meat to his own plate, and add several more slices for good measure. 'I suggest it if only because it will help my recovery.'

Hargood considered the pile before him as though an estimable Providence, not his own hand, had supplied it. 'My dear Silas, we have already plotted a course and it is under way. You are making progress, albeit slowly. Now you wish to diverge?'

'I merely . . .'

'I am the navigator in this matter, and my answer is no.'

'I do not question that you have plotted a good course. I only believe that taking up my duties now will assist the fine work that you have already done.'

Hargood resorted to his own knife and fork. He cut a piece and raised it to his mouth, chewing carefully. 'My dear Silas, let us not forget one aspect. In this matter, for the time being and until further notice, you are the patient, I am the physician.'

'For the time being, I agree.'

Hargood raised his eyes towards Grange, studying him carefully. 'For the time being, then, you are in my care. And as we have agreed, it is the physician, not the patient, who plots the progress of that cure.' He paused again to raise another piece of meat to his mouth and chewed contemplatively. 'The convention of our profession is that it is the physician who may say when that course has ended.'

Grange said, 'I must thank you again for taking upon yourself the care of my patients. You have given me precisely the rest I needed. Now I must begin to take up some of the burden myself.'

Hargood chewed, raised another slice, masticated slowly. 'And if you faint upon your duties?'

'It is a risk, I agree.'

'You have already experienced a relapse.'

'Out of deference to your wishes, I will not go visiting other houses for several weeks, but I will begin to receive patients in my study. Mrs Thompson will be at home.'

'You are lucky to have her. More wine?'

'No, thank you. I acknowledge my good fortune with Mrs Thompson. That is why, if I pass out, we will have capability at hand.'

Hargood filled his own glass and considered the rolling, dark-red depths. 'Then I give you my final warning, sir, and I say that you are responsible for your own actions. And speaking of Mrs Thompson – have you consulted your housekeeper in this matter?'

'Consulted?'

'Have you asked her opinion?'

'Is she also my physician?'

'She observes you as closely as anyone.'

Grange smiled to himself. 'A moment ago you made the case that it is the physician who charts the cure. Now you wish me to consult Mrs Thompson?'

'I do not ask you to consult her. I ask you whether, in assessing my own opinion, you have also spoken to her.'

'Much though I admire her attributes, I do not choose to consult her on the matter of my cure.'

'On the matter of attributes . . .' Hargood shifted his ground again and proceeded now to drive home the point. 'I do not see why such a handsome widow should replace her hope of a husband merely to keep house for a dry ascetic such as you.'

'Hargood,' Grange said, 'I do believe you change the subject . . .'

'Do I?' Hargood continued to eat, shifting the meat from one set of molars to another, pausing to set down his knife and withdraw a strand of gristle with his fingers. 'It seems to me they are part of the same subject.'

'What subject is that?'

'Mrs Thompson's relations with yourself.'

'I see no connection.'

'Do you not?'

Grange was forced to smile at Hargood's solid intent, his pursuit of a single line. 'I do not see the connection between her own motivations in remaining with me and whether I should consult her on my cure.'

'No, indeed,' Hargood insisted. He paused to consider, masticating his food meanwhile. 'Yet I know several gentlemen of good standing who would be only too pleased to take it upon themselves to make a proposal of marriage to her.'

'Then why do they not do so?'

'Perhaps,' Hargood said, 'because they perceive the depth of her zeal, the strength of her commitment to you.'

'Mrs Thompson is free to stay or go as she chooses.'

'Oh, do not mistake me,' Hargood told him. 'I do most earnestly believe that she does choose. She is a woman who knows her own mind and chooses most carefully. I merely consider what her motives may be in choosing to keep house for you.'

'You shift your ground, Hargood. I believe I still do not understand.'

'Do you not?'

Hargood's persistence caused Grange to smile again. 'It is perhaps because she does not harbour hidden motives to marry herself off to another man that she stays with me.'

'I believe your answers have a certain neatness. However, like good soup, they are not entirely satisfying by themselves. They lead instead to other questions.'

'What other questions?'

'I do not think any man should believe he knows the motives of a woman,' Hargood said.

In repose, Hargood had the natural torpor of a predator, his eye a calm meditation on the world. Yet to Grange there was something fearsome in it. It was not merely the leonine gleam of the eyeball. If there was a key to Hargood it lay in this posture, the observation of the world as he sat, his head to one side, considering his guest out of a surfeit of well-being. It seemed to Grange, in the light of this beneficence, that there are those whom contentment moves towards passivity; but with Hargood, active by nature, contentment was simply the ground on which to launch his next enquiry and assault.

Despite the warmth of the surrounds, Grange felt a chill inside him. It might have been his own breathing, or the movement of air which circulated in the room, the flames of the candles, a dust of lights on the glasses and window-panes, the curtain breathing softly, like an animal.

'There are those Frenchmen', Hargood said, 'who regulate *amour* through a code of behaviour, who have mistresses who are a part of their formal arrangements.'

'You wish us to emulate them?'

'We emulate the French in many things, do we not?'

'Perhaps so.'

'If France sneezes, it is said, England catches cold.'

'I did not know you admired our continental cousins,' Grange said, 'or granted them such high esteem.'

'It is not a question of emulation. It is a matter of practical sense.

Our continental cousins, as you call them, are masters of the art of life. Who knows, more than they, the robust and delicate arts of living, the pleasures of the table, or the bedroom?'

'More recently, they have become masters of the art of death.'

'The Revolution is an aberration,' Hargood said with something like certainty. 'A terrible aberration, to be sure. Order will be restored in the fullness of time.'

'Will it? You do not think this killing is the dark side of the same nature?'

'What do you mean?'

'Such widespread use of the guillotine. The sensual nature carried to excess?'

'My dear fellow,' Hargood said. 'It seems we change our positions. You, a radical, are apprehensive about France. I, a Tory, am not.'

'Why are you not?'

'Because, as I have mentioned before, I see the Revolution as an aberration.'

They continued to discuss through the evening the various aspects of the French Revolution which had affected them. Grange in particular was not displeased that the subject had moved from the question of Mrs Thompson's devotion to him, or the reasons why she seemed disinclined to consider offers of marriage from other sources. Though he liked to stalk Grange on the subject, Hargood's implication was clear – that Mrs Thompson's final hope was that Grange himself in due course would succumb to her practical charms.

It was perhaps a measure of Hargood's subtlety that he never directly expressed this view. He preferred to move around it, to hint at it, to cause in his younger colleague a sense of hotly defending something which had never been directly stated and in other ways to hunt the fertile ground without actually killing the quarry.

When Hargood finally became silent, resting his head on the table in sleep, as he was increasingly inclined to do, a part of Grange regretted his generalisation, aware that Hargood's thoughts had less to do with his housekeeper and more with Mrs Quill. Hargood implied – and Grange did not need his direct expression to work out the fuller implications – that Mrs Thompson waited in the hope that the effect of Mrs Quill upon him would recede. In this, it seemed to Grange, both Hargood and Mrs Thompson had common ground.

Not long afterwards Hargood began to snore loudly.

Grange stood up and walked into the interior of the house. In the small waiting room off the rear hallway, Simmonds was sleeping in front of the fire, nodding occasionally. Some intuition on the part of the faithful servant caused Simmonds to stir. He opened his eyes. Grange said softly, 'I am about to leave, Mr Simmonds. Dr Hargood rests comfortably asleep on the table. There is no need to stir yourself.'

'I should see you to the door, sir.'

'I shall see myself out, Mr Simmonds.'

He turned and walked away before the old man could remonstrate with him or pursue him with courtesy.

In the hallway Grange lifted his heavy cloak off one of the iron pegs and swung it over his shoulders. Now that his health was returning he found that he relished the prospect of the walk home. He lifted the large metal latch and stepped out into the darkness. The sky was clear and he needed no lamp. He swung the door to and set off. Ahead of him the pathway glimmered faintly with dew.

CHAPTER 26

Dear Leman,

In the evenings, when my younger colleague visits me, after I have consumed much good meat and red wine, I lay my head forward on the table and fall asleep in my chair. We are sufficiently at ease in one another's company that he takes no offence but, on the contrary, since it signals a temporary respite in my disquisitions upon his affairs, no doubt he considers my removal from immediate consciousness a blessed relief. Taking his leave, he sets back home upon his walk and leaves me to my slumber. Thus, sir, we bachelors form our habits and continue in our incorrigible manner, uncorrected by the sweeter forms of female temperament.

Perhaps my resort to a temporary sleep at the end of the evening is a sign that at my age I cannot carouse as I did in my youth. Yet I find the behaviour oddly fortuitous to my current circumstances. For after I wake up in the early hours my mind is a little clearer and, when I rouse myself from the table, somewhat refreshed from my slumber, it has become a secondary habit of mine to take myself up to my bedroom, set myself down at my writing desk and compose a letter to you for an hour or two, before retiring to my bed for several further hours of sleep. So I write now, sir, my window open to the cool night air, my mind a little more coherent than when I fell asleep, though still pleasantly befuddled with the fumes of wine. The quietness of the hour and the solitary nature of the task in hand suit my mood. I turn my attention to more serious matters.

Since Mrs Quill left, it is strange how the society of which she had become so much a feature, indeed a cornerstone, has reacted to the news of her departure. It is as if her absence has become, through its very strangeness, a talking point among local society. At first they thought that she had taken a holiday or rest from her good works, perhaps that she visited her daughter in Winchester. Later, as her absence became prolonged, certain sources found that the house had been locked and the usually well-kept gardens have begun to look unattended. I dare say certain people, under the impulse of paying her a visit, have called by the undefended property and glanced through the windows, and there observed the absence of her furniture. Not long after several such parties had made the discovery that her house is boarded up, her disappearance began to be the talk of society. It is sometimes said that you may judge the strength of a character by the weight of his absence. In the case of Mrs Quill, her absence here is so powerful it has become a veritable presence.

Still, not much is known, least of all among those who make it their business to know. There is a great deal of guesswork among our local families of good standing and certain circles who are closed to me have become more open, as if they believe I may add some clue to the general consternation. In support of this new standing I have been invited to partake of dinner in several houses where previously I was, at the most, an infrequent guest.

As the story of Mrs Quill's departure has become more widely known, it has spread from the female population to the male, from wives to husbands, from sisters to brothers, from daughters to fathers. Like a person who hears an echo, I have become privy to the story in another form and – since it is reported from a masculine view – with different inflections. Several of my male friends and acquaintances, having become aware of my colleague's involvement in her departure, though not entirely apprised of the circumstances, now perceive him as a less detached and passive being than they had previously considered him. His earlier connection with Mrs Quill, though to all outward respects a happy association of mind, had become the subject of local discussion and amiable gossip long before she left. But now, after her departure, I understand that at some dinner-tables it has become the only subject of discussion. After her departure they have heard of his illness and self-imposed isolation. Putting such matters together, they have assumed that in some manner he was wronged, or at least slighted, by her. And, Leman – this perhaps is the measure of our masculine temperament – in various obscure fashions they have made known to me, as his senior colleague and his effective physician, that they would wish him to exact some form of recompense or retribution from Celia Quill for what they consider to be the humiliation of being wronged by her. I mention it because they are not certain how she wronged him. They have drawn the conclusions from the barest facts – that she has gone and he has fallen into illness. That association seems to be enough to engage them in this matter. The mere suggestion that it was her departure that has caused his illness is sufficient, in their eyes, for their own sex to be traduced by her behaviour.

It may be that I myself was partly of that view, at least in its most superficial aspects. It is only later that I have come –

without fully realising it – to take his own side, to understand that such a response is inappropriate to the occasion, and that perhaps it may even take on the character of weakness, or perhaps of self-indulgence. For my younger colleague has intimated to me that if he was 'deceived' by her, it was only because he assumed certain things about her which he had no right to assume. He has said that he entered upon a companionship with her quite knowingly and willingly, in the face of my own warnings that he should exercise caution. Why, then, should he wish to be revenged for what is in effect merely the consequence of his own behaviour?

I do not know what passed between them when he visited her on the last occasion before her departure. It was, I do now believe, a fateful occurrence. Mrs Thompson informed me that he left the house quietly, while she worked in the kitchen. I have reason to believe her ears are unusually sharp in respect of the movements of her master. Yet on this occasion she was lulled by her own assumption that in his state of physical weakness he was incapable of attempting any journey outside the house. Indeed, she believed him capable of descending the stairs only with great difficulty. Armed with these certainties, she continued her work of preparation in the kitchen while he slipped out of the house. So, while her attention was thus diverted, he made his escape and conducted his rendezvous.

Mrs Thompson continued to assume that he was peacefully asleep in his chair by the window several hours later, when I arrived to pay my daily visit. She even cautioned me on my arrival not to disturb him more than was necessary.

When I called out from the landing that he was not there, she advanced up the stairs in a state of excessive agitation and in her excitement pushed past me to examine the empty room. At first, such was her amazement, she assumed that in some manner I must have been responsible for his disappearance and turned towards me with angry eyes. Perhaps she saw, in my own perturbed expression, the mirror of her own, for she immediately demanded that I should conduct a search for him.

Understandably perhaps, she blamed herself for lack of supervision. He was in a state of extreme weakness through loss of blood and in no condition to traverse the house, let alone the distance to Mrs Quill's. When she discovered his loss, her agitation was further compounded by another consideration. I believe she had convinced herself that he had gone down to the marshes, as he was inclined to do in more equable times. I suspect that she even feared that in his state of profound depression, driven by his own fearsome will, he might have gone there to do away with himself.

When I had quietened her, I set out on horse to take the paths down to the water's edge which Mrs Thompson believed he would follow. I saw no sign of him. It occurred to me that he could not have walked for long in that state of health without succumbing to exhaustion, and this led me to suppose that he had instead gone out with a particular destination in mind. I should have admonished myself for not sooner reaching the conclusion that he had visited Mrs Quill's house. It would have been the place where he had last seen her. He would have gone there if only to assure himself that she had left – for what lover believes his love has departed from his life unless he witnesses the evidence with his own eyes?

Having searched the foreshore at Oxey Barn and Pennington without success, I then hastened towards her house. This meant that – Lymington lying between Oxey and her house in Walhampton – I returned to the High Street. It was there that I saw, at some small distance, the cloaked figures of two women approaching the stagecoach. One of them I believe I recognised as Mrs Quill, for she has a way of walking which is stately, regal almost, despite the heavy outer garment. The other figure seemed to be her daughter Jane.

They were perhaps two hundred yards distant and already about to mount the skirting board, assisted by the ostler. The groom had placed her hand luggage in the outward box. As I watched, the door closed, the driver flicked his reins and the stage began to move up the High Street away from me in the direction of Winchester. I could have overhauled the vehicle and asked Mrs Quill if she knew my younger colleague's whereabouts. But, my dear Leman, I would have been forced to stop the stage, for no reason other than to approach one of the passengers – a most respected lady – and interrogate her within the close sight and hearing of the other travellers about the whereabouts of my younger colleague. You must know how swiftly gossip travels, and with what haste any sense of crisis may be transmitted.

I was thrown into a quandary. My immediate task was to find my colleague, who by now might have fainted somewhere, or become incapacitated by weakness. On the other hand, the fact that Mrs Quill and her daughter had departed now increased my determination to visit her house. For it seemed to me increasingly likely that he had suspected she was about to leave and had attempted to see her. Accordingly, I decided to increase my pace across the toll-bridge to Walhampton and the shoreward path to her house, in the hope of meeting him on the way, or intercepting him in the course of his errand.

I saw no sign of him on my journey. When I arrived at Mrs Quill's house I walked the garden, in case he had fallen or fainted there. I knocked at the door and pulled the bell. When no answer came, I tried the front door, which was locked. I was about to turn and leave, and had already begun to curse myself for not hailing the stage, when it occurred to me that he might have gained access to the interior by the back door. On an impulse, then, I went round to the rear of the property. The door was stiff but did not appear to be locked. At my shoulder's brief insistence it gave way.

My first impression was that the house was empty, that all important items of furniture had been removed. I called out my younger colleague's name and heard the echo of my voice in the empty rooms. Since I was trespassing, albeit in an unoccupied house, my movements in the interior were limited to my intention. Because I am, as you know, a respecter of property, I allowed myself only a brief exploration of the rooms to satisfy myself that he was not on the premises. I was about to leave, when I caught sight of a faint movement of shadow that caused me to turn and glance towards the front hallway.

My younger colleague was in the forward part of the hallway, almost in the shadow of the main door. He was half leaning, half lying against the wall. I saw by his composure that he was in a state of extreme fatigue. His expression was lacking in emotion, at least that I could see. But if I had expected some terrible mishap, I was mistaken. For a while it seemed he hardly noticed me, so lost did he appear in thought. Then he came to himself. I persuaded him to put an arm around my shoulder, and helped him towards one of the trunks which awaited final removal in the hall. He was weak, and half sat, half lay across it. For perhaps a minute he did not speak. His pulse was faint but steady. His silence allowed me to consider my position. Rather than assist him in walking back to the High Street, I determined to settle him as best I could and then return with the fly to transport him to his house. I believe that, after she had departed, he might have been capable of making his way back. But instead he had chosen to remain in the house, perhaps standing in the same position in which she had left him, cast into deep thought. He was exhausted by then, and I believe only an effort of will saved him from passing out.

I spread out some old cloths on the floor of the hallway and persuaded him to lie down. His face was deathly white. Having settled him as comfortably as I was able, I left him and rode fast towards my house. Reaching there, I set up the fly with the help of my servant Simmonds and returned within the quarter-hour to help transport him to his own house.

The task was difficult. My younger colleague has one of those long, bony frames which seem to impede rather than encourage assistance. He did not utter a word as I helped support him through Mrs Quill's garden towards the fly, or speak when he was finally laid on the seat. By the time we reached his house he had succumbed to a fainting fit, and Mrs Thompson and I began the task of carrying him to his room. We worked as swiftly as possible. Neither of us, for perhaps understandable reasons, was keen to attract a crowd of onlookers. We carried him inside as soon as we could and rested for a short while in the hallway. Because of the length of his frame, we negotiated the stairs with difficulty. I carried him under the arms and proceeded backwards up the stairs, like a crab. Mrs Thompson braced her arms under his knees. Thus we proceeded upwards with our charge, until we reached the landing and were able to pause there, breathing heavily and exhausted from our efforts.

When we had recovered we put him to bed. Apart from faintness, his pulse seemed even and his breathing was constant. I had enough faith in Mrs Thompson's supervision to leave him in her good keeping until morning. The poor woman had been distressed enough by his unannounced departure not to feel grateful for his return, in however weakened a state. In due course I left her sitting by his bed, gazing down upon his face, in the knowledge that, having lost him once through an oversight of attention, she would guard him now like a mother her child.

The following morning I returned. Mrs Thompson reported that he had become feverish during the night. I returned to bleed him, after which his fever seemed to subside, and he became more restful.

As to Mrs Quill, I can only speculate what he might have said to her, or she to him. Who knows what passed between them? That he had travelled there hoping to meet her I do not doubt. He must have had some intimation she had returned to her house. I believe he may have confronted her. Perhaps they exchanged the final words in their strange courtship, after which she left, and he was struck into that haunted repose in which I found him.

Yet, since that incident several months ago, there has not been the slightest inclination on my younger colleague's part to inform me or Mrs Thompson of what transpired between them, or even if any words were spoken. He refuses to speak, and no encouragement will loosen his will.

So, my dear Leman, the final incident, at least in its physical aspects, was laid to rest, and we began, over the following weeks, to assist him in his recovery. Except for one last matter, which I now relinquish.

I do not know whether Mrs Quill was fully aware of the frailty of my younger colleague's state at that final meeting, for in leaving him in his condition at her house while she departed for the stage, we might speculate that she displayed an uncharacteristic callousness. In mitigation, then, of an impression that her behaviour may have fostered, I record the following.

Mrs Thompson was so much opposed to Mrs Quill, and her influence upon her master, that I did not hear, until a few days later, that on her way to the stage Mrs Quill had called by at my younger colleague's home and, knocking upon the door, informed Mrs Thompson of his presence, in a weakened state, at her own house.

She told Mrs Thompson that he was resting, that he was safe and in no immediate danger, but that he required direct assistance in order to return. I was by then already away, searching for him on the marshes and Mrs Thompson had no means of immediately acquainting me with this fact. She was tempted to set out for Mrs Quill's house herself, but determined that she could not assist him as well as I could. Instead, she set herself to wait, with some considerable impatience, for my return.

When I knocked upon her door in due course with my younger colleague waiting in the fly, we became so much embroiled in the immediate task of moving him to his room that I believe the fact of Mrs Quill's visit slipped from Mrs Thompson's mind.

I did not ask for this information, though it was a few days late in coming – for Mrs Thompson informed me of it on one of my visits to the patient. I can only assume that she, excellent woman that she is, had taken a decision to acquaint me with it so that I might not be unfairly prejudiced against Mrs Quill's reputation. I thanked Mrs Thompson, but at the time my attention was sufficiently arrested by what she had told me that I did not think to ask whether Mrs Quill had given any other indication of the contents of the meeting with my younger colleague.

In due course, on one of my visits to his house, I drew Mrs Thompson aside and asked her whether Mrs Quill by chance had communicated any other aspect of the meeting when she had called to inform Mrs Thompson of his presence at her house. Mrs Thompson said, 'Mrs Quill seemed distressed.' When I asked how she ascertained this, Mrs Thompson answered, 'I saw a trace of tears in her eyes and believed she had been crying.'

I asked her whether, in the course of this communication, Mrs Quill had indicated anything further of the meeting. To which Mrs Thompson said, 'No, sir. She simply informed me of my master's whereabouts and then departed to the stage.'

We were standing in the doorway of the kitchen downstairs, where we had withdrawn in order to remain out of my patient's earshot. Mrs Thompson regarded me with characteristic directness, as though considering the effect her information would have upon me.

We are two people with separate motives, though with a common interest in my younger colleague's welfare. I thanked her for this description of Mrs Quill's state and left shortly afterwards for my own house, though in somewhat thoughtful mood.

I have written for longer than I intended. Already I hear the first faint sounds of bird-song outside my window. I will return now to my bed and shall hope for several hours of sleep before waking.

I bring my missive to an end, sir, and remain,

    Yours most sincerely,

      Hargood

CHAPTER 27

They were walking fast, two solitary figures upright on a long horizon, on a level foreshore which stretched from Hurst Castle towards Lepe. Hargood said, 'I have gathered a few crumbs, though I do not pretend that they make a cake.'

On a small rise, no more than a mound, Hargood halted and, Grange silent by his side, looked out over the saltings, towards the Solent. The tide had receded, leaving grey mud banks and green weed.

'So I will proceed to tell you about her,' Hargood said, 'or rather, to give you an account of an account. I judge you well enough to hear what I have to impart.'

Grange was silent, waiting for Hargood to continue.

'After she departed our town, like you, sir, I have heard no further of her for the three months, other than that odd sighting in London. By chance, however, I happened to come across another small piece of information.'

On the foreshore a group of small waders, sanderlings and a few snipe, rose in sudden alarm, like leaves blown in a storm.

'My fellow physician Harding came to visit me for a half-day perhaps a week ago. In the course of our conversation he commented that he had seen a handsome woman walking down the street in which his surgery is situated, and remembered that he first observed her while visiting me in Lymington. I asked him whether he knew her, whether she was a social acquaintance, and he replied that he had seen her only once. My suspicion was aroused at so deep a memory of so thin an encounter. He described her appearance in some detail and, since the surface aspects fitted so well, I began to suspect the mysterious personage's identity. When I asked how in particular he had remembered her, he said, if I recall rightly, that she had "an attitude of calm deliberation". I replied there were a number of women who could be so described. He said, "I never saw a woman so self-possessed." It is strange, is it not, how a phrase, often an innocuous one, reveals the complexity of a person? "An interior woman," I believe he called her. You will suspect, sir, that harboured inside the interior of that phrase is perhaps Mrs Quill herself. I began to think we were talking of the same woman.'

Grange was silent, looking out over the fields and water-meadows. He might not have been listening. But when Hargood halted, Grange's eyes turned towards him quickly, as if impatient.

'Silas, you dissemble. I know that every word I have spoken about her has been absorbed by you, that you will store and sift what I have said, that you will search for some hidden meaning. Keep her memory, if you will, fix her in your mind. Hold her as deeply as you wish. But in the meantime, sir, your mind should be fixed on your recovery.'

Observing Hargood's taciturn recognition of his interest, Grange turned away again. He stared over the marsh. 'I do believe you are right.'

'I know also that you speak to humour me, that inside you there is no lessening of your . . . intensity.'

'You know me too well, Hargood.'

They looked out to where several small rowing-boats plied in the Solent, spreading a net between them, the floats bobbing on the surface.

Hargood said, 'When next he visited me I asked Harding, should he have occasion to write to me on other matters from Winchester, to mention whether he should ever happen to see Mrs Quill again. I received his letter yesterday. There was no mention of her whatsoever. Harding is a meticulous man. I assure you he would have recorded the fact if their paths had crossed a second time.'

'And what do you deduce from such a sighting?' Grange spoke softly, without a sign of animation on his face, but Hargood was arrested for a moment by the weight of interest.

'That she was visiting Winchester, that its significance is simply that it is also a stage in the journey towards another place. And if I draw a line, so to speak, between Lymington and Winchester and extend that line, why, sir, I believe that we may see that its final projection is London. Therefore I deduce it is towards London that she is finally bound. If we unite that with the further possible sighting as recorded by my mistress, I believe we see now where she has ended. She has sought the most populous place on earth in which to hide.'

Grange nodded, though without conviction.

Aware of the concentration of his companion's silence, Hargood said: 'You realise, Silas, that she has moved beyond your reach? In London she will disappear. She could take lodgings anywhere, perhaps in some outlying part. After that, depending on her immediate financial position, she will sooner or later look for some form of occupation for which she is fitted and she will become one of those grey women, those who turn quietly into middle and old age.'

Hargood might have believed that Grange had drifted away again, but he was surprised by the note of detachment in his patient's voice. 'The London sighting is mysterious and perhaps can be discounted. If that is so, you are basing a great deal on one crumb of information – that she passed through Winchester.'

'Yes, indeed. Do you have an alternative?'

Considering, perhaps, the rhetorical nature of the question, Grange did not reply. Instead he asked, 'What is the second crumb?'

'The second crumb?' Hargood was momentarily startled.

'You said you had "crumbs" of information, I believe. You had mentioned the plural.'

'Did I? You listen well, sir. You do persist. But you are right. My second crumb of information is this. That I have asked my mistress to correspond with me on any further matters relating to Mrs Quill which she may hear from her London acquaintances. My mistress, as you know, is one whose ears are attuned to gossip. She has heard nothing so far.'

'That is another crumb?'

'Why, Silas, I believe I do detect again that fierce and silent mind. I wondered when it would reappear. A crumb is exactly what it is. She has returned to London quietly, without fuss. That is what the information conveys, at least to me. I suggest to you, sir, that this will be the pattern. She will live in quiet circumstances on the fringe of polite society, keeping her own counsel. And if you should be unwise enough to seek her, I believe you will not find her.'

Hargood paused to consider Grange's response. In front of them a heavy cloud moved across the marshes and beneath its grey underside white gulls turned in the light. The surface of the sea had a strange calm. Several rowing boats were putting out to a merchantman which had anchored off the Lymington river. The light breeze was offshore, and since the merchantman could not tack under sail in the confines of the channel, it would require a tow upriver to its berth. They could see a group of men working on the capstan of the vessel. Others were putting new staves so that they could lend their weight to breaking the anchor out of the mud. The crew milled like ants about the machinery of the capstan. Fresh hands placed staves in the engine and added their weight. Gradually the iron anchor, with its wooden cross-brace, rose from the water. The rowing boats swung stern to the merchantman and towing ropes were flung. On each craft the helmsman made fast the towing rope. Slowly, taking their rhythm from the helmsmen's shouts, the men began to strike down with their oars and row.

They watched the oar-blades sweeping, like the tentative legs of an insect, without immediate effect. Then the merchantman's bow swung upwind and the slow procession began to make its way upriver. There were hardly any waves from the light offshore breeze and the surface of the water seemed sulphurous with light. The oars rose and fell. An uneasy light put silver in their edges.

Hargood turned towards his colleague, and observed that he was lost in his own thoughts. He made his own deductions over Grange's prolonged silence, then turned away.

'My mistress will pass me any information concerning Mrs Quill which she can find. In the absence of that, you must recognise, finally, that Mrs Quill is gone. She may be a few days' ride from where we stand, but in her personal disposition she could not be further from you than if she had removed herself to the furthest deserts of Arabia.'

'Should I disagree?' Grange asked.

Hargood smiled, despite himself. 'My dear Silas, lovers personalise matters. Even the most adverse circumstance is turned to their advantage. You will assume she is fleeing from you. That you are individually responsible for her flight. In her very absence no doubt you will find complicity and cause for subtle hope.'

'Who else might she be fleeing from?'

It was asked softly and Hargood was conscious of the weight behind it. He was aware, too, of the sudden, real surveillance which had been turned upon him. 'Shall I treat that as an earnest enquiry?' he asked calmly.

'It is earnest.'

Silence seemed to fall between them, as solid as a door. Hargood had intended to make a light reference to Grange's persistence, but the words died in his throat. Beside him, his companion was preparing calmly to speak again.

Grange said, 'Who else, then, would she be fleeing from?'

It was the cold intensity of the question, enhanced by the calmness of the repetition. Hargood experienced a faint tremor of apprehension, for the truth was that he felt uneasy at some deep level. He sensed that the concentrated regard of his younger colleague upon him was based upon an intuition and a part of him hoped it was no more than that.

'From herself,' Hargood answered at last. 'From her past.'

In the circumstances it was a skilful and deflective answer. Yet still he felt the lamp of Grange's attention upon him, turned up to its fullest extent. And for several minutes while they walked, Hargood sensed, striding in the soft evening light beside his younger colleague, the chillness of obscure culpability.

CHAPTER 28

'Let us construct a hypothetical background,' Hargood said, after a few minutes.

Grange nodded. 'A fiction?'

Hargood continued, 'I believe that fiction is not only the prerogative of liars and certain novelists, but may also, in highly limited circumstances, become the tool of honest men.'

'Please proceed.'

'Since I am asked to provide a base, so to speak, upon which we may build, I say the fiction of which we speak is likely to be something of this nature. I compound it of other matters and incidents which I have heard from my mistress concerning Mrs Quill's past. As the sources of this information are various, I do believe that fiction, most aptly considered, is the best account we may put forward. Afterwards we may refine our story in the light of evidence.'

Beside him, Grange nodded.

'Let us begin, then,' Hargood said, 'with the initial premise. A young woman, of poor but perhaps genteel parents, comes to London and is employed at a milliner's house, or some such place. Let us say that she meets a man who flatters her and in due course she takes him as a lover, not out of cynicism but in the belief that in the fullness of time he would marry her. Instead, as is often the way, he merely leaves her with child. I know of several such incidents, but this account is a composite of them. Now, sir, having a child outside wedlock, it becomes difficult or impossible for her to marry, for, in the society in which we live a lover's child is not the best pathway to respectability. Perhaps, when she insists that he make good the outcome of their relations and marry her, he takes offence. Perhaps, if she is a woman of character, and insists further, he will find himself obliged to cast her out from his protection. Again, I have heard of several such incidents.'

A peculiar silence descended upon them. Grange waited patiently for the next instalment.

After a few moments, Hargood continued, 'I believe that, if she is a woman of spirit, then rather than live in quiet shame, she might strike a show of independence. Now, sir, what show of independence might she make against that man, and perhaps men in particular? What courses of action are available to her, who feels herself wronged? Could she run away to sea? Could she take to preaching sermons for the Church? I jest, of course, merely for effect. These are all avenues allowed only to men. Perhaps, having taken a cynical view of men and their proclivities, she decides to turn the matter to her advantage. Perhaps she might become, by due degrees, a madam.'

Hargood halted. They were still staring out over the marshes. The merchantman was entering the second bend in the channel, pulled slowly by the attendant rowing boats. Hargood said, 'What do you think of my fiction so far?'

'It has a curious interest.'

'Do you not find in this account an odd irony, that she should take what ruined her – men's lust – and turn it to her advantage?'

'Ironical, yes. But suppose – to take your fiction further – that this woman were gifted with a fine mind. It would seem a strange profession for one so educated.'

'I have met madams, sir, who were the very soul of respectability, and others who could converse as learnedly upon a subject as any scholar. I knew one who lived in permanent sobriety and was dressed in black in mourning for her husband, and who was more chaste and kind of heart than almost any other woman I have met. I knew another . . .'

Grange smiled. 'You seem to have a good knowledge of the general terrain, Hargood.'

'As, I believe, do you, my dear Silas. I should perhaps remind you, sir, that in your own youth you were something of a rakehell, or so I have gathered from mutual acquaintances.'

'A mere amateur to your professional,' Grange murmured. 'A summer swallow compared with your permanent eagle.'

'I do believe you attempt to flatter me, sir,' Hargood said. 'Since we have entered a veritable bestiary of allegation, I shall retaliate in kind. If I am an eagle, I think you are a fox, scuttling for your lair after a diversionary tactic.'

'You have given me much food for thought, I promise you,' Grange said.

'Good. I shall accept your protestation at face value. And now, since we have walked a good eight miles or so to this point, I believe we should consider that we owe ourselves some fare and take ourselves to an inn.'

CHAPTER 29

My dear Leman,

I pray you are well and that God will grant you the patience to continue with my account.

My younger colleague continues to make progress, though it becomes increasingly clear that his advance towards health is independent of my supervision, and arises from some interior whose aspects I do not know – if indeed he knows them himself. For he appears fortified by a conviction that he will one day meet again with Mrs Celia Quill. Why he should believe so, why he should assume that to acquaint himself anew with the cause of his malaise will prove beneficial to his well-being, I do not know. But as his conviction increases, so his health seems to improve.

You have met him, I do believe, several years ago at Lymington, though as I remember your acquaintanceship with him was sufficiently brief that perhaps you cannot remember him in detail, except as a kind of abstract. If my memory serves me, he attended a meal at my house for yourself and several of your colleagues who were passing through from Wareham to Southampton on a tour of the surgical facilities of the southern coastal ports for His Majesty's Navy. If you retain any recollection of the event at all, this abstract may consist of an impression of a person who is tall, and nervous, and withdrawn into himself – that, I would say, is a means of fixing the animal in your attention, at least in his external and more rudimentary aspects. That is how I think of him too, as some remote creature who remains by his own volition on the periphery of social intercourse. Whenever he is not occasioned by the direct address of another he becomes silent and seems to drift backwards, as it were, into his own territory. It would appear that he uses this appearance to dissemble, so that he may retire without allowing his perceptions to be too much affected by the world. But there is another self, which is also present, and which is less amenable to description. I believe that it is this mysterious inner man which now begins to show.

Whatever I may say of this inner being, one thing is certain. He is watchful. I do not think I have ever been in a man's company where I sense my thoughts and expressions so carefully surveyed, so parsimoniously sifted, albeit in a most subtle and innocuous manner. Yet it is precisely this watchfulness that causes me to consider in like manner what I say to him most carefully. For he hunts my own speech for clues, as if I myself might not know the implications of what I say. And sometimes he questions me on a statement in comparison with one that I made several days ago, and whose form I cannot clearly remember. He appears diffident, as I say, yet when his curiosity is roused he recites my recent statements to me in their most precise configuration as if a written record had been kept. As a man of this world, with some experience, I know that great passion is exact, and keeps its secret and precise accounts.

This, then, is my dilemma. That even as I arrange his cure, it appears he is regarding me, not with the external gaze of a spectator, but with some inner eye which, it seems to me, perceives the shape of my thoughts and formulations in an unblinking gaze. And for my part, as I stroll with him (for we ramble over the countryside), I must remind myself that I am walking not with a tame dog of a companion, but with a detached wolf.

The other day I found myself in possession of some loose information regarding Mrs Quill's whereabouts. My mistress had written to me and I attempted to interest him in it, in the hope that we might arrange an exchange of information. But, sensing the direction of my negotiation and not wishing to impart any such himself, he refused to show interest in my own information, even though (as I sensed) the full beam of his inner concentration was upon me, and he was most wakeful and attentive for clues. Thus, in the course of our amiable conversations, I find ourselves manoeuvring like two wrestlers who watch one another for the first signs of a hold.

I hope you will forgive this digression, which I may excuse, if it may be excused at all, only on the grounds that it leads to another thought, closer to the heart of this matter. When I think of his attachment to Celia Quill, I consider that what she ascertained in him were some signs of hidden life, which are not obvious to others. I am willing to concede that she at least observed something there, something that altered her own course and perhaps even caused her (extraordinary woman that she is) to founder or fall.

Leman, my dear fellow, this is the strangeness of dealing with my younger colleague, that everything seems reversed. For I had thought he was drawn towards that remarkable woman like a filing to a magnet, or like some hapless insect to a flame. Yet I can see that this may be regarded in another light entirely. For perhaps it was she who was impelled towards him. Her own social position, the result of not much more than a mere three years of living in these parts, was (as a consequence of both her character and good works) of such solidity that I would say it was almost impregnable. Her authority was natural and graceful. Yet she risked everything that she had won, in some sense, by engaging with a stranger who was once my colleague and is now my patient. I have thought of him as the moth and of her as the flame. But now I perceive that the flames have had no final effect upon the creature I once thought was their victim – that the moth, having passed through fire, has an invisible presence, which beats always before me, both stronger and more silent than before.

Other matters develop their own momentum. I mentioned earlier the effect of Mrs Quill's disappearance upon the community in which she had become a central figure. And in speaking of spirits, we have been subject to a visitation, from an earnest representative of our communal religion, who approaches me as his parishioner and seeks my assistance in clarification of certain matters.

Recently I was approached by the Reverend Gilpin, a vicar of these parts, who senses that I know more than I am able to impart of Celia Quill's departure. I met him as he returned from giving a communion service at Boldre, one of the neighbouring areas of Lymington, where he presides. As I am one of his side-wardens, he drew me aside and asked me when Mrs Quill might intend to return, since it seemed that half the charity of the town, directly or indirectly, was upon her shoulders. Although she left advice and instructions with her acquaintances and helpers, and had made an orderly retreat, yet he gained the impression that she had left under the impulsion of events. We were standing outside the church, among the gravestones. It was becoming a hot day, and in the course of his sermon he had grown somewhat heated over the subject of divine love, that blessed love which Greeks call *agape*, so much so that now he stood beside me mopping his forehead and surveying me with his shrewd eyes. He is a likeable man, who is not afraid to describe the majority of his forest parishioners as pagans, not least to their faces, and he is not above imbibing some liquids in companionship. He was perplexed, and was inclined to hold me responsible for not conveying to him at least the gist or germ of an explanation of Mrs Quill's departure.

It was clear that he had been deputed by certain members of society to approach me and to discover whatever clues may be necessary to form an opinion. For nothing is more heinous a crime to society than that it cannot form an opinion of someone upon whom it feels entitled to sit in judgement. The good man set about questioning me, albeit in friendly enough fashion, about the circumstances of her departure. And I, as befits someone of my responsibilities, in guarded fashion set about providing as little information as I could, which was not too difficult, since there is precious little to impart.

What perplexes those of her former circle more than any other matter is that she has not communicated with them since she left. Knowing her good works, my questioner expressed his view that it was out of character for her not to correspond, so to speak, with her former acquaintances, and at least enquire after their health and disposition. He made much of her unremitting efforts on their behalf. It was a terrible temptation not to enlighten the good man, at least to the extent of reassuring him that she had been subject to events outside her immediate control, and that her behaviour in not communicating with him and others should be excused on those grounds. But that would only have led to further enquiries. I know enough of social intercourse to be aware that the imparting of limited information is likely to be treated as greater provocation than none at all, for no other reason than that a carefully limited account implies a knowledge of the whole. They would not only blame me for retaining what I knew, but their worst expectations of her would be confirmed – that at the base of her leaving there are facts that are being withheld from them. At present, then, all I could do was agree with him that the manner of her departure, and her subsequent silence, were uncharacteristic of her. As you may imagine, he left dissatisfied, inclined by charity against forming an unfavourable judgement of her, yet lacking the evidence upon which to answer those who had consulted him.

I return, then, from this digression upon Mrs Quill's departure to my younger colleague, who has not retreated, but in some sense has held his own ground. (You see how these things turn – she departs, as though struck down, and he remains, damaged and still healing, but yet perhaps in control of the disputed territory of their former life.) I had thought him to some extent susceptible, perhaps even culpable, for that which has afflicted him. But now, as I have recently observed, I continue to revise my view. Observing the determination of his return, the implacable belief that he will meet her again, I acknowledge that it is not his weakness which has caused him to suffer these trials. Rather it is some subtle strength or hidden quantity in him which women, perhaps more than men, are able to perceive.

I observe these things and, as I do so, my own position is subject to a subtle change – for are we not all of us merely the sum of our intimate feelings? If what I first considered to be weakness in my younger colleague is increasingly changed into a form of strength, then what may I say of my own observations? Perhaps, in regard to my behaviour and the righteousness of my responses, there is some necessary change or addition. For I am aware that at each shift in my perception of him, so my perspective is subtly altered, and I am forced to view my own feelings in a new light.

These are difficult matters and ones which, though they require resolution, yet continue to impede my clarity. I must give them my most careful consideration and, when I have examined them as much as I am able, I will attempt to return and, in so doing, try your patience again.

With these thoughts, sir, I wish you farewell, and remain,

Yours sincerely,

Hargood

CHAPTER 30

Mrs Thompson piled logs on the fire in the drawing-room, seasoned pieces of beech, spruce and oak. Breathing deeply against the strain of leaning over the grate, she lit the dry leaves and kindling with a burning twig from the wood stove and watched the thin flames flicker among the brushwood she had laid between the logs. She was an active woman, not given to lingering, but certain recent events caused her to pause for a few moments, watching the flames as they began to gather and rustle between the logs.

'Mrs Thompson?'

Grange stood behind her, his presence breathing a calm agitation.

'Sir?'

'I see we have an extra source of firewood.'

Mrs Thompson stood up and brushed down her skirts, turning to face him directly. She nodded, though she did not speak, so he attempted again to prompt her.

'You have an explanation?'

'Dr Hargood ordered an ox-cart full of wood from his own estate to be brought here, sir.'

Grange paused, as though struck. Mrs Thompson, taking brief advantage of the interval, asked, 'Is something wrong, sir?'

'It is a charitable action, no doubt.'

'I believe so, sir.'

'Nevertheless –' Grange chose his words carefully '– I am inclined to resist such gestures from my senior colleague, however kindly motivated.'

Mrs Thompson asked, in what seemed a heartfelt perplexity, 'Sir?'

Grange said, 'I am nervous of incurring too many favours from Dr Hargood, Mrs Thompson.'

She considered him closely. 'I do not understand.'

'Do you not? There are certain favours which place the receiver under a debt of gratitude.'

Grange wondered, not for the first time, about Mrs Thompson's deeper motives. He had assumed, perhaps too easily, that she would understand that it was precisely such gestures on Dr Hargood's part which would later become items of account in the courteous but prolonged struggle between them over the nature of Grange's cure. But it occurred to him that since Mrs Thompson appeared to be of the same party as Dr Hargood over the details of that cure, perhaps she did not consider the acceptance of such gestures as hostages to fortune. On the contrary, since she was so much in agreement with Hargood over his prescriptions, in her view perhaps any favour owing to him was likely to be beneficial. Now she said simply, 'A debt of gratitude, sir?'

'Precisely, Mrs Thompson. My older colleague attempts to impress upon me the importance of his views in the matter of my own treatment and cure. I believe that he has influence enough upon me without his position being improved by my gratitude over other matters.'

'I am sorry, sir. The wood arrived, and I assumed you had approved.'

The wood had arrived, perhaps conveniently, when Grange was out walking with Hargood himself and Mrs Thompson had taken the opportunity to order the elderly drover to off-load it in the garden at the back of the property. Before Grange returned, and to ensure that the task was completed as swiftly as possible, she had taken the trouble to put on an overcoat and assist the drover to pile the logs, choosing as their location a position at the rear of the garden against a south-facing wall so that they would dry more easily. With some justification, she suspected that her master, with his passion for independence, would refuse the gift if it had been offered directly and thereby create an incident. Having taken possession of her master's welfare, she was concerned not to leave the matter to chance, since she took the view that no sane man would risk creating a greater incident by returning a gift once it had been accepted. It was not her task to make the decision, she would be the first to agree, though it might be that she was more than willing to supply the circumstances in which any other decision became impossible.

When Grange had returned later that afternoon, seating himself on the wooden bench in the hall to remove his dust-covered boots, the wood was neatly stacked against the south-facing wall, the cart had disappeared and Mrs Thompson could refer with some satisfaction to the extra supply of fuel for the fires, leaving him to consider how he might deal with a question that had already been resolved on his behalf.

'Is there anything else, sir?'

Grange, stirred out of his consideration by her question, was unable to reply.

Having imparted her information and receiving no positive response from him, she nodded and was about to turn and leave for the kitchen. It was her sanctum and he knew or suspected that once she had reached it, the matter would be closed, or at least difficult to raise again without a sense of returning to old ground.

As she was in the process of turning, Grange called: 'Mrs Thompson!'

She halted, then swung towards him again, her face composed against any hint of satisfaction or justification.

'I am at a loss. Did Dr Hargood ask you directly about the delivery of firewood?'

'No, sir,' she answered with truth.

'But you accepted it when it arrived.'

'I assumed, as I said, sir, the matter had already been decided between you.'

'Dr Hargood is inclined towards generosity,' Grange observed. 'In future, kindly enquire with me before gifts are accepted.'

'Indeed, sir,' Mrs Thompson said, ignoring the casual irony.

Grange was certain that the matter would not rest there. Like one of those underground fires, it might be put out in one area, but the certainty was it would break out again, in a different form, in different circumstances.

After the perturbation of their confrontation, he felt himself subject to a fit of coughing, but was equally determined not to exhibit too many further signs to her of physical frailty. With his lungs already beginning to heave in protest, he walked through the hall and up the stairs to his own study. There he closed the door. In the privacy of silence, leaning over the metal washbasin, he allowed the racking fit to take its full effect.

CHAPTER 31

My dear Leman,

There is another woman who has been to some extent at the centre of these events, and whom I have mentioned before, though somewhat briefly and in passing. I have treated her as a secondary actor in this strange affair. Perhaps it is time to direct our focus more closely upon her, for I do admit that she may know our patient better than I do myself.

My colleague's housekeeper, Mrs Thompson, is a handsome woman, indefatigable in his defence, protective of his privacy. She is past the first flush of youth, but she has regular and pleasing features, a fine figure, and a liveliness and strength of character all of which, when taken together, would make someone a most excellent wife. If I were to convey a picture of my younger colleague's current circumstances, it would be incomplete without some direct and perhaps fulsome acknowledgement of her presence in his affairs. As his housekeeper, she guards his privacy like a vixen her cubs. Throughout his illness she has contrived to survey his activities at every turn and, keeping her judgements to herself, has attempted to effect in every possible manner his recovery. Though she might have been suspicious of my intentions at first, and unsure of my role in the matter of Mrs Quill's departure, she has become my accomplice and collaborator in our mutual efforts. I have a suspicion that she withholds her final judgements upon me too, though no doubt in so strong-minded a character they are present beneath the surface of her duty. It is a strange thing, but when I meet her I find myself intimidated by her presence, for she observes me with not much less conviction than she observes her master, as someone who must be helped and, if necessary, chided to do the right thing. We have established between ourselves a certain mutual but often wary collaboration, which extends no further than a professional interest in the recovery of the patient, but which makes me suspect I may take her more into my trust, not least in the hope that she may herself offer some enlightenment on other matters.

This leads me to ask a question, perhaps of a rhetorical nature, which has its roots in what has been accounted in previous letters regarding the effect of my younger colleague upon the female sex. Are strong women attracted to a certain type of man, one whose strength is hidden? Certainly, I am rendered somewhat reticent in reaching a conclusion. But our patient, it seems, is not. He takes their attention as a kind of due and shows no fear of them, even of their most formidable personages. If he is a lamb, then he is a strange lamb, for he walks among our female wolves without trepidation.

In our conversations before he fell from health, he informed me of a belief which he has, that young women are moulded by men, and that, as they grow older and begin to perceive the world for themselves, they become purer by virtue of casting off the illusions which were previously placed upon them. I distrust theory, as any good Tory should, and my first suspicion is that he merely justifies what he feels – just as I, owning a certain amount of land and property, would be provoked in the defence of it to provide any justification necessary for my continued enjoyment.

Yet if he thus merely defends what he prefers, I may begin to ask myself, why should he hold that preference in the first place?

I had thought when young women gave themselves into the protection of older men, men of property or rank, they did so out of recognition of strength. But perhaps the weak are drawn to the weak, for beneath this structure of privilege, perhaps the man who employs it is also lacking in that final confidence which would claim the attention *de naturo*, as of right. I begin to think that those of us who seek such privilege, and employ it for our gain, are perhaps without that final assurance that we should act for ourselves alone. That is certainly not the case with our patient, for I observed that one of his peculiarities is that he employed no privilege over women, he exerted no leverage or patronage, and yet his character is such that he appears to command their interest and concern.

My dear Leman, you find me, having committed so many stray thoughts to paper, none the wiser for my deliberations. I have become prone to doubts not only about my own role in this affair, but also about certain tenets in which I believe. In so doing, I hope that I have not tempted your generosity towards me beyond enduring. Perhaps, out of the kindness of your heart, you will forgive me once again for thus using your kind offices.

In the interim, sir, I remain, as always,
Yours most sincerely,
Hargood

CHAPTER 32

'For you, sir.' Mrs Thompson raised her eyes from the letter towards Grange.

He had an intimation that she knew from whom the letter came. 'Thank you, Mrs Thompson.'

His fingers closed over it and he felt the slightest resistance from her hand. He was about to nod and excuse himself in preparation for retiring to his study, but it was Mrs Thompson who turned away, pivoting with grace and unexpected speed on her heel. He looked in some surprise at the empty doorway into the kitchen where a few seconds earlier she had been.

Through the open door he heard a clatter of pots and the pouring of a jug of water.

He walked up the stairs and entered his study, taking care not to close the door too peremptorily while his fears and desires rose inside him. The sound of his heart was heavy in his ears and threatened to engulf him. Out of the turmoil, he observed his fingers calmly split the seal and the opening of the single sheet in his hand.

He had recognised the writing on the outside. His habitual faintness, rising up from beneath his ribs, overtook him, forcing him to lean back against the table for support. At first he could not bear to look at the letter. He expected some neat avowal of resettlement and an injunction that she was happy in her new state. Perhaps it was some final anger lying beneath the certainty of his suspicions, or an inner revolution against his own fear, that caused him to unfold the letter and focus his attention upon it. In so doing he became aware of the familiar clarity of the hand, the economy of the sentences.

Dear Silas,
I pray that you will forgive me for writing to you at this time.

Having departed Lymington on the terms which I did, I do not expect either your tolerance or forgiveness for my behaviour. I sincerely hope that what I do now does not strike you as more surprising still.

You think of me as deliberate and perhaps as calculating. There is much that I cannot explain to myself in my own terms, let alone that of others. To one such as I, much of whose past has been inflicted on me by forces outside my direct control, there is a struggle to make the present and future conform more closely to the terms of that which I may hope or desire. I shall not continue longer in this vein, except to say that I do not ask for your understanding, but merely wish to inform you of certain facts and occurrences which, considered separately, may supply a basis and explanation for my gratitude.

Since leaving my house I have received, sometimes by rather diverse routes, several letters from my acquaintances in Lymington. It happens that one of them has given me a report of your illness and partial recovery, for the latter of which I am exceedingly grateful. If there is one aspect which had exercised my most profound regrets, it was the state into which you had reportedly fallen.

If I have one further reason for writing it is that I wish to impart, as best as I am able, the following expression. The letters I have received from various parties assure me of one thing, for which I have to thank you directly. Those who have corresponded with me may be both perplexed and suspicious of my behaviour, yet they hold only the vaguest of views as to the reasons for my abrupt departure. They appear to associate my leaving with you and perhaps with your illness, but are unable to place any more precise association upon it. Having no clear intimation or knowledge of my reasons for leaving, they are bound to speculate, and indeed one or two of the letters I have received contain enquiries demanding an explanation, and even raising directly the matter of your condition. This is to be expected. Yet it is clear, from the very fact that they have been obliged to ask such questions, that your colleague, Dr Hargood, and yourself have kept whatever reasons I may have had for departure from others, and that is why I am compelled to write, to thank you both for your silence and the protection of a reputation which, though it does not deserve protection, yet has been left in some sense intact.

With regard to my own future intentions, I do not expect ever to return, for reasons which I cannot explain. But if it were within my compass to do so, it would be with the deepest and most profound gratitude for your continued discretion.

There is little else for me to add. I could attempt further to explain my actions, but to do so would require the consent of another party, to whom I believe I owe silence, and even if it were possible, or advantageous, for you to know something of the background, it is not in my gift to supply it. Should the fates ever allow our further discussion, I would still be unable to proffer an explanation. If the protection of my reputation means anything at all, it is that other party to whom you must, in the fullness of time, address such enquiries.

Both Jane and I are in reasonable health. I write this letter after some contemplation, in the knowledge and foreboding that to communicate with you at all is unwise. Yet if there was a second motive in my writing, I desired above all to wish you well, to express my deepest hope that you are not too severely damaged by events and to trust that in due course your recovery will be complete.

You must not to attempt to seek me, or to find the address from which this letter was written. I believe that in the course of time you will forget what has occurred and that fate, being often just, will grant you a full and contented life. I pray that once you have fully recovered your health, you will discover in yourself not only the fortitude which shall grant you that peace, but the terms and conditions of a deserved happiness.

I remain,
      Most sincerely,
         Celia Quill

A peculiar sensation of hollowness entered Grange's legs, as if they had become insubstantial. He sat down, breathing coldly and heavily. Downstairs he heard the clatter of Mrs Thompson's plates, but the sound hardly disturbed the perturbations of his own mind.

There was so little, and so much, in the letter that he could grasp at or understand. For several minutes he could only wait while the thunder of his heart lessened. His breathing was difficult. With tight fingers he loosened his cravat, then leaned forward, placing his elbows on his knees and his face in his hands. For another minute at least he remained in that position. When he was no longer short of breath he raised his face from his hands.

After a while he stood up and walked to the window. He drew down the upper casement on its sash, so that he could take into his lungs the clear, cold air.

CHAPTER 33

Dear Leman,

I hoped that my most recent letters, regarding the gradual improvement in communication between myself and my younger colleague, would allow a time of reconciliation, upon which we could build our collaboration. But in the midst of my renewed hope an event has occurred which threatens to affect profoundly the relations between us.

There is no news I feared so much as that which has now arrived. Our patient, whose recovery is almost complete, insofar as any such may be ascertained, has received a letter. The letter is from Mrs Celia Quill, who I both hoped and believed had departed the field in perpetuity, leaving him at last to take possession once again of his life.

From my own perspective as his physician, the missive is unwelcome. Yet to attempt to ignore it would be foolhardy. It has come, and I too must now adjust to its presence upon our scene.

The change in him, I am certain, is not a change in his previous concerns. On the contrary, among its other effects, the letter seems to have sharpened that enquiring eye with which he regards the world, and which he sometimes turns upon me in particular. After first informing me that he had received a letter from Mrs Quill, for a certain time he kept its contents to himself. Throughout the following afternoon he walked beside me, lost in thought, but at the same time alert to my own conversation and commentary, as though he struggled to balance the niceties of our discourse with his own inner concerns. In short, he acted like a man who, by withholding information, hopes that his companion may be tempted to explain some aspect which he does not understand.

It may be that I have misjudged his behaviour. Perhaps we are guilty in this life of attributing to others our own inner thoughts. For myself, not yet having read the letter, I noted his careful observation of my response to the news that he had received a communication from Mrs Quill, as if he considered me from a fresh perspective. Though the evidence of this new worldliness in my colleague may cause consternation, I for one was relieved in the first instance at his state of mind, for I had feared above all that he might sink again into that terrible dejection which had characterised his first reaction to the news of her previous life.

In the latter stages of our walk, as I have mentioned, he gave me the letter to read. As I did so I sensed his eye on me with such intensity that I felt uncomfortable. It was only by an effort of will that I prevented myself from turning away at the last moment, so that he could not read the doubt and fear which contended within me.

. If I had worried about the effect of the letter on him, my concerns were perhaps misplaced. I should instead have been more perturbed about its effects on me. There are phrases in it that terrify my soul. Only I know their import – though my patient, with his rapid and discerning intelligence, suspects that I hold some key to their explanation. I handed it back and nodded, and though I hope that I was not visibly shaken, my mouth was as dry as paper. Praise God that I was able to show as little of my own disturbance as was possible in the circumstances. He took back the letter without comment and, though by then I had recovered something of my superficial repose, I sensed he registered the tremors that had shaken me.

He will not press me immediately, I know; it is not his way. But from henceforth I must recognise and attest that everything I do or say will come under his closest scrutiny.

We have walked far today and I must see several patients, so I am forced to post this communication in its incomplete form, in the hope that you will forgive my haste, having accounted at least for the outline of the event.

In the meanwhile I have much to think about and will return in due course to these reflections.

I remain, sir,

    Most sincerely yours,

      Hargood

CHAPTER 34

It had been raining for nearly half an hour when Mrs Thompson heard the knock upon the door and made her way briskly to open it. She could not remember such rain.

As she moved through to the hallway she saw a flash in the windows, followed almost immediately by a peal of thunder. In her haste she struggled with the latch.

Her master stood against the dark afternoon. His hair had been plastered down by the rain and his bony features seemed to be set in an expression of detachment. He appeared to be in no hurry to enter, but stood for several seconds with the overflow of the gutter upon his head and shoulders. She watched in consternation as the water flooded him and streamed down his neck and cravat. He seemed to be almost entirely oblivious of his state, looking upon his own existence as a stranger might who had returned from a long journey.

She swallowed and opened the door wide. Almost reluctantly, he entered and walked over to the small bench where he habitually sat to take off his walking boots. He set himself down carefully and leaned forward to unlace his boots, but as his fingers went about their familiar task, on his right boot then his left, his eyes stared directly ahead of him. She could smell the damp of clothes, but in his mood of concentration she hesitated to address him.

Her instinct was to chide him, as she had done when he returned home from the salt furnaces, soaked in sweat. But he was in such a strikingly composed state of mind that she believed he would be impervious to her strictures. Instead, she took one boot, then the other, and put them aside on the stone tiles.

He stood up in his stockings, removed his tailcoat and handed it to her. She searched his face for some loss of colour, which at the least would provide her with the excuse to chide him for being out in the rain. But he seemed in good health. There was no sign of the faintness which until recently had often overcome him at the end of a walk.

Having divested himself of outer garments, standing in shirt and breeches and stockings, he gave his head a brief shake like a dog.

Perhaps this odd gesture released his hold upon himself. He appeared to return from his trance and smiled at her almost apologetically for his detachment. She, for her part, was too grateful for his arrival to criticise him. Instead, she carried his wet clothes through to the pantry and went in search of fresh, dry ones.

In the course of the afternoon and evening, Mrs Thompson considered whether to complain to Dr Hargood for allowing him out in such weather. But she guessed he had left Hargood's house before the storm and the sudden onset of the rain.

In this surmise she had been close to the truth. After their habitual afternoon walk, Grange had left Hargood's house and travelled for a quarter of an hour towards Walhampton, relieved of the peculiar tension of their mutual suspicion. He felt, on his solitary walk, a certain light-headedness. But at the same time he became aware of the odd closeness of the day, the unexpected darkness which proceeded from the Hurst Narrows, the sudden cool wind that set leaves fluttering. In a clearing above Hundreds

Hill he noticed that a mist of bees were streaming downwards into their hives at the base of some tall elms.

He paused on a promontory to look out towards the Isle of Wight. Tendrils of lightning flickered in the low hills behind Yarmouth. The thunder rolled like a heavy battery. Behind it there came the slow, rising whisper of rain.

The storm drove animals and men under cover, and Mrs Thompson was right to imagine, perhaps, his exhilaration at being left alone in the countryside as the storm struck. Sheets of rain beat upon the trees, the houses and farmsteads. Falling water splashed beside the road. A group of sheep were huddled under some oaks at the edge of a meadow. The darkness which came was like the onset of night, so much so that a number of pheasants and partridges seemed to have taken an early roost in the branches.

The rain fell so heavily it obscured his vision over the Solent. The Isle of Wight disappeared entirely behind a curtain of water. He had been soaked through in the first heavy fusillades and the moisture which had collected in his clothes was already being warmed by his body. He turned briskly down Hundreds Lane, taking a detour along a footpath that meandered at the river's edge.

The rain continued unabated. Fierce gusts of wind swept through the trees. It was so dark that with the obscurity of the water, he moved carefully down the increasingly slippery path towards the river bank. In the valley there was some respite from the wind, but the thunder continued to bellow.

He loved the sound of heavy rain on water. The water birds at least were in their element – coots, moorhens, dabchicks continued to feed as the surface around them was turned to froth by the rain. He noticed the sudden thrust of a cormorant's neck above the surface on the far side, an eel wriggling in its beak. With a series of jerks and flicks of its head the bird aligned the eel head first down its throat.

The causeway at Walhampton was deserted of its usual traffic when he walked across it alone. Gosport Street too was empty in the fierce downpour. There was no sound except for the creaking of the signs of the inns in the increasing gale. Devils of rain spun down the street, so that on several occasions he was forced to lean forward against the wind. Weak light shone from windows where the inhabitants had lit lamps in order to pursue their daily chores.

On the High Street, heavy runnels of water flowed down the cobbles. Yet whatever temporary discomfort he might feel, his enjoyment had turned to a kind of ecstasy. The import of Mrs Quill's letter had signalled something to him. It had given him a morsel on which to chew. At least she had not disappeared entirely without trace. She had remembered him. When he finally knocked on his own door and waited for Mrs Thompson to open the latch he was impervious to the weather. It might be weeks or months or even, perhaps, years before he set sight upon her again, but it was, to his own mind at least, the end of his isolation.

CHAPTER 35

My dear Leman,

An episode in my life that I thought was over has emerged to haunt me.

I believe you may know of what I speak, but I find myself unable even to write it, so deeply have I suppressed my memories. It is as if I have struck out deliberately an area of my past that no longer fits with any degree of comfort into my present.

As my younger colleague appears to heal in both body and mind, so he begins to question me more consistently and directly. Some sense, some instinct perhaps, suggests to him that I have not told him all I know of Mrs Celia Quill. Sandwiched between other matters, he asks me whether I was aware of the reason that Mrs Quill came to settle in Lymington, when she might have chosen equally half a hundred other small towns within a similar distance of London. It appears an innocent question, but I have become fearful that he sniffs some scent and follows a line.

I have made myself a promise that though I will withhold

what is private and personal to me, I will resist telling a lie. In response to his question as to why she settled in Lymington, I avoided the necessity of answering the subject directly, by asking in return whether any of us knows precisely why we inhabit a certain place. Maintaining a certain lightness in my response, I attempted to turn his attention to other matters. But the uncomfortable fact remains, I do have an idea why she came to Lymington. For the truth is she came originally, I am almost certain, because I am here, though what her plans and reasoning might have been, assuming she had such plans, it would be beyond my powers to guess.

In confessing this, I also confess another thing, which follows inexorably from my information. I knew Mrs Quill before she arrived in Lymington.

Having informed you thus, I am bound to disclose the circumstances in due course. You will know that I mean my younger colleague no harm – the very opposite; I wish to preserve him from knowing what may harm him. Above all, I wish to protect him from whatever knowledge will reopen those wounds which over the past weeks and months have healed.

Yet in certain senses he has more than healed. Watching him progress, day by day, it is almost as if he remakes himself, that the being he fashions is not an exact copy of his former self, but something newer and stronger. He used to quote Hume to me, but now he is silent on the subject, either because he does not trust his former guide, or because he no longer relies upon any counsel but his own. It is difficult to say precisely in what this change consists, but I believe it stems from his meeting with Mrs Quill, and his survival of the crisis which he has suffered following her departure. I have a sense of a peculiar sharpening of his presence, as though much that was more delicate has burned away. Hume may have gone, but is replaced by a stronger spirit and a greater determination. He no longer requires or places his faith in the authority of some external agent, however elevated and inspired, but lives within the ambit of his own skin and five senses. It is as if his mind, unleashed from its yoke of learning, travels towards me, seeking some answer.

This letter, like my last, is written in haste, between other matters. I must go now. But until I am able to write again, sir, I remain,

Yours most sincerely,
Hargood

CHAPTER 36

Dear Leman,

I have spent the day in the greatest anguish. Some stone in my soul, having been edged off the ledge, has now begun to fall and tumble downwards.

What I shall tell is in the strictest confidence. It is like one of those knots which, if you are to understand its fullest extent and dimensions, must be untangled in its entirety, or not at all. I pray that you will not judge too harshly what I am about to report. For myself, I deserve no mercy, and will accept what befalls me. It only remains for me to trust that, in the process of its telling, you may begin to understand something of the background and constraints to which I am subject, and under which I have suffered. I shall assume that even now, since your mind is swift, you have an intimation of what I am about to unfold, for it concerns my own youth and requires a certain digression into my past. In this, too, I pray you will grant me your licence, for in recalling it I proceed to uncover my own soul.

When I was in my young manhood, as a bachelor who owned a house and several hundred acres, I represented, I do believe, a reasonable prospect for certain younger members of the fairer sex. Over a number of years I had engaged in several affairs of the heart with some of the women of Lymington. You will know that in principle I agree with the admonitions of our profession against involvement of the emotions with patients and I have never so engaged. Those with whom I had formed relations were not patients, but younger women among our local gentry of marriageable prospect. Though I expect no mercy from you in the matter of mine own state of mind and past proclivities, these courtships, in the sense that I saw them as preparatory to marriage, were conducted in good faith. This is not to say that I was successful in my final aim. In each instance, when it came upon me to fulfil my suit and tie myself in the bonds of matrimony, I found myself balking at the idea, as nervously as a horse who has smelled some strange scent. It was partly that I valued my independence and perhaps also that I had found no hand gentle or persistent enough to help me to that final barrier. There is little more to be said, except that it is a situation which is not unknown among young men who have been sufficiently blessed to inherit a small fortune, and who have lived well enough without marriage to distrust, somewhere in their hearts the curtailments of liberty imposed by the institution.

Although these courtships of local womenfolk with a view to marriage were no more than those undertaken by many young men who, so to speak, play the field in the hope of finding a true partner, I began to perceive that in the aggregate they ran against the tenets of my profession, not least insofar as they were perceived by others. For I began to discover that I was achieving, among the parents and relations of the young women, a reputation as a breaker of hearts; if not a rake, then what the French call a *roué*. You know, from our youth, that I have always been robust as far as reputations went and have been happy to ride roughshod over small unfairnesses to my own in particular. If it were not for the fact that I was ambitious to achieve a moderate success as a physician, I might have continued in my search among the local maidens for a mate who would inspire me sufficiently to make a marriage. But in the absence of such a resolution my professional practice started to suffer. I began to perceive that in a community as small as ours, and as addicted to gossip, certain alliances were forming against me. At first there was never any hint of direct criticism, but that is not how such campaigns either begin or proceed. They seem to form spontaneously, as though by some form of collective instinct, and to perpetuate themselves as if by their own momentum. Though young, I understood that once begun, they are difficult to halt.

It happened that certain women would no longer visit me for consultation for fear that, by mere association with me, their reputation suffered. And since most men are bound up with womenfolk too, in the form of wives, daughters, sisters, cousins, for whom they feel in large or small part responsible, they also began to exert a broadening effect upon the general movement. What begins as a few whispers among one or two families may soon turn into a tide. The tide in question started to move slowly about me. I knew of its existence not least because the number of my patients, which had grown so solidly and satisfactorily in the course of my earlier career, was declining most markedly.

The result was that after a certain time I considered my position and, after much thought and some increasing irritation at the curtailment of my services by certain men who should have known me sufficiently to perceive I was no threat to the modesty of my female patients, I decided to take such actions as I could, and make a careful expiation of what were increasingly perceived as my sins against the female community. Thus it came about that I ceased my courtship activities in the local field for a considerable period.

Slowly, over perhaps the next several years, my behaviour was noted and judged by the powers that be in our local society. Since I believe I carry out my professional duties as well as any other, those among my clients who previously had shown hesitation, reconsidered their position in regard to my trustworthiness and, since it began to be believed that my behaviour was no longer, of necessity, the subject of close scrutiny, after a certain while my practice began slowly to return to its former state, and even to grow again.

Leman, if I had resolved one matter to my own satisfaction, and perhaps to that of the community, there was another which I had not. I believe you know me well enough to understand that I would seek some outlet for those natural desires which in a marriage are sanctioned, but which our society regards with some formal disapproval outside the bonds of matrimony. I considered taking some housekeeper, or female servant, for the benefit of physical attraction as much as performance of duty – which is much the habit in these parts, though it is equally much denied. But local matrons, still suspicious of my treatment of the fairer sex, would sooner or later have discovered the true nature of my relationship. The gossip of matrons on the proclivities and courtships of young men is to be expected, but in my chosen profession and with my past reputation – which in the nature of things could so easily be revived – I remained peculiarly vulnerable to such assertions. At the very least, it would have awakened the interest of several mothers who, having witnessed their daughter courted by me without matrimonial result, might observe in the installation of a comely young woman in my household a special provocation to their sensibilities.

You perceive, perhaps, the conditions and outer limits of my dilemma. It is a circumstance to which young physicians are prone. And you, as a surgeon, no doubt experienced some similar misgivings. But though I may recognise my responsibilities, at least in their outer form, I am of a practical nature, and the question became one of finding a solution rather than moping in defeat.

Since I had been blessed with good connections in London, and in particular with one or two patrons among the senior fellows of the Royal College of Physicians, I was called there on professional matters several times a year. Sometimes I delivered a small paper on a medical subject to an audience of my peers. Sometimes I agreed to certain secretarial or clerical duties on behalf of the College which my more illustrious colleagues were content to leave to my small capabilities. Given that I had just cause to visit the capital on a number of occasions each year in the performance of my professional duties, it seemed to me that one means of alleviating my condition was to take a mistress in London.

Ideas are often not realised unless the physical conditions are propitious. For the best part of a year, still chastened by my experiences of losing the patronage of a substantial proportion of my patients, I either was not sufficiently determined upon my course, or found no opportunity to put my principles into practice. In the early spring of the following year, when I went to London, it happened that I noticed among the servants of the College of Physicians a young woman who, at the time of which I speak, was hardly seventeen. I remember clearly that she was a scullery maid and that her labours were such that she remained in the servants' quarters, undertaking a variety of menial tasks. Only occasionally did she enter the main corridors in the natural course of her duties. She was tall, somewhat slender and her name (which I draw from the past like some ancient and beautifully preserved relic) was Cecile Duchamp. I understood that she was French and that she was an offspring of one of the genteel families whose house had been burned in one of those earlier agitations or uprisings that preceded the Revolution. Her father had died in the fire attempting to protect his possessions, and her despairing mother, ruined by events, had sent her daughter abroad. It seems that not long afterwards the mother herself died.

I took a liking to this tall and slender girl, carrying with her as she did a history of tragedy. You may smile at my ingenuousness, but in addition to her physical appearance, there was in her some aspect of her disposition which almost approached reserve. I would have said that (had it not been for her unfortunate circumstances) she was of a studious nature. I understood that her deceased father had been a physician in Paris and that there were others of her family who had subsequently been sent to the scaffold. I was led to believe, further, that partly out of obligation to the offspring of a fellow physician, and partly out of charity, the overseers of the buildings at the Royal College of Physicians had taken pity upon her circumstances and employed her as a menial in the kitchens.

You will understand, I trust, that I set myself a strange and difficult task in attempting to court her. She was reticent, and the misfortunes which had befallen her had rendered her suspicious of strangers. My ambitions would require a certain tact and some deployment of patience. I could more easily have

146

taken up with some young strumpet, who would have been only too pleased to set aside drudgery for a room and sufficient to live on, to exchange her rags for some reasonable clothes and the role of mistress. Instead, out of what feelings I do not fully understand even now, I chose to pursue, most carefully, the favours of Miss Duchamp.

She proved no easier a target of my ambitions than I had suspected. In the event, my courtship of her lasted perhaps a year. I will not recount the details of my pursuit. Suffice it to say that when she acceded, it seemed to me that it was not entirely out of acceptance of material gain, but rather that, in the course of our meetings and my careful but persistent pursuit, she had taken an affection to me. This is not, I believe, mere vanity on my part – though I am as vain as any – but rather, the circumstances of her acquiescence played a role in what I will recount.

In the course of my careful pursuit of her I began to perceive not merely her physical attributes and a certain shy charm, but the stamp of a certain quality of mind which I had only dimly recognised before. I would visit in a small room that she shared with two other maids. While she waited for me she read avidly of philosophers and essayists. There was a library in the main building of the College of Physicians to which she was allowed a limited access. She had impressed the librarian with her hunger for knowledge and in the light of her sincerity he allowed her to remove certain works for her own consumption. Since the works were the proper reference for the members of the College, he had stipulated that the volumes in question should be returned within a forty-eight-hour period. So she read avidly, with the spur of this particular proviso upon her. This then, was the young woman whose form and character I pursued during the course of the following year, with the result that in the end she consented to leave her employment and take rooms which I found her. I made her a promise that I would encourage her studies and even provide her with a small library of her own. When she was installed in her new abode, she gave me lists of certain books she wished to read and, for her own edification, I bought others with which I believed she should become acquainted.

I will not try your patience further, my dear Leman, with details of my own hopes and expectations in this affair, but it seemed to me that I had found a rare companion and, if I were honest with myself, my own feelings were closer to affection than simple passion.

I had searched for a spouse among the young women of Lymington and found none. Now I searched for a mistress, no more and no less, and soon found myself developing those affections for her that are more normally directed towards a spouse. Such are the strangenesses of our fate.

I set her up in a small house in Chiswick, with one elderly female servant and sufficient funds to allow her that modicum of material well-being which may not be genteel, but which is nevertheless sufficient to preserve a small decorum. I was true to my promise to build up a small library, which I know she treasured. These limited conditions were aided by the fact that she was frugal in what she did, and sensible. In order to keep her occupied during my protracted absence, I encouraged her to take lessons at a small *forte-piano* which I had installed in the household and to develop a talent for singing. Some books of my own library that were not in immediate use, I transported to that modest house which she occupied, so that when I visited I had some recourse to the written word, but also so that in my absence she could read further if she wished. Yet having made arrangements for these genteel distractions, which were aimed at providing an occupation for her during my long stays in Lymington, I do believe I never met anyone so studious, or with so natural a propensity for knowledge.

I commenced taking a positive, indeed increasingly zealous, interest in her education. Thus a good three years passed, in which I started to feel that I was happy. When I stayed in London it was as much her conversation, her music and the prolonged discussions that I enjoyed with her, as her other attributes that held me to my chosen course. In short, I had never conceived that patronage could be such a variegated satisfaction. She was like one of those courtesans, whose gifts extended far beyond that which was necessary for simple pleasure.

148

I began to take a pride in her accomplishments. We would visit the theatre, attend operettas, concerts and plays, and her appreciation made them such a consistent pleasure that I believe I came to consider the benefits of my native culture more than I otherwise would. My encouragement seemed merely the initial aspect of a process, a set of conditions, so to speak, in her development. She set herself tasks of learning and would throw herself into a course of study until she completed it. At each visit to London I marvelled at the strides she had made in these, her chosen subjects. She studied Latin and, since so many of the classical works of medicine are in that language, she could even assist me on finer points of translation or meaning in the medical texts and proceedings for which I acted as one of the agents or secretaries to the College. I myself changed under the light of her influence, for when I was with her I found time to read in her company. My mistress became, you might say, not merely my paramour, but my scholarly accomplice.

There were certain limits to our social activities, which I did not resent, though I acknowledge they were present. It was known that she was a woman whom I had found, so to speak, and set up in a house for my own purposes. I might go to the theatre with her, but I could not easily invite her to polite table with a colleague and his wife. My friends and acquaintances would tolerate a mistress, indeed congratulate me on my choice, but they would not approve the prospect of her presence in the company of their own wives and families. In this I think we differ from our great lords, whose social position allows them the latitude to exhibit their mistresses in open society as much as they wish.

The truth was that she accepted these limitations and was herself conditioned to their persistence. She seemed, insofar as I may attempt to describe the disposition of another soul, contented with her situation. For the circumstances of her independence, combined with her own studious nature, were such that she had no great need of outside company. Her books and learning, her music and singing lessons, appeared to be sufficient to concentrate her mind when I was not present in the household. She seemed, indeed, to welcome a certain solitude, for the improvement of her skills and knowledge. I grant perhaps an impression of someone not lacking in will, or character, but whose own virtues and inclinations were such that they commended an obeisance to her circumstances.

Thus my life continued in apparent contentment. I discovered in due course that my work for the College increased, and that my visits to London became more frequent. Since much of my work included the perusal of learned tomes to find points which aided my seniors in discussion with others, I was most happily abetted in this by my mistress. Indeed, if I mentioned that I was obliged to search Galen for certain passages about flows in the bloodstream, or Harvey for doctrines of subsidiary circulation, she was as able as I to find the reference. Such collaborations brought us together in an intimacy which was above that of mere man and mistress, much though I value the latter. For myself, I counted the days until I would see her.

My dear sir, I have written at length upon the circumstances of Miss Cecile Duchamp because, as you shall see, it bears closely upon what follows. However, having spent some considerable part of the morning in the composition of this letter, I am forced by circumstances to continue my missive at another time. An engagement with a patient presses. Since the heat and pain of my confession is upon me, you may be sure that I shall write again as soon as I am able.

In the meantime, sir, I remain,

    Yours sincerely,

       Hargood

CHAPTER 37

It seemed to Grange sometimes that houses were built around silence, that there was a core of stillness at the heart of each house which was as substantial as the bricks and mortar of the building itself. It was said blind men recognised the quality of this silence, that as they moved from room to room so its nature changed. He tried sympathetically to imagine himself in this lack of sight in which other senses reached out towards the world.

But it was the blindness inside him, a sense of something missing, that caused him to pause in thought, searching for some circumstance that he had omitted to consider. He remained in this state of mind, perplexed and quiescent, but able to carry out his few domestic duties with a careful conscience, until almost the mid-morning of that day.

Before his collapse, much of his practice had concerned those who worked in the salt industry. In the furnace houses, men suffered from burns, from heat exhaustion and water loss. Working parties of exhausted furnace-men tramped across the marshes, labouring in shifts so that the furnaces could be used throughout the summer. The summer sun was the first engine, coal the second, human sweat the third. On certain nights, when the wind had died, the doors were opened for ventilation and some of the presiding roof was removed, the effect being of numerous fires that were like white stains on the surface of the darkness. During the night, at the height of summer, looking out across Oxey and Pennington marshes, it seemed that the whole sea-shore blazed.

In autumn, as the majority of the furnaces closed and only a few remained, he would stand at the window and consider the view, watching the few thin streams of smoke rise into the pale sky. These were the limits of his small world, the boundaries of that consciousness he had developed to span his work and his amateur concerns – the interests to which, in his lucid moments, he yearned through his illness to return.

CHAPTER 38

My dear Leman,

I have found a further respite to continue my story, which I now commit to paper with a certain trepidation, in the knowledge that what will transpire may arouse your silent condemnation. I hope, sir, that you may come to forgive me in due course for what I am about to write.

Though I did not know it at the time, there were other matters that concerned my mistress, Cecile Duchamp. Her former status as an orphan was genuine, though she was not entirely without family connections. Unknown to me, she was pursued by a blackguard who called himself her brother, though he was at most a half-brother, a certain Henry or Henri Duchamp, who had become a minor clerk in the offices of a merchant, but who perceived that by a mixture of threat and pleading, he could obtain more for less work by preying upon the conscience of his relative. For though she was herself parsimonious and sparing in her own expenditure, she was indeed inclined to be generous with her good fortune towards those she felt were deserving.

When she was set up in her new household, it was he who, pursuing her improvement of circumstances, demanded some part or portion of her good fortune. And if she hesitated to comply with the scale of his demand, he was of such a nature that he was inclined to threaten to expose her background as my mistress to all who knew her. She was of sufficiently strong a character that she was unlikely to be influenced by this threat. But he posed another, that was more complex. He was, I understand, some eleven years older than she, and on this fact alone he was able to exert his petition. For by the terms in which she had been committed to an orphanage, the survival of an older male relation in sound body would have made her his dependant, until such time as she reached the age of twenty-one. That this same relation had refused to undertake his responsibilities in supporting her previously and had thus far ignored her entirely during the time of her greatest need was another matter. Thus the very man, who did her the initial injury of ignoring her plight, was the same who would later attempt to blackmail her for not disclosing his existence when she was able to establish a life of her own.

I did not know of him for almost eighteen months, and there was no sign during that time that she had overspent her allowance. On the contrary, she lived so frugally I became suspicious precisely because it seemed to me that some portion of her allowance was unspent, and therefore missing. I learned from her servant that when I departed she would not burn candles where it was not necessary to her needs, although I had left her sufficient tallow to light the house well. The servant did not attempt to betray her mistress but rather praised her for her frugality. I learned further that while she allowed the servant her own measure of heating stuffs, my mistress's own consumption of wood and coal in the main portion of the house was hardly enough to maintain the place above freezing. I began to take note of the fact that her wardrobe, which I expected to grow steadily under my careful largesse, contained only a few dresses, that were artfully maintained by her.

When I took it upon myself to confront her with these oddities of expenditure, she would not stoop to deny the matter, but refused to speak, and thus confirmed my worst fears. Though she might keep certain details from me, the honesty of her disposition was such that she would not tell a direct lie when challenged. As I continued to pursue her on the subject she saw no escape from my enquiry and admitted all, pleading with me that her relative was a deserving case, and the fact that he attempted by dubious means to influence her did not gainsay the fact that he also required support. I was outraged that my funds for her well-being were being spent on a blackmailer, and raged against her and him, as though they were both accomplices who had conspired against me. Even though he were her notional relation, I threatened to take my sword to the man. Although at first she seemed calm, and willing to receive my censure in the belief, perhaps, that I would not condemn

her for the sin of helping to support a relative by savings she
had herself effected in her household, she grew increasingly
alarmed at my temper.

This gave rise to another aspect of her reasoning, and
perhaps of the female sex in general, whose circumstances and
nature we must consider further. Although she allowed she had
given money to the scoundrel, yet she had stayed within those
expenses which I had allocated her, and thus in her view had
kept her bargain with me. At this I began to rail. That she
should become my mistress was one matter which we had
agreed between us; that I was supporting a second dependant
without my knowledge was another. Would I, in the normal
course of events, elect to support a blackmailer? She surveyed
me, in a kind of calmness, frightened at my rage, but
apparently determined that once my temper had reduced I
would begin to see sense. But her persistence merely inflamed
me further. She not only gave my funds to the blackguard, but
was prepared to defend him in the face of my enquiries. Damn
me, I remember shouting, was she defending his actions and
rights over my own?

Now, sir, let us prepare ourselves for another aspect of a
woman's reasoning. For it became clear in the course of these
discussions that it was not Henry Duchamp whom she was
supporting, but his wife and five children, who lived in direst
poverty in Cheapside. She hoped that by means of this
disclosure she could calm me. But instead, my rage knew no
bounds. I shouted that I was not here to support a blackmailer,
no more than a dog is bound in faith to every flea which
attempts to live on him.

Now that matters had come to this pass, I began to observe
her spirit. She had sat down before my display of rage. Now
she rose up from her chair and assembled her courage to face
me directly. She said that the children were not fleas, but
innocents betrayed by circumstances not of their own choosing.
I believe that in her mind she saw those waifs crying, not
because they were the victims of a dissolute father – which was,
I believe, the real cause of their distress – but because she could
not help them. Despite my anger, she continued to press her

case in the intervals between my rages. The savings did not affect me, she said, as much as they affected her. Was not the house perfectly well lit when I arrived to stay? Was not the fire properly stacked? What did it matter if she chose not to consume fuel when I was absent? Was she any the less a good companion to me? If she had chosen a few dresses, rather than many, had I ever complained about the paucity or impoverishment of her appearance? In what sense, then, was I affected?

I marvelled at her effrontery, and the quiet passion with which she committed to her case, yet my rage at her allocation of my funds to one of whom I disapproved was in no sense allayed. For all I knew the wretch used what she gave him to buy drink, and I suspected that not only did he not grant any portion of his earnings to his wife, but arrived home drunk and disorderly as well. This was the probable sum of the contribution she had made at my expense; that it inflicted a yet greater burden on the poor woman and her waifs.

Now, when I had spoken in these terms, I observed in my mistress a certain quiet, and even began to consider that some of my observations had struck home. She grew more tranquil. I waited for her to respond to me with a sufficient and due respect. And for a short while it seemed that she was ashamed enough to do so. But, instead of her apology, she told me that it was for precisely this reason she gave only a proportion of the money to him, and donated the rest directly to his family, for their food and provisions.

This was wilful indeed, you will agree. This was not what I had set her up in good living to undertake. It was not blackmail of a weak-minded young woman, no, but active consorting with the blackmailer's family.

Since she could not deploy her money responsibly, I told her that I would adopt exactly that strategy in respect of her own funds that she had adopted with the aforesaid Henry Duchamp. I would buy her clothes directly and supply her also with her pieces of light, and the elderly servant (whom I trusted) would henceforth be given a budget for the heating and the food, which she herself would exercise. My mistress would no longer hold sway over the expenditure of the house. Thus I would prevent all future attempts at largesse with her master's funds.

She seemed struck at last by her predicament. I perceive she may have begun to concede not only the depth of my anger, but her misuse of my hospitality.

Now, however, I still faced the problem of this rogue, who I believed would continue to plague her. For I deduced that as soon as I left the scene he would return and, like the parasite he was, attempt once more to milk her of funds that were not hers to dispose of in any manner she pleased. I considered that I could deal with him in peremptory fashion, by taking a lawsuit against him as a common blackmailer, or by directly confronting him and threatening to administer a beating if he so much as showed himself in the vicinity. But I perceived that while it was one thing to withhold my own funds from further abuse of trust, it was quite another to threaten harm against her own flesh and blood. I knew her sufficiently to realise that such actions against her own family would have turned her against me. After due consideration, therefore, I informed her that there was something else that I required if we were to continue in our present disposition. I would set her up in a house in another part of London, under another name, so that she might be free of her half-brother's importunity.

She began to remonstrate, but I was adamant. If she did not agree, then she herself would forfeit my patronage and my largesse. I would give her sufficient for several months, so that she might have time to find employment, and I would write a reference in respect of her many gifts and talents. For at the very least I believed her education was now such that she could find a position as a governess. But that would be the end of my obligations concerning her welfare.

I remember her expression as she considered me. It seemed that she was in part at least in love with me, and she did not believe that I could show such resolve over a matter of principle. Sometimes a man and a woman will see themselves in their true light only in certain extreme circumstances. It may be that what she observed in me shocked her. Perhaps I was different from what she had imagined or sensed. Once expressed, my decision was impossible to change or remit. I was too strong in my feelings, and too far gone down my singular road, to consider any alternative path. I told her she should sleep on it, and give me her decision in the morning.

I did not adopt my usual habit of sleeping in the double bed that we had shared so amicably for several years on the occasions of my visits, but ordered the servant to make up a bed in the side room, in order to show I was in earnest, and to allow her time and solitude to consider the error of her ways.

My dear Leman, I do not know what she thought about during the course of that night, but the following morning she was pale, and I do not think she had slept more than a wink. I believe that if she had not loved me she would have left, for she was strong-willed. But when I asked her what her decision was, she raised her head towards me and, biting her lip, merely nodded. I nodded too, relieved and in certain respects almost saddened at the success of my headstrong decision. For though men may conquer women in material terms, it is only afterwards we realise we have suffered our most grievous defeat. What use is the winning of an argument if, at the very moment of our victory, we forfeit the heart of the one we desire? We were both silent for some seconds, then she turned away. So it happened that the decision was fulfilled.

Thus I arranged to place her in another house in Chiswick and gave thought to a new name that she might call her own, and that would represent her in her new station in life – what writers I believe may sometimes call a *nom de plume*. You may guess what that name was, if you have not already uttered it aloud. I sat down with a pen at my desk and wrote it on a clean sheet, as if I were some catchpenny novelist or playwright creating a character in a drama. I would give her an English name and thus complete the transference into English society which I thought her accomplishments deserved. I believed that this transference, if it could be achieved, would be an added inhibition on the depredations of her half-brother. She had been named Cecile and it happened that certain of my distant female relations had been called Celia, a name that held an appeal to my own ears. I paused for several seconds and, in the course of my considerations, I glanced at the pen I was holding, and so the conjunction of words took hold of me. Thus her full name was conceived, and afterwards she became known as Celia Quill. Suffice it to say that I chose it and she consented to it, and so we proceeded to live together on the terms we had agreed.

These memories have so engaged my emotions they have tired me. I find myself once more embroiled in the past. Returning, I have revived those feelings and sensations which I had thought long ago were put aside. In re-awakening the emotions that I felt, I am compelled not only to live them again, but to consider them with the benefit of hindsight, which renders my assumptions perhaps more painful. Even so, the distance of time intrudes an element of objectivity. For I perceive now that there existed, in the seeds of our conflict over her half-brother and his dependants, much that was to affect the final outcome between us. The change of name I insisted she adopt in order to protect her from a common blackmailer may have alleviated one aspect of her situation, but at the same time it may have worsened several others, not the least of which was that it strained the relations between us, which until then had been of the finest.

You will, I trust, forgive me if, my hand being tired, I bid you farewell until such time as I am able again to put pen to paper. The recollection of it has taxed the emotions, against which the duty of setting it down in some form is much the lesser pain.

I hope and trust, sir, that these disclosures do not shake your faith in me too much. I thank you again for the kindness of your interminable silence, and hope that out of your goodness you will grant me lenience to continue in due course.

In the meanwhile, sir, I remain,

    Yours sincerely,

      Hargood

CHAPTER 39

Hargood had brought the fly, so they could walk out into the country.

They drove down Lymington High Street, then across the causeway and toll-bridge to Walhampton. On the other side, Hargood snapped the reins and the roan began to trot. They moved north along the bank of Lymington river, then onto the steep track up Hundreds Hill, the big roan pulling ably, until they reached the flat roadway above. There Hargood drew the fly into a small patch of grass beside the track and put on the brake. The roan could eat grass and was strong enough to pull the fly with locked wheels a short distance to further patches of greenery.

Hargood said, 'Let us walk, sir.'

There was water on the paths from a downpour the previous night, but it had the effect of dampening the dust, and the air was clear. After settling the horse and fly, they set out in the direction of Boldre.

'What is strange about your opinions', Hargood said, 'is that you harbour no ill will towards her.'

They had reached a stage in their conversation where they could raise the subject of Mrs Quill without mentioning her name, as though she were a constant between them.

'Why should I?' Grange asked. They were walking along the roadway side by side, at a reasonable pace. Flies and occasional bees streamed between the trees. Sometimes their wings caught the light.

'Because of the injury she caused you.'

'She caused me no injury. My injury was to myself.'

'That may be so, Silas.' Hargood paused to gather himself, assuming an air of patience. 'But is it healthy to be so dispassionate?'

'Is it healthy, on the other hand, to feel aggrieved for no good reason?'

'Yes,' Hargood said, suddenly and grandly. 'I will face you directly and say that it is. I believe that grievance has very little to do with reason. That is my point. Reason itself is not a cause of grievance. The causes of grievance lie beneath reason. Grievance is its own justification.'

'Would you say so?'

'I do say so. And I would be obliged if you did not continually answer my questions with your own. Grievance, my dear sir, is a state of the emotions. Reason is a state of mind. The two are incommunicable.'

They walked for several seconds in silence.

'So.' Grange paused. 'If I may ask a question, what is it you ask me?'

'I seek your health. As your physician, I ask whether it would assist in your recovery if you could allow yourself a little anger, a certain spleen.'

Grange smiled. 'I do not feel anger, so whether I could allow it or not seems to me outside the terms of our discussion.'

'It is a view about the world. If a man is discomfited, perhaps he has a right, even a duty, to expend a little anger.'

'It seems to me that in order to feel this grievance, I must believe that she did me harm . . .'

'Did she not?'

Grange paused. 'I do not know.'

'Do you not?' Hargood was astonished. 'It is surely the most simple and elementary of assumptions. She caused you to fall into a crisis. Your health deteriorated alarmingly. This is harm, is it not?'

'That is my point. When you say she "caused" me to fall into a crisis, I can only repeat that perhaps much of the cause was in myself. You yourself have said that I was predisposed towards it.'

. 'You absolve her, then, of all involvement in your current circumstances?'

'If harm is done unintentionally, without malice, there is little cause on my part for grievance.'

'Yet you do not entertain the view that there may have been intent?'

'That she is malicious? I never saw her malicious to anyone else. And therefore, I ask myself, why should she be so towards me?'

'For various reasons. Perhaps you discomfited her, or threatened her equilibrium. You said that she was passionate in deflecting your offer of marriage to her daughter.'

'It would appear she had every reason to be so in what she considered the best interests of Jane. She had a marriage which, though it may not have been a source of great happiness or content, at least gave her some comfort and stability.'

Hargood paused suddenly, arrested. 'You say her daughter's marriage was not happy?'

'I believe so.'

'You did not tell me previously.'

'Did I not?'

'No, sir, you did not.' Hargood appeared incensed. 'It seems there are many facts and attributes which you have kept to yourself. My dear Silas, your reticence in these matters does not help us. Certain facts emerge, without warning, in the course of the conversation, that are necessary to our discussion. If they tend to arise somewhat randomly, like pieces of driftwood that float to the surface, it is because you keep these matters to yourself.'

Grange allowed himself a brief smile at Hargood's apparent outrage.

Hargood said, 'Should I express surprise, then, if you keep so much from me that we are unable to reach further into the matter?'

'Whatever you may choose to believe, Hargood, I do not deliberately withhold information which may be useful.'

'No, sir, you do not. It is another general principle that you act upon. At the same time, you do not disclose information unless it is specifically asked for, or unless it is uncovered by another line of enquiry.'

Grange was silent. Satisfied that he had expressed his view, Hargood said, 'Let us continue, then. You say her daughter's marriage was not happy? Allow me to ask, if you will, who informed you of that?'

'Informed?'

'Yes. Was it mother or daughter who informed you?'

'I believe it was Mrs Quill.'

'She told you that her daughter's marriage was not happy?'

'As I remember, it was part of a conversation. We were discussing women in general. Or rather, she was talking on the subject. She said that many marriages were not satisfactory. Shortly afterwards, as though by way of an example, she raised the instance of her daughter.'

'She raised this matter before you met her daughter?'

'Yes, I think so.'

'So that when she introduced you to her daughter, you knew both that her daughter was married and that she was unhappy in her marriage.'

'Yes.'

'After which, she encouraged you in your affections towards her daughter.'

'Hargood, you do her an injustice.'

'An injustice? I merely pursue the facts.'

'The facts are superficial.'

'Indeed, sir. Now the facts are superficial.'

'What matters, I believe, is the heart.'

'The heart now. What matters is the heart.'

'You seem agitated.'

'I am agitated, sir.'

'Why should you be?'

'Because it appears there is the hand of manipulation in this matter.'

'Whose hand?'

'Mrs Quill's hand.'

'I see no such hand.'

'You see no such hand.'

'It seems to me that you constantly repeat me.'

'It seems to me, sir, that you will only understand the nature of your replies if I repeat them for you. I believe that precisely by repeating them, sir, I am determined to shame you into some form of reasonableness.'

Grange smiled. 'I believe I am able to perceive the nature of my replies at the first airing of them.'

'Then let us proceed', Hargood said, 'as though you do.'

'Please proceed,' Grange said.

'Mrs Quill informs you as a general principle that certain women are unhappy. She raises, as a specific example, that her daughter is

162

unhappy in her marriage. Subsequently, she encourages your attentions to the young woman. You see no manipulation in that?'

'No,' Grange said.

'No?' Hargood asked.

'In the first two cases – that women, certain women, may be unhappy and that her daughter is unhappy – I see merely statements of truth. In your third and final case – that she encouraged my attentions to her daughter – I observe merely generosity and trust.'

'Generosity and trust,' Hargood said.

'It seems to me', Grange said, 'that you are determined to repeat me again.'

'It appears to me that you will admit no malice in the world. No evil.'

'That is not the case. I will not attribute malice unless it is the only explanation.'

'But that is absurd,' Hargood stated. 'Surely one should attribute evil intent if it is the most fitting, that is to say, the easiest explanation.'

'It is nearly always the easiest explanation. If we are struck by lightning, we say it is the angry intent of God. If people die without apparent cause, we say it is the evil intent of malignant spirits. It seems to me that most, if not all, of our function as physicians is to reject the easy explanation of malignancy in favour of the true.'

'It seems to me', Hargood said, 'that truth is a mistress with whom you are not necessarily on the most complete terms.'

Grange saw that this was to be Hargood's final admonition, at least for the time being, that his companion wished to consider his own thoughts. Hargood signalled his intention with a change of pace. Until that time, their walk had been leisurely. Now, Grange felt himself drawn along by the greater energy which the older man applied to his stride. He wondered whether Hargood was attempting to establish silence in the ferocity of his speed, or perhaps to punish his younger colleague for his insolicitude.

Whatever Hargood's motivation, Grange too was content to be silent as they traversed the long meadows in the direction of the foreshore, swung right along the shore line, and proceeded for several miles towards Beaulieu, taking the path that skirted the panning pools inshore.

CHAPTER 40

They had reached a long valley or declivity. To one side were woodlands, on the other an open meadow and several fields planted with oats or barley. A stream ran down the centre of the valley. In front of them, a haze of mist rose off the damp grass of the meadow.

They decided to rest for a few minutes, in the shade of a copse of oaks.

Grange stared across the meadow at a wave of summer light against the furthest bank. He saw a hare there, sitting upright. An odd notion took hold of him that the beautiful creature was female, and that her upright posture, so calm and watchful, was sentient. The animal moved back a few feet with a piece of white on her flank, then continued forward, springing suddenly in high bounds, her hind legs like a single limb, single then double then single. She halted, her left foot braced flat against the ground, head down, serious. She began to graze, moving slowly from tuft to tuft of grass. As they watched, she drifted further and further away into the obscurity of the light.

Hargood said calmly, 'It is sometimes said that the hare is a pagan emblem.'

'A female deity,' Grange replied, then added, as though to dissipate the force of his assertion, 'So it is said.'

The intensity of his concentration on the hare had caused his eyes to ache. For temporary relief, he allowed himself to glance around him. Bees drifted across the clearing, alighting on the small purple flowers at the edge of the field. There was a smell of decay. In the undergrowth the carcass of a rodent heaved with blue flies.

Grange raised his eyes again and tried to pick out the hare's still shape against the glimmering fields. Suddenly, alarmed, she leaped forward, her legs smashing down, her shadow beneath her rising and falling in soft loops. He observed the curling and uncurling of her spine, until her body and its shadow had fallen beyond the furthest sheen of field.

They stood in silence for several seconds. The disappearance of the hare seemed to have broken a spell.

'Let us continue,' Hargood said.

They began to walk down the long meadow. There was a broken, disused house in the clearing and beside it the husks of several old farm carts. An atmosphere of silence pervaded the place. Clouds moved behind the rusting machinery of an old water wheel across the nearby stream.

In one corner of the clearing stood a number of dilapidated beehives. Grange assumed they were abandoned, but there was a rising mist or smoke above at least two of them. As they drew closer the insects seemed more like pellets or lozenges, wild oats, mere specks of dust. At the further edge of the woodland, a long field of barley stretched out, sloping towards a stream. Grange gazed out at the hush of the long declivity.

Hargood said, 'I believe we have a visitation.'

A swarm of bees moved like a ghost above the hives, a whirlwind with a drunken lean, or perhaps some animal without a skeleton. At a distance they had seemed as faint as a scent or aroma, but close to they vibrated and hummed, the individuals moving so fast they appeared like blurred amber meteors. Now the clearing was crossed with traces of golden fire. Their mad music transformed into individual, staccato pulses.

Grange felt the first stab of pain in the flesh of his hand, the second beneath his eye. Shortly afterwards he and Hargood, like a single panicked animal, were running jointly and comically with knees up across the bracken, the misshapen shadow of bees in pursuit, Hargood shouting, 'Damn the brutes, sir, damn the brutes,' as they descended the high mud bank in a sliding rush and struck the surface of the water with their knees and elbows, shattering its sheen.

Like falling clouds, they were submerged into the stream, into a calm and timeless silence.

The clear water was chill, the sun reflected from a rill of golden gravel. Grange broke upwards into the air, breathing in deeply. The swarm still darkened the water. Around him, the horizon seemed subtended. Only Hargood's head showed above the light-coloured surface, his overcoat across his face like a hood. The maddened moan of the bees pressed downwards, then the skewed shadow left them suddenly, as if, for some inexplicable reason, boredom had taken hold.

In the sumptuous light, Grange reached back and pulled his coat off his head. He raised himself cautiously above the surface and looked around, turning towards his companion.

Hargood's hair was as close to his skull as an otter's, parted neatly by the water; his eyes had a hunted look. 'There are few things that move me, sir, more than a swarm.' Relief rendered him eloquent. 'The collective passion of the crowd, the sense of hunger for your flesh and tender parts. I believe, sir, there is little that is more exhilarating to the senses.'

They looked around the clearing carefully. The insects appeared to have departed. Cautiously they waded towards the overhanging bank.

There was a narrow furrow down to the water which animals used to drink. They climbed up the furrow, Hargood leading the way. On the bank they were both overtaken by coldness. Calm sunlight fell on their backs. They removed their boots and emptied the water from them. Grange felt subject to an unexpected shudder, the almost palpable sense of calm that he felt after performing surgery or amputation, his body's voluptuous sigh of relief after danger.

There were still bees, soaked from their immersion, clinging to their coats. They spread out their wings to sun themselves, and one by one took off.

Grange imagined the subtle machinery of life in the garden, the singing insects, the flowers which closed or opened to the light of the sun. He envisaged the mechanism of bees, the closely working wings, like one of those remarkable clocks.

Hargood said, 'I can brush them off, if you find them disagreeable.' But Grange, raising his hand for peace, continued to watch the last stragglers take to the air.

Sunlight beat down upon them. The sudden plunge had brought a sense of focus to their state, which their shivering did not dispel.

Hargood said, 'I believe we should take ourselves off to my

house, before we catch a chill.'

They trudged across the fields, their boots squeaking with water.

CHAPTER 41

It was perhaps a mile back to the fly and another to Hargood's house. The sun warmed them fitfully. Blackberries were beginning to appear on the bramble bushes beside the slanting ditches and hedgerows.

When they reached Hargood's drive, they descended from the fly and Hargood tethered the roan. Then they approached the house like tramps. Grange had a brief vision of being ejected by Simmonds as ne'er-do-wells.

Hargood raised the handle and opened the door. 'Simmonds,' he called.

'Sir?' The faintly querulous sound came from inside.

'We have had a dunking,' Hargood bellowed. 'We require, immediately, two fresh sets of clothes.'

Simmonds appeared in the doorway, nodded to his master and peered briefly at Grange, at the swollen bulges on his face, the violent discoloration beneath his right eye.

'A bee-swarm,' Grange explained. 'We were forced to retreat.'

Simmonds nodded again and said, 'Forest bees, sir. Very unpredictable,' before he turned and disappeared into the interior in search of two sets of clothes. Grange observed his bowed form fading into the obscurity.

Hargood and Grange both moved into the hall. Hargood closed the door behind them. They were still sufficiently drenched to leave puddles upon the floor. The situation was not so odd that it prevented Hargood from enjoying a small homily on the nature of certain insects: 'It is strange, is it not, that if you tread upon a wasps' nest, they will rise up and attack and sting you. But if you retreat or run away, they will not follow you *en masse*. Bees, on the other hand, are the very devils, and appear to be excited by the chase.'

'What are your conclusions?'

'I believe that nature divides herself into conservatives and radicals, sir. Wasps will become angry if you unsettle their property, but there is an end to it. Bees, on the other hand I believe, have a touch of fanaticism in them. I would say that bees are radicals at heart.'

'You think we were the object of an attack by radicals?'

'I do indeed. Let us remove our outer garments here,' Hargood said in the hallway. 'I expect there is a fire burning in the study.'

They abandoned their jackets, breeches, shirts, cravats on the hall chair, and went through to the large inner room where Hargood worked and kept his accounts.

In his woollen underclothes, Hargood resembled one of those large, white, virulent larval forms which live beneath the bark of trees. The remains of a pale fire were burning in the grate. Hargood threw on fresh blocks of beech wood and rubbed his hands. He took hold of the bellows and added some fierceness to the fire. 'A glass of brandy?'

Grange nodded, cast into his own thoughts. Noticing his preoccupation, Hargood handed Grange a full glass, then set to inflating the fire once more with the bellows. He said, 'I believe we were touched by a malign presence, sir.'

'Do you?'

'No doubt you will tell me that those damned creatures meant us no harm, that their motivation is benevolent.'

'Perhaps we disturbed their equilibrium.'

'By entering the clearing? Damn me, I believe we have a right to cross a clearing without being attacked by the inhabitants. They behaved, if I may say so, like a Paris mob.'

'If we touch their world, Hargood, perhaps they have a right to inflict themselves upon ours.'

Hargood, having finished fanning the fire, turned towards him, and it seemed as if he would offer a reply. But Grange had fallen into a respite, studying the shifting lights of the liquid moving in the glass.

'What a singular fellow you are, Silas,' Hargood said. 'We have escaped a mob with our lives, enjoyed a brief swim, and you show no relief. Instead, you sink once again into contemplation of your beloved.'

CHAPTER 42

'Where is that damned Simmonds with our clothes?' Hargood asked. 'He is too meticulous. He will be standing at the wardrobe examining half a dozen possible combinations, unable to make up his mind.'

He stood up from the fire and walked from the room. Grange heard him calling, then some kind of reconciliation with Simmonds on the stairs. He listened to Hargood insisting loudly that the new changes of clothes were not entirely appropriate, then gently haranguing Simmonds about another choice. They both ascended again to the master bedroom, where Hargood continued to admonish Simmonds on the correct combinations of jacket, breeches and cravat. In the interval, Grange was left alone at the fireside.

The draft up the chimney pulled the warmed air out of the room. Since Swann had immersed him in the flames of the salt furnace, all fires seemed to him smaller replicas of the one great fire. This, he knew, was the same physical phenomenon, observing the flames with a warmed front, while cold gathered like a premonition at his back. He considered for a moment (standing up from his chair so that he could kneel in front of the grate, arranging the logs carefully with a poker) the oddness and continuing intensity of his feelings for Celia Quill: to be burned in the heat of his emotions and chilled at the same time by the mind, by the rational processes that were constantly at the back of his thoughts.

The fire flamed under his attentions and settled slowly. After a while he stood up from his kneeling position at the grate and sat down in the chair again, his long legs set awkwardly. He let his head lie back against the rest and continued to stare into the flames. Occasional sparks rose like eyes in the fire-blackened wood. Heated red lines spread like the lines of mouths. Fire devils began to appear from his imagination, with their creased brows and red jaws.

His thoughts drifted. The fire seemed to reach into the inner recesses of his mind. He considered notions of loyalty and compliance. Hargood was right in one sense at least. There was no lessening of his obsession with the circumstances of Celia Quill's departure. Time had no effect on the process. It constantly renewed itself, drawing its heat or energy from some deep portion of his being which lay outside his immediate purview. He wondered how long these thoughts would continue to burn in his mind, what circumstances would be required to stop the flow of fuel. While his mind moved restlessly about the subject, he remembered Swann saying that the men who lived with fire in the salt furnaces learned how to empty their minds, to live like Hindoos. It seemed to Grange that this was what lovers did: they allowed themselves to be flooded by fire, to float, not merely by volition but because to hold back the flames would be a greater effort still. They knew instinctively that to attempt to staunch the flame would be to risk being scorched, burned, injured, fatally consumed. Sometimes he wished he could explain to Hargood that to give in to his obsession was to take the path of least resistance, that of least damage to the mind or body. In the meanwhile he could resolve merely to let the process take its effect, to let the flames burn, to submit his mind and his emotions before it and hope that at the end he emerged without too much injury.

Hargood said, 'You sit so quietly I am inclined to think you asleep.'

'I was merely thinking. The fire burns well.'

'Indeed. And what do you consider?'

'I continue to meditate upon your notions of Mrs Quill's motives.'

'It is wise of you to consider my notions on any subject,' Hargood said with approval. 'Here now, is a fresh change of clothes.'

He set out clean undershirt, velvet jacket, cravat, cream breeches, stockings.

'Come, sir, let us remove these damp undergarments.' Hargood led by example, slipping his own undershirt over his head and removing his breeches. Grange saw fur-covered chest and belly, heavy genitals, the impression of a rubicund, Pan-like body. Grange stood up and raised his own undershirt. By comparison his own body was thin-limbed, white, long-boned, forked. Hargood handed him a clean, dry undershirt.

They dressed briskly facing at right angles to one another, in deference to one another's presence.

'My dear Silas, I may disagree with you about her motives. But whatever doubts I have about Mrs Quill, I promise you that I do hold her privacy sacred. You understand me, do you not?'

The question seemed to Grange rhetorical, but he nodded his assent and continued to dress himself.

Hargood leaned down to tie his breeches. He was moved to continue. 'We must never allow the rumour of her departure to take hold among the populace. Though the individuals of this borough may be benevolent in their singular selves, yet their collective will is not so beneficial to our cause. I will speak to any man directly, but the murmuring of a crowd, one whisper magnifying the other, is the onset of hell. No, I promise you that such matters as we have discussed will be resolved between us, by us alone, in our individual souls, before God, without the terrible accession of the common will.'

'Now you make Lymington sound like a revolutionary mob.'

'I believe the individual may be benign, sir, but all collectives are potentially dangerous. If I have some thing for which to be thankful, it is that I was born on this side of that water, and that I live in a civil society which respects the individual and his eccentricities.'

'So long as he does not impinge upon the eccentricities of others?'

'Precisely so.'

'Yet any concern with the collective is unhealthy?'

'So I do believe.'

'But', Grange objected, 'surely it is the notion of the collective good which drives the ideals of our own most able legislators.'

'I cannot speak for politicians,' Hargood said.

'You think there is a difference between our profession and that of politician?'

'Indeed I do.'

'Are we not both concerned with bettering the human lot?'

'There is a great difference between the two,' Hargood insisted, 'which can never be bridged.'

'What difference, precisely?'

'Medicine treats the individual, politics treats the mass.'

'That is the difference?'

'It is a profound difference, sir. It is all the difference in the world.'

Grange sensed Hargood had gathered behind some redoubt and would make his last stand here. 'And you believe this difference is absolute?'

'You know that on the other side of the Channel there are those who have allowed this collective will to break out, who actively encourage it? I am not speaking of some peasant rabble-rousers. I speak of learned men, lawyers and legislators, even certain physicians, who believe the entire state and its functions should be predicated on the collective will.'

'You disagree?'

'When the collective will is separated from the individual, and it begins to rule over the individual's own interests and wishes, it becomes a strange and dangerous entity. It becomes as capricious as that damned bee swarm.'

Grange smiled. 'I believe that bee swarm will haunt you, Hargood. You will be chased through your dreams by crowds of winged radicals.'

They finished dressing and, after Hargood had persuaded Grange to accept a second glass of brandy, Grange made his goodbyes and departed for his own house, reeling a little from the effects of the brandy on an empty stomach, his mind busy working out his excuses for Mrs Thompson regarding yet another dunking. He marshalled the explanations he would be forced to give for this second change of clothes and attempted to rehearse his story sufficiently to render it convincing – truth, it seemed to him increasingly, being another kind of fiction, which happened to fit with the facts. He considered that the flesh wounds he carried on his face (the stings now turning to impressive blues and green in places) would provide sufficient physical evidence of their fracas with the bees and give some validity to the story, at least so that Mrs Thompson could not accuse him of leaping into the cold river for the express and specific purposes of annoying her and endangering his health.

CHAPTER 43

Strangely, despite his comment to Hargood about being pursued by winged radicals, in his sleep that night it was Grange who dreamed of bees; of the faint hiss of their industry, their segmented forms, their compact bodies and jewelled, glistening wings. He imagined them in their deep hives, in that state of preoccupation which is like dreaming. He envisaged the faint trace of luminous light through the wax of their combs; their shrouded, mummified existence and the clean caskets of their young. There was no meaning to their activities, only perpetuation. The hive was a cycle of youth to age, and then youth again. Yet each generation enjoyed spectacular transformations. The parched skin and muscles burst forth new wings and shiny, segmented bodies. They were like angels, ascending in a cloud of oscillating, amber balls that moved under their own volition. But in their collective state they were also rapacious and excessive; he had experienced their violent and narrow-minded anger, the way they crawled into clothes and facial hair. He imagined them taking several shapes: the forms of animals, a house, a cloud, a hingeless door. He envisaged them rising from hives like steam, thick with outrage, and woke up in a dream of sinking into water, with cold sweat on his forehead and the dark cloud receding.

CHAPTER 44

Mr dear Leman,

Now that I have begun, I am obliged and compelled to
continue with my story.

My mistress and I had reached a state which both caused a
new understanding in our relationship, and also brought in its
train other aspects, perhaps a certain detachment or fragility,
which in turn was affected by what I will now relate.

After I had insisted that she change her name and address to
avoid the further unwarranted attentions of her half-brother, we
set up in a new house. There we continued in like manner, she
with her studies and her music, for several more years. She was
by now in her early twenties, a handsome young woman of
great acuity, who had already begun to impress upon all who
knew her the weight of her character and the breadth of her
knowledge. I believe that she lost a certain liveliness after the
incident which I last spoke of; she became more reserved, but
she applied herself with greater determination to her studies. My
admiration for her increased. I knew that I had found, in this
humble girl, a companion of the mind, if not the soul. I may
say now, in hindsight, that I admired her mind and character
as much as any, though at that time I merely blessed my own
good fortune and percipience for obtaining such a mistress.

Whereas before I had wished to display her to the world, or
to my companions, I now preferred to keep her in my
company. When one starts to accept the true worth of such a
one, the views of third parties are no longer necessary to
conjoin. I believe that, though there were signs of a certain
hesitancy or coolness resulting from our altercation over her
misuse of the funds which I had granted her, if a certain
maturity on her part had entered the relations between us, this
had no effect other than to increase my respect for her.

So we continued in the new circumstances for what was
perhaps another two years. And then a matter occurred whose

results affected my pleasant *ménage* in such a manner that further relations were changed beyond repair.

I spoke of a condition in which I had not found any companion of my soul among my acquaintances. My decision to take a London mistress, who was separate from the operations of my work and day, had fulfilled its function admirably. I no longer was a threat and scourge to the local maidens of good family. Indeed, if the matrons had cause to complain, it was that I had mended my ways too well and, apart from the obligations of society, showed no vital interest in any of their daughters. This itself might have been cause for comment, but my restraint was hardly a reason for scandal. Thus I continued to prosper in my profession. I took precautions, so that even my numerous visits to London were conducted under the auspices of the College of Physicians, in whose affairs I continued to play my role. My improved standing among the citizens of Lymington was no hindrance to my increasing involvement in the College's affairs and I was thus, to all intents and purposes, above suspicion.

These were days of happiness for me, and I thought of my mistress often during my activities, though it seemed to me I never entirely knew her mind.

After our change of household and address, I heard no more of the wretch Henry Duchamp. I can only assume that he returned to his previous occupation and, if he did, I believe his change to respectable employment was beneficial to his person and the instruction of his soul. Thus it seemed to me that although my mistress may have held my action against me, the tender hearts of the female sex are sometimes not the best guide to social affairs, and a brisk display of temper on a man's part, properly controlled, may help to disperse much of the confusion that attends their good intentions.

I believed I had set our relationship upon a proper basis and, if the consequences were a certain coolness on her part, then that was the necessary price of our equilibrium. So, having weathered the storm, we settled down into an equable condition. At a certain point I restored her to control of the finances of the household, and in every aspect thereafter she proved a satisfactory caretaker.

I do not wish to congratulate myself too fully on the state of affairs, but so we proceeded, for a number of years, into a tranquil life as man and mistress. In writing to you of this account I have opened up, so to speak, a chapter in my past, which must be completed before we arrive at the present day. The telling of that which occurred next is painful, but I must negotiate it and set it down, not least for the shriving of my soul. But for the time being my duties call, and I must regather my resources before continuing. Since much of what I shall communicate is still painful to me, I am grateful for the respite. And so, sir, I bring to an end this small missive, and shall write again in due course.

In the interim I remain,

    Yours sincerely,

      Hargood

CHAPTER 45

Standing on the marsh, Grange addressed Swann directly. A south-west wind was blowing the couch grass flat. Sometimes the wind whistled so much they were forced to raise their voices. 'I have experienced a furnace at night and have seen the conditions under which the men work. But suppose I were to wish to see a furnace at close quarters by day, in order to study more fully the detail of its operations, what should I do?'

'You'd have to observe it discreetly.'

'Discreetly?'

'The furnacers would be highly suspicious of any wishes to view their operations for any length of time.'

'Why?'

'On account of the Salt Officers.'

'But I am not a Salt Officer.'

Swann considered Grange briefly, as though wondering whether the show of innocence regarding local matters was deliberate. Deciding the physician's perplexity was genuine, he said, 'They would think you might pass information back. The Salt Officers have used spies in the past.'

'Spies? This is absurd, Mr Swann. You speak as if it were some war.'

'Is it not, sir?'

'Swann, I believe you exaggerate. I myself have seen Salt Officers engaged in their functions when I am out walking.'

'Functions, sir?'

'I have observed one or two consider the marshes through telescopes . . .'

'Surveillance, I believe it is called.'

'They supervise and regulate, in the natural course of their duties.'

Swann regarded Grange carefully and decided to shift his point of attack. 'There is a higher tax on salt, as regards its value, than any other thing in the kingdom. The salt-makers resent it badly.'

'That is understandable. But I do not see why it should lead to the state you describe.'

'That is why the powers, in order to collect the tax, see fit to install such a body of men to oversee the work.'

'In the form of Salt Officers?'

Swann paused to choose his words. 'If they were simply there to collect the taxes, why do they need so many boatmen and riding officers at Lower Woodside Green? A few clerks would do.'

'And you say this entire body of men are engaged in spying?'

'Spying and apprehension, sir. Everyone on the marshes knows that, except . . .' Swann halted.

'Except perhaps a certain physician, Mr Swann?'

Swann licked his lips. 'You do not live on the shore, sir. You only pass by on your walks.'

'But you do live on the shore,' Grange said. 'And so you know.'

'The value of salt to manufacture is nearly one shilling a bushel. Salt Tax is ten shillings a bushel. The tax is ten times the value of the thing that is taxed.'

'What point do you make?'

'That is the source of the friction.'

'Why, then, are the taxes so high?'

Swann shrugged. 'The Crown, sir, is greedy of the profit.

Perhaps it is because the furnaces are observable. They are a part of man's activities that can be watched and regulated and milked, if anything can.'

'And the salt-makers, they flout the law?'

'The temptation is always there. For every quantity of salt they sell without paying tax, they save themselves ten times the price.'

'I see.'

'Do you, sir?' Swann asked innocently and Grange wondered whether perhaps he detected a little impertinence.

Grange swung his glance swiftly towards Swann and saw that, instead of the expected presumption, Swann's eyes regarded him with a certain benevolence. He felt a brief stab of guilt at having doubted his companion's motives. 'Let us return, then, to my original question after this interesting . . . digression. How would I observe a furnace at close quarters?'

'Discreetly, sir, like I say.'

'You would help me?'

'I believe I would.'

They began to walk back towards the shore, skirting the ditches and canals that ran between the furnace houses.

'And how, then, do they avoid the tax?' Grange asked.

'Every way you can imagine.'

'Let us keep to specifics.'

'The local regulation says that all the salt must be transported first to the Salt Office at Woodside. There it must be weighed precisely, before it goes inland to be sold.'

'And how might this be subverted?'

'There is a continual movement of coal to the furnaces during the day. When the empty carts return, sometimes salt is shipped out hidden in them.'

Grange nodded.

'The riding officers put in men to check the empty carts. Another method is to use the barges that sometimes ship coal directly to the furnaces at high tide along the narrow canals. They come in carrying coal, and go out with secret caches of salt. When this was observed, the Salt Officers installed boatmen to check the outgoing barges.'

Grange considered the curious battle of wills that had evolved around the imposition of a tax, the efforts to avoid the law, the cost of men to supervise and prevent, the fresh efforts to subvert, and the additional costs of the increasingly complex administration as various loopholes were exploited and filled. 'And so all the means have now been prevented?'

Swann smiled again. 'They took to smuggling out salt at night, under cover of darkness.'

'And what remedy was effected?'

'More officers, sir – a full night watch.'

Grange had a brief vision of a new strain of Salt Officer that could see in the dark, perhaps secretly bred on some deserted wharf on the Isle of Dogs.

'They brought in the regulation that there could be no traffic between the shore and the furnaces between nightfall and morning.'

'I see.'

'Which they now rigorously enforce. There is a curfew on the movement of all carts in the dark and anyone caught shifting even a pocketful of salt at night is subject to prosecution.'

'You intend to inform me of yet other means.'

'There are others – less direct.'

'What are they, if I may so ask?'

'The salt that is exported to foreign ports is free of duty, sir. That is another path.'

'How so? If the Salt Tax has not been levied?'

'They load the salt onto barges for export. A Salt Officer accompanies the shipment to the ship. The salt is sealed in its containers and the ship sails for America. But at night the vessel halts near another part of the English coastline. The salt is smuggled ashore, sometimes at Christchurch, sir, or in Lyme Bay.'

'You no longer surprise me, Swann.'

'That was a very effective method for a number of years, until the Customs and Excise got wind of it. Then Commander Case put a stop to it, in the local area at least.'

'Commander Case?' Grange remembered him, a short, square man with a heavy, diagonal scar across the side of his face.

'He runs the Excise cutter. They say he is not susceptible.'

Grange was amused by Swann's speech. 'Susceptible?'

'To bribes, sir.'

'So another route has been closed.'

'Not entirely.'

'I was beginning to suspect.'

'After they found it too risky to smuggle ashore locally, they began to offload the salt outside Commander Case's jurisdiction. He operates between the Needles and Swanage. Beyond Swanage is another matter.'

'How do the Salt Officers deal with this new transgression? Or do they not know of this latest method?'

'Oh, they know, sir. They insist on proper paperwork from the American importer. That is why they installed extra clerks at the Salt Office.'

'Yet more men.'

'Yes, sir. And now, in addition, they send a man or two aboard ship, who will supervise the weighing of the salt on arrival at the destination.'

'You educate me, Mr Swann, I do believe.'

'I try to make the point, sir. If we are to survey the work of a furnace we will have to run a few hurdles. And I believe it is best done at night.'

'I think I will have to overcome a problem of supervision in my own affairs which is even greater than that of Salt Officers and Excise cutters.'

'Sir?'

'Mrs Thompson,' Grange said.

He observed Swann's wall eye enlarge a little, then a slow blink. 'I begin to see the dimensions of the problem now, sir.'

At the house, seated in front of the fire, Grange thought again of the curious, intensive battle of wills on the marsh, that was carried out secretly and stealthily. His mind drifted uneasily to David Hume, towards the logic of a single precept – a tax that was ten times greater than the value of the thing it taxed – leading, by a natural extension of human action, to a complex and self-perpetuating war. He wondered whether the Crown, in the prosecution of its duties, had considered the full cost of the means of collecting the tax and whether, if it could be calculated, the imposition and means of collecting it outweighed the revenue gained. He attempted to consider, as a means of achieving some insight into the matter, whether such a finding would deter the agents of the Crown from seeking their share of an industry in whose productive aspects they played no part. But, as he stared into the fire, watching its flames move slowly about the wood, it seemed to him that greed, like love, might be infinite.

After a further time spent in thought, he rose from his chair and kneeled before the fireplace, stirring the logs with a poker. He considered, for a final few minutes, the nature of the industry itself. But his mind could find no purchase for his further consideration of the problem of taxing an item at ten times its value on the open market. Behind the intricate behaviour of the Customs men, the flames of the hell mouths opened, shadowy figures raked the furnaces with long poles tipped with iron, the flames rose pure white against the governing night. He sat back in the chair and, closing his eyes, fell to thinking again, while under his eyelids a shower of raked sparks flew upwards and disappeared into darkness.

CHAPTER 46

My dear Leman,

It was in the midst of my contentment with my mistress Celia Quill that the event occurred which both changed our previous relations and caused me to modify my habitual ways. For the truth is, lacking any expectation of marriage and content with my lot, wholly unexpectedly, I fell in love with a Miss Eleanor Wright, the daughter of a local landowner, Mr James Fenton Wright. Since I do not profess to be acquainted with the mysteries which cause one soul to become enamoured of another, I shall not attempt to explain the sudden and unexpected depth of my infatuation. It was a complete and consuming passion, my first and perhaps only experience of what is sometimes called love.

I hold it strange, and somewhat ironic, that when I had looked earnestly for a young woman to marry I found none to inspire me. And when I found myself utterly content, with a female companion whose character I admired and whose company was a pleasure to me, I should fall in love with another. I do not mean to wax philosophical, but merely record life's strange incongruity, and proceed to the matter of my marriage.

My intended was, though beautiful to my eyes, somewhat frail in her constitution, and in my heart my most earnest devotion was mixed with a desire to preserve her from all further vicissitudes. Her father warned me that in his view she was sufficiently vulnerable that she would not bear children without the most severe detriment to her health. I assured him, with the fullest of hearts, that I recognised her frailty and would do everything I could to preserve her.

I had desired children, it is true, not least an heir to my name, but these considerations were small compared with my regard for her. She and I became engaged. We would be married at the nearby church at Boldre, where her own parents had been wed, and in whose graveyard several of both her and my own antecedents were buried.

Leman, you may perhaps consider the course of men. I know a number of my acquaintances who, living far distant and keeping two distinct households, would not have informed their mistresses of their private matters. It seemed to them that the less the two separate worlds should meet, the better for all parties. For is there not always the fear, among those of us who keep a second house, that an offended mistress may inform the wife of her husband's infidelities? Do you remember that something such happened to our good friend John Claridge, who kept his mistress in ignorance of his marriage for some six or seven years, by which time he decided to move on to another mistress? And when his current mistress heard, out of revenge she proceeded directly to inform his wife of their relationship. And you will perhaps recall that his wife, once informed, took proceedings against him, and returned to live with her father, which I do believe she continues to this day, wearing black like a widow.

It may be argued that I had no need to inform my mistress of so private a matter and, except that I held her in too much respect not to tell her of my intentions regarding Miss Eleanor Wright, I might have continued to keep her in ignorance. But I had become too used to informing her of my inmost thoughts. Besides which, I believed that her educated mind, her comfort in her current role, combined with the benefits of leisure for her studies, would all conspire to assist her in the realisation of her own advantage in continuation of our mutual arrangement. Thus, on my next trip to London, I duly visited her and, as soon as seemed propitious, carefully and soberly apprised her of this new eventuality. I told her that I intended to marry another, but that I proposed to continue to maintain her in the house, that I had grown to respect her and deemed her companionship a privilege. For my own part, I foresaw no reason against perpetuating our relations. I believe, in this respect, I behaved more honourably than many.

Perhaps, having been witness to my account of her character, you will suspect what happened next. For while I spoke, she gazed at me without talking, and continued thus in absolute silence for a certain time after I had completed my speech. Her silence disquieted me. We ate much of the meal without speaking. She showed no clear reaction, except that she continued to administer the meal, with much calmness, albeit without eating a great deal herself. Though we maintained good relations, at least in their external aspect, this silence between us, on the most delicate of matters, though it seemed natural in the first instance, began to unnerve me. I started to fear something which before had never been explicit between us, that she had been hoping, and perhaps preparing herself, for my final acceptance of her as my wife. In my defence, I should add that though I respected her, I had never given her hope of my marrying her. For it was one thing to keep her, under an assumed name, in some modest household beyond the purview of my social circle, and another to bring her into the centre of my life where her past as my mistress could be examined.

As if to tie our two selves together in our mutual regard, there was another bond between us, for which reason I felt honour bound to continue our arrangement. It had become clear over the past few months that she was with child. While she watched me without comment, I told her I would honour the child and take all care to provide him with material welfare until such time as he was old enough to find his own way. And when that child was born, I would in fairness treat him entirely as my own flesh and blood, in everything but name.

Leman, I say again, that many men, having had their way, would have cast her out, or arranged a transfer to some work as a servant or governess, and perhaps even insisted that the child should be placed in foster. It seemed to me that I had been honourable with her, that I had never promised her marriage and that, having announced my intention to marry another, I offered reasonable and practical terms both for the continuation of our relations and the well-being of her offspring. In due course, it seemed to me, she would adjust to the new circumstances.

Even then, I put her silence down to the fact that she had become acquainted with certain new facts, which by their nature deserved her most earnest consideration. It did not occur to me that she would do other than accept the terms of our continued relationship. I did not expect enthusiasm for the new circumstances, but in the light of her previous adjustment, I had reason to hope that eventually she would accept the inevitable with a show of equanimity, which would mature in the course of time to acquiescence. In the calculation of motive of which I (as a creature who must live with others) am the victim as much as the perpetrator, I believed that the prospect of abandoning my protection with her child would hold such terrors for her that she would see sense. The very constraints imposed by the infant would, if nothing else, render her sensible to the importance of maintaining the advantages of the current arrangement. She would elect to stay in material well-being, among a community which accorded her a proper respect. I suspected there would be some tears and scenes while she adjusted to the altered circumstances, but I have known what it is to be subjected to them and was determined to stand my ground.

You, my dear Leman, being perhaps wiser in the ways of women, or possibly having gained from my account some knowledge of the nature of my mistress, will understand a little better than I what she did next. To be precise, in the very first instance it was nothing. Having maintained the decorum of the meal, she did not attempt to speak to me on her own account for the entire evening, though she answered my questions sensibly and with brevity. Having made my peace and eaten my supper, I repaired to the nearby fireside, as was my habit, and sat there, while she took her own chair opposite me. There, in silence, she gazed upon me. There was nothing that indicated excess emotion in her outward appearance, except perhaps the continuation of this same quiet reserve, as though she were assessing me from a perspective of which she had previously been unaware. After some time in this domestic configuration she requested, with all show of calmness, my permission to absent herself from the room, and departed to her bedroom.

I did not follow her. It had been my custom to join her there, but in respect of her state of mind and her need to consider the new circumstances, I decided I would overnight in the other room. Accordingly, I instructed the servant to set another bed. There was, after all, a precedent for my actions. It had been a hard ride to London and, though I felt some concern for her, I was determined that she should accept the conditions that had imposed themselves upon us. I had no energy for violent argument, and assumed that in the course of the night she would consider her position. Tired from my journey, I slept peacefully, and the result was that I woke up a little later than was usual with me.

I dressed myself and shaved and, on reaching her door, I found it closed. I knocked upon it and received no reply. I could hear no sound from her and she did not seem to be inside. Mindful of her privacy, I did not attempt to enter. I was not yet perturbed, for it seemed she might have taken a walk while she waited for me to rise.

I went downstairs and questioned the servant, who said that she had seen no sign of her mistress that morning. In some alarm, I returned to her room, knocked again upon the door and, receiving no reply, opened it.

The room was empty. In haste I glanced around. A wardrobe that had held her clothes swung open. I saw, with increasing consternation, that it was largely bare except for one or two pieces of clothing that appeared to have been flung aside. There were a number of other objects that were personal to her – a brush, a mirror – that were missing. Now I was truly fearful. I ran downstairs, calling out her name, and pushed my way past the servant to the hallway door. Outside, in the street, there was no sign of her. I turned this way and that in panic. I thought she might be waiting for a coach and began to run towards the nearby hostelry. But Leman, even as one pursues a wraith, so there was nothing that remained of her but an empty street and the few shreds of her discarded belongings that were left in her chamber.

In my heart I knew, given the power of her nature and her decisiveness, it was the last that I would see of her. She had made her avowal, and the abrupt and final nature of her leaving transmitted to me the true and full import of it. Though I might rail against the event for weeks and months afterwards, and still hope that it might be resolved in some other fashion, I knew in my bones that she had taken her final decision.

That, indeed, was the last I saw of my mistress for many years. What she bore in her mind I do not know, but she also bore inside her my child which, as the months went by, I reconciled myself to the view I could now expect never to see.

You may imagine my despair, and that anguish which increasingly I felt over my behaviour towards her, which in the light of her leaving seemed to me still to be both sensible and honourable. After all, I had not deceived her. On the contrary, I had taken every pain to inform her precisely of the situation that had befallen, and to reassure her of my continued responsibility towards her welfare. I persuaded myself that I had made the unpardonable sin of overestimating her good sense and laid too much emphasis on her calculation of her future, to foresee that in the excess of her emotion she might cast such advantages away. I learned from it, I believe, one salient fact: that one should never trust a woman to exhibit good sense, particularly where the exercise of it conflicts with her own emotions.

I must close this account and return once more to my duties. In the interim, I remain,

Yours sincerely,
Hargood

CHAPTER 47

In the late afternoon light, Hargood had approached his patient unseen, tethering his horse on a heavy driftwood log and walking out across the couch grass to where Grange stood, a single figure staring out across the water. At first sighting, Hargood had seen two figures of almost absurdly different height facing one another in what appeared to be animated discussion – his younger colleague as tall as a pole, the other party squat and bulky. As Hargood began his stalk, the smaller figure had nodded, shaken hands and separated. Hargood was surprised at the speed with which he had disappeared into the rising evening.

When Grange turned finally, Hargood said, 'I saw you engaged in earnest discussion with a man who I believe is a former ship's mate.'

'My patient, Mr Swann.'

Hargood turned to look out along the marsh wall, but there was no sign of him. 'You maintain an eye upon his health?'

'He is as much an acquaintance as a patient.'

Hargood smiled, though he did not speak further. Instead, they found themselves discussing other matters, lapsing into a mutual silence while the sun descended like a dark rose in the western sky.

Towards Hurst Castle, a single curlew called out on the marshes beside the water.

The name of Swann occurred several evenings later when Grange visited Hargood for an evening meal.

'This Swann,' Hargood said. 'You are beginning to see your patients again?'

'I merely take note of the after-effects of his amputation.'

'As I watch over your own own recovery.'

Grange smiled. 'You find us similar?'

'Similar?' Hargood studied his glass, the shape of shadows moving inside the wine. 'Similar in this, perhaps, that whereas his arm has been removed, it is your emotions which you seem to have jettisoned.'

'I do not follow you.'

'Your own amputation, I do believe, is more of the spiritual kind.'

'You remain obscure.'

'Do I?'

Grange waited for edification. But Hargood, it seemed, had gone to earth. He remained at the head of the table, bulking huge, though it seemed to Grange that his mind roamed elsewhere, somewhere out of the room.

'Hargood, you amuse me. I have read an account, in the published journals of the East India Company, of lions when they hunt. To confuse their prey, so it is said, they make a low roar, which appears to come from no particular direction and gives no information to their prey, except that it serves to frighten the quarry into the lion's jaws.'

Hargood's eyes studied Grange. 'It sounds a most interesting technique.'

'I believe you use it, sir.'

'Indeed?'

'And that you are hunting tonight.'

'You flatter me, my dear Silas. Since I am not so sure of this hunting technique myself, perhaps you will explain it to me.'

'You say I am like Swann, and draw some broad comparison between physical amputation and the curtailment of the emotions.

Then you refuse to make the connection explicit. This is your low roar. You intend me to run into your jaws.'

'Do I indeed, sir?'

'Perhaps you merely hope, by concentrating my mind, that I will do your work for you.'

'That, as I understand, is the technique,' Hargood said with satisfaction. 'Perhaps it is mere laziness, or sloth on my part, to hope that you might contribute towards your own edification. But since you have roused me, may I continue?'

'Please do.'

'Then let us address the central matter. This detachment you desire. Is it not achieved through some form of amputation – some amputation of the emotions?'

'I believe my emotions are intact.'

'Intact, sir, but like the pizzle of a gelding, not much in use.'

'I believe they are in use. Indeed, I believe they drive what you call my detachment.'

'How?'

'I suggest to you that detachment is an active, not a passive, quantity, that it requires the utmost effort of will. It is not achieved by cutting off the emotions, but by disciplining them, balancing them, perhaps – in the process – even intensifying them.'

'They are present in the background, perhaps. But surely we should apply our emotions hot, directly to the events?'

'I believe mine are present at events – hot and ready.'

'Yet somehow you remain hidden, disguised, latent. It is as if the world must be filtered through some other zone, some climate of coolness, before it reaches the heart.'

'That coolness is surely only the external impression created by the reasoning mind.'

'Or is it some philosophical principle, behind which a person may hide?'

'You expound again, Hargood.'

'What would happen, my dear Silas, if you removed the reasoning mind from these equations?'

'I believe I would become an animal.'

'An animal?' Hargood raised an eyebrow, as though the notion appealed to him. 'An animal, indeed.'

Hargood refused to expound further, but continued to survey him. Grange had the impression that his host once again had emitted his soft, low roar and was expecting Grange's panicked thoughts, like some nourishing prey, to run into his jaws.

CHAPTER 48

My dear Leman,

In some curious manner, which I still do not begin to understand, he waits for something, like a man who is watching the weather, hoping for some change.

His waiting infects me. As his strength grows, so our walks lengthen. He can maintain a pace which sometimes leaves me breathless. And because we are able to cover ten or fifteen miles in an afternoon now, without much respite, we have ranged increasingly widely through the New Forest and the shores of the Solent, along footpaths and narrow tracks with which I was not previously acquainted.

We walk through some strange territory, that I do not know. I hear dogs barking, and suspect a settlement, but cannot find it. We enter a deep forest and the leaves are so thick the light is put out above our head. It is as if we are underground. We walk through unknown groves and find that there are fissures in the ground and small valleys there. In one such valley the layer of rocks above us so resembled a roof that we might have been in a human habitation. Indeed, there were signs of an old fire which indicated that certain beings lived there.

In the late afternoons the clouds pour across the land, so that the shadows cover the roofs, the sun is quiet on the earth.

In his company, I sometimes feel as if the world is an engine, a beautiful machine, that its processes are natural and quiet, that sunlight and leaves will continue to rain down softly after I die. One may say such things easily, but I feel it in my bones. Each day that we walk, it is as if I must wait for some process of maturation in his mind.

But in my heart I know that he not only waits, but is ready to receive certain information which it is my responsibility to impart. I have seen how, beneath the surface of good relations between us, his soul hungers. I remember from a few weeks back, when he had fallen prey once again to his fevers, the ferocity of his grip upon my wrist as he lay upon his sickbed. I know that for which he waits, and must steel myself to tell him. If until now I have withheld it on the grounds that it might precipitate a further crisis, I believe that time is nearly past. What I lack now is the courage to impart it. For I am certain that once I have done so, our relations will be changed, perhaps for ever. These considerations weigh upon me, but they do not alter the central fact that when he has reached full health again, he will have an absolute right to know of the circumstances that pertained between Mrs Quill and myself.

So we proceed, walking towards our destination, our motion carrying us through the afternoon. One day moves into another. Each day that passes is some moment in the eternal mind. I wait for what I know shall one day come, and steel myself for the inevitable.

In the meanwhile, sir, I remain,

Most sincerely yours,

Hargood

CHAPTER 49

Grange opened the wooden gate off Barrows Lane and entered an area of quietness.

The house was hidden behind a line of elms. There were no signs of Mrs Quill's attention to her garden. Rainwater had collected in a basin beside the sundial. In adjacent beds the heads of flowers had withered without being cut. Creepers had grown away from the wall.

He began to walk down the familiar paved path until he rounded a yew hedge. The house came into view, shuttered, with its uncut lawns. Clouds crossed the sky behind it.

He moved towards the door. A sensation of faintness overtook him as he approached it. He tried the door handle, but it had been bolted from the inside. He went around the edges of the house, to the rear porch. His hands felt for the key that he knew had been hidden once in cracks in the masonry. But his enquiring fingers found only the empty edges of the brick. He pressed the door, but it too had been locked. He gained a sense of the emptiness of the house, its coldness enclosed, the solidity and weight of silence.

After a few moments he retraced his path. On the lawn in front of the house he paused. There was a fine view of the Lymington river and the Solent to Hurst Castle. A sheen lay on the surface of the water. He could smell the faint odour of decaying weed that the lightest of breezes brought up from the foreshore.

Perhaps, on the point of leaving, something had caused him to turn – the rustling of a bird or small animal in the undergrowth. In the herb garden the soil had been turned. It lay, thick and rich. He looked more closely. There were signs of tending. Several small plants had recently been earthed. He felt a slight catch in his breath.

There had been a cook, whom he had seldom seen. Did she return now to cultivate the herbs in the garden, perhaps for her own uses? He did not know her name. But it occurred to him suddenly that her mistress might write to her, if only to enquire about the state of the house and garden, and perhaps to ensure that a friendly eye might supervise the property. And if Mrs Quill wished to be advised on the condition of the house, would she not leave some form of forwarding address to her correspondent and former employee?

He wished he had thought of it before. Yet at first sight it did not much advance his cause. Who would know the cook's name? He himself could not remember her, except once or twice as a plump shape moving in the further recesses of the kitchen. He could not recall even a detail of her face. His mind began to race. He looked down at the ground again, the turned earth slick against dark soil. The shrubs he could see were most of them immediately identifiable: mace, marjoram, thyme. For several minutes he stood in contemplation, but despite his attempt to remember some detail of the cook, he could proceed no further with identification of the source of the carefully turned earth and small plantings.

CHAPTER 50

They had returned from their afternoon walk to Hargood's house. At his invitation, Grange seated himself in the chair.

Hargood moved to the mantelpiece, placed a hand on it, turned to face his guest. 'Silas, I have watched you grow more healthy. I have observed you make your repairs. And in my surveillance of your state I have preserved one final piece of news against the day when you might best receive it.'

'Concerning Mrs Quill?'

'I promised myself that when you stand apart once again from this incident, I would inform you of it.'

Grange nodded, cautious, not wishing to speak in case he disrupt the flow.

'You asked me if I knew why Mrs Quill came to settle in Lymington. I did not answer you, though in defence of my own behaviour I say that I cannot explain this fully, even now. I never knew her mind entirely.'

Grange watched him, attentive.

Hargood observed the intensity of his companion's listening, as if every word was sifted. He proceeded with caution, picking his words: 'I believe, nevertheless, that what I know in part is also a partial explanation. The fact is, in her younger days, I enjoyed her acquaintance.'

'Hargood . . .' Grange's face froze. In the fervent calm he could hear the precise ticking of the mantelpiece clock, even the faint hiss of the turning mechanism.

'Let me continue, since I do not wish to falter. I speak of facts. The fact is, that in the distant past . . . she was my mistress.'

Again Grange was afflicted by the sudden blankness of intense thought. Hargood seized the moment of calm, and proceeded, 'I do not expect you to excuse my tardiness in explaining this simple fact, or my silence until now. She was my mistress over a number of years, a period of great happiness to me, even though I may speak of it only in retrospect.'

In that watching silence, which Hargood had come to fear, there was no emotion in Grange that he could see, though it was precisely in this lack that he was drawn to finish his message.

'I had the deepest regard for her. I settled her at an address which was respectable in every manner. In order to continue these proprieties, I visited her as her guardian – a not inaccurate description of my function, for in all ways I sought to help her achieve that respectability which she both sought and deserved. She had the most remarkable mind, even in her youngest years. Though I could not appreciate them fully, yet I understood enough of her gifts to consider how best to give them some latitude in expression. I watched over her, in short, like a father with a gifted daughter.'

Grange stood up suddenly. It was not, it seemed, out of anger or an intention to confront him, but a cold eructation of anguish. Hargood said, 'My dear Silas.' But Grange walked to the other side of the room, as if in peering out over the Lymington marshes, towards Pilewell and Sowley, he could perceive something in the pallid exterior which would assist him in this new arrangement of facts.

How long did Grange stand at the window? Hargood could not remember. It occurred to him that Grange had turned away not least in order that the expressions on his face might not show.

In the ensuing silence, Hargood himself was subject to a series of emotions. He had been interrupted in his flow of discourse, and felt that common and understandable slight at not being allowed to complete his address. He understood the younger man's agony, but was concerned now at the way in which it might express itself. There was something in Grange's movement that was agitated and at the same time precise. He had stood up suddenly, as though his thoughts had made him rise, composed himself sufficiently to move silently to the window and there stared out in intense concentration.

For several moments neither moved. Grange had reached

forward with both hands to hold the two handles of the window, as though he were intending to drive the sash upwards and let in the pure air. He stood, arrested in his thoughts. Hargood watched the slender, bony fingers folded over the handles, the ligaments and tendons showing white. For the time being, at least, he seemed in no mood to turn around, or to take account of Hargood's own agitation.

When Hargood had recovered a little he found his throat was dry with tension. He swallowed, breathed out, glanced up at the ceiling and brought his gaze down again to the same figure at the window, a figure who to Hargood's mind was as much a mystery as ever.

CHAPTER 51

Grange peered through the window at the shore, at the shifting configurations of light there. Several fishing boats could be seen above the line of shrubs and holly to the south of Hargood's property. It was one of his fascinations that the light above water was always changing, almost from moment to moment, as if two fluid elements magnified one another's evanescent properties.

It was not anger at Hargood's reticence that animated his emotions so much as astonishment that he had never once considered the possibility of his involvement with Mrs Quill. It was a monument to his own selfish concerns that it should never occur to him that such a relation might exist. Anger at his own failure was followed in turn by fear, the sudden visceral sense that if he had miscalculated in this, perhaps he had done so in other things, too. The flux of emotions caused him to breathe more deeply. He had thought of Hargood as fixed, as solid, as immovable. Now that he found himself between two fluid elements, his turmoil magnified.

Behind him, Hargood cleared his throat.

Grange turned to speak, as though to a different man. His customary caution came to his assistance. 'Hargood, I must consider my position.'

Hargood nodded. He searched Grange's face for signs. 'Will you not stay for dinner, sir?'

'Thank you for your kindness. I believe I should leave now, and that we should communicate again in a little while.'

Hargood, for once, was nervous of speaking, as though all words were inadequate, and to speak would be an intrusion. He nodded again, and stood up.

They walked down the main passageway in silence. In the hallway Grange, as though to forestall his host, reached for his cloak hanging on the heavy oak hook and swung it about his shoulders. For several moments Hargood thought Grange would depart without saying another word. But at the last moment the younger physician reached forward and, as though to preserve some form of communication between them, shook his host's hand with a cautious formality. He stared briefly into Hargood's eyes, then bowed slightly, before he departed through the open doorway.

CHAPTER 52

Dear Leman,

It is three days since I wrote. I communicate with you now under the inspiration of pain.

Do not be alarmed, I most earnestly entreat you, at my condition, or concerning what I now recount, for the fact that I am able to mention it is a sign that whatever threat or danger was implicit has now passed.

The day before yesterday, on our habitual walk, my younger colleague struck me so hard with his fist on the side of my face that I lost my footing and tumbled down a small slope. The force of my fall winded me into the bargain, so that when I came to rest and could begin to count the damage, I found that I had sprained my ankle as well. It was my mind, more than my body, which was in shock at what had happened. I cannot easily describe the weight of his anger. For it seems that when we are disturbed at our roots, our violence rises through us like an insupportable force. He followed me to where I then lay and, as he descended the slope in his cold ferocity, I feared that he was determined to complete what he had begun. But whatever had provoked his mind and arm to such sudden and extravagant expression had left him without immediate intention of extending it. For by the time he reached my side, he was detached and almost withdrawn in his treatment of me and, when he had ascertained I had recovered enough, he assisted me to my feet without any further sign of rage, but also without apology, for some part of him seemed to feel that what he had done was just.

When you have been struck with the full force of another's anger, it is not merely the physical impact, but also perhaps the fervent transmission of one shocked mind to another. For in the light of an argument, such a blow is not merely a physical expression, but a violent communication between souls. Yet when he had approached me and his own rage seemed to have dissipated, having recovered some of my senses, I felt no anger or wish to retaliate. In such strange manner I sensed that what he had effected was done under extreme provocation. I forgave him his immediate action and, on our return to my house, with him assisting me in my halting and somewhat hobbling walk, the subject of what he had done was not mentioned once, as though by tacit agreement between us it had been consigned already to the past.

Yet if we did not speak of it, the physical consequences remained with me. For two days subsequent I lay in my bed with a fever and a headache, my cheek and jaw swollen, my ankle (which had been stretched in the fall) bound in cloth, and in some subsidiary discomfort.

I have left aside in this account, as though it were a mere detail, what precisely it was that gave rise to his fury, or at least occasioned it. The previous day I had explained to him my reasons for withholding the information that Mrs Celia Quill had been my mistress during my younger years. I had expected some outbreak then, but he walked calmly to the window and stared out for what seemed several minutes. I believe it was the clearest demonstration of his self-control. When he turned back to me he merely requested that, in our future discussions, I should inform him of everything I knew that directly affected his circumstances. I should have taken that as a warning of any further transgression against his own state of mind and disposition.

Perhaps I placed too great a faith in his self-control. For when, the following day, while we were out walking, I mentioned the circumstances in which Celia Quill and I had parted, he seemed to accept what I said, if not with equanimity, then with that outward calm which is characteristic of him. I proceeded in my tale of the detailed conditions in which she left me, and he listened with all his concentrated intensity, but no immediate sign of animadversion. It was when I recounted that she was bearing my child that something inside him seemed to break. He struck me suddenly, without warning and with the utmost ferocity. I forgive him, as I say, because his rage surprised and overwhelmed him as much as it did myself. I forgive him also because it was perhaps the first time in our acquaintance that I have seen him lose control of himself. And in partial mitigation of his action we may at least perceive some sign of that fallible being which lurks within us all.

It is uncomfortable to write further, given my circumstances. But I should here repeat what I have stated before – do not be alarmed by this report of my condition. For though my physical being has been rudely surprised by it, yet in my mind I feel no more anger than if my horse had thrown me badly, and on gathering my senses I perceived that, though I might be bruised, I was without broken bones. I have a certain sense of relief after the event, as though things might easily have been worse. The fact remains that I have a good constitution, which will repair me in due course. Thus, considering the matter in its entirety, I write now with a sense of some small forgiveness and even a modicum of patronage towards my younger colleague, who at last has shown his hand. For another, I am convinced sufficiently that in expressing some extreme action we may at least help to diminish the motive of it.

There is another aspect to this affair which may, however,

provide occasion for some regret. I have tried my best to take over from him the burden of his patients, so that he might recover more quickly without the extra strains imposed upon him by his profession. Indeed, I have insisted on accepting the responsibility for his patients as part of my duties in his recovery. Now, while I do myself recover from his inflicted transgression, for his own part he must accept for a few days at least the full sum of our combined duties. Thus, there are consequences, albeit more gentle ones in his case, of his own action, which I hope will conspire in due course to concentrate his mind on any further such intemperance in his behaviour.

There are even one or two aspects of the matter which give rise to possible satisfaction. In taking upon himself this extra load, which he shows no sign of shirking, he has been provided with an opportunity to prove to me his own improved fitness. He has taken to visiting me each day while I recover, as though I am merely one of his patients and, while he gauges my progress, I am able to assess his own well-being.

How strange is life, that by means of some brief, albeit violent, episode, there is a sudden precipitation of circumstances. I have cursed my temporary discomfort and inveighed against my confinement following the incident. But it too has given me an opportunity to consider other matters, which my routine and the burden of my patients had prevented or foreshortened. I have much to trouble me, but in this enforced leisure I at least begin to address my fears. With regard to my younger colleague, I do believe that the incident has served to acquaint him of his own inner man, and it brings certain aspects of his mind forward, into the light, so to speak, and thus into our account.

These sir, are the summaries of my communication – that I am struck down, and am strangely grateful for the insights it confers, while my younger colleague, who struck me, must find room in his own conscience for his actions. In the meantime he has an opportunity to show that he is at least partially restored to health.

As soon as I am able to resume the burden of my patients, and his own, I will insist on a further month at least of recuperation on his part, to consolidate the grounds of his advance, and to make certain that he does not regress into a fevered state again. I believe that, affected by a certain remorse regarding his action, he will grant me this request.

My own fears are more complex. What has happened in our latest episode is that he has seen some cause for development in his relations with Mrs Quill, and in the explanation of her behaviour. I know in my heart that, far from satisfying him as to her background and the cause of some of her behaviour, he will now proceed with his investigations even more fiercely than before. Thus, sir, I believe I must brace myself for further upheavals.

I will write again as soon as I am able.

In the interval, I remain,

    Sincerely yours,

      Hargood

CHAPTER 53

When Hargood had recovered sufficiently to take up his duties, Grange visited the Poor House.

Mrs Quill had supported the impoverished and disadvantaged. She had aided the crippled and the sick. As she had become known for her charity, so the domain of her action had expanded. There seemed to be no limit to her commitment to the unfortunate of the parish. If there was a single area in which she had held most sway, it was here.

It was a substantial building, with its work-rooms, the long boards pit-sawed from giant oaks, the strong beams of its sloping roof shingled in slate and various additions that had grown to accommodate its activities. Both the outer and inner doors had been left ajar to allow a soft breeze to enter on this autumn day. Grange sensed her presence in the sanguine walls, her calm like a shadow.

'Good day, Mr Cruitt.'

Joseph Cruitt, her former lieutenant, sat at his desk by the entrance. Grange observed his long jaw and cold eyes in the interior gloom.

Considering his visitor, Cruitt raised his face carefully, like an old dog, and stared without speaking at Grange. He swallowed once, in a manner which might have been slow and agonising, were it not for the traces of ham pie lying on a white plate beside him. 'You called, sir.'

Grange said, 'I should like to see the registers of expenditure for the last three years.'

Cruitt regarded him for several further seconds without movement, while a variety of expressions passed behind his eyes.

'Sir,' Cruitt replied at last, as though he had come to a decision. He stood up, bowed towards Grange in melancholy admonition, then turned and walked into the dark recess at the back of the room. He raised a calico curtain and drew it close behind him. Grange watched the commotion of grey material as Cruitt entered his interior domain.

In the ensuing silence, Grange glanced about him. The place had the smell of institutions. On three sides the walls were exposed brick. The fourth wall was little more than a board partition. The wooden floors had been scoured with a stone and vinegar, and bore the fine traces of the stone's passage. In the corner were several piles of belongings – though 'belongings' was perhaps too strong a word for so abject a collection of old clothes and artefacts, since they clearly now belonged to no one. No doubt they were the last few chattels of poor vagrants who had passed on.

There was another commotion of grey cloth in the interior. Cruitt returned with several heavy leather-bound ledgers held under his arm. He placed them carefully on the desk between them and then, raising his face, looked at Grange again, as though daring him to speak. It seemed to Grange that Cruitt had the attitude, pitched delicately between obedience and insolence, of a former Navy clerk.

'Anything in particular you would like to see, sir?'

'I should like to study the ledgers in some detail.'

Cruitt hesitated. Grange was reminded more acutely of an elderly dog, who has a bone but is not inclined to share it.

'At this moment, sir?'

'Now, if you please, Mr Cruitt.'

Elementary courtesy suggested Cruitt should have offered a visiting physician the small inner office in which to read. It was Grange, more than Hargood, who had taken up the burden of the health of the Poor House inhabitants. But when it came to outside supervision of his small domain, it was Cruitt's custom to provide nothing that was not asked for. Grange, for his part, was determined not to throw himself too determinedly upon the meagre shores of Cruitt's hospitality.

The ledgers lay between them like disputed property. With a nod and a final look at the piles of vagrant clothes, Grange drew up a chair to the desk, settled down and hauled the volumes towards him across the desk's scratched surface. He opened the first ledger. Without looking up, he began to turn the pages.

Cruitt was left standing uneasily, looking down at his visitor.

'I'll leave you to it, then,' Cruitt said, after a few moments, though he hovered on the other side of the desk.

Grange continued to turn the pages, determined to repay Cruitt in his own coin. He looked up now only to exhibit surprise at his host's continued presence. 'Good-day, Mr Cruitt.'

'Good-day, sir.'

Cruitt drew the curtain behind him. The swirl of his white hand was like a fish in the gloom of a pond.

The pages of the ledger were beautiful, the entries clean and clear. Their cream surfaces had the scent of learning. Proceeding to examine them more closely, Grange understood why Cruitt regarded the ledgers as his own. All the petty dealings, the to-and-fro of the Poor House, were registered there with the loving attention of a scribe. Here, the sordid details of humanity were reduced to a clear and calm distinction. In the past, whenever Grange had brief recourse to the ledgers, his heart had softened a little towards Cruitt. Each man had his own domain. In these pages, with their precise and careful entries, the angry, silent overseer of the Poor House brought order to his life. No wonder there was something like resentment towards the visiting physician as he split the ledgers open with his thin fingers and proceeded to exclude Cruitt entirely from his study of the contents.

There were a number of mundane entries:

1 doz. lbs Salt Butter	*9s od*
To the wife, child of Wheeler committed	*3s od*
Paid for 2 cwt 3 qrs 12 lbs old junk	*10s od*
To bad copper being received from overseers	*16s 6d*
Nails and virrils	*10s 6d*
A pair of spectacles for Lucy Barnes	*2s od*
A quarter's quit rent for Buckland Cottage	*1s od*
3 gallons of mint water	*11s 10d*
Nicholas Read in the palsy	*7s 6d*

As the morning progressed, Grange worked carefully through the cryptic entries, glossing page after page, running his finger down the margin, searching for signs. Apart from a set of annotations in the margin from the parish clerk, each entry was in Cruitt's fastidious hand. The capitals were high, the numerals flowing and precise. For perhaps two hours Grange was absorbed in his search. Once there was a brief scene of consternation behind him when an elderly woman appeared unannounced at the door, demanding to see her husband, who was quartered somewhere within the building. Grange would have attempted to help her himself, but at the last moment Cruitt appeared from the interior, placed a claw-like hand on her shoulder to calm her, and escorted her up the spiral wooden staircase into the dark air of the upper floor. Grange heard their progress across the boards, Cruitt's old feet dragging slightly, to an upstairs room where her husband, having been found drunk and riotous the night before, had been tied to a bed against his will and subdued by isolation.

Grange heard several thumps as the prisoner kicked out in gagged silence against the wooden wall. Then quietness, a sense of bruised air. Grange was distracted, despite himself. The silence seemed to draw him upwards. After a while the woman uttered a low imprecation that Grange could not fully discern, then she began crying in a low, gathering howl. Grange assumed it was reconciliation, of a kind.

There were further entries.

Grange's heart stopped: his mind seemed to hover:

Mrs Celia Quill for supplying tutelage, Chorleys   9s od

There was a leather marker in the ledger. Grange placed it on the page and continued his searches. Once or twice Cruitt emerged from the interior and passed through the room on his errands, carrying articles of clothing and pieces of furniture. No word passed between them.

'Where are the Chorleys?' Grange asked finally.

Cruitt seemed arrested, holding several pairs of old breeches and a much-patched jacket. 'There is no such place.'

'It is here,' Grange said, 'in your own hand.' He turned the ledger towards his host.

But Cruitt ignored the pages and regarded him in the gloom, as though attempting to discover his motive for the question. 'It is a family.'

Grange nodded. 'A family.' He waited patiently for further elucidation.

Cruitt hovered, swallowing several times. At length he coughed, though it was more like a bleeding of stale breath into the air between them, and appeared to choose his words carefully. 'If one could call so loose an assemblage a family.'

Grange could have smiled at the strangulated outrage and its agonised precipitation into such quaint expression. He had already formed the impression that Cruitt was something of a scholar, and felt a certain sympathy for these vapours. 'This assemblage, then. They are in Lymington?'

'No, sir.'

'They live freely, then.'

'Freely, sir?'

'Like the birds, perhaps. In a state of nature.'

Cruitt ignored the irony. He paused, his hesitation predominant. The obscurity seemed to settle around him. He appeared about to bring forth something, considering perhaps its consequences first.

'Pilley,' Cruitt said.

'Pilley, you say.' Grange knew enough of Cruitt that he would gain little from questioning on extraneous matters. He waited again, determined carefully to draw out Cruitt's own words by maintaining adherence to a single line of enquiry. 'This is a family from Pilley?'

Something cleared in Cruitt's mind or throat, some blockage or impediment; then his sudden vehemence about the location surprised Grange. Now Cruitt was speaking briskly: 'A band, more like, united by blood. A tribe would be better, though the only thing they hold in common is that they are all ne'er-do-well. And their beliefs . . .'

'What beliefs would those be?'

Cruitt coughed again. 'No beliefs that you or I would recognise.'

'Pilley is an appropriate setting, then.'

'Sir?'

'I have heard that on the outskirts there is a pagan settlement.'

'Dissenters?' Cruitt was shocked.

'Not Dissenters. Pagans.'

The word had no meaning for Cruitt. Grange continued, 'There are more than a dozen families there who resemble gypsies. One cannot tell the full extent of them because so many are vagrants. They have their own laws.'

'Is that so?' Despite himself, Cruitt was drawn.

'As a physician I have been called to one of those families only twice. They seem to apply their own remedies, too.'

Cruitt had come to the end of his anger, perhaps even now regretting his outburst. He appeared to advance towards saying something further, then retreated. The effort of swallowing made his eyes loom, but for several seconds he did not move.

'Thank you, Mr Cruitt.' Grange indicated the ledgers. 'I should like to study these a little more.'

Cruitt nodded, turned and left. He was already about to enter the interior when Grange called after him: 'Mr Cruitt?'

'Sir.' Cruitt halted, framed by the heavy cloth.

'These are beautiful ledgers. You have the hand of a scholar.'

Pausing in mid-turn, the master of the Poor House pinched his mouth against expression, nodded again without looking directly at Grange and exited through the solace of the grey curtains.

*

Grange became lost to time. Once, during the course of the following hours, he edged the desk a few feet across the floor to take advantage of the shifting light that streamed through the single window on the east side of the room. Outside, he heard faint bird-song and the trilling of insects. His concentration dissolved time. The thin ticking of the watch that depended from its chain in his pocket reminded him vaguely of the dry brushing of insects' legs.

Towards mid-morning, without announcement, Cruitt emerged from the interior with a jar of ale and placed it with emphasis on the writing desk; beside it he put an earthenware mug. He took no notice of Grange's 'Thank you, Mr Cruitt'. After he had perfunctorily filled the mug, he shifted away again, his gullet moving in the dark like a complicated, bony fish.

The entries were a strange slice of life, as if an axe blade had laid bare the roots and details of its circumstances. The poor were housed and cajoled, the indolent warned, tradesmen pursued for unfulfilled work. Discipline was meted out to indigents, favours to benefactors. Supervisors were repaid in meals and ale.

Hargood had once said, 'But for the Poor Laws, we would have followed the example of France into revolution, of that I have no doubt.' Grange, determined not to allow his older colleague to claim the Poor Laws as a shrewd Tory reform, had asked, 'That was their motive? Not to offer charity but to forestall revolution?' Hargood had replied grandly, 'The motive and the effect are two different things.' He had closed his eyes as though considering the efficacy of this comment, then, perhaps reassured that he had given a definitive reply, his head had sunk to the table, as it was increasingly inclined to do after an evening of drinking. Grange's attempt at further conversation was met by a series of voluble snores. Sometimes Hargood's snoring had halted, though it was only momentary, in order to change position slightly. Shortly afterwards, in the process of draining his own glass preparatory to leaving, Grange had been obliged to move his chair smartly backwards as a mug of wine, disturbed by Hargood's restless but insensible fingers, fell over on the table, and the liquid moved across the wood in a tide as dark as blood. He had watched it spill to the flagstones beside his own hastily withdrawn legs.

Grange turned a page.

Evidence of Celia Quill's goodness began to appear. An annotation stated that Mrs Quill had personally collected the following items for sale:

3 silver teaspoons	*4s 2d*
A striped silk handk.	*1s 6d*
2 shifts	*4s 0d*
A calico sheet	*4s 6d*
A muslin handk.	*2s 1d*
5 caps and a muslin handk.	*3s 8d*
A silk gown	*9s 3d*
An old silk inner garment	*2s 7d*
A red cloak (old)	*1s 3d*
A good petty coat	*5s 8d*
4 other old petty coats	*4s 0d*
A silk bonnet	*1s 0d*
A box	*1s 1d*

Mrs Quill's contributions seemed uniformly benign, set against the normal duties of the Poor House. There were other, more ruthless gestures than that of simple care and charity. Part of the provisions of the Poor Law was that the parish officers could return to his place of birth any man, together with his family, who became chargeable to the rates. The fear that certain disreputables would lodge with them for ever on their charity instilled such fear in the minds of the parish authorities that they exercised their powers harshly and often at substantial expense.

Coachman to carry Richard Dean and family	*£17 3s 0d*
Returned to Huntingdon. Travel expenses	*£1 12s 7d*

'Mr Cruitt!' Grange called.

After a suitable pause Cruitt emerged from the curtain.

Grange waited until he approached the table. 'This entry here.'

'Which one, sir?'

'Coachman to carry Richard Dean. These are high costs merely to return a man.'

Cruitt coughed, moved his mouth. 'It is considered by the overseers that the longer the journey, the less likely the person is to return.'

'A longer journey is a good investment, then.'

Cruitt ignored the trace of sarcasm. 'The overseers have emphasised their belief in long journeys, sir. It is for me to make the arrangements.'

'And this?' Grange raised the matter discursively. His finger indicated the entry.

> *Matthew Chorley not returned. Inquiry upheld.*
> *Expenses of*   *£3 13s 8d*

'What are you asking, sir?' Cruitt wished to know.

'If there is no travel, why such expenses?'

'Justices of the peace, sir. After the inquiry, they were fed and entertained.'

'And this?'

It was the reason he had summoned Cruitt, though he was determined to raise it casually and obliquely.

'Which, sir?'

Grange's finger pointed at the entry just beneath.

> *Expenses defrayed courtesy of Mrs Celia Quill.*

Cruitt looked up, swallowed. 'What aspect of it, sir?'

'Who is Matthew Chorley?'

'Matthew Chorley?' Cruitt paused on the edge of suspicion, but appeared to find no ground on which he could prevaricate further. His lower jaw drifted, it seemed to Grange, independently. He moved his mouth again, seemed to struggle for expression.

'Mr Chorley,' Grange reminded him softly.

'He is the son of Mrs Quill's cook.'

'What is her cook's name?'

'Mary Chorley, sir.'

'Mrs Quill interceded on her son's behalf?'

'He had taken some trouble upon himself.'

'What trouble would that be?' Grange asked. He was determined

to give Cruitt no chance of hesitation. Some of his mannerisms –
the elaborate swallowings, the pained rectitude, the careful and
meticulous parsimony – appeared to his questioner as further
techniques of delay.

'He stole, sir.'

'Stole what?'

'Some objects, sir. I do not recall.'

'From whom?'

'From Mrs Quill.'

'But if he stole, was it not a criminal matter?'

'Mrs Quill . . .' Cruitt was swift at least in this, apparently aiming
to forestall. 'Mrs Quill made him return what he had taken and
wrote to the Magistrates herself in apology for his misdeeds.'

'Even so . . .' Grange knew the consequences of theft, from long
imprisonment to deportation to a penal colony. He said, for
emphasis, 'If there was a charge of theft he would be tried for it.'

'She used her influence to obtain a written apology from the
youth. She stated that he borrowed the items from her, and was
merely tardy in their return.'

'The Magistrates accepted her intervention?'

'She was the affected party, sir. No charges were preferred.'

It was another indication of the force of her character and the
calm zeal of her self-righteousness.

'Then why did the overseers attempt to transport him from the
parish?'

'The overseers', Cruitt said, 'took a stricter view of him than Mrs
Quill.'

'When no legal charges were preferred, the overseers took
matters into their own hands, is that what you say? And arranged
for him to be deported?'

'Until she confronted them herself,' Cruitt said, 'and pleaded his
case.'

'Pleaded again?'

'They only accepted her plea on his behalf if she would promise
surety on the boy.'

'Which she did?'

Cruitt nodded.

And so Grange approached the question. 'This woman, the boy's mother, she lives locally?'

'Sir?' Cruitt was surprised at the sudden switch in direction. His Adam's apple bobbled alarmingly and it seemed to Grange that he heard again the strange movement of internal forces, the slight clack of Cruitt's tongue, spittle sliding down his oesophagus. Cruitt examined him now, one eye incredulous – this cold interloper, who seemed prepared to frighten those he did not impress.

'These are the same Chorleys of Pilley?'

'Sir.'

'The place of pagans. The street?'

'I could look it up, sir, in the supplementary listings.'

'You have a scholar's memory, Mr Cruitt. I place my faith in your recollection.'

Cruitt's strange physiognomy moved again, the engineering of his jaw, tongue, the flutter of his throat, his obscure sense of outrage at the line of questioning balanced against his curiosity, challenged now. 'Hendon Lane. The first of the three cottages. On the right-hand side after the turning into Hendon Lane.'

'Thank you, Mr Cruitt. I return the ledgers to your good offices.'

Cruitt nodded, swallowed again and with a solemn intensity watched the tall physician turn and leave. He observed Grange pass through the inner and outer doors like a draught of cold air, as though suspicious he might change his mind and return to interrogate him again.

CHAPTER 54

My dear Leman,

Now that I have reported to you my more immediate news, and the circumstances in which I have recovered my physical equanimity, I believe it is incumbent upon me, more than ever, in the respite to which I am temporarily confined to continue with the story of Celia Quill – that fiction of my own mind, who became flesh and blood, who returned thereafter to remind me of my past sins, and whose most recent chastisement of my soul has been a bruising on my face and a sprained ankle, administered by her former lover and protector.

I have forgiven him fully for his intransigence. I believe he was overtaken by the speed of his own thoughts and vented the conclusion upon my person. These are the barest disclosures. In mitigation of his behaviour, I see now that there were other thoughts that might have exacerbated his reaction. For among them there might have been the notion that the child she carried away in her belly was the same young woman for whom my younger colleague had developed an infatuation, without knowing that she was perhaps my daughter. For such are the complexities that now return upon us.

I have told you the rest, as much at least as I believe you would wish to know. I was struck down and am now almost fully recovered, though I feel the persistence of some bruising occasioned by my fall, and a certain stiffness in my bones and joints when I ride a horse.

But these are mere physical aspects of a somewhat minor nature. There are other matters which shall continue to haunt us. You may judge the distant nature of the relations between Mrs Quill and myself after she came to Lymington, and my observance of her privacy, when you consider that despite all my curiosity on the subject and the hopes which I had of an offspring, I did not conceive that I had the right to ask her if the young woman who is her daughter is also mine. From this you may also consider, after all that had passed between us, the strange depth of my respect for her independence. For though my paternity may be in question, yet I do consider that she, having raised her child without any outside support, holds the right to the young woman's future, and it is I who must stand aside in order to allow a natural justice in the matter of priority.

You will understand the turmoil I felt when I saw that young woman and attempted to perceive in passing whether her own features or spirit bore any resemblance to my own. These impressions now rain upon me.

Such memories are like confessions. They raise the former terrors of my soul. I am exhausted by the expression of them. You will forgive me if I cease from further toil at my letters this day, for my current discomforts absorb my energy as though they were a sponge.

In the meanwhile, sir, I remain,

Sincerely yours,

Hargood

CHAPTER 55

While he hunted for traces of Mrs Quill, the salt furnaces continued to haunt Grange's imagination. They formed a kind of background or backcloth to all his activities. In the remaining three furnaces, even at night, the white shadows of men fed the fires. At the height of the season forty tons of salt had been produced by evaporation every day, nineteen bushels of coal burned for each ton. Fire, oxygen, water, salt – these were the elements of perhaps the greatest single concentration of industry on earth. Lymington was its black lung, and he who, more than any other, had been its presiding physician was now once more confined to a spectator's place, observing the remaining three fires burn like white stains in the darkness on the foreshore.

He was occasionally provoked to pursue a more active role. On one of the walks that it had become his habit to take in the evening he was crossing a stile gate across a footpath, when a strange odour touched his nostrils; rancid, tinged with smoke and sweat, unmistakably human. He thought it might be some poor vagrant or vagabond, lying in a ditch. On emerging on the other side of the stile, he had already begun to cast his eyes over the terrain with the vague aim of identifying the source of the odour when he heard a jingle, as of keys and, looking up in the direction from which it came, saw, perhaps some forty feet away, faintly outlined, a group of men in the half-light. They had no energy or animation and seemed to him more like ghosts. Perhaps because of his own appearance, they had drawn to a halt beside some elder bushes. As his eyes adjusted to the darkness, he began to perceive, from the wretched state of their clothes, that they were a gang of furnace workers returning to the marshes. Standing a little to one side, observing him, was the overseer, whose features he now recognised as those of Jacob Reynolds, a local Pennington man.

With the light behind him, Grange would have been visible to Reynolds's eyes, whereas the overseer and his party were largely invisible to him against the dark mass of the land and trees behind. Having seen him cross the stile, Reynolds appeared to have halted his group with a raised hand and waited for the tall physician to pass. Yet the fact that Reynolds and his men stood off at a little distance, as though avoiding proximity, excited some attention in Grange, some call to investigate the source of their behaviour. He approached them carefully.

'Mr Reynolds?' Grange enquired.

The overseer did not answer, but merely nodded his head in brief affirmation.

'You are on your way to the furnaces, I see.'

The overseer was silent.

Grange looked at the men behind him. Several were leaning to one side. One appeared to hold on to another for support. The strong stench of sweat and beer affronted his nostrils.

Grange said, in affable observation, 'I believe your men are so filled with alcohol they can hardly stand.'

Reynolds nodded briefly, as though acknowledging a melancholy truth, then he added, 'But they can walk, sir, as you see.'

The line of men stood staring morosely forward over one another's shoulders. They were partly lit by light from the marsh furnaces on their faces and hands. Grange continued, 'They do not seem to be in much of a condition to work, however.'

'That's a matter of opinion,' Reynolds said.

Behind the overseer the men were as still as shadows themselves, as if waiting for the outcome of this confrontation. They regarded Grange without emotion.

'You vouch for them?'

'They vouch for themselves.' Reynolds stared at Grange implacably.

'Given their state of inebriation,' Grange persisted, 'I believe you should allow them a day at least to recover.'

Reynolds coughed. 'That's as may be, sir.'

'You disagree?'

Grange noticed the hardening in Reynolds's jaw, the trace of tension in the moonlight. 'If you would be so kind as to step aside, sir, we will proceed to our work.'

Grange said, 'You have not answered my question, Mr Reynolds.'

Reynolds paused and for a moment Grange thought that he was about to push past him. But there was something intimidating about the tall physician, who stood dark against the flames of the three furnaces behind him, his gaunt body outlined by light, his face in partial shadow.

'Why do you not ask them directly?' Reynolds suggested suddenly.

It seemed to Grange that he had no choice but to accept the challenge. He nodded to the overseer, then stepped past him and walked down the line.

The smell which assailed him was a blend of wood smoke, sweat and alcohol. He wondered if this was how the ancient slaves had offended the air, trailing in chains after caravans, or working in forgotten mines.

Grange announced aloud, 'Your foreman gives you permission to return for a day and rest.'

'Without pay,' Reynolds called out into the night air.

'Without pay,' Grange conceded.

There was hardly a whisper. Grange had never seen figures so immobile. The silence was unsettling, not least because he began to observe in it the first signs of the imposition of Reynolds's will over his men. To gain time, as much as anything else, Grange began to walk further down the line, so that he might address the stragglers at the rear. As he moved past them he examined the faces as best he was able in the fading light. He recognised several as former patients. One in particular – a middle-aged former cobbler – he had attended on several occasions in the man's cramped house. As he moved down the line the men stared back at him. The features on which he looked were partly lit by the fires on the marsh, their faces darkened by dirt, their eyes reddened with weariness. Several were too far gone in drink to hold his own gaze.

One of the sub-overseers at the rear, taking advantage of the pause, casually turned sideways, reached inside his clothes for himself and began to urinate copiously on the path. If he were to continue his line of inspection, Grange would have been forced to walk through the vitreous, glinting stream. As it was, he turned calmly, as if by his own independent volition, and walked back without haste to the foreman.

'I believe you have won this day, Mr Reynolds,' Grange said, 'though I do not approve of your use of artillery.'

'I was once a bombardier, sir,' Reynolds acknowledged. He spat out a stream of saliva.

'Indeed.'

'We learn to use what weaponry we have.'

Grange nodded. He stepped aside. Slowly the column began to move and the men drifted past. Several of them glanced at the tall figure of the physician as he leaned on his cane and surveyed them, one side of his face lit by the light from the marshes, the other in darkness. No one laughed or sneered at his defeat, if only because they did not possess the energy.

CHAPTER 56

Hargood wiped the black dust from his window-sill, tracing Lymington's history. 'We are directly downwind of the salt furnaces here.' He turned to face Grange. 'Here in my manor house, in its own country, in its private grounds, yet I might be in the smoke of the capital.'

'Given the attractions of London to one who keeps a mistress there,' Grange said, 'that is surely a compliment.'

Hargood smiled, but proceeded unimpeded. 'This layer of grime that overlays everything – everything that we touch – it is like the notion of sin, is it not?'

'How so?'

'Sin, the inexhaustible pollutant. Yet I find its traces strangely comforting. Perhaps that sounds odd. It is as though, if it did not exist, I should have to seek it elsewhere.'

'In London perhaps,' Grange suggested slyly.

'London indeed. No, my dear fellow, that is merely where my mistress finds herself, as the French say. That is not where I seek my sin.' He looked at Grange's face. 'I see you hardly comprehend me.'

Grange did not speak, so Hargood continued, 'I believe that I carry my sins with me, as we all do.'

'I am not so familiar with the notion of sin.'

'As an atheist, then, you have no private sense of sin?'

'In the sense that there is someone who will judge me, none whatsoever.'

'Not even in the most basic sense, of tempting some outside order?'

'None.'

'Your conscience?'

'My conscience is internal. It is part of myself. It will perish with me.'

'I do not know whether you are fortunate or unfortunate,' Hargood said. 'My sin, on the other hand, is in the mind of my Creator and, I suspect, eternal.'

'No wonder, then, that it is so attractive.'

'Attractive?'

'When you sin,' Grange replied, 'you register in some great eternal mind. If I sin I merely flout my own small conscience.'

'My own arrangement is the better, it seems to me.'

'I believe Mrs Quill had something to say on the matter.'

'She did?' Hargood was surprised to hear her mentioned so directly. Her presence continued to underlie much of their conversation, but after their more recent exchanges Grange seldom brought up her name without direct incitement. Yet now he was prepared to raise her name at will.

'She claimed that the presence of women in high office would bring gentleness, harmony. The mothers of men would not send them to war.'

'And what of our great queen, Elizabeth the First? What of

Boudicca? Whenever women reach high office, we may enjoy a brief period of greatness, it is true – but of war and agitation, not harmony.'

'Is that so?'

'Who is France's greatest woman? Joan of Arc, no less – who so badly misunderstood the English, and who so rudely curbed our little forays onto foreign fields.'

'She was not a monument to the pacific, I grant you.'

'I will say this. Women look at the problems directly, with greater honesty than men. As we have said before, sir, if Elizabeth had not taken upon herself to institute the Poor Laws, and had not made it the duty of every parish to provide for the impoverished within our boundaries, I dare say our land would have gone the way of France, and subsided under revolution.'

'She brought harmony, then – though in the longer term.'

'The longer term!' Hargood was incensed. 'Every imp and devil of a dissenter claims to be able to bring harmony in the longer term. The French revolutionists claimed the goal of a future harmony – though in the short term, of course, they must manufacture blood in every hedgerow.'

'You speak with vehemence.'

'I lost several good friends in the Quiberon expedition.'

To shift the subject from this impasse, Grange said, 'We are losing individuals almost weekly to the salt furnaces.'

Hargood paused. 'Directly?'

'Few of them perish on the marshes, it is true. I have attended their bedsides when they were shrunk from loss of liquid. They develop other complications: a yellowness of the skin, which seems to herald some disruption of the liver.'

'And then they perish?'

'If they continue to work and replace their liquids with alcohol.'

'They know the risks they run.'

'As did those, I believe, on the Quiberon raid,' Grange said. 'If there were some means of arresting those who have reached a certain state . . .'

'These are free men, sir,' Hargood replied. 'It is part of their liberty to abuse their own beings. I may mourn the dead of the

Quiberon, but I do not prevent them from doing what they conceive to be their duty.'

'But I have attended to these abused beings. And when I recommend desistence from the habits that cause their condition they use exactly the argument that you do.'

'That they are free men? There is much that is robust in our workers.'

'They are not so robust when they are dead.'

'We are all good Englishmen,' Hargood stated. 'We know that our liberty has a price, and most of us, when we come to it, are prepared to pay it.'

At first it seemed to Grange that the remark was merely another generalisation designed to annoy or enrage him, and to cause further entertainment for Hargood. But he had an intuition that Hargood meant something different by it from simple provocation. It was only afterwards, on his way home, that he began to wonder whether the price Hargood believed every Englishman had to pay for freedom had a particular significance for his host, a personal significance that extended, perhaps, beyond mere rhetoric.

CHAPTER 57

Dear Leman,

I have not spoken much before of Lymington, for we take for granted what is familiar. Yet each day that I gaze out over my surrounds I find the scene is changing. Though I know that it is my mind which changes, yet I perceive it in those terms which are the simplest and perhaps the most childish, as if external circumstances do arrange themselves to fit my moods.

I have spent a happy life here. For as long as I may remember, the salt furnaces have burned through our summers, and the dark cloud, the shadow out to windward, has been a source of reassurance to me, as evidence of our communal life and our continuing commerce with the world. I ask myself even now, what would we be without it, except a small hamlet by a river whose harbour mouth is daily more silted? That is how I have regarded such manifestations. The poor wretches who work the furnaces may deserve our sympathy, and the acrid smoke which falls on the town may sometimes blow into our eyes and ears. But in this world there are few gains without losses and fewer achievements without sacrifices. *Sufficient unto the day is the evil thereof.*

We have other blessings, for which we should be grateful.

The land here is not flat, but flows in gentle hills, covered with meadows and woods. I have regarded this bountiful hearth, with grass on her slopes and cheeks, as the repository of my hopes and the ease of my fears, for are not we English embedded in such gentle earth? Is not the very word 'gentleman' also *de facto* much the same as 'landed'? I do not mean by 'landed' the same thing as ownership – I mean rather the broader privilege of living in the rural community, of taking some part in it and drawing peace from its ancient traditions. These verities, I earnestly believe, arise from that mystical communion of land and nature, the one feeding the other. And so I ask this: lying beneath our religion (which is of a pragmatic and somewhat dispassionate nature) is not our local earth our deeper saviour? And when we measure our lives, shall our souls be emptied of these glimmering moments we have spent upon her surfaces?

When I repeat these verities to myself, when I seek to reassure my own doubts, I find that same mind which I address is not listening, is not attentive, as though some part of it is focused on another place. Since this audience is myself who, in normal circumstances, am inclined to see common sense, and since no one is more sensible of the virtue of my own arguments than I am, I should expect myself to be persuaded. But I am not. A doubt lingers, and that doubt seems to grow, like a cloud on the horizon. Since I am not persuaded, a part of me begins to despair of both reason and instinct.

The clouds pass over us, but they do not leave us untouched. I have mentioned to you before that, like those shadows which are thought to loosen from the earth and drift away, something of me is loose. I remember that the Marquis de Puysegur, that follower and disciple of Mesmer, has spoken of the second mind, that secret mind that lies beneath our thinking and our spoken thoughts. I am drawn to that image now, if only because whatever is loosened is not immediately clear to me. I must await its consequences and assess its dispositions upon me. I, who am impatient of anything that does not flow directly from my own actions, whose daily habit has been to rise and impress himself upon the world, must now begin to acquiesce to circumstance.

These are trying times, my dear friend, and it requires some struggle in me to achieve that patience which is now required of me, and to which I have not had much recourse in the past. And this is why, to return to the subject of these letters, I continue to observe my younger colleague with such careful attention. For there is something in both our behaviours which leads me to suspect the truth of de Puysegur's dictum. The second mind, which lies beneath the first, inhabits each of us. It is more secretive, perhaps more obscure, and we must come to terms with its hidden workings.

In the meantime, sir, we all must play our role in life and I suppose that it is the true burden of my belief that the role we play is everything, that it gives us our position in society, our standing and, at the same time, our obligations and responsibilities. I did believe, and much of me still does, that there is nothing beyond this role – indeed, that anything which subverts it is inimical to the natural order. The notion that there is a second presence beneath the manifest exterior is an uncomfortable one, for it suggests, too, an alternative disposition to the prevailing arrangements.

These thoughts, which exercise me as I write, would not have made much impression on my former self. To the extent that they do so now, I believe that they are themselves evidence of my changing circumstances.

I shall not seek to trespass further on your time and patience with more disquisitions, but shall post this to you in the hope that you will forgive me these additional transgressions.

I remain, sir,

    Most sincerely yours,
      Hargood

CHAPTER 58

In the final part of September there was an easing of the weather, a late extension of the summer. For two weeks the days grew thick and hot.

Grange made his way up Hundreds Hill in the gold light that fell through the maples. Crossing the top of the rise, he could see a bend of the Lymington river, and the flash of metal in the traffic of carts and horses on Lymington High Street. The earth seemed warm from the sun; he could feel the glow of it on his forehead, cheeks, wrists, hands.

There was was no central track or highway through Pilley; rather, it was arranged in so random a manner that one path might lead to another, and the individual walker who knew the district less well could easily become lost. In the gardens or plots of the small cottages, women worked or sometimes leaned on the fence and looked towards the setting sun. He passed a number of smallholdings that held enclosures for cows, sheep, chicken, goats; nearly all had pigeon cotes and beehives, the latter always to the south of the houses, in the warmest places. He walked briskly, but the earnestness of his endeavour could not alter the geography of the place, the way that one path seemed to drift into another, or the manner in which the same path would round a house or hedge and depart in another direction towards a wood or a meadow, as if it had been taken by a different mood.

Unwilling to ask advice in any form, he was forced by circumstances to seek directions to the Chorleys' house. When they saw his formal dress, his informants seemed to pause and spoke carefully, choosing their words, as though to someone who was lost, or perhaps to a child.

He was aroused from his meditation when a lurcher dog ran across the pathway. It glanced back at him, as though he were an intruder, opened its mouth as if to bark, then seemed to think better of it and disappeared through an unseen gap in the tangled hedgerows. He heard voices of women working in the fields, though he could not see them. Sight seemed detached from sound.

He searched down several paths for the Chorley house, asking the occasional passer-by for guidance. Directions again were sought and given, as if to a child, and he pursued the diverse pathways they had specified.

In due course he found what at first appeared to be several mounds and were in fact cottages. As he drew closer, he saw that they had thatched roofs, but there was so much ivy, grasses and ferns, they almost merged with the unkempt garden plots. He knocked at the door of one of them. At first there was no sign of the inhabitants. He turned to look around at the surrounding plot. Disused and scavenged wagons lay, wheel-less and axle-less, in the fast-growing weeds. While he waited, staring out at the sunshine falling through the straggling oaks that lined the periphery of the garden plots, someone must have raised the latch quietly and surreptitiously because, while he had turned away, slowly the door had opened, apparently of its own accord.

The creature who stared back at him – at first he could hardly see whether she was a woman – merged into the dark interior of the hovel. He could glimpse only her eyes.

'Mrs Chorley?' Grange asked. The doorway was so low that he was forced to crouch.

She did not speak, but surveyed him carefully. He was aware of her studying the details of his clothing.

Grange said, 'Are you perhaps . . . ?'

He cut himself short. As his eyes adjusted to the gloom in which she stood, he could see in the face blackened with soot that she herself was younger, far younger, than Mrs Chorley could ever be. At the same time the figure in the doorway seemed to have taken stock of him. At last she volunteered. 'You want my mother?'

'Is she here?' Grange asked, and then, perhaps a little too earnestly, 'May I speak to her?'

'She isn't here.'

'Could you tell me when she might return?'

'What business was it you wanted to speak on?'

'Her son, Matthew.'

Grange was aware again of her intense inspection of him.

Then something happened inside the hovel. Some further presence he had not suspected moved across the wooden floor. He could hear the faint shuffle of feet. He was aware of a shadow that seemed to spread across the door jamb. Then the door slammed, suddenly and hard.

He stood out in the open, breathing deeply to steady his violent surprise.

CHAPTER 59

Dear Leman

Several times since my last communication I have attempted to put pen to paper regarding my actions in relation to Miss Celia Quill, but the memories again reared up so fresh that I found myself lost in a kind of contemplation, and my anguish in turn was so intense it seemed to expunge the thought of writing from my mind.

Several days have passed, and I have recovered my composure sufficiently to continue.

What helped in my discomfort after the abrupt and final departure of my mistress was precisely that other event in my life which replaced it – namely, my marriage to my betrothed, Eleanor. I attempted to displace my distress through my attentions to her.

In the emotions, it is said, we should use fire to burn out fire, water to drown water, air to displace air. The ardour of my attendance on my future wife was not diminished, but enhanced by, the loss of my mistress. Thus in the two months before we would be married I was especially considerate of her and visited her every day as soon as my duties were over. She was the most charming of souls, high in spirits despite her frailty, a most perfect mate and equal. I watched the colour rise in her pale cheeks when she saw me, and her beautiful eyes that regarded me with both emotion and amusement.

The days proceeded towards our marriage. Eleanor, as I knew only too well, was popular with our local society, who valued her for her gentleness and consideration. She had gained her friends and accomplices through natural kindness and acts of good character. Even among those in whose stocks I had never been high, owing to my prevarication before marriage, I achieved a rare enhancement of my reputation.

Thus, we advanced our preparations. We were married in Boldre church by the Reverend Gilpin. Her father gave her into my safe keeping, and I proceeded towards my home with my new bride on my arm.

I believe that, taking into account the measure of human weakness and frailty, our marriage was as happy as ever I could have expected. There were days when she was frail, sometimes too frail to rise from her bed, and I would sit by her in a state of happiness and would read to her from a novel or play cards. I had never entertained the greatest hopes of a spiritual union in marriage, but once I had experienced an intimation of that true union of souls, I discovered I had practical cause to change my mind. For if a marriage is blessed, I believe that some part of the woman enters the man's spirit and character. It is difficult for a man, particularly one such as I, to speak easily of love, but I experienced that yearning of one soul for another, which is only fulfilled when they are conjoined in one another's company.

Our language may convey depression and despair, rage and fortitude more easily than the subtle beauty of life, which is as intense as it is fleeting. For where pain is fierce and specific, happiness would seem to lie in subtler and more harmonious relations. But if to describe happiness is beyond the poor efforts of this writer and this pen, I record merely that for the first time in my life I was fulfilled, and had no further expectations than those which I already felt. So we started to settle to our existence, and I began for the first time to invest the full meaning and terms of my days in another's company.

Her health continued to be fragile, and I believed with her father that we could not contemplate the idea of children. Before we were married, he warned me of her frailty. He made it clear that he was passing on a sacred charge, from one to another, and in turn I assured him, with perfect sincerity of heart, that I intended to patrol my responsibilities with the utmost care. But Eleanor was determined upon a different course. She was set on having a child, even if it put her life at risk. If there was one difficulty between us, it was this. As a physician I warned her of the extreme danger to her state of health, and quoted to her, when occasion demanded, the terms of her father's trust in me. She merely smiled at my determination and reassured me that, for the time being at least, we would desist from raising a family. Thus, with this temporary conjunction and agreement, we were able to avoid for several years what seemed the hidden threat of her desire for children.

I have said that I believe these were the happiest years of my life. I do not know what your views may be on such fulfilment, but since I have had time to consider the matter, and to differentiate between that and other times, it seemed to me that for once my character was whole, that my very disparate worlds became united, that I moved without a barrier from my work to my household and the community among which, suddenly, I began to feel a part. I cannot remember that happiness in any other existence. It had no centre. Perhaps because it lay not in any concrete thing, but in the abstract relation between so many aspects of my life, I could not grasp its essence and cannot do so now. Though its presence moved about us, like the invisible wings of an angel, it is not etched, like certain pains or vicissitudes, on my memory. I can only perceive in retrospect, by means of what you might call deduction, or rather by the memory of its effects, that it existed it all.

Our happiness might have lasted, but events conspired to place barriers in our path. Some time into our marriage I started to observe the symptoms of a changed state in my wife, and to realise that Eleanor was with child. I questioned her and she told me it was so. I remember that she looked into my face when she told me and studied my expression, searching for those doubts which I had uttered regarding her soundness of constitution.

Now began a time of waiting, for she was both nervous and exhilarated. I had never seen upon her face such calm joy. Her father shared my nervousness, but he did not blame me, since he knew as well as I of her desire for a family, irrespective of the risk.

My own fears increased as the pregnancy continued. I could see that she suffered more than usual from sickness, though she bore it with a calm demeanour. But however much her spirit might triumph over the circumstances, when it came to the final days the complications ensued and began to multiply. Suspecting such beforehand, I asked Dr Ignatius Harrison, a foremost authority on childbirth at the College of Physicians, to visit us from London for a week. As her confinement drew closer, he agreed to stay on for a few more days. It was he who supervised her delivery, and I may at least swear that if any one person were to save her, it would have been he.

These matters I now record. The baby, a girl, was stillborn. My dear angel of a wife died after eight days of pain, during which she grew progressively weaker. I remember her face, void of all emotion, as she settled into death.

Of the days of happiness all that remains is a vague presentiment of its elusive presence. What I remember is my beloved's final hours, at her bedside while her life ebbed away. There was no life in her eyes and, while I waited there through the afternoon, I felt only the last faint pulse in her hand.

I cannot remember much of the two or three months which followed. I must have continued a routine, for there are entries in my notebooks, though I recall writing few of them. We learn to survive as we must.

Leman, since writing in the aftermath, I attempt to justify my behaviour. We each of us have a sufficiently detached view of the affairs of our fellow man to be unsurprised at the dispositions of life. Throughout my life, I wished for a wife towards whom I would direct my affection and respect, and a mistress for my bodily needs. These delineations are arbitrary, I would agree, but are they any more arbitrary than that other view – that a single woman should be both our respected partner and the object of our most physical desires? If my own wishes were impractical, is not this latter ideal – that one woman shall embody everything – even more unlikely?

I believe still that a man may seek more than one woman in his life. It is a theme, perhaps, which runs through our male disposition. You, who understand this, will also understand that within three months of the departure of Celia Quill, and in the first month of marriage to my beloved Eleanor, I had installed a second mistress in the house at Chiswick, a young woman who had grown tired of the role of governess, and who was happy enough to exchange her straitened circumstances for a set of good clothes and a measure of material security.

You may wonder at my disbursement. Yet we make what we can of our lives. I made a promise to my dear wife's father that I would not harm his daughter's health with my physical demands, and I attempted to be true to my promise by the best means that I could achieve on this imperfect earth. My mistress was not a close companion of my mind, like Celia Quill, but she satisfied those physical needs, and I was thus better able to fulfil my role as Eleanor's protector. I believe still, and am haunted by the notion, that if she had not been determined to have a child, my good wife and I could have continued thus for the duration.

Who knows what strange accounts one manages with our Maker? I have set down a few thoughts on the blessed memory of my wife, and I believe I do truth no disservice by describing a goodness which amounted almost to saintliness in her. Yet if I took what care I could to save her, did she not herself jeopardise our marriage by knowingly risking her life in favour of a child, despite all advice to the contrary? Such matters are not my account, but must fall to the mercy of our Maker. In my own terms I took whatever precautions were necessary to protect her whom I held most dear.

Thus I bring to an end these disquisitions on the passage of my marriage. For though I may be affected by the virtue of women, I am also in essence the same, and it is this same colleague and acquaintance who now bids you adieu, and sends you his deepest respects.

I remain, sir, as ever,
    Sincerely yours,
        Hargood

CHAPTER 60

In October the weather began to harden. Mrs Thompson insisted that Grange put on extra leggings and heavy winter topcoat. Without the burning of the salt furnaces the eye found nothing to attach on the horizon to seaward – merely the cold grey sky. The mind sought vainly for relief across Oxey and the Pennington marshes. Only the fort of Hurst Castle intervened, and the thin grey streams of smoke from three of the furnaces that continued their work into the autumn.

The town, too, became cold, huddled in upon itself. In the afternoon long cold shadows spread across the street.

'Your broth, sir,' Mrs Thompson said.

Since he had forgone red meat, she surveyed his recovery with scepticism, assuming his thin diet would soon weaken him. He sipped the hot fish soup with as much show of apparent relish as he could muster, enjoying the double incentive of maintaining his diet against Hargood's recommendations, and of annoying his own strong-willed housekeeper.

On leaving the house, Mrs Thompson would say, 'I go now, sir, to the harbour market,' as if reminding him of the incongruity of his determination to continue with such a diet.

The fishermen brought mackerel and cod, halibut and bream, to the Lymington quay. There, beneath the clouds and crowding gulls, who feasted on the entrails carelessly spilt by the fishwives on the black cobbles, Mrs Thompson haggled for the freshest produce. Shrimps and whitebait lay in baskets and iron tuns. Sea-trout spread in rows on the black wooden boards gave off their delicate, dying bloom. Eels and sardines swam in barrels. The cloud of gulls turned in the thin sunshine.

Not wishing to bring the stink of fish into the hall and drawing-room, Mrs Thompson would enter discreetly by the back door of the house. She was not above rattling her boots against the grate with sufficient force to remind him of the absurdity of her mission before, with a deep sigh, she entered the kitchen.

'If men were meant to catch and eat nothing but fish, sir,' she told him, 'I do believe the Almighty would have given us fins.'

'Mrs Thompson,' Grange replied, 'I have noticed that the healthiest of our men in Lymington are precisely those who live on fish. They do not suffer from a variety of common ailments. There are few who are victims of overweight, or gout, or sudden attacks of the heart. If I lived entirely within a community of fishermen, instead of salt-makers, tradesmen and farmers, I believe that I would soon be out of my occupation.'

'Perhaps it would be a just and proper punishment, then,' Mrs Thompson said, 'for such a pitifully thin diet.'

He watched her return to the kitchen.

'I hear from a very good source', Hargood said, 'that you persist in your diet of fish.'

'I do indeed.'

'Do I not deserve an explanation?'

'There is a Statistical Survey of the Edibles of the Sea, from Aberdeen University, which indicates that fish are the healthiest of foods.'

Hargood drank, set his glass down, returned to knife and fork. 'Aberdeen is much reliant on the occupation of fishing, I do believe?'

'It is,' Grange confirmed.

'I merely note the fact,' Hargood went on, with a calm exterior, though some hint of something more than affirmation.

Grange allowed the pause to settle. 'I fail to see what you are driving at.'

'It is an unusual coincidence, is it not, that Aberdeen is a great sea-fishing port and, this being so, there should issue from Aberdeen University a survey which indicates that a diet of fish is the best for all men.'

'Are you suggesting complicity?'

'No, I am raising an interesting statistical fact, as connecting one matter with another,' Hargood told him with satisfaction. Implication was a mode he took up sometimes, as occasion allowed. It gave him the opportunity to create the maximum damage with the least risk to his own reputation. 'It is you who raise the subject of complicity.'

'In answer to your inference.'

'Your own inference,' Hargood insisted, well pleased at the course of his attack and inclined to polish off a few more foot soldiers of meat. 'Your own inference, I do believe.'

'It seems to me that in these assertions and inferences the original subject matter has become buried. Whether Aberdeen is a fishing port or not has little or no effect on the truth or otherwise of a statistical survey.'

'An interesting theory.' Hargood nodded. In the course of answering his colleague, he was always willing to grant to Grange's statements a speculative turn. 'Nor should we forget that Aberdeen is in Scotland.'

'Hargood, I fail . . .'

'In Scotland,' Hargood repeated, 'that source of wisdom at whose fountains you seem to drink a very considerable amount of liquid.'

'It is true that I was educated at Edinburgh, but that alone is not perhaps sufficient of itself to . . .'

'To indicate your affiliations? To establish the broad compass of your sympathies?'

When Hargood raised his glass to a toast, Grange noticed his host's eyeball observing him above the level of the liquid, like a calm sun above a horizon. The sun blinked several times. The glass was replaced on the polished surface with a certain tenderness; the heavy, handsome head sank downwards. It had become a ritual between them. As Hargood's temples touched the solid table wood softly, the dregs of wine wobbled in his glass, as from a mild but noticeable earth tremor. There was silence for a while. Then, a few minutes later, there issued from Hargood's mouth the sound of heavy snoring.

Grange finished the last few morsels on his plate, wiped his lips with his napkin, stood up quietly and walked towards the area of the kitchen where Simmonds and his wife were usually to be found.

He informed them what they no doubt surmised already – that their master was sound asleep and should not be disturbed. He was familiar enough with Hargood's habits to know that he hated to be woken and helped to bed. When Hargood woke of his own accord several hours later he would lift himself from the table, take one of the candelabra and in his own time go grumbling up the stairs to his sheets.

Simmonds accompanied Grange quietly to the door and handed him his greatcoat. 'It is cold, sir,' he whispered.

Grange nodded. Simmonds raised the cross-piece on the oak door and Grange stepped outside. In the porch Grange swung to face the old man and lowered his voice: 'How long do you allow him to sleep?'

'He usually wakes up of his own accord,' Simmonds answered, 'in an hour or two.'

'And then he sleeps in his room?'

'No, sir,' Simmonds replied. 'I believe it is his habit to write.'

'To write?' Grange had seldom been more surprised. It occurred to him briefly that if anyone had touched him with a feather at that precise moment, he would have laid his six and a half feet out flat and cold upon the boards.

Simmonds seemed impressed by the effect of his information. He was naturally kindly and, since he believed, perhaps rightly, that he addressed Hargood's greatest friend, he assumed that any knowledge of his master's habits would be treated both benevolently and circumspectly. 'I leave his fire burning in his bedroom and I think he writes, sometimes into the small hours.'

'This is a recent habit?' Grange asked. He wondered whether Simmonds would consider his interest too precise and demur from further discussion.

'A month or two, I believe.'

It seemed to Grange that if there were further evidence needed of a changed state in Hargood's mind it was surely this. Some aspect of his surprise had communicated itself to Simmonds, who watched him with his kind, shrewd eyes.

'Thank you, Mr Simmonds. I hope that you yourself are able to reach sleep without being forced to resort to writing.'

'I believe I can reach sleep by almost any path,' Simmonds said. 'Though I prefer some over others.'

The sentence had reached past Grange before he realised it was an amiable sexual innuendo, perhaps even a mild boast.

This was too much rich information in one night. Hargood the reclusive and secretive diarist; old Simmonds the satyr. The prospect of Simmonds capering atop the buxom Mrs Simmonds was an image Grange would normally have excluded from his mind, but now it merely brought a smile to his face.

'I am glad that life amuses you, sir.' Simmonds regarded him steadily from the door.

'You have been most considerate,' Grange said. 'I believe I shall depart now.'

Simmonds nodded. Grange turned and began to strike out along the pathway. Out of courtesy, Simmonds waited a few seconds before he closed and bolted the heavy main door behind him.

Dewfall on the fields had frozen and turned them white. Stars shone in a clear black sky, like an accusation. Perhaps, Grange thought, they represented clarity, the scientist's presumed state of mind.

CHAPTER 61

My dear Leman,

After the perturbations of the last week my younger colleague has sealed into himself again. A surface of good relations has been established between us. He becomes drier still – more internal, more withdrawn, more driven.

He has accepted, no doubt partly in recompense for his outbreak of violence, my injunction that he should desist from returning to his patients for another month, on the grounds that he should allow his constitution to settle. Though he makes good physical progress, he accepts that it is the interior wounds which now must be provided with an opportunity to heal.

As I have recovered from my own physical chastisements, I have had a chance to reflect on my situation. I believe violence is the most basic of human communications, that final resort of the fearful and frustrated soul, and I have resolved to do all I am able never again to place him in that position – of feeling, even for a terrible moment, that it represents the only expression between us of his private torment. In the meanwhile, having been given an advance warning, so to speak, against withholding information from him, though our relations remain cautious, there would seem to be a new clarity of understanding between us. This in itself is not a settled matter, but takes the form, rather, of an expectation of good behaviour on both our parts.

Such clarification, bought at the price of some suffering, raises other perspectives. On several occasions now, my younger colleague and I have discussed the view of the Marquis de Puysegur on the 'second mind'. In the course of our walks we have joked between us on the subject. I have objected to his obsessive sense of privacy, to his protection of his thoughts, and demanded, in the interests of advancing his condition, that he be less circumspect in his communications with me. Yet in considering that strangely rich allegory of de Puysegur, I am struck by the notion that the violence which my younger colleague committed against me, which seemed to rise from a part of his character beyond control, perhaps represents that primitive communication of the second mind. For it reached out like a strike of lightning between us. And when I had recovered from its sudden and terrible assault, when the first stench of burned air had receded and I found myself still alive – though somewhat chastened – I considered myself to be the witness of an expression of that second mind.

But I have a further view, which follows from the reverberations of the first. We humans use what means we can to come at the mystery of our existence. I begin to wonder to what extent de Puysegur, that secular scientist and rationalist, is engaged in pursuing the same notion as we Christians when we mention the soul – that other being which lives beneath the outward physical expression, mysteriously directing our deepest desires. And I wonder, again, to what extent the great and rational Marquis, in an excess of enquiry, has provided my younger colleague and myself with a means of communication concerning the same thing.

I digress again, sir, upon philosophy. Suffice it to say that in the meanwhile I have recovered some of my equanimity. And though my colleague is no less mysterious to me, I believe that some barrier has been crossed between us and that in future, fate willing, we may proceed towards a closer understanding of the views that continue to divide us.

I remain, sir, as always,

Yours sincerely,

Hargood

CHAPTER 62

Winter took hold of the Lymington foreshore, turning it grey and gold.

Gulls and petrels drifted like the storm-lost. In the bay and around the river a grey sun picked up the glint of their wings.

On the shore at Oxey lay the heavy animal ribs and shattered timbers of a work boat. Pots, old boots, the remains of a smock, a horsehair mattress, floated in and out with tide. Along the foreshore hovered the putrid smell of rotting fish. Clouds of flies moved among the green weed. Beneath the surface glimmered white oyster shells.

Grange watched the herons, driving their spear points downwards into the grey. He paused, hovering. Some undertide, the itch of memory beneath the surface reflections, caused him to linger. But he found no purchase on his discontent. Whatever lurked shyly in his mind seemed to crouch hidden there.

He shook himself free of his temporary introspection and walked across the wide, empty marsh. The wooden houses on the foreshore were built on stilts, against the ingress of the high tides. Further out on the shore, spirals of smoke wound upwards from the salt furnaces.

'I do not know his calculations,' Swann stated, 'but it is said that he believes his investment is better used.'

'If he burns throughout the winter?'

Swann nodded. He looked out towards the shore. A swarm of gulls hovered above the easternmost of the three remaining boiler houses that were still in use. Sinking down against the dark land, the birds became almost invisible, until they rose up against the western light. An evening stillness had settled on the marshes.

'What interests you about them?' Grange asked gently.

At first Swann did not answer, but continued to gaze out to sea. 'I watch the boiler houses as I go about the shore.'

'But you have a specific in mind.'

Swann glanced at him, then away, speaking beneath his breath: 'It is a nice calculation, I think, that puts men's lives against profit.'

'The furnaces are dangerous?'

'Dangerous?'

The word was perhaps too large for Swann. Everything in his world contained its dangers. Grange saw that Swann had tried to assert something delicate, a doubt, and that Grange himself had sabotaged the intended meaning with too ambitious and perhaps too crude a word.

Ahead of them a furnace door was open, showing the hot heart of the flames. A line of white light limned Swann's cheek-bones, eye-sockets, the line of his forehead.

'Around each house,' Swann said, 'down to leeward there is a black area, where the grass has caught light from the sparks and burned away.'

'Fires have been started?'

'There are too many cross ditches and pieces of standing water for the fire to spread far.'

Grange paused to consider. 'Then what is dangerous? The furnaces?'

'The wind, sir.' Swann struggled with expression, or perhaps a complexity of emotions. 'They are landsmen. They don't know much about the wind.'

'You say that as a seaman?'

'Seamen, sir, do not often play with fire.'

'You speak in riddles, Mr Swann.'

Swann seemed to gather himself, assembling some argument before turning himself outwards again. 'The wind is seldom constant. It is full of holes and eddies. That is what they do not understand.'

'Why not?'

'They test the breeze, find it is small, then open the doors wide to bring more air to the flames. But the wind is not predictable, sir. It breathes in its own way.'

'Breathes . . .?'

'For example, it happens that the breeze often decreases before a gust.'

'I see.'

'They open the doors then, to let in more air.'

'It is a natural response, surely, to maintain the flow of air over the coals.'

'When the gust strikes, it brings more air than they had calculated for and the fire burns more fiercely. I believe you have seen once or twice a flame travel outwards from the doors, a long, soft flame like an angel's wing? It lasts hardly more than a second or two.'

'I have seen it,' Grange confirmed.

'Then you know of what I speak.'

Grange nodded. 'I have also seen the men move out of the boiler house when it occurs – at a run, admittedly.'

'They can do so when the flame occurs only once.'

Grange experienced an odd prickle of interest, an intuition. 'There are sometimes secondary flames?'

'The men know enough at least to keep to windward of the first flame.' Swann paused. 'The first flame seldom harms.'

'Why not?'

'If they close the doors, then the flame burns away the air, the fire is starved for a while, so the flame dies down.'

'Then,' Grange said, trying to follow Swann's thought, 'the

236

process would seem to be self-limiting.'

'For a few seconds, sir. Without a fire, the new air that rushes in does not burn immediately, except at a certain point. But when the hot coals ignite the fresh air that is now in abundance, the result can be another flame, only bigger than the last.'

Grange was held, for a moment, by the first strange intimation of the poetry of destruction. 'You say the danger occurs when they return and open the doors once more to the fire?'

'Depending on the wind. If the wind gusts as they open the doors to let in new air, a greater danger arises.'

Grange no longer prompted. He began to understand the infernal sense of rhythm, the fire taking its own breaths, the transformation of physical processes into some almost animate being. He stared out across the marshes, where the water was lit with the flame. 'That is what concerns you, then?'

'I have seen the process repeat itself several times, each time the pause is greater and the flame is larger. It becomes a kind of bellows, almost like an engine. I don't know what the end would be.'

'An explosion?' Grange was absorbed. 'You have seen an explosion?'

'I have seen men hurrying to close the doors. That is how they bring the process under control, by starving the fire of fresh air for the next flame.'

'So you have not observed the worst consequence?' Grange asked. 'In practice it is sufficiently controllable.'

'Most things are controllable, if we watch over them.'

Despite himself, Grange felt a sense of relief, as if cool air blew over his own heated imagination. He breathed the sea air. 'Swann, these discourses are very interesting. I believe you have a penetrating turn of mind. But even if those who work the furnaces do not understand the principles, or the unpredictable nature of the wind, it seems that they are able to take measures which prevent the final accident.'

'That is true, sir. There is much we control that we do not understand.'

Grange said softly, 'I believe that may be true of medicine as much as the manufacture of salt.'

Now the gulls around the furthest boiler house seemed to have dispersed. A stillness had settled over all the marsh.

'The point is, sir, there are fewer men now than there were in summer, a skeleton crew, and they are more tired and incapable.'

'Why so?'

Grange had asked the question almost out of courtesy. He believed he had interrogated Swann enough today. He glanced at his timepiece, and was about to bid Swann goodbye and turn for home, when Swann spoke again with an unexpected vehemence.

'They burn with a banker's economics.'

'Economics?' Grange was concerned not to sound surprised at this sudden intrusion. 'That is why they burn in winter?'

'Indeed.'

'To make profits?'

'I believe so.'

'Yet if profit were not a motive, the furnaces would not be there at all.'

'But they are there on reduced crews, sir. That is the economics. One day the men will not have the resource or strength to rush to close the doors.'

'The owner is not aware of the dangers?' Grange asked.

'Mr St Just?'

It seemed to Grange, in the silence that followed, that Swann was about to laugh, or even perhaps to utter some imprecation. A flicker in his eyes indicated the movement of another thought, tangential to the first. Swann spoke quite calmly, choosing his words: 'Mr St Just is a gentleman, sir.'

He was about to say something further and hesitated. There seemed to be some extra hidden criticism in the words. Grange suspected irony.

'What is your import?'

Challenged, Swann paused again, considered. 'Being a gentleman, sir, the actual machinery of the thing is not his business.'

Grange ignored the implied rebuke. 'His foreman, then. If Mr St Just lives in his own gentleman's heaven, should we not put our trust in his representative on earth?'

'Each foreman does the best with what he has.' It was

spoken without vehemence, but Swann's words were enough to carry force.

As a rule, Grange was slow to emotion. What he felt now was a general unease, sufficient to disturb him. Its location was the former sailor. Swann's intractability began to seem almost reasonable. He sensed he had been cornered by a crude but persistent consistency of argument.

Out on the marsh, someone must have stoked the fire. Sparks started to drift from the open door like a sheaf of fireflies. Grange watched the embers flying downwind. There was no grass there that had not been burned and nothing for the fire to catch. The sparks drifted across scorched earth and came to rest. It seemed to him again that certain processes were capable of controlling themselves, and this thought at least gave him a momentary respite in the aftermath of Swann's reasoning.

CHAPTER 63

My dear Leman,

Each day plunges me deeper into memories, and I am forced both to rehearse and to re-create the past in these limited letters.

In the continuation, I shall endeavour to give you an account of a development that arose during the time of my marriage, and which touches in turn upon the recent aspects of my life. For if you will forgive my examination of this matter, it has a bearing upon what follows.

During the time of my marriage, and in my widowerhood, I began to hear rumours of a certain lady who called herself Mrs Celia Quill. Since the addition of a 'Mrs' in front of her name clearly indicated a married woman, I did not at first consider, even idly, that this could be the same person who had left me in the circumstances I have described earlier. Besides, if she had married, according to custom, she would have taken the surname of her husband. These facts, taken together with the remoteness of the original surmise, indicated to me that the strangely familiar name was an incidence of mere chance, or what is sometimes called coincidence.

I heard that the personage in question was a woman of unusual charm and discretion, who ran one of those houses, numerous in London, which men of good fortune may visit to seek entertainment and relief. There were many other rumours and much gossip in the capital concerning such establishments in general. The faintness of this particular report provided no immediate incentive to investigate its truth.

In the course of the next few months, on my visits to London, I occasionally heard the name in conversation concerning the same married woman or widow. The reports accumulated slowly, but certain aspects began to excite my curiosity, and acted as a kind of counterweight against my predisposition to ignore the matter as an example of mere coincidence. I was visited by a faint unease, nothing more, concerning certain features of the subject. I knew my own Celia Quill well enough to believe that she was capable of almost any task or enterprise to which she might put her mind. At the same time, I did not believe any possible connection with the occupation of madam, for at the very least it seemed incongruous with her character that she would enter such a profession. There was something incorrigibly fine in her, on which I believe I have reported at some length in my previous correspondence. I had it firmly in mind that she would use her learning over some seven years as my mistress to find herself a post as governess in a reputable household and perhaps, thereafter, within this lowly paid but respectable calling, she would seek for herself a suitable husband – someone of a quiet disposition, who would accept her first offspring. I believed, as I believe now, that there was some power in her for goodness, a moral force that I had offended and which I suspected at a later stage would reassert itself in the establishment of her new life. For I have observed that if that which is truly fine is offended, it tends not to corrupt itself but, on the contrary, merely grows stronger.

There seemed, I repeat, no reason for me to investigate the rumour in its earliest manifestations. At the time it first reached my ears, I was in love with my wife and had installed my new mistress in my house at Chiswick, and thus I was, I believe, for a period of two years or so, a man at peace with the world. Though I regretted my former mistress's departure, the wound of her leaving had been healed, at least partially, by the resumption of my good fortune in other matters. I was simply a man who shuttled amiably and contentedly between Lymington and London, between true love and pleasure, observing the most auspicious aspects of both.

When fate acted against me and my wife departed this earth during childbirth, I was for several months plunged into despair. While I continued to maintain my mistress, during this period I did not call on her. (No doubt some would regard it as odd that I could visit her happily while my wife was alive, but curtail my visits after she died. But who among us knows the strangeness of human sentiments?) I believe the young woman was not insensible to my distress, and so there was something of a truce between us during that time, despite my lack of attention. She continued to receive her monthly allowance and in due course I started to see her again. So I settled once more into my old pattern of bachelorhood, even though I was considered a widower.

My practice prospered as much during this period as it had ever done. In the eyes of the community I had married, and it was only misfortune which had prevented me from living the contented life of a husband and father. There were those who were inclined to forgive my past indiscretions, now that I was a widower, for I have learned that in this country there is no greater excuse for respect than venerability. If we live long enough, sir, we may not only survive our misfortunes, but find that our lives are subject to a general reinterpretation. I received the deputations of sympathy from the matriarchs of this parish, who previously had no good to say upon my name.

If my past sins against the female sex were expunged, at least in the eyes of the community, there was yet another aspect which continued to haunt me. With the progress of time, and no further news of Celia Quill in any other respect, I became increasingly alerted as the rumours of this madam grew fuller, the designations and descriptions more exact. There were certain aspects of the reports which vied for my attention. For, compared with certain others of her profession, it appeared that this same Mrs Quill conducted herself both modestly and amiably, insisting on good manners towards her 'young ladies' and an atmosphere of some gentility in her house. I heard that when her young women were not in company they took lessons in music and needlework and, by these and other means, turned themselves into persons of refinement. If men sought lewd bawds, they went elsewhere. Whatever might be the common practice, the pleasures of this same Mrs Quill's establishment were reported to be more gentle. I heard one of my colleagues in London claim that in the drawing-rooms of her house there was such unaffected decorum he would hardly object if his own wife and daughters were raised in such an atmosphere.

Now, Leman, it began to seem to me that there was a pattern of fate in this which I started to perceive as wilful, if not ironical, though at the time I could not easily identify the direct source of my disquiet. I started to observe the trace of an outline, the shape of a sensibility which I recognised yet could not easily define. It occupied my mind in certain spare hours that this Mrs Celia Quill, this madam, might indeed be my own Celia Quill, whose name I had invented, yet who, despite my best efforts, had escaped my protection with such abruptness and certitude.

Several months after my dearest wife's death, when I was still in mourning, I chanced, while on a visit to my mistress in London, to be in receipt of a letter from my colleagues at the College of Physicians. I was requested to stay over the best part of a week in order to assist the translation and expedition of several new ordinances of the College. These concerned the policing of certain physicians who, the College considered, had become too strongly influenced by developments on the European continent, not least those of Monsieur Anton Mesmer, the Viennese physician who was then practising his strange cures in France. They were matters mainly clerical and administrative in nature, but since they concerned the agreed boundaries and confines of our common medical practice, they required some discretion in their execution. Despite such complexities, it happened that the duties were of a routine nature, and I discharged them somewhat sooner than expected. Thus, I had several further days before my planned departure. Since my current mistress, Miss Harriet Weaver, though amiable, was not of a learned disposition and did not engage with me in my work, once the initial pleasure of her company was fulfilled, my thoughts wandered once more to the question of Celia Quill, whom I had not seen for some seven or eight years now and whose companionship I believed I had missed.

So it was that one morning I decided to take a chaise from my mistress's house in Chiswick to Mrs Quill's supposed establishment in Cheyne Walk. I do not remember a great deal of the journey, except that I was much taken up with various aspects of my own thoughts, and in a short time found myself in the locality. I alighted on the pavement of a street of good-sized residences, gained my direction from several passers-by, and advanced down the street until, in a slight bend by the river, I came upon the house in question. I opened the wrought-iron gate and walked up the path to the main door. There I raised and let fall the knocker, and waited for a few seconds. Standing there, I must admit that I was subject to an odd perturbation. A maidservant, a dark-haired girl of good manner, opened the door. I was unaccountably nervous and had to gather myself before I was able to ask to see the householder. The servant enquired politely whether I had made an appointment. I told her my name and asked her to convey my compliments to her mistress. After a short while she returned and informed me that her mistress was engaged in some paperwork, but that if I were inclined to return in an hour's time she would be pleased to receive me.

Thus cautioned, I removed myself to stroll along the river bank. But the prospect of meeting Mrs Celia Quill again so engaged my thoughts that I walked the streets for the best part of that hour, hardly aware of the passage of time. When

I returned, the maid, on seeing me again, asked me to enter.

The establishment was as I had been informed: a gentlewoman's house. The servant showed me through to a drawing-room that lay off the main hall and asked me to be seated. I waited there, as though for some lady of consequence, and again I fell into a strange reverie. I sat for perhaps a quarter of an hour. In due course the maidservant appeared, announced Mrs Quill, and stepped aside. I heard the footsteps of her mistress in the hall. You will perhaps appreciate that I did not know fully what to expect, and at that stage a good part of me still considered this matter was entirely coincidental, and would be put to rest with the appearance of my hostess.

The servant stood aside, and the lady in question emerged from the hall into the drawing-room. She was tall and of a stately countenance. She paused, and for several seconds stood gazing at me in calm contemplation. During the time of her quiet consideration of me I was unable to speak.

I knew she would be nearing thirty-five years of age, but I had not prepared myself for the figure who now stood in front of me, either for her dignity or the calmness of carriage. Perhaps I thought she would be discomfited to see me, whom she had deserted with such precipitation all those years before. No such emotion showed on her countenance. There was something in her that had not changed, and that I may only describe as a concentration, or purity, of outward disposition. I was afflicted with the most terrible conflict of impulses. A part of me wished to step forward and embrace her. But her very composure informed me that this was her own ground upon which I trespassed, and that in the circumstances any gesture of affection would not be returned. She considered me for several seconds without moving, then nodded a brief welcome, as though acknowledging a fact of existence, and held out her hand, maintaining, so to speak, the requisite formalities.

I cannot speak easily of the intensity of my emotions. There was much that I could have said to her, but I myself was held in check by contradictory impulses. I took her hand briefly and released it, she watching me steadfastly meanwhile.

Out of a sense of courtesy more than any warmth, she invited me to sit down, and seated herself perhaps ten feet away in an upright chair. I was able to study her more closely. She had the same fine frame and figure that I recollected, except that she seemed, in her modest dress, more detached and calm than I had remembered. Her comely features had lost their initial plenitude and appeared now to have settled into their final character. She was soberly dressed, in black fustian with simple white lace trimmings at wrist and neck.

At what might be called a suitable distance, therefore, we conducted what seemed to me a genteel, almost stilted discourse which, while it contained sentiments of a formal nature, admitted of no real consideration of our past relations. But if it allowed no sentiment, it was at the same time not lacking in content in other matters. You must understand that within her character was a directness which was almost disconcerting. It was part of that transparency of character which is like goodness, insofar as it can be assessed. There was about her, perhaps even more than I had remembered, such manifest honesty and nobility of purpose that it seemed to incite, in those she addressed, a similar disposition. After we had exchanged formalities, I cleared my throat and asked her directly how it was that she had come to set up such an establishment.

For several seconds she did not answer. It occurred to me that I might have exceeded my welcome, and that she would now suggest the meeting be curtailed. But instead, she was regarding me directly, in no sense perturbed by what I had said, but as though considering what sort of answer I might understand. It seemed to me that she made her own calm calculations on my state of readiness for what she might be inclined to impart. In what follows I report merely the essence of her reply.

She informed me that she did not regret her earlier life with me, but that in the course of it she had developed the hope that one day I would take her for an honest woman. Her prolonged stay with me had demonstrated to her that, if her own relationship was nothing more than that of a mistress, then she would make that relationship, which men preferred of her, to be both more formalised and public. Thus she indicated that she saw no wrong in the commonly held surmise that men should pay for the pleasure of a woman's company as, in a sense, I had paid for hers by keeping her. But if that were to be so, there should be no pretence of affection. It was this to which she objected, and which she determined to banish from her future affairs.

I was at first incredulous at what I had heard. I wished to remonstrate that it was she who had left me upon a whim, not I her. But in the very moment that my objection rose inside me I knew, or rather guessed, her counter; that I had left her companionship for a new wife, and that in leaving me she was merely putting into effect, so to speak, that abandonment which I had committed already upon her.

Sir, in my heart I had hoped to see, within the reserve of time, some sign of affection, some recognition of more than half a dozen years together. But I saw none. She examined me with what seemed to me an absolute and objective equanimity as I struggled with my emotions. Seated in her own house, at the mercy of her goodwill, I was powerless to object to what she said. I sat in her drawing-room, under her gaze, and we discussed with a kind of detached decorum the views she held, and which she had attempted, under her own auspices, to put into practice. After perhaps another quarter of an hour, in which we exchanged further formalities, our conversation seemed to reach a natural end. We had no more words between us. I felt obliged to take my leave. I stood up and thanked her for her courtesy. She also rose, bowed briefly against my deeper bow, and followed me to the door of the drawing-room with every sign of detached goodwill.

She accompanied me into the hallway. There she held out her hand to me, then the maidservant opened the door. I turned to depart. Passing through the main door, I paused there briefly to glance back in the hope of seeing her one last time. But she had already turned and, quietly, was walking away from me into the interior of her house.

I admit that I was somewhat shaken by our meeting. The

reason and clarity of her response was beyond question. The servant closed the door behind me, I walked down the pathway to the wrought-iron gate and then I was outside. I was so perturbed by what had passed that for several seconds I was arrested there, and could hardly breathe for the complexity of my thoughts. I had been interviewed by my former mistress, calmly informed of my faults, reminded of the injustice of my treatment of her and, having thus been apprised of her philosophy of life, had been courteously and formally dismissed.

I remember that it began to rain and that several women who passed in the street raised the hoods of their coats against the steady downpour. There were lightning flashes over the south side of the Thames, and the rain grew heavier. I raised my arm against the deluge and, shielded thus from the eyes of others, I departed in strange mood, subject to feelings which alternated between anger and astonishment, admiration and outrage.

Without knowing fully what I did, I walked away from the river, towards Fulham, and there found a chaise for the journey to Chiswick. I was so much lost in my thoughts that I cannot remember the precise details of my journey back to my incumbent mistress. I remember only that after a while I found myself in my own familiar neighbourhood.

I emerged from the chaise, paid the driver, and entered once again the private and closed atmosphere of my thoughts. Another wave of emotion overtook me, whose source I do not even now begin to understand. I had been soaked by the rain and, having passed the journey in a somewhat bedraggled condition, perhaps had the beginnings of a chill. But I am one who prides himself on the strength of his constitution, and a little water had never harmed me before. Not long after the chaise had departed, however, while I walked towards my mistress's house, I began to tremble as though with the palsy. My limbs started to shake and my teeth chattered uncontrollably. I felt I was suffering from the early visitations of a fever. Then, to my own surprise and embarrassment, I burst most unexpectedly into such a loud mirth of surprise at the completeness of her victory over both me and her own circumstances, that several passers-by were startled by my expressions, and drew back as though from a madman. Their reaction did not halt the unpredictability of my mood. My laughter, which was nervous in its nature, seemed to grow on what it fed, though it must have further alarmed several of those who saw me in the grip of emotions which I could not control. I remained doubled up while I allowed the remainder of my fit to pass. I must only hope that, since it still rained, when I stood up and looked about me, those who witnessed me were oblivious to the nature of the copious tears that now, equally unexpectedly, began running down my cheeks.

My dear Leman, you have been patient enough to read these pages. At the risk of appearing both self-indulgent in my manner and somewhat episodic in my discourse, I must take my leave of you again. My thoughts and memories have been disturbed, and rise once more to claim my attention. In the meanwhile, I will look to regain my composure, so that I may complete this account in reasonable order, and bring you in due course to the present day.

I thank you again for your patience, for I do believe that to write this is also in part to exorcise my mind of its strange proclivities. And if for no other reason, I beg your forgiveness, and remain, sir,

 Yours sincerely,
 Hargood

CHAPTER 64

At Hargood's house Grange said, 'My patient Mr Swann reminds me sometimes of the salt-workers. You have seen their burns?'

'I have treated a number.'

'It is a strange thing,' Grange went on. 'Those workers would tell you that it is the harshest of all occupations, worse than mining.

They will inform you of the scalding heat, of the loss of weight and appetite, that the body seems like a scarecrow at the end of a single day. Yet it is from the very horrors of their industry that they derive their pride.'

Hargood nodded. 'Their pride is like a phoenix, rising from the ashes.'

Grange continued, 'I have seen them raise their shirts and show me scars from wounds that should have killed them – not so much out of vainglory, but out of reverence almost, at what their occupation has inflicted upon them.'

'We respect what is most dangerous.' Hargood turned the fluid in his glass, watching the shadows that moved inside it. 'Perhaps in the emotions too.'

Grange smiled at his host's persistence. 'Hargood, you constantly return.'

'As I believe I should, sir.'

'You lead always towards a single subject.'

'Mrs Quill is not merely a subject. She is the name, sir, the name and title of your condition.'

'And yours?' Grange asked.

'And mine too,' Hargood replied.

Towards the close of the evening, Hargood's huge fingers enclosed the base of the decanter, so that the wine moved like blood in his open hand. He had filled it twice in the course of the evening and most of the contents he had consumed himself.

'You are not drinking,' Hargood noted.

'If I drink, you refill as fast. If I were to obey your well-meant injunction, I should need to drink as fast as you were able to refill.'

'Then I shall fill my own glass, which I can trust to empty itself.'

Hargood lifted the decanter and watched the red liquid fall into its own darker depths. 'Drinking is based upon experience. I do admonish you to learn from mine.'

'I have a good master.'

Hargood swung the liquid in the glass. More than ever, it seemed to Grange, he deliberately drank towards insensibility. Now he seemed to rouse himself with an effort. 'Tell me. Since you accuse me of always returning to a single topic, let us choose another. You raised the subject of your amputee.'

'Swann?'

'Yes. He seems in good health?'

'I believe so,' Grange replied.

Hargood leaned back. 'You study his recovery?'

'From what I can see, his condition is remarkable,' Grange said.

'You marvel at his powers of recuperation?'

'Indeed.'

Hargood drank from his glass, considering. 'To what do you think he owes his recovery?'

Grange paused, perhaps a little nervous as to where Hargood was leading him. 'A sound constitution, I do believe. But also, perhaps, a certain attitude of mind. It is as if he has a will towards health.'

'"A will towards health",' Hargood repeated. 'That is, if I may say so, an interesting phrase.'

'Why so?'

'Would you say you possessed the same?'

Grange was cautious. 'I attempt to make progress.'

'I believe you do. I believe you do. But the phrase lingers.'

'You wish to apply it to me, then?'

'In what manner?'

'You think I might myself be lacking – in my deepest motivation, perhaps?'

Grange had grown used to gentle chastising by his mentor, and had learned that the best means of dealing with him was to meet him head on. But Hargood ignored the counter-attack, and turned aside. 'On the contrary. It seems to me your recovery proceeds apace. No.' Hargood gulped his wine. 'I wish to apply the phrase to myself.'

'To yourself?'

What did Grange notice in that moment, he would ask himself afterwards, that he had not noticed before? The line of Hargood's jaw seemed no different from usual. The weight of Hargood's shoulders, bunched beneath the jacket, appeared no less forceful or assertive than previously. But it was as if some core, as mysterious as that notional centre of gravity Newton had defined, had moved or emigrated.

Hargood raised his head and for several moments considered the ceiling. 'It seems to me that I have lost my own impulse to health.'

'Lost?' Grange asked, astonished.

Hargood did not move, but continued to contemplate the ceiling. Now he lowered his gaze and considered Grange, as though from a distance. 'I say "lost" because we lose most easily what we do not know we have.'

'You surprise me.'

'And when it is lost,' Hargood continued, 'we do not easily recover it.'

'Hargood, these are unusual and – if I may add – somewhat morbid thoughts . . .'

'I do not ask for your sympathy, my dear Silas. I merely record a fact.'

'Nevertheless, what you say agitates both my private and professional concern.'

'I shall attempt to take precautions. You may be assured.'

'Then perhaps I may ask you: to what circumstance do you believe this is due? Is it a physical affliction?'

'I believe it is because I am not so much in the present, but find myself falling into the past.'

'Which past?'

Hargood seemed to recover and waved his hand. 'It is nothing. A perturbation of the spirit. I am allowed a brief season of melancholy.'

'Is it some private matter? What is it that ails you?'

'Does one need reasons for ailing?'

'One searches for the causes,' Grange suggested. He would apply Hargood's medicine to Hargood himself. 'That, after all, is the physician's task.'

But Grange was unable, that night, to proceed further with his line of questioning. It was Hargood's usual behaviour to fall asleep. But this evening he seemed to sink instead into somnolence, leaning back in his chair, tilting his head and staring upwards at the ceiling. After a few minutes Grange stood up from the table.

Hargood, observing his movement, smiled. 'You leave, sir?'

Grange said, 'Do not get up, Hargood. I shall find my own way out.'

'I am inebriate. I believe I would fall over if I attempted to rise.'

'You are comfortable?'

'Bless you, sir,' Hargood said. 'When you have departed, I shall sleep a little while on the table, and recover sufficiently to take myself to bed.'

Grange nodded and made to leave. He, on the other hand, felt curiously well after a long night of drinking. It was a sign of his recovery.

Grange stood up. He found that he could do so without faltering or swaying. Hargood remained seated at the centre of his room, occupying his chair like a wounded or incapable monster, and for the first time Grange felt a pang of sympathy for him. It was followed almost immediately by a surge of guilt at his importunity for extending such an incongruous feeling towards his great mentor. As he bowed to Hargood, evoking a smile of acknowledgement from his host, Grange wondered what was the source of his guilt over such a natural emotion. He remembered that Hargood once had admonished him that sympathy for his patients was an absurd notion, that – in Hargood's resounding phrase – 'sympathy is a mechanism for making two people unhappy where only one was unhappy before'.

Having completed the formalities, Grange turned and walked into the hall. He put on his cloak and let himself quietly out of the door, leaving his host to a silent household and his own private thoughts.

CHAPTER 65

When Grange raised the knocker at Hargood's front door on the morning of the following day, a Sunday, his host had recently returned from Matins. He appeared in the doorway with his cravat already loosened from the formality of the service and his dark frock-coat replaced with a russet hunting jacket. He seemed, to Grange's eyes at least, not much the worse for wear.

Hargood opened the door wide and, before inviting Grange

inside, stepped out himself. 'A clear, cold day, my dear Silas.' Hargood indicated the light sunlight that lay on the frosted fields. He glanced beyond Grange, but could see no tethered horse. 'You came by foot?'

'I walked off some of last night's food,' Grange said.

'You should have come to church, my dear fellow. A fine service from the Reverend Gilpin. Such stirring words on charity, such a paean to gentleness of heart. An excellent start to a day's hunting.'

'Hunting?'

'Come,' Hargood said. 'Your physical recovery is nearing completion. I have something to show you.'

He led Grange round the side of the house, along a line of hedges, to a high wall that threw them into shade as deep as water. Hargood, temporarily blinded after the cold sunlight, felt for the latch. 'This way, sir.'

He opened the side door for Grange, a rectangle into pure light. A stone path led through a herb garden towards a further gate. Hargood raised the oak bar and swung it open. They walked through an open field of couch grass which sloped down the meadow to a small tidal inlet.

The sunlight was so pale that it was almost silver. Frost whitened the dark green of the foliage. The shine on the couch grass appeared to lift upwards, adding its sheen to the air.

At the lower end of the meadow Hargood guided him through several screens of holly which had been planted to provide a screen against the shore.

Small ripples lapped at the sides of the inlet. Grange stared down.

'Here she lies,' Hargood said.

The vessel was so low in the water it did not seem a row-boat, more a canoe or a river narrowboat. It was longer than a working craft, slimmer and pointed at both ends. A strong tripod construction was fixed at the bow, with a brass aperture to take some heavy, central weight. On its mid-sections, carefully laid across the ribs, was a flat wooden platform, long enough for a body to lie on. The varnished gunwales gleamed. Two thole-pins, which would serve as rowlocks, were in place on both sides.

'Built by Inman's yard,' Hargood murmured. 'Designed precisely for its intended use, a perfect and most literal construction.'

There was something almost military about the attention to detail, the strange completeness. The vessel was as sinister as a coffin. For a moment Grange thought this might be its function: a floating bier for a hero's body. He entertained himself with the thought that Hargood intended to be buried at sea.

It was chill at the water's edge. The water was cooler than the land. Small ripples touched the curved topsides. In his contemplation of the floating device, Grange experienced a faint shiver at his spine.

'You do not recognise a wildfowl punt?' Hargood asked.

Beneath Grange's gaze the delicate vessel rearranged itself, like an insect emerging from its chrysalis. The function of the strong tripod at the forward end became clearer. It would brace the heavy fowling gun. Grange felt like exclaiming aloud.

'Having slaughtered so many animals ashore, Hargood, you intend now to take your battle to sea?'

'You guess my intention admirably, sir.'

'And there perhaps die a solitary hero's death.'

Hargood's attention on the vessel was rapt. He murmured, 'It can be used by one, but is best operated by two.'

'Two?'

'One to scull the boat, the other to aim the ordnance.'

'You suggest . . .'

'I do, sir,' Hargood confirmed. 'You will be my crew.'

Grange hesitated. 'Press-ganging is, I understand, rife among the fleet . . .'

'A necessary evil.' Hargood brushed Grange's objections aside. He raised his arm and pointed out to sea. 'If you were to look at the horizon through a telescope, where the shine of the water meets the air, you would begin to perceive, I do believe, the faintest of horizontal lines, a mere indication of darkness. Do you see it?'

'A line?'

'The intimation of one.'

Grange said, 'I see only light . . .'

'Delicate. A dark raft like a shadow.'

Grange adjusted his eye to the horizon. He believed he could distinguish a faint line, extending outwards from the shore. But it was nebulous, merely a suggestion.

'Geese,' Hargood stated. 'Several thousand pass by here each week on their way south. The heavy weather brings them.'

Towards Hurst, Grange perceived the further trace of a shadow, a tenuous continuity along the edge of the water. But it was elusive to the naked eye, and he wondered about the suggestion of the mind.

'You intend to engage them?'

'I seek a rendezvous, my dear sir.' Hargood gazed out at the faint luminus of the cold horizon. 'No more than that. A meeting.'

There was a glare on the surface. The shadow on the water seemed to recede. Grange searched the thin light for a further sign of the floating flock. His eyesight was good, but it appeared to him that the birds, if they existed, lived in some realm of their own. 'What if I refuse to join you?'

'I am your physician,' Hargood informed him cheerfully. 'It is my decision. This shall be a part of your cure.'

'To stalk geese?'

'To involve yourself with the world once more, my dear Silas. To observe both life and death.'

'At sea?'

'At sea. But first, we must practise.'

In one respect at least, Grange discovered, Hargood had been accurate. There was room enough for two, lying side by side on the floor of the craft. Hargood gripped the scull oar in one hand and moved it gently, working his wrist, feeling the blade shudder as it gripped the water. A shimmer of life moved through the hull.

Grange could hear Hargood's slow breathing beside him as he manipulated the oar. Almost imperceptibly the boat eased forward.

They were so low that, from the craft itself, they seemed to be in the water. Only a few inches of topside separated them from the surface of the sea.

'Closing on the quarry on the intended line,' Hargood said, 'one should sweep less. Approach at an acute angle, slightly sideways, so that the moving scull oar is hidden by the body of the boat. These are refinements, of course. But each little thing helps. Here, take the oar.'

Grange gripped the haft as instructed.

'Edge it back and forth.'

The boat rocked clumsily with Grange's efforts.

'Now, sir, let me demonstrate. Move the wrist like so. This, sir, is feathering.'

Grange attempted several more movements. The hull swung again but did not move forward. 'Practise, sir, and I will lecture you. You begin to perceive how important is feathering. When you have practised a little more, I will teach you steerage. Do you see that piece of flotsam a little off the bow? See now if you can move us towards it.'

Hargood was patient. For almost an hour Grange worked the oar under his tutelage. It was several minutes before, by feathering, he was able to take some grip upon the water. Imperceptibly at first, the craft ceased to rock and began to glide softly forward at Grange's manipulations.

Hargood said, 'In the final stalk, it is not necessary to propel the boat at all. If we lie quiet, the flock will drift towards us. Our own stealth alone will close the distance.'

'Then,' Grange asked, 'you fire?'

'You wait. If you fire while the flock is sitting, you will hit at the most a few birds. When they are on the water, their folded wings protect them from the pellets. And since you are on the same effective plane as they, the ones in front will shelter those behind. The best advantage is the first part of the flight, when the flock leaves the water for the air. That is when their wings are open, when they seem instead to crowd every available space in the three dimensions. That is when they expose themselves in the densest concentrations.'

Grange edged the boat forward, sweeping his wrist, feeling for the drive in the blade. At the end of each stroke he turned and feathered the blade at a new angle for the return sweep.

'Now, sir, move your sight along the surface of the water. You see the smaller tower at Hurst? Subtend a line between ourselves and it, but move a few degrees to your right. What do you see?'

A pencil line of elusive contemplation, a little closer than before. At least now Grange could make out individual objects, hardly more than points.

'Those are birds, sir,' Hargood said. 'Not geese, but gulls and guillemots. I do believe they consider us, as we consider them. Their senses are better than ours. It follows that we cannot surprise them with our stealth. Rather, if we wish to stalk the geese that lie behind them, we must allow them no excuse for alarm. If you will forgive the metaphor, it is not unlike the seduction of a woman of temperament. She may have a considerable suspicion of your intentions, but as long as nothing you may do is too sudden, the end may be achieved.' He turned again towards Grange. 'Now, sir, since you have managed the first rudiments of propulsion, we may return for the ordnance.'

CHAPTER 66

The day was cold, but in the concentration of learning to work the oar, Grange had put aside the numbness of his feet. Hargood set in the thwart, they took up position seated side by side, and together they rowed the punt back to land.

When they reached the shore, a clear but febrile sun hardly heated the air.

'We will partake of a light lunch, sir, which I believe Mrs Simmonds has prepared, before we set out on our mission.'

They returned to the house. The table had been laid for two by Simmonds. Silver salt-cellars had been set beside each plate, along with heavy napkins.

'Mr Simmonds,' Hargood called into the interior. 'I believe we are ready to receive our fare.'

Grange could hear the shuffle of the old man. The lunch consisted of two partridges each, followed by an intermediary of beef stew, then two heavy haunches of venison as a main course, followed by lamb soup. Grange felt obliged to follow Hargood in his carnivore's repast but, unlike his host, he did not have seconds. He felt bloated nevertheless. That he did not feel faint as his stomach came to grips with the huge meal was perhaps a further sign of his general recovery.

After a brief respite for digestion in front of a strong fire with beech logs, accompanied by a little port, they walked to the gunroom at the rear of the house where Hargood kept the majority of his fire-power. Together they lifted the heavy fowling piece from its braces on the wall. Simmonds attempted to help them but Hargood waved him off. 'Be so good as to open the door,' he requested.

Together he and Grange lifted the armament across the lawn to the little creek. Two men were needed to carry it even a short distance. By the time they reached the vessel Grange was sweating with the effort, despite the cold. He extracted, nevertheless, a certain satisfaction from Hargood's assumption that he was capable of a little labour.

The surface of the shore-side puddles were turned to ice. To the south, the thin sun raised itself above the Isle of Wight.

Hargood placed the stock of the fowling piece on the ground, beside the punt, and raised the barrel with both hands, so that it pointed skywards. 'Now we will load on land, since it is almost impossible to reach the end of the barrel when we are at sea. Hold the gun vertical, if you will.'

Hargood raised the lid of the powder horn with his thumb and tipped a charge of powder into the barrel. Taking the rod, he rammed it down the length of the barrel, then drove in a wad to hold the powder. 'We must be methodical,' he said.

'And if we miss our target, how shall we reload?'

'We will have only one shot,' Hargood replied. 'That is the traditional custom and limitation.'

He poured lead shot into a metal cylinder the size of a small glass, carefully levelled the top, then decanted the measure down the barrel.

'How many pellets in a single measure?' Grange asked.

'Several hundred, I should say, each sufficiently large to bring down a goose on a direct hit.'

Hargood rammed down another wad to hold the shot in position. He stowed the rod on the underside of the gun. 'Our fowling piece has the power of a small cannon. If we shall have only the one opportunity, I do believe we shall be obliged to do our best.'

He kneeled down on the ground beside the floating vessel and, with Grange's help, together they placed the heavy fowling piece on its tripod and set the barrel on its forward brace; the brass pintles engaged.

'There, sir.'

The punt lay sleek and sinister and restless, armed like a man-of-war. Lazy ripples lapped its sides. Hargood rubbed his hands against the cold and again gazed at the thin line of the horizon.

A short while afterwards they returned once again to the house, and put on heavy greatcoats against the biting cold, scarves and several layers of woollen stockings. Strong leather boots would hold the moisture at bay.

Hargood placed the temporary thwarts across the boat. They sat side by side, took an oar each and pushed off from the bank. The boat rolled gently as they settled on the thwarts. Carefully, easing themselves this way and that for balance, they began to row out of the tiny creek. As they touched open water they swung to starboard, then across the Lymington river mouth.

There was a channel platform called Jack-in-the-Basket, because it was the habit of the women to row there and hang out the lunches of the fishermen, who did not have to return into the river at midday and thus forgo valuable fishing time.

Several sacks hung from heavy nails driven into the wood. Hargood said, 'There is a story of a woman, Mary White, who used to hang out food for her dead husband. No other fisherman would touch it, out of superstition. But always, when they returned the following morning, they found the food had been eaten.'

Out they rowed towards the Pennington marshes and Hurst, into the glare, into the hungry, empty light. Edging towards the Hurst spit, a faint swell from the narrows rose and fell, a distant memory of storms.

Sound carries across quiet water unimpeded. They could hear cattle lowing, the single shout of a drover. At Woodside three thin plumes from St Just's winter salt furnaces rose into the air.

Off Oxey the bells of Woodside church seemed to rise from the water, as if they tolled beneath the sea. After half an hour they rested. Their cold breaths streamed.

'A little brandy.' Hargood withdrew a flask; then, deciding he should test the contents himself, he swilled deeply. 'By God, sir, but that is fine.' He handed the flask to Grange.

The hot liquid touched Grange's stomach and seemed to turn to flame inside him. Beside him, Hargood raised his telescope to his eye and began slowly to quarter the shining surface of the water.

Condensation had gathered on the topsides. A small pool was forming in the bilges.

'I see nothing,' Hargood said, swinging the telescope. 'Nothing except light and water.' He continued to peer. 'My view is obscured. There is a mist on the Keyhaven marshes. I believe the geese lie beneath the earth's curvature.'

Grange could see the mist, as light as breath. They drifted into the white silence.

'It is fortunate,' Hargood told him. 'We are being assisted by the last hour of the ebb tide.'

They continued to row towards Hurst. After another half-hour Hargood halted and raised his telescope again. The hull of the boat drifted; a small swell rolled slowly beneath them. The mist had begun to move in towards them, leaving a few clear patches to the westward.

Beside him, Grange sensed Hargood's shoulder stiffen with excitement, like a gun dog. An interval of several seconds passed.

'Damn me, sir.'

More time, more floating seconds.

'They are present,' Hargood announced. 'Like the host.' He handed the telescope to Grange. 'To the left of Hurst, a good twenty degrees towards Keyhaven.'

Following his instructions, Grange settled the telescope on Hurst

Castle, then swung the field of view across the burnished surface towards Keyhaven.

'Further,' Hargood said. 'Upward a little. There. Do you not see? In the shadow of the land. A few hundred yards from the reed-beds – a stain on the light?'

The shine lifted towards the shore. Grange swung the telescope, then swung again. He saw a smudge on the surface, then, as he watched the outer periphery, several distant protrusions like sticks; necks and heads.

'You see them?'

'About a mile away, I believe.'

Even from this distance they seemed alert. The line appeared to be in constant gentle motion, forming and re-forming.

Hargood spoke softly: 'Their hearing is acute. When we are stalking them, they can swim as fast as we can travel.' He murmured as if to himself: 'There is a case for trying to trap them against the land. Otherwise, they have such acute senses that they would simply drift back towards the open sea as we advance.' He paused, glancing around at the cloudless sky. 'We run the risk, however, that by manoeuvring them against the land we may panic them. Since we are not ourselves mere abstract observers in this matter, our own position influences the game.'

Amused at these fervent speculations, Grange said, 'I look to your guidance, Hargood.'

Hargood was not to be rushed, however. 'On the other hand, sir, if we approach them from the landward side, we ourselves will be more difficult to perceive.' His meditative eye moved from one horizon to another. 'I believe, on mature consideration, there is too much clarity in the day to approach from the sea.'

Hargood took the telescope from Grange and studied the flock again, assessing their disposition. He paused, removed the hip-flask from beneath the thwarts, took a swill himself, and wiped his mouth in deepest concentration. 'I believe, all things considered, we should approach from landward. Here, my dear fellow, since it is the Sabbath, I believe you should take a last shine of spirit. It is customary before the final phase. We have a long stalk ahead of us.'

The day seemed to spread outwards, like shadow. Grange swilled the brandy and replaced the top. Hargood stowed the flask carefully under the thwarts.

They began to row again, at a tangent, towards the shore that merged the coasts of Pennington and Keyhaven.

After perhaps twenty minutes they halted. Hargood was breathing softly and heavily, more from excitement than fatigue.

'Let us unship the thwarts.'

Hargood set the thwart along the bottom of the vessel and lay across it on his front. Grange took up position beside him.

The spare oar was stowed lengthwise between them. They removed its thole-pins to reduce all projections.

Grange placed his oar in the U-shaped slot on the starboard aft gunwale and took hold of the haft. He moved it carefully backwards and forwards, swinging his wrist gently, judging the placement of the blade, feeling for the balance of the stroke in the oar's responsive shudder. When he paused they drifted forward slowly; in moments of respite, he used the oar to adjust the heading of the boat.

'Now we are settled,' Hargood whispered, 'I believe I shall arm the weapon.' He raised the frizzen covering the pan and poured in the priming powder. With his finger he delicately wiped away remaining traces of powder on the upper barrel. Carefully he lowered the frizzen and eased the flintlock down until it found its point of rest. 'Good. We need only to raise the flint before firing.'

They settled down to sculling, drifting, waiting. Now that they were on the same level as the birds, the flock had disappeared beneath the curved surface of the water.

A placid swell raised and lowered them. They had to trust to direction, maintaining the keep of Hurst Castle and the red conical lighthouse a few degrees to port.

Through the afternoon they edged forward, their eyes fixed on the glare ahead of them, the shore a black line. The castle keep and a cluster of smaller buildings were the only objects in a clear day, a speckle of relief on a flat horizon.

Somewhere ahead the geese moved within their own flickering lights; a wave of animal sensibility, a net of instinct.

The cold crept into Grange's bones. Thinner than Hargood, he felt the damp more deeply. Sometimes he paused from sculling to hold his hands to his mouth and blow warm breath across his fingers. A thin pool of water moved in the bilges. His feet were numb in their heavy leather boots.

Grange returned to his sculling. Then, for a few minutes, at Hargood's instruction, they waited. As the sun lowered, the surface of the water became imprecise, abstract. They seemed to float on light. He was about to whisper to Hargood when his companion, in calm emphasis, touched a finger to his lips.

They were among the geese. Perhaps a hundred yards away, necks periscoped out of the water. Heads turned sharply, alarmed.

Beside him, Grange sensed Hargood tighten with anticipation. With cautious, slow movements Hargood edged forward on the bottom of the hull, resting for several seconds at a time, until his cheek touched the stock of the fowling piece.

Grange watched, resisting the temptation to blow again on his frozen hands. Hargood squeezed forward a few inches further, feeling for final position. His jowl lay on the wood, his finger felt for the trigger guard, his thumb on the flintlock. Slowly he shifted weight, arranging himself so that his body merged with the stock. Now Hargood and the heavy fowling piece seemed like a single construction; half animal, half weapon.

The birds were all around them. Grange did not move his head, only his eyes. Wherever he looked there were birds, beautiful heads craned. It seemed to him the geese were speaking softly with one another. Their voices were gentle, inhuman, like goddesses.

Slowly, attempting not to make any brisk movement, Hargood raised the flint with a concise click, an audible precision. The voices of the birds halted.

The small sharpness of the sound seemed to add an explosive charge of silence to their world.

Without warning a gander barged across them, leaving a flaming rooster tail. Trains of water crossed and recrossed. Ahead of them the surface erupted into flailing bodies.

Grange's mouth dried. Still Hargood did not move. The panic was not yet general, but seemed to move in diagonal lines across a still quiescent flock. The bow of the boat drifted across slowly.

Around them there was a continued accumulation of energy. The geese ahead thundered upwards into light, turning the sky dark; they were in a tunnel of drumming wings.

Grange heard the click of the flintlock, saw the flash like a worm of lightning. An explosion wrenched the vessel backwards. Over the bow a hole opened in the air. A piece of sky shuddered, separated from the rest, then began to fall like masonry. Individual fragments churned the surface of the water.

The remainder of the flock was still rising, snowflakes hit by a gust. The cries of alarm and beating of wings faded, until its lamentation was a memory, and all Grange could hear in the fervent silence was the beating of his heart.

Hargood turned towards him. A faint streak of powder lined his eyebrow and the bridge of his nose. He reminded Grange of an illustration of an animal he had seen in plates by Kessler or Cuvier, both comical and sinister.

Hargood grinned. 'I believe we have struck a harvest, sir.'

Grange struggled to remember the illustration; an American racoon.

Grange lost count of the bodies they hauled into the boat.

When they had recovered from the explosion, taking deep breaths of air, they raised themselves, installed the thwarts and oars.

Grange rowed the boat to the feathered corpses, while Hargood leaned over and gathered them in. Having hauled them aboard, Hargood broke the necks of any struggling or wounded birds with a single, heavy flick of his wrist.

Each bird weighed perhaps eight or nine pounds. As they piled them in the bilges, so the boat sank lower, until a bare two inches separated the gunwales from the surface of the water. Afterwards they discovered they had piled into the vessel beside them the bodies of some twenty-seven geese.

They rowed slowly back through the afternoon, thankful that there was still no wind on the winter day.

Hargood sat beside Grange and took up his oar. The tide was flooding gently, and they might have struck out further into the channel. But they were nervous of taking aboard water, since there were more likely to be waves where the tide ran swiftly. In order to make the safest progress they kept as close as they could to the Pennington shore. They stopped occasionally to rest and to massage their frozen fingers.

When they rested from their efforts, Hargood showed Grange how to press his fingers into the flesh beneath the wing joint of a bird, where the warmth was greatest. Grange felt the warmth ebbing from the bodies of the slaughtered birds.

They finished the contents of the brandy flask and began to row again.

CHAPTER 67

For some time afterwards Grange would remember the lamentation of the departing flock, like the murmur of souls.

Years before, some sense of this, of the need of individual souls, had driven him towards the profession of physician. He considered the curved pile of heavy bodies now; in some of the birds, the pinion feathers extended upwards like hands. Enormous ingenuity had been applied to this, the simple death of innocent creatures.

Hargood observed Grange carefully surveying the feathered horde. 'Your heart is full, sir.'

Grange looked down at the blood on his hands. 'Such an extinction of fine, fervent life.'

Hargood smiled in happy exasperation. He had a target for his outrage. 'Damn you, Silas. You are like some Hindoo. Because of our efforts, some twenty or so poor families will have a fat goose for Christmas. They shall rejoice in their Maker.'

But Grange had felt the life ebbing, the beautiful, passive life in his fingers.

'You learn something, perhaps,' Hargood said. 'Life is light. One breeze and it is snuffed out.'

Grange nodded.

'But perhaps it is not enough to know it in some dry

philosophical sense. You must feel it, here . . .' Hargood patted his chest. 'In your living self.'

Grange did not answer. Out on this waste of water he was at temporary ease, though not at peace. A white arrangement of sunlight and water appeared to fill his soul. He seemed strung out between fire and light. Staring out to sea, he could not forget the death that lay on his hands.

They had drifted close to the land. A slow swell was breaking on the shore, an obscure band of white where the flow of trees moved down the shallow valleys. Between them Grange could observe meadows, shining fields.

He stared towards the land at Oxey and Pennington. On the shore line was a stand of several aspens, further inland a group of Norway spruces, the rest mud flats and marsh grass interspersed by small estuaries. Seen from the sea, the few struggling streams of smoke from the salt furnaces were like campfires. From this vantage, out at sea, he could see the strange effects of the salt industry – sea walls thrown up here and there, a complex tracery of water passages, small windmills with their sails removed against the winter gales, their blades lashed down, standing disconsolate. Around them lay the machinery of lock gates and tidal channels leading to the large flat pools in which evaporation had taken place during the summer. Further inland were the deeper storage pools of brine which, having been raised from the evaporation pans and stored throughout the summer, were now in the process of being evaporated by the heat of the few remaining winter furnaces.

A blue sky poured down its soft light. The shore line had the look of an industry stricken by seasonal fluctuations. Hargood was moved to speak again, not so much by natural beauty as by the provocation of Grange's silence. 'The tide will turn against us within an hour.'

They began to row again, striking blades into the water. But progress was slow with the load in their bilges, their overall weight substantially increased by their slaughter.

Slowly, after much sweat, they had passed around the Oxey marshes and reached the mouth of the Lymington river. There was a small cross-current there, caused by the outflow of the river mixing with the tide. Once or twice a disturbed swell lopped over the gunwales into the bilges. They were tired, but the prospect of sinking added incentive to their efforts. Neither spoke through their labours, though they both watched the slop water rise and the gunwales sink a little lower with each intrusion of water.

Hargood said, 'A few more swells and I believe we shall be in a position to beach her.'

The waves increased slightly in steepness as they neared the shallows. They were almost there when a soft green tide entered the boat and they were filled, suddenly and completely. The coldness of the winter water struck into Grange's legs. It came to him, with a sense of forbearance, that he might now drown, but Hargood said calmly, 'I believe we are safe, sir.'

He slid off the boat and his feet found bottom. With a gasp he raised his shoulders above water. The cold struck into Grange's chest. Beside him, Hargood floated out with seraphic calm, tested the shallow gravel bottom for a foothold and, standing with his arms and chest above water, held on to a thole-pin.

With one on either side of the boat, they walked the flooded craft through the shallows with a tide of geese floating gently in her bilges. Cold and exhausted, they beached their coffin in a narrow inlet. Crawling up upon the shore, they sat down for several minutes, gathering their breath.

They were silent in shock and gratitude. They lay on their backs to recover their breath and equanimity. The final remnants of a weak sun made an effort to dry their outer clothing. Staring up at the sky, Hargood said, 'This is the second time, my dear Silas, that your company has led to an unintended ducking.'

'You blame me, Hargood, for untoward events?'

'I myself have not received two such in twenty years of being out and about on this land. I believe it calls for some comment. Now, in your company, it threatens to become a habit.'

'What do you deduce?'

'I imagine it is your exasperated and atheistic spirit, which extends outwards into nature, and incites her to chastise you.'

'An interesting speculation,' Grange said. 'At least this time we have no bees to attend us.'

'You complain, sir? I believe that what we have just witnessed was another vibration of nature, provoked by your ungodly thoughts. I think your intellectual mind, sir, strikes nature like a tuning fork, though at a perfect counterpitch, and we will have rogue waves or radical bees in response.'

'Your theories have a certain mystical quality.'

'You are unassuaged?' Hargood asked. 'You wish to provoke yet further events?'

'You yourself seem none the worse for our immersion.'

'It is good for the circulation.' Hargood replied. 'Particularly if it is followed by copious supplies of port.'

When they had recovered their breath, they began to fling the bodies of the geese higher up the shore, where they were safe from the incoming waves. They removed the heavy fowling piece, hauled the boat partly out and turned her on her side to drain her. Blood and feathers clung to the thwarts. They righted her again. Having lightened her, they could drag the vessel up the shore to beach her properly, then lay her upside down on the marsh grass.

'The tide is starting to ebb,' Hargood said. 'The water will rise no further.'

Grange nodded.

'I believe', Hargood told him, 'the geese will be safe here for a few hours. We should proceed to my house, and revive ourselves. Afterwards, when we have celebrated our achievements, we can return to carry the birds.'

CHAPTER 68

When they came back for the geese it had already begun snowing. It took them a good half-dozen trips each to the shore to carry all the birds to the house. Hargood might have called the gardener and the stable-boy to assist them, but it seemed to Grange that this was his host's attempt perhaps to assert his own physical primacy over the traditional pursuit of hunting.

In due course, Grange took his leave. He was nervous, if he delayed too long, of incurring Mrs Thompson's disfavour.

When he reached his house she was preparing his supper, and

took a little time to wipe her hands and remove the apron, before walking through the passage and hallway. Opening the door, she could see him only faintly in the dark. To her eyes at first he appeared to be holding two large objects, almost the size of valises. She put up her hand to shade her eyes against the light from the lamp which she had hung outside the door for his arrival.

'Two geese, Mrs Thompson.'

He held them by their legs, so that their long necks and heads descended.

She stood aside to let him in.

Grange walked through the narrow hallway into the pantry and set the two great birds down upon the oak kitchen table. Mrs Thompson, at a loss for words, sidled in behind him.

Grange said, 'I was press-ganged by Dr Hargood into a hunting expedition. I blame him entirely for diverting me from my expected walk.'

'Hunting?' Mrs Thompson asked.

'We used Dr Hargood's punt to stalk the poor creatures, and were unfortunately successful.'

Mrs Thompson could see the advantages almost immediately. The two birds, set across the table, were a gander and goose. 'You will eat them yourself?' Mrs Thompson ventured hopefully.

'I believe we will have one ourselves at Christmas. If we hang them in the cold-larder, they will be ready for plucking a day or two before.'

'And the other?' Mrs Thompson asked.

'The other?'

'The other goose?'

'I shall give the other to a family.'

'Which family would that be, sir?' Mrs Thompson asked.

'I believe I do not yet know,' Grange answered.

She could only nod to herself, in the pretence that what he said made sense, since there was clearly no other way of negotiating with him that she could imagine. He arrived on the doorstep unexpectedly with two large geese, intending to give one of them away to a family of whose identity he was not, currently speaking, aware. Occasionally, it seemed to Mrs Thompson, she was forced to remind herself that she was dealing with the careful and rational acts of a reputable physician, as opposed to the random actions of a madman.

For a moment they faced one another, the two dead birds on the table between them.

Grange said, 'I ate a substantial meal of meat today, Mrs Thompson. Despite the bad effects of animal flesh on my constitution, I have experienced no fainting fit. My health appears to be improving. All the more reason, it seems to me, to maintain my fish diet.'

This raised other aspects of his behaviour which contributed to her view of him as a perpetual mystery. He had held to his diet of fish now for several months, in spite of both Dr Hargood's and her own dire predictions. Against their own prognostications, in his body he grew steadily fitter, his fainting fits had been superseded and much of his colour had returned. If he were to break his fast of fish finally, she knew now that he would do so himself, not by succumbing to any pressure on either Hargood's or her own behalf. It was another small hurdle he had overcome in his attempt to regain control over his domain.

Though he might feel some small satisfaction in the progress of his health, he did not dare tell Mrs Thompson that he wore a fresh set of clothes supplied by Hargood, because he had received another ducking that day, a full immersion in cold salt water, and that the clothes he wore even now were being rinsed by Mrs Simmonds in fresh water to remove the salt, prepatatory to being dried for several hours against a fire in Hargood's study. She would have insisted that he depart straight to bed, and he could be certain that in this respect at least she would have carried the day.

In the circumstances, it was a special pleasure for him to be able to say, 'I intend to visit a certain house later this evening,' without being contradicted or chastised for recklessly endangering his health.

'A visit?' Mrs Thompson asked. 'It has started to snow.'

'Indeed,' Grange said. 'That is why I believe I should set out in good time. I would appreciate an early supper.'

'Sir,' she agreed, though she was determined to watch him carefully, while certain suspicions remained. His thin soup of fish and vegetables was boiling on the stove. Mrs Thompson returned there to supervise his meal and consider the matter further, her uncertain temper only partly mollified by the thought of her forthcoming preparations to cook the Christmas goose.

CHAPTER 69

By the time he left, perhaps two hours later, the snow had fallen heavily. Avoiding the worst of the drifts, Grange pulled his greatcoat around him. Flurries moved along the fences, drifted upwards, tugged at him. He was reminded, in the howling, feathery tunnels, of goose wings.

The lantern he carried was constructed on the principle of the storm light, with the minimum of ventilation to protect the wick. Nervous that its tiny flame should pass out and leave him stranded without illumination, he had filled the base with the best quality spermaceti oil.

Grange folded both hands around the warm reservoir of oil to warm his fingers and held the hooded lamp close to his chest to afford some further protection of the flame. His height and thinness both increased his own instability in the stronger blasts. Stooping against the wind, he walked the pathways towards Boldre as if in prayer.

Sometimes, at a fork or cross-gate, he was obliged to hold up the lantern in order to observe the way more closely. But for the most part the whiteness of the snow retained the light. He had views of pale fields, above which dark flakes drifted across the moon. Crossing Boldre bridge, he swung left into a smaller lane that was hardly more than a cattle track.

At the heavy gate of St Just's house at Boldre, Grange halted. He pulled the cord of a bell which sounded in the gatekeeper's cottage.

There was no sign of movement. At length the stooped figure of an old man emerged from the side door, swung the door closed and approached the great wrought-iron double gates. Grange could not see the face because of a cowl that covered his features almost entirely, except for a pair of unusually penetrating eyes, which now stared out at him. The small figure's hands, bandaged against the cold, touched the convoluted iron between them. 'Dr Grange?'

Grange nodded.

'Mr St Just expects you, sir.'

A heavy key was turned and the gate was pulled aside. Grange waited until it had been closed again and the locks slid home. He followed the frail shape across the whitened paving stones, until they reached the porticoed entrance of the main house. There the gatekeeper hauled on a bell-pull. Grange heard the chimes in the house. Glancing around him, he saw the man was already disappearing down the path towards the gate cottage.

He was slightly distracted by the rapid and unexplained departure of the gatekeeper, and did not hear the door open behind him until a voice said, 'Dr Grange. I am honoured by your visit.'

Grange turned and observed a heavy, somewhat bony face in the darkness of the doorway.

'St Just,' the figure said. 'I am pleased to make your acquaintance.

'You have had an opportunity to consider my letter, sir?' Grange asked.

'Indeed,' St Just answered.

'Then I thank you for seeing me.'

In the tallow light of the hallway, Grange could see his host better. Henry St Just was tall, white-haired and handsome, of a strong build which was turning a little to corpulence. His features were regular and incisive. His handshake was stronger than Grange expected.

St Just said, 'Be kind enough to follow me.'

In the gloomy corridor, it became clear that St Just's left leg was shorter than his right, and that he dragged his right heel as he walked. As he flung himself forward, his head and shoulders bobbed and heaved with the effort. The strain caused Grange's sympathy to rise a little in his favour.

The walls of the corridor were oxblood red, which made the white frames of the doors stand out. At its end, St Just opened a tall oak door. 'My study.'

It was a substantial room, bound by three large windows in which the curtains had been drawn against the night. Piles of papers were pinned with solid brass paperweights. A heavy clock in a glass case was balanced on a mantel. There were no decorations on the walls, which were also painted a deep, oxblood red. Grange guessed this was St Just's throne-room, where he conducted his business and controlled his interests.

The central table, set almost in the middle of the room, had been placed a little towards the windows for light. It consisted not so much of a desk, more of a library table. While St Just manoeuvred around it, dragging his foot, Grange found an opportunity to look at the piece more closely. A much enlarged version of a keyhole desk, its function was to allow two people to sit facing one other. In St Just's case, Grange surmised, it would permit him to dictate while a clerk, facing him on the other side of the table, wrote down his thoughts.

'Be seated, sir.'

St Just himself made his final advance to the far side of the table and sat down, pushing out one leg. As he settled, a flicker of pain crossed his face, a transitory acknowledgement of the discomfort with which he habitually lived. As though seeking relief, St Just shifted on his chair, closed his eyes and seemed to compose himself. Then, as he recovered, he turned his concentrated stare on his guest. Grange began to appreciate the cause of his watchfulness. He was one of those men who live so closely with a chronic affliction that it settles into the skin and bone of their expression.

From his position at the head of the desk, St Just nodded, as though signalling his guest to make his case. 'Please speak, sir.'

'What I should like to enquire', Grange said, 'is perhaps a minor matter. I hope that you will forgive my curiosity.'

'No question of detail is so minor that it is not worthy of consideration.'

'I raise, then, one small detail of your enterprises – the salt furnaces.'

'That is a broad canvas, if I may say so. At present I am in ownership of seventeen furnaces in all. To which of them do you refer?'

'Not to any particular one, but to the general practice of continuing to use several of them well into the winter.'

'And what precisely do you ask, concerning that practice?'

273

'It is unusual, is it not?'

'Indeed,' St Just replied. 'But what may be unusual and what may be wise are sometimes not wholly unconnected.'

Grange nodded. 'Then perhaps, sir, you might be kind enough to inform me a little about its wisdom.'

'Certainly.' St Just inclined his head. 'I believe it is incumbent upon us to make the best use of the resources in our keep. Among the seventeen furnaces which fall under our ownership, there are three in particular which have made no profits during the last few years, and whose losses must therefore be sustained by the profits of others. Accordingly, we are obliged to consider the circumstances concerning these three unprofitable furnaces.'

St Just contemplated him while he spoke. 'At first estimation the furnaces in question did not appear materially to be much different from the other furnaces. They seemed of identical construction and dimensions. I therefore drew the initial conclusion that the cause of their continuing losses was not physical, but human.'

'Human?' Grange asked.

'Perhaps I might add, sir, that I believe another employer would have begun by dismissing the foremen and crew of the unprofitable furnaces, and replacing them with a more effective work-force. But I believe myself to be of a more rational nature and, before effecting their dismissal, I wished to consider the matter further. It seemed to me that I should treat each of the possible causes in turn and set in train a number of experiments designed to expose more precisely the nature of the cause. Accordingly, I exchanged the three foremen with others from the profitable furnaces. After a season's burning, somewhat to my surprise, the exchange had caused no significant difference in the performance of the furnaces. I assumed, therefore, it was not the original foremen's fault.'

Grange nodded, perhaps a little tentatively.

'Having isolated one such cause,' St Just continued, 'and found it wanting, I proceeded to another. Next, I exchanged the working crews of the three furnaces with the crews of other, profitable furnaces. After another season's burning I found there was no change in output. It became clear to me that the three furnaces did perform unlike the others for reasons which could not be attributed to human fault, and therefore my original surmise was incorrect.

'After two seasons of experimentation, I had not reached any useful conclusions. However, almost by chance, it happened to occur to me, when looking at a map of the area, that the geographical location of the three furnaces which were unprofitable had something in common. They were each further from the water than the others. I began to believe that, set at a larger distance from the shore, they might suffer from a greater protection from the wind. Receiving less wind, the furnaces would not burn so fiercely. This hypothesis, if verified, at least would have a beneficial result. I would resolve not to build any further furnaces at a distance from the shore.'

St Just surveyed him, as though attempting to assess these reports upon his guest.

'Another employer, I believe, having granted two seasons' grace, would have settled that the furnaces could not benefit from man-made changes and would have closed them. But as I say, sir, I hope that I am of a more objective disposition. I considered yet another alternative – to extend their time of operation. According to my calculations, by burning through the winter, their product is approximately doubled, though overall expenditure is only extended by two-thirds.'

Grange said, 'If I may enquire, sir, how can you manage so admirable a result in winter – if not by reducing the crews?'

'Not only by reducing the crew. In summer, we are forced to pay higher wages because of competition with the other furnaces and other types of summer employment, including farmwork and harvesting. In winter, where the supply of available labour is much greater and the competition is less, we are able to pay less. It makes, as I say, economic sense. Now, sir, since you have asked me a question, which in all good conscience I have attempted to answer, perhaps you will permit me to return the favour. Why do you enquire?'

'I have a former patient – a seaman by trade – with one of those minds that would perhaps, if educated, prove capable and even original.'

St Just smiled.

'Last winter, owing to incipient gangrene in his left arm, I was forced to amputate it at the shoulder. His physical recovery has been remarkable, though I believe it is due not so much to my small efficacy as his own prodigious constitution. He works on the foreshore now. He has a small naval pension, and he supplements his income by wandering there to collect driftwood and other offerings of the sea.'

'This driftwood . . .'

'He uses it to supply his own fire and sells the surplus to householders in the town.'

'I am pleased that he has survived and now prospers. But why do you mention him?'

'During such time as he patrols the foreshore, he has noticed, in the remaining furnaces which burn through the winter months, a series of events which, he humbly submits, if not attended to may in due course exert a deeper cost than lack of profitability.'

'A deeper cost?' St Just moved in his chair, adjusting to the thought. 'This former seaman . . . is expert on salt furnaces?'

'As a former second mate on a sailing ship, he is an expert on wind – on its properties and peculiarities, to be precise.'

'I fail as yet to perceive a connection.'

Grange gathered himself, preparing to strike out with courage. 'He says the pattern of wind during winter months is different. There are more gales and greater fluctuations. He informs me that during those months he has observed gusts of wind to strike at such intervals that they cause certain of the furnaces to flame and expire. This, he believes, is not itself so great a danger if the gusts are limited. But it would appear the gusts and hollows of the wind may sometimes generate a rhythm in which the flame increases at each round. As each flame goes out, so new air is sucked in by the vacuum and the resulting flame is larger. He says that, by a process of continuous exaggeration, at each successive gust the flame will return and grow greater, until the admixture becomes dangerous.'

'Dangerous?'

'Both to the furnace and the men within it.'

He was aware of St Just considering him. The banker had folded his hands together and his eyes had taken on a concentrated, almost hooded expression. In the ensuing silence Grange wondered whether he had lost his host's attention. But St Just seemed to rouse himself from the thoughts into which he had sunk, and now he said, from a depth of apparent contemplation, 'Please continue, sir.'

'The pressures which build thereby, stage by stage, may reach a point at which they become . . . explosive.'

Grange observed in St Just's face that faint habitual twitch, that smile of pain, with which he was becoming familiar.

'An interesting observation,' St Just commented, 'though in the absence of fact, somewhat fanciful, perhaps. There was, I believe, under the previous ownership, an accident in one of the furnaces, though its origin was obscure. But I have no means of knowing whether what you suggest is related.'

'I understand from Swann that the normal means of control over these events is to close the doors. This starves the process of air, until the combustion is able to settle. Then the doors may be carefully opened again.'

'I see.' St Just nodded. 'And if they are able to control the process by the use of the doors, what is it you wish to tell me?'

'These methods may be efficacious in the summer months. But as the season proceeds, the greater gales and gusts in the autumn and winter months, in combination with a skeleton crew . . .'

'I believe I see you now, sir,' St Just observed. 'I believe I see you clear.' Grange was about to speak again, to add more detail to the general argument, when St Just raised a hand as if to quieten him.

'You have a theory, sir, which is both interesting and entertaining. An accident may happen, but it has not happened yet. You believe this hypothetical accident may occur and you describe admirably the conditions under which it might occur, but not the measures by which it may be met. Now, I am always willing to consider most seriously dangers both to men or property, particularly when the description is precise. For example, at Keyhaven, on the weather side of the salt furnaces, there is a sea wall which is in danger of breaking under winter gales. It shows first signs of wear at its base for some two hundred and thirty yards of its length. Should it be strengthened now, against the possibility of breakage? Or should we expend our funds elsewhere, and live in constant hope that there will be no great storm to sweep away our efforts and carry away the four most western of the furnaces?'

'Sir, that is not my interest or my plea . . .'

St Just raised his hand again, in calm authority. 'Nevertheless, I am compelled by circumstances to decide whether to use my limited resources to strengthen the sea wall. If no great storm arises, then it will be considered a grievous waste of resources that were better spent elsewhere. I may expend a large amount of capital to shore up the defences in a certain area, only to find that they are breached in another place. The weighing of risk is a difficult and complex matter.'

'I understand the complexity,' Grange said. 'But in answer, it may perhaps be said that storm and flood do not so strongly threaten life. A storm gives warning and crews may be advised to leave the site until the worst is past. What is being suggested is that the rhythm of the flame, breathing fast and fierce like an animal, may pass out of the ordinary in very short order. It could take a crew unawares – the interval between smaller and succeedingly greater flames may occur after only a few seconds.'

'I see you, sir,' St Just said, though Grange began to suspect that he did not – or rather, that what St Just was beginning to 'see' now, developing from the argument, was his authority usurped. The faint smile of pain again, an expression of conciliation and perhaps a little patronage. 'And what recourse do you suggest?'

'Recourse?'

'What reform have you in mind?'

'I raise the matter with you merely for your consideration.'

'For my consideration,' St Just repeated. 'I am grateful indeed. But, suppose, sir, that having received the theory proposed by your seaman, and having given it my closest consideration, I see no reason to change current practice?'

'I would hope that you might perhaps consult the men who . . .'

'The men would be even less likely to wish to change current practice than I. You may, perhaps, understand their reticence. They and their ancestors have been working the salt furnaces from time immemorial, using certain methods. Why should they change their practices?'

'Before, they have always burned in summer . . . ?'

'You think a mere extension of the season would be sufficient reason, in their minds, to change their practices?'

'My point is that extending the season, against all prior habits and practices, is itself such a change to previous practice that it perhaps should be considered . . .'

'Shall we put it to the men?' St Just suggested suddenly. 'Shall I tell the foreman to warn them of the risk, repeating what you say, and ask them whether they wish to continue under the present conditions, or to cease their labour?'

'Cease their labour?' Grange was lost for a moment and determined to recover his equanimity, if only to pursue the case. 'That would be most considerate of you. But as I understand, they have no alternative labour . . .'

'That is their business,' St Just said calmly. 'It is our privilege to offer them employment in the difficult, unseasonable months of winter, in order to extend the working life of the furnaces so that we may begin to make a profit. Will you be satisfied if I instruct the foreman to put to the men the question whether they wish to be so employed? In view of the risk, I do emphasise that the choice will be theirs entirely as to whether they will continue to work the winter shifts.'

It seemed to Grange that he had heard a similar argument from the foreman leading the replacement shift towards the furnaces. It appeared to him the final refuge in the face of any proposal in favour of a particular reform to current practices. Ask the men whether they wish to be employed or not.

Grange said, 'Can you not increase the crews, in order to build a margin of safety . . . ?'

'A margin? Oh, indeed I can, sir.' St Just regarded him. 'But then I must follow the consequences, which are exact. By increasing the crew, on one or all of the three furnaces in question, the furnaces will become unprofitable once more. If this is so, the consequence is that I shall be forced to close those same furnaces in winter. And it follows therefore that such extra employment as we may presently offer will be forfeited.'

'These matters are outside my scope or knowledge . . .'

'But they are within mine.' St Just paused. 'Again, sir, let us be precise. Let us face directly what you suggest. Let us, above all, not be shy of rigour. The direct consequence of increasing the crew will be to make any such operation unprofitable, and thus force the closure of the three furnaces in winter.'

'But assuming you are right . . .'

'We are quite right about that, sir,' St Just insisted. 'But that is not the end of the matter. For there are other consequences, which I believe we should also consider. When we remove the hope of profitability, we are forced to consider the next step. That is to say, that since the furnaces in question will have no hope of profitability in summer either – that, after all, was our reason for extending their use through winter – we must close them down not only in winter, but in summer too; that is to say, in perpetuity.'

St Just watched him. Grange observed again the flicker of pain, now more than ever grown unconscious, like an ox flicking off a fly.

'Allow me, then if you will, to rehearse and summarise the consequences. By loading the winter furnaces with extra men, not only will the winter shifts lose their employment, but the summer shifts on those same furnaces must also be curtailed.'

Grange breathed out. St Just, as if his case were proved, sat back calmly to hear his response, laying his arms along the arms of his chair, and studied his guest dispassionately.

Grange said, 'If you will forgive my temerity in suggesting an alternative, your winter furnaces are an arm of the general body of furnaces that you own. May you not support the extra crews in winter out of the profit that you make on the others?'

St Just shifted restlessly in his chair, as though a certain part of his pain, though not its entirety, were caused by the argument itself. 'Sir, perhaps I could remind you of the consequences. Already you have reversed the entire reason for attempting the winter shifts. It is to make a profit. With a profit in hand, I can employ workers. Without a profit I am forced to decrease the scope of the operations.'

'It is a small matter of adjustment, surely,' Grange said.

'Adjustment, sir?' St Just asked. 'You suggest that I subsidise the winter saltings out of the profit of another part of these industries?'

'Since you ask,' Grange answered. 'Yes, sir, I do believe that is what I suggest.'

St Just smiled. 'I have committed myself to the discovery of the precise effects of subsidising one part of the industry with another, and have worked the calculations. I am in a position to tell you what the exact consequences may be. If we subsidise the losses of the three furnaces out of the profits of the remainder, then the likelihood is that other furnaces cannot make a sustainable return, or will become unprofitable. The consequence is that we must close yet more furnaces.'

So it continued, for the best part of another hour, in which arguments were refined and rehearsed, conclusions ineluctably reached, until Grange felt himself drawn through the fine machinery of commercial logic.

'If I may commend a principle,' St Just said, 'it is this. The industry is like a sea wall. By taking the strength from one part to support another, you merely weaken the wall at other places. Thus, far from strengthening it, you risk the failure of all.'

Grange said, 'I respect your arguments. But I should like to appeal to you as an employer, sir. Their fate is surely your consideration.'

'It is indeed. And therefore, recognising my responsibility, perhaps I may ask you a question. How many people do you yourself employ in some form of enterprise?'

'I believe you may know the answer beforehand, sir. I have a domestic housekeeper, but apart from that, none.'

'Then since you so kindly inform me of your own position, perhaps you will permit me to explain to you how such matters work. The reason I am able to offer employment is because I make a profit. By being rigorous in this matter, I offer more employment, whereas those who feel tempted occasionally to advise or criticise me for my efforts in most circumstances appear to offer no employment of any substance. I hope you will forgive me for pointing this out to you, my dear sir. I mean you no disservice. The inescapable fact is that profit is the motor of employment. Lack of profit is the death of employment.' St Just smiled. 'The profit of the employer is the friend of the worker, not his enemy.'

Grange nodded. 'You have made your views clear.'

'And yet you do not agree?'

Grange said, 'I have done my duty.'

'Indeed, sir. You have done so admirably, if I may say so. And is there anything else you should wish to discuss?'

'No,' Grange replied. 'I cannot do more than say that I believe, on the grounds I have indicated, that there is a risk of an accident. If that should occur, my own services, which are in the alleviation of suffering, will perhaps be requested. Until then, I believe I should thank you for your hospitality, and for your most interesting exposition of economic principles.'

'Your intentions are good, sir,' St Just said, with firmness but something like equanimity. 'And I thank you for your interest in my affairs.' Having presented his views, he was now concerned with his duties as host. 'Would you not like some port, before you go?'

'You are kind to offer.' Grange stood up. 'But I must depart.'

St Just inclined his head, drew himself to his feet and walked around the desk to the door. Grange noticed that the tips of his fingers rested a moment on the corner of the desk for support. There St Just paused, breathing with the effort of rising.

'You have heard of the philanthropist Mr James Elstead?'

Grange nodded, though surprised at this new direction.

St Just paused a little longer before moving ahead of him to open the door of the study. 'Mr James Elstead, of Northumberland?'

'I believe I have heard of him. The inventor and owner of mills.'

'An admirable man.' St Just seemed to drive himself forward towards the door of the study by an effort of will.

They began to walk down the panelled corridor.

'James Elstead owned perhaps twenty cotton mills. He is the inventor and former patenter of the Elstead Slide, a device that greatly facilitated the turning of cotton into linen and for which he is justly renowned. As his banker and financial partner, I supported him in his efforts. Even after the day on which he began to practise philanthropy, I was faithful to him and his great enterprises.'

St Just was driving himself forward, leaning heavily as he placed weight on his shorter leg.

'He was an idealist, sir. When his fortune was amassed, he took account of his conscience, and turned his prodigious mind and energies to the alleviation of circumstances among those who worked for him. He was determined to provide for his workers the finest conditions of living of any such in the land. His fervour to help his own workmen was so great that he began upon the construction of not one, but three model villages. As his adviser I

282

prevailed upon him to start on one, and so lessen the risk to himself, but he brushed my objections aside. I admired him. But perhaps it was the case that his principles overcame his good sense. I blame myself in large part for supporting him in this endeavour, for I watched him proceed to that point where the process could not be reversed. As his adviser, I should have warned him more forcibly. But among my faults was this, that I admired him, no, worshipped him too much, too whole-heartedly, to convey to him the full truth of the conditions in which he found himself. Perhaps the circumstances would have been averted if I had made my views clear to him in good time. But I was in awe of him. His vision was too great, his judgement too profound for me to countermand it. By spring of the following year I was forced to tell him that he should forgo the building of two of his planned new villages if he were to weather the storm that was gathering. But he was equally determined that these were merely temporary conditions. He pressed ahead regardless of my counsel.'

They were by now in the hall, standing at the doorway. Grange turned towards St Just to shake hands with his host. St Just was breathing slowly and heavily.

'The result of my endeavours to support him was that he was bankrupted within the year. I tried to save what was left of his considerable estates, so that the kernel of the skilled work-force which he had assembled over his lifetime might be maintained, but it was precious little when compared with the whole. Nothing of it remained in Elstead ownership. Most of it was sold in lots to his neighbouring owners – to lesser men in every way. Your coat, sir.'

'Thank you.'

St Just's breathing had deepened and become more regular.

'I offered him the use of a cottage in these poor grounds, but he prefers to live his declining years in some employment, however small. He himself gave work to several thousand men and their families, but there is no one who will employ him now, an old and broken man. I prefer not to witness him directly.'

Grange experienced an odd intuition. 'He is here?'

'He is the gatekeeper, sir.' St Just swallowed once, twice. 'If you will excuse me, I will ring this bell for him and then depart before he arrives at the door to escort you.'

'Forgive me, I do not understand.'

'The fact is, sir, though I may worship him, he cannot bear the sight of me.'

Grange hesitated. 'He feels ashamed that you should view him?'

'No, no, sir. I believe it is the admiration that he still perceives in my face, in my countenance – that is what unnerves and anguishes him.'

St Just pressed the push that would summon Elstead from the cottage, and bowed briefly.

'Good-day,' the banker said. He turned and moved off down the corridor, like a solitary minotaur, leaving Grange to the elderly doorkeeper, whom he could now see making his way across the garden from the gatehouse.

CHAPTER 70

Following the gatekeeper through the snow towards the main gates, Grange sensed the scene had turned lighter around him. The blizzard had halted. A cautious moon lit the edges of the snow.

Ahead of him, Elstead seemed shrunk into his coat, a moving wraith. He unlocked the gates and Grange waited for him to step aside so that he could pass through. At the same time as having his curiosity aroused, Grange was shy of staring too closely into Elstead's face. He was aware, at some instinctive level, of the privacy of despair. Yet some part of him also lived in the hope that he might see in abject failure a greater humanity than he had observed in St Just's success.

Having opened the gate, Elstead drew apart into the shadow, and Grange was uncomfortably aware of being surveyed himself, of his entire person being subject to the concentration of a singular mind.

'Thank you,' Grange said.

In the shadow of the wall Elstead made the slightest inclination of his head, and waited for Grange to turn and go. He paused until Grange had passed through the gateway, then he emerged from his shadow and swung the gate closed. Grange heard the locks turn behind him.

Moonlight made the snow fields luminous.

It was strange that nature, with her unpredictable moods, would turn such a serene face to his sombre thoughts. He was disturbed, though it was a little while before he could place an explanation upon it. It seemed to him that he had seen in the rigour of St Just a state peculiarly suited to his own character, as if his own commitment to precision had been extended to its logical conclusion in the exactitude of the banker. Perhaps fate had shown him, in a lucid insight, the final direction and destination of his own character. His mind was agitated, subject to a fierce ferment of uncomfortable irritation and conjecture. The fact that the wind had now dropped, and was at most a light breeze, allowed him to concentrate on his thoughts even more fiercely and obsessively than on the outward journey.

At one stage on his walk, the landscape being obfuscated by its blanket of snow, he passed the turning to the footpath that would take him past the ancient Durlston rings into Lymington, and was forced to retrace his steps for several hundred yards. When he found the place again, and put the familiar mound of Durlston on his right, his thoughts continued to churn unabated until he arrived at his house.

'Will you take something more to eat, sir?' Mrs Thompson asked.

As he sat at the small bench in the hallway and removed his boots, the message in her own eyes was that of genuine concern. He had returned shaken from his visit. She could sense the disturbance in his mind.

'I have had my fish broth, Mrs Thompson. What more could I need?'

'Against walking in the cold, sir? Some meat, perhaps.'

'I have done well enough without meat until now.'

Mrs Thompson nodded. 'I have stoked the fire for you.'

'Thank you,' Grange said. 'I believe I shall be going out again this evening.'

'Sir . . .' Mrs Thompson began to object, but thought better of it.

There was something that had agitated him, that had stirred inside him. She knew or guessed that in his present state of excitation Grange would treat any attempt to restrict his comings and goings with singular brusqueness. She allowed herself to say, as though, merely in commentary, 'That is twice in one night.' She refrained from saying precisely what was on her mind, which was that he would catch a fever.

But, as though suspecting her question, Grange said, 'If I have not caught a chill on one journey, I do not think I will catch it on another.'

'You may have already caught a chill,' Mrs Thompson demurred. 'Though it might not yet be upon you.'

'Then another walk will do me no further harm', Grange said, 'than I have done myself already.'

She considered him carefully and left in silence for the kitchen.

CHAPTER 71

After he had put on his greatcoat, Mrs Thompson handed Grange a heavy scarf and watched as he wound it around his neck. She lifted the oil lantern off its hook on the wall and gave it to him. He nodded to her and raised the wick a little to increase the radiance. Then he set one hand on the door latch and picked up the bulky canvas bag in the other.

In the open doorway the cold struck him like a body. Mrs Thompson drew the door closed behind him.

Outside, his boots crushed the snow. He stared down the glittering street, lit partly by moonlight, partly by rush burners stationed at intervals along the walls. Behind the street the white mass of Walhampton Hill reared softly on the other side of the Lymington river. Fresh snow had fallen that evening, but now the air was clear and cold. Water had refrozen on the paving stones, turning them slippery. He began to walk down the High Street, choosing his way carefully between the frozen sheets.

The faint, soft roar from the rush burners was a companionable sound but, turning left along Gosport Street, he entered a zone of comparative silence and darkness. At the end of the street he swung right and crossed the toll-bridge, nodding at the white-faced visage of the toll-keeper behind his small winter window. His exemption as a physician from toll dues produced the customary reaction – a searching glance, followed by swift withdrawal of the face, as though the toll-keeper, having established his identity, had just witnessed something vaguely inexplicable and unmentionable, and was not willing to bestow further attention.

On the Walhampton side of the river, silence extended across the snow fields. The lantern cast a faint light, only enough to illuminate the next few steps. He caught glimpses, through the trees, of the reaches of snow that curved down to the river; and of the moon, which breathed outside the mysterious circle of light.

There were several paths that he might have taken, but he chose to walk up the incline to Barrows Lane. At the top of the slope a tall, geometric fir was covered in snow. He turned into Barrows Lane itself. The path was familiar now, but the need for caution on the slippery roadway engaged his attention until he was broadside to the familiar wooden gate, and could see in the moonlight the line of sentinel elms behind which Mrs Quill's house stood, now empty at its heart.

He had followed a path to her gate without being fully conscious of his reasons for doing so. It was intuition, more than precise purpose, which had led him. Staring across the empty snow towards the deserted house, attempting to justify this late-night visit, he remembered a quotation of Hume, in which the sense was that the rational mind is the servant of the emotions. Standing silent in the snow, he recalled another – a passing remark of Hargood's – to the effect that a ghost is nothing more or less than an intense absence.

He walked through the gate and stood at the place where he had first found freshly dug earth, and had suspected that someone still tended the empty house. Snow covered the area in blankness. Beneath the line of beeches he stood in the cold silence for several minutes, attempting to collect his thoughts. It was then, staring at the ground, that he realised the peculiar unconscious efficacy of his mind.

The herb garden, over an area of perhaps eight feet square, had been recently cleared of snow. He raised his lantern to survey it. Someone had used a board or branch to brush the snow from the herbs themselves. Grange bent down and looked more closely at the disturbed surface. The heads of small plants showed through on the cleared area. When he examined them more minutely, there were signs that several had been clipped. On his knees he hoped, prayed, suspected, that whoever had cleared the snow had left imprints. He stood up again and raised his lantern over the surrounding reaches. The small flame flickered for a moment, then spread a sincere light about him.

There were indeed a number of footprints around the area which had been cleared. For a moment he considered their size – a large child's or perhaps a woman's footmarks.

His mind, unleashed from its hesitation, started to work on several fronts simultaneously. The snow had fallen only a few hours earlier, in the late afternoon and evening. It appeared that the visitor had come with the purpose of clearing the snow from the herb garden and taking back certain herbs. It seemed to Grange, from these broad deductions, that he or she had left only a short while previously. It occurred to him that the person might still be in the garden, having withdrawn at his approach, and perhaps was surveying him even now. He suppressed a faint shudder at the thought of an invisible witness, and turned to consider more immediate matters.

Another question taxed him more closely. When he had entered the front gate he was certain there had been no footsteps alongside his own in the virgin snow. How, then, had the visitor entered the garden? He glanced around at the pallid walls of the empty house and back along the pathway that led to the gate. He raised his lantern, and confirmed that he could see no tracks other than his own leading to or from the front gate.

These points established, he began to circle the area, searching for further tracks. Almost directly opposite the path from the front gate, he saw some prints leading from the other side of the garden towards the herb garden and, almost simultaneously, another set of tracks from the same small shoes leading away from the cleared area.

Holding his lamp ahead of him, he followed them. They moved directly towards the house itself and his mind brushed against the thought that the visitor had a key. When the tracks reached the front of the house, however, they diverted onto a side path that led down the south side and round the back of the house. There, hidden in a yew hedge, was another side gate. He leaned down carefully to open it. He was engrossed in examining the latch, and establishing that the gate led onto the footpath down Walhampton Hill, when there was a sudden flurry in the hedgerow beside him. The skittering paws of an animal, a hare or fox, that had been sheltering on the other side of the hedge, moved away. For several seconds, while he waited for his heart to quieten, he considered that the visitor must have left some little while earlier, long enough at least for a wild creature to take up shelter and settle down in the hedgerow near the gate.

Beside the gate there was an odd indentation in the snow which, on closer view, showed two footprints close together and in parallel. Their inner edges almost touched one another. He sensed that the visitor had stood here for a while, perhaps while he or she warmed his or her hands after clearing the snow. To his surprise, the tracks led not down the footpath to the river but inland, across the empty fields. Determined now to track down the prints to their destination, he raised the wooden latch, opened the gate, closed it carefully behind him and began to follow the indentations across the silent snow fields.

CHAPTER 72

It was by chance, perhaps, that he had felt compelled to go out into the night and pay a visit to Mrs Quill's house. Yet his pilgrimage had not been entirely random. He had hoped, without even allowing the thought to gain a clear and exact form in his mind, that there might be some signs of visitation by the person she had asked to oversee her property, at least in the form of vague prints in the snowfall of the day before. As it was, he had felt a sudden access of gratitude, even a faint flush of pride, when he discovered that the prints were not only present, but that the visitor had appeared on the same night and had left a clear indication in the new snow. It seemed to him that a small tide was running in his favour. He might be following the vague imaginings of his mind, but some providence had placed in his path a part of the evidence that he sought.

For half a mile he followed the line of prints across the field, then for several hundred yards along the side of a lane. They seemed to be taking a line parallel to the Walhampton shore and towards Sowley. He was beginning to accept the validity of this assumption when they stopped abruptly, as if in mid-air, and for several steps he was walking in virgin snow. He halted, at a loss. The visitor appeared to have taken to the air like an angel or a devil.

Standing still, so that he lost no further ground by unnecessary panic, he swung the lamp and stared around him. A yard or so to his left a small stream, no more than an overflow of ditchwater, ran alongside the outside edge of the road where the ground was lowest. It was a dark, oozing flow. The cold was not yet sufficient to freeze running water. But he noticed that the small persistent rivulet had removed the snow beside the road in its course. It occurred to him that his quarry might have stepped into the moving water, leaving no tracks. But where, then? On both sides of the road were high hawthorn hedges, impossible to surmount.

Without moving, he considered his surroundings for some time. A peculiar notion occurred to him, a thought so odd he would have dismissed it in any other circumstances except those facing him now. Perhaps the person, after halting in the snow, had deliberately walked backwards, using his own prints to disguise his retreat. He attempted to follow the logic. Since it was, he surmised, extremely difficult to do so without falling out of the tracks, there would be a point, not far back, where footprints once again diverged. He walked back along the path of the tracks perhaps twenty yards, looking to left and right for some avenue of escape. Finally, glancing to his left, he saw on the other side of the small black stream a break in the high hedge and an old oak cross-gate. By raising the lantern as high as he could, and peering through the slats of the gate, he could just discern the trail of footmarks leading away across a field.

He breathed out a sigh of surprise and relief. The visitor's deliberate stratagem seemed to him both wilful and inordinately cunning. There could be no doubt that he or she was nervous of being followed and had taken elaborate precautions against being tracked. The ruse (if that was indeed its purpose) at least had the effect of alerting Grange to other possible decoys. As he had surmised, the water flowing alongside the roadway was no more than a few inches deep, hardly sufficient to threaten the integrity of his boots. He crossed it and raised himself on the step above the cross-gate. Descending, he found himself in a long meadow whose furthest extent could be perceived only dimly by the moonlight on the snow.

The track passed over the long sloping meadow towards the eastern end, crossed another gate, then joined a footpath running north and south, parallel with the field. It was clearly a well-used way, probably between two settlements, though he was sufficiently disorientated now not to have a clear idea of the exact direction of the pathway. He experienced another moment of doubt when he saw that there were several other tracks on the path – the large footprints of at least three men. As he approached them more closely, he saw that the smaller footprints had disappeared into the larger ones.

If it had not been for the earlier change of direction, he might have abandoned his search. But now he was becoming used to a certain active cunning. To his mind, the exposition of the visitor's character had been set out upon the snow a short while back, by deliberately walking backwards in the existing footprints. He tried to place himself within his quarry's thoughts. How would he react to the footprints which also ran on the path? It seemed to Grange that such indentations would be perceived as yet another opportunity. He could envisage in his mind how his quarry now proceeded, taking care to disguise smaller prints within the large footprints.

The assumption placed a fresh dilemma on him. He was now forced to consider in which direction his quarry had gone. It seemed to him that the general movement of the visitor's tracks, taking into account the changes in direction, was inland, directly away from the Lymington river mouth and the Solent foreshore. So he decided to follow the path northwards, and hope that if and when the prints diverged from the large marks, he would be sufficiently alert to find them.

At length he arrived at a point on the footpath where a line of footprints separated from the path towards another cross-gate. But to his consternation they were not the smaller prints he expected, but one of the larger ones. He was at a loss. In whose footsteps would his quarry choose to hide now – in those on the common path, or in the single set of larger divergent prints? It was the third occasion that evening on which he was compelled to place his own intuition against the cunning of the visitor. It seemed to him once again to balance largely on a matter of general direction. If his quarry was making steady progress inland, the divergent trail was the more northerly, the more inland and therefore potentially the more promising. He decided he would follow the latter for a while, for a few hundred yards at least, but would have no hesitation in doubling back if he sensed he had made the wrong decision.

The prints led through another field. It occurred to him that the task of keeping one's own tracks within those of a single trail would be more difficult on virgin snow than on a general trampled path. A single or momentary loss of attention would leave a tell-tale sign. As he proceeded, he searched the trail for any sign of such a lapse. For several hundred yards he found no indication of any other track.

The meadow through which he proceeded was long and relatively narrow. To his right was a substantial wood of oak and beech. He was about to consider returning to the footpath when the prints reached an obstacle in the field and and moved around the squat shape of a lonely gorse bush. It was there that he was subject to another of those particular intuitions or convictions that had assailed him that evening.

It seemed to him that perhaps the unexpected change of direction of the original tracks around the gorse bush would have unsettled his visitor. Perhaps, in concentrating upon placing footsteps within the existing ones, he or she would come upon the sudden change of direction unawares. As the original larger tracks made their sudden detour around the offending object he found, set on the borders of two of them, the overlay of a smaller shoe or boot. He kneeled down and, drawing his lamp closer to examine the evidence, for the first time that evening allowed himself the faint trace of a smile.

There were no further clear divergences until the gate at the lower end of the field. There his quarry must have decided that sufficient effort had been made to hide his or her tracks. The larger swung left. Emerging from them, the smaller abandoned their larger parents and moved off at a tangent.

He suspected that this display of increased confidence was perhaps associated with the fact of being near the visitor's own dwelling. Staring up through the dark, he could just perceive, several hundred yards ahead, the bulk of what seemed to be several cottages, piled up in dark outlines against the clear sky, though there were no lights that he could see.

Grange halted to stare around him and take account. A roadway approached the group of cottages from the right. His impression was of haphazard habitations set broadly about a winding country track that had expanded by usage into a narrow lane. The image raised a memory in his mind. He had been here before. He saw now that the prints had led, by a diverse route across the fields and byways, towards Pilley.

As he approached the habitations his heart beat a little faster. He had emerged from his search with the same sense of mild satisfaction that he derived from scholarly research or exegesis. The radiance of the lamp swung softly over the snow. He began, at the same time, to feel some of the physical tiredness from his long pursuit. The bag in his other hand seemed heavier. Finally he stood outside the low front door of one of the small dwellings. He rapped twice on the door and waited.

CHAPTER 73

He heard a shuffle inside, the sound of a large bolt being drawn, then a baby crying.

The door swung open. In the several shapes and layers of darkness he detected the outline of a figure, almost certainly the same young woman he had encountered before. Perhaps she recognised his own tall shape, because she stood within the doorway, surveying him suspiciously.

Grange said, 'Miss Chorley, I seem to remember?'

The figure moved off, like a fish into the interior of a pond.

He wondered whether the door would again be slammed in his face. But a short while later another figure returned with a tallow lamp. The light was brought close, almost to his nose. He believed that – though he could not recognise her against the blinding light – he was face to face with Mrs Chorley at last.

'Dr Grange.' It was not a welcome, merely a confirmation of identity. For several seconds, it seemed to him, the woman studied his features with relentless attention.

He could see her better now. Direct eyes in a face burned dark with sun. He believed he recognised in her features some trace of the cook he had seen once or twice at the back of Mrs Quill's house on those occasions when he had visited her – a small, quiet, active woman who hardly ever spoke.

Grange said, 'Is your son here, perhaps?'

'Which one?'

'Matthew?'

The pause that followed was like darkness, an absence of feeling. 'Matthew doesn't live here.'

Grange did not express any outward emotion at the evasion. He was used to conducting his investigations with what the College of Physicians liked to call a 'closed face'. She, on the other hand – if the records of the Poor House were reliable – was used to persecution from the Customs and perhaps some harassment from other officials of the parish in regard to her son's activities. Grange said, as gently as possible, 'That was not my question.'

The light came closer still, so close he thought the iron contusions of the lamp would be pressed against his face. He could feel the heat of the flame on his cheeks and forehead, and experienced the faintly rancid smell of the burning tallow. Now the flame seemed to occupy his entire vision, its light and heat a single ball of fire, like the sun.

This was intimidation of a kind. He had read that certain notorious criminals would hold a lamp close to a traveller's face in order to blind him when he entered their domain, so that he could be more easily attacked from behind or from the quarter. Determined not to blink or give ground, he waited. The flame seemed to burn itself into the roots of his eyes.

Without warning the lamp was drawn backwards, the door was hauled open and he was invited into the interior darkness. Out of courtesy, he put down his own lamp outside the door and, holding his heavy parcel, was forced to duck low beneath the lintel. For several moments his eyes saw nothing. A stronger smell of cooking and sweat assailed him. Holding his head low, he felt his way along the adjacent wall with his hands. If there were blackguards waiting for him, he would have been as much at their mercy as a blind man.

The door creaked and slammed behind him. Inside the hovel, layers of darkness became visible, unfolding slowly. Gradually his vision returned. Vague shapes drifted on the outer periphery. The tallow lamp which had been used to intimidate him was hung in its place from a heavy roof beam. In its faint radiance, a baby's head was moved from a single, huge breast. The voluptuous white shape was covered silently.

'Mrs Chorley?' he repeated.

He heard, in some other room in the hovel, the click of a latch, felt the drift of a current of air against his face, and knew that Matthew had escaped to the exterior.

Mrs Chorley allowed no trace of triumph to enter her voice, though a note of sententiousness seemed present. 'What was it you said you wanted, sir?'

'I brought you a gift, which I hope you will do me the honour of accepting.'

Grange reached inside his bag and drew forth the bulky body of a goose, a little stiff, now, after its transport through the cold night. 'I had hoped it might be a small addition to your Christmas fare.'

'Our Christmas fare?'

'With my compliments,' Grange said, 'to you and your family.'

His eyes could see a little better now. She regarded his gift with an expression of manifest suspicion. He watched her eyes narrow and, in the changing circumstances he observed perhaps the faint trace of discomfort which followed her hoodwinking of him over her son's escape. She paused and he thought she was about to refuse his offering. Inside, a part of her seemed to flinch against him. But perhaps because she had mistreated him, or out of an unexpected access of kindness towards him, or possibly on account of simple relief that her son was now outside and already at a sufficient distance not to be easily pursued, she reached forward and took the bird.

'I must go now,' Grange said. 'Perhaps you will be kind enough to give my regards to Matthew?'

She half nodded, as though considering what he had said.

There was just enough light for him to feel towards the door, using the lintel of the window as guide with his fingers, and from there to the frame of the door. He lifted the heavy wooden cross-piece and swung the door open. In the frame he was forced to bend almost double again, before emerging from the cottage.

Outside, as the cold struck him, he was able to rise again to his full height and ease his spine into straightness. Behind him the door was firmly closed, though it seemed to him not quite with the same ferocity as on the previous occasion.

Freed from the dank interior, the sudden, flowering complexity of his thoughts brought to his face the trace of a smile. What had caused him to take one of the beautiful feathered carcasses and deliver it to her? An instinct, perhaps? Or something more subtle, a little darker?

Inside the house, he had a sense of the various members of the family gathering around, as though the goose were a mine, fearful to touch it, quietly watchful. He imagined even the suckling babes momentarily distracted from their mothers' breasts, their tiny brows garnered in thought. Despite Mrs Chorley's misgivings about its source, he felt certain that in the end she would pluck and cook the bird. They would eat the proffered gift – if only because to do otherwise, to reject his offer, would be to grant his gesture an even greater meaning and portent than it already held. And so, like a Trojan horse, his intentions would infiltrate their Christmas in the form of a fat and magnificent goose. And at every mouthful they would consider their maltreatment of him.

Charity, he knew, was complex.

CHAPTER 74

Outside, there was a clear sky and a good moon. His own lamp, which he had set down before he entered the hovel, burned softly beside the doorway. He picked it up and set off towards Lymington.

It had begun to snow again. White flakes filtered through the black light, yet there was no sign of cloud. Using a more direct route than the circuitous one he had taken to Pilley, he found his way more or less easily along the lanes that led back to the Lymington river. A half-hour later, emerging from Hundreds Lane, he came to the banks of the river. A night breeze had risen. Gusts of wind furred the water, and smaller, lighter feathering eddies detached themselves and drifted like pale spats across it. He watched a flurry of snow dissolve in the river's dark surface.

Following his knock, Mrs Thompson unlocked the door. Seeing him, she opened it quickly to let him in and shivered at the body of cold air that entered with him. She closed and rebolted the door.

Grange said, 'I believe my errands are over.'

He removed his coat and scarf, and sat down on the small bench in the hall so that he could withdraw his boots. She considered him carefully, wondering at the source of the smile that played upon his lips. He handed her first one boot and then the other, and she took both so that she could place them in warmth beside the stove.

He seemed, at last, exhausted and, at her suggestion settled down in front of the fire.

297

'You gave the goose?'

'Indeed, Mrs Thompson. To the Chorleys, who live at Pilley.'

'It is a kind thought. Pilley is a long distance on foot.'

He did not respond. Exhaustion seemed to have taken hold of him. When she looked more closely, she found that he was already asleep in his chair by the fire.

CHAPTER 75

My dear Leman,

In my past I was not usually subject to dreams of special intensity. But since I have begun to return to my former loves and deepest passions, and to evoke them in greater detail than I had ever wished or countenanced before, the disturbance of my equilibrium has given rise to some fearful and lurid imaginings. I am not one who sets much store by dreams, but several of them seem to carry with them a faint echo of my past, and one in particular seems to project, like a shadow on the wall, an odd, distorted simulacrum of my previous behaviour.

It seems to me that such dreams rise through the mind like an intimation, and give the everyday a strange light, or perhaps darkness, as though the earth itself became part of the reflection.

I dreamed last night that I rowed out in the wildfowling craft with my younger colleague, and we set about stalking some geese that lay along the horizon. (Thus, it seems to me, in dream we mix our memory, for I had no less than a few days earlier undertaken just such an expedition.)

After a long stalk we found the birds and drifted silently, until they were all around us, alert and alarmed but not yet inflamed with that sense of panic which would set them off the surface, belling like hounds. We were among them, and I began to feel a strange tranquility, as if we shared more than some space and light with the beautiful creatures, but even certain feelings or sensations.

Their agitation at our presence did not cause them to fly. Indeed, it seemed that they drew closer to observe us, turning their heads this way and that to gain a view, and all the while we drifted among them I felt the sensation of ease spread through and about me, as though their presence and close association began to affect me.

How difficult it is to describe the sensation of a dream! Despite their tranquillity, or perhaps because of it, I experienced a strange sense of foreboding. I started to feel that they had cast a spell upon us with their delicate beauty, with the calm but alert progress of their bodies alongside us – even that, in some strange manner, they escorted us towards an unknown destination. I cannot begin to describe this destination, except perhaps in terms of the sensations to which I increasingly felt subject. If I may attempt to clothe such an obscure sensation in words, it seemed to me that we were moving towards some paradise, some haven. I had only to lie there, patiently quiescent, and this beauty would be revealed to me.

Yet something else arose in me, which at first I could not name, and even now do not understand. A perturbation, a slow fear gripped me. It had no outward cause, yet lay in some internal sense or conviction that somehow, though I might be drawn unresisting towards paradise, my own senses were betraying me. I sensed, with what apparatus I do not know, that I was entering a dream from which I would not wake. (Thus, in dreams, it seems, there is no contradiction that we may dream of ourselves while dreaming.) It was precisely this musing, this feeling of moving towards that strange peace, that caused my deepest consternation.

I say that I was gripped by a form of fear or panic, that in remaining passive I seemed to be leaving behind something of my own sensibility. I sensed there was some price to pay for this sensation of bliss, and my nervousness was based upon a notion of what this price might be. I feared perhaps that if I lay quiescent and passive as paradise approached, as pleasure flooded me, I would begin to lose control even of what I was. Though my companion was silent, I knew he too had entered that state of strange communion with the birds and with that intuition or foreboding which is a property of such dreams. For this was my dilemma: that my companion seemed complicit in that feminine paradise, and it was my conviction that he, unlike me, would offer no resistance to the final commingling of beings in a state of bliss.

The creatures were gathered around us, they accompanied us and, though all were silent now, by means of some communication between us it seemed that in our calm progression we were approaching that state of final peace towards which all souls are thought to long.

My dear Leman, I say that I was affected by terror, which grew in proportion as we approached our destination. While this sensation expanded in me, I decided upon my final resistance to the dissolution of my soul. For there, a few inches from me, lay the crude mechanism by which I might absolve myself from fear. I began to crawl towards it, and raised the firing hinge of the heavy fowling piece. The single click which caused it to settle into its primed state became the simple focus of my will. At the sound of it the birds grew nervous suddenly, as if they sensed betrayal, and began to show signs of agitation, and then to dart and move alarmedly, and finally to take off from the water, leaving confused tracks. Thus afraid, they swung into the air, and their panic flung them upwards, until the density of their wings was as dark as a cloud. It seemed that they would take my light and dissolve me into darkness. At which I pulled the trigger, the flint came down in the firing pan, the gun rocked against me, and the flock of souls began to tumble downwards into the water.

I believed I had saved us, my colleague and me, from the loss of our senses to these sirens. Now at last he had woken, and we roused ourselves to gather in what we had done. But when we went to collect them I perceived a strange transformation. For the beings that we dragged over the gunwales, with their feathery thighs and the warmth of life still in them, were not geese but women – naked maidens. I was gripped by a terrible awe, but not contrition, for what I had done. I was determined to bring them inboard. Beside me my companion did not speak, but helped me silently with the work of dragging the corpses into the boat.

As we gathered them in, I gazed into their faces, and I saw in them not merely the abstract features of beauty, but in one or two the traces, the hints, the outward characteristics and particular features, of several of my own former mistresses. I looked, I searched, for some trace of horror in their passive expressions at what I had done, but they were at the height of their beauty, their expressions calm in death, as though in some final sum I had released them.

My dear Leman, perhaps you emerge from the contemplation of my dream with a faint intimation of its effect upon me. For what may we communicate of so strange a flight of sensation in the form of words? Perhaps, in the crudeness of my enterprise, I suggest that dreams are often overlaid with memories. On the day of our stalk, when we had gathered in the feathered tribe, I saw that my colleague's hands were cold, and calmly I showed him how to warm them by placing them in the joint between the wings and the body, where the last heat remained. So now, in the midst of my contemplation of these maidens, I observed that he was cold and heard myself advise him, in a voice with no less calm, to place his frozen hands in their warm armpits.

Floating there, among the corpses of these murdered women, I felt weak suddenly and fainted forward, and the final image that I carried from the dream was the impression of lying in the bilges of the craft among my dead mistresses.

That was when I woke up, sweating in my night-shirt, and reached for the hooded candle that I increasingly keep beside my bed, so that after one of these nightmares I can concentrate for my repose upon the small light of a single, wavering flame.

Sir, these are my thoughts, which I have written down as though in a trance, and from which I now depart, having expressed something of them to the best of my ability.

I will continue with my narration once I have had a little time to recover. Now I am a little too much distracted for comfort, and for the sake of easing my tension I will absolve myself of the need to expound further on this strange matter.

Until I write again, sir, I remain,
    Yours sincerely,
        Hargood

CHAPTER 76

The weather continued cold for several days. It was a clear night, a night of perfect peace, though the land was still covered in frozen snow, when Grange visited Hargood's house again. He had recovered from his exertions of several nights before without being subject to a chill or a fainting fit. As he progressed beyond Walhampton Hill and struck inland, he felt a sense of contentment in the rhythm of his walking.

Hargood himself opened the door. He seized Grange's cold hand, drawing him into the warmth of the hall. 'You are frozen.'

Thin moonlight fell through the panes and edged along the floor. A great fire burned in the main room. At the sides of the fireplace, fresh logs had been placed to dry out before burning.

Hargood said, 'If I had known you intended a visit I would have picked you up in the fly.'

'You would indeed, and I would have thanked you. But that was why I walked.'

'You would like a little wine, perhaps?'

'If I could rest a few moments,' Grange told him, 'I would be grateful.'

'This is not a night to be out,' Hargood said, 'walking alone on the roads.'

He followed Grange through into the great drawing-room, admonishing him on the way. 'Be seated, sir.' He drew one of the tall-backed chairs towards the fire. 'At the very least you should rest a while before our dinner.'

'Dinner?'

'You must dine with me, sir. I insist.'

Hargood moved along the wall, taking up a position at the fire with his back to the grate. Grange was disinclined to argue the point. He found the angularity of the high-backed chair suited the rectangles of his tall body. Seated, he looked up at Hargood staring down at him. He noticed the high cheek-bones, now lined by light, the hieratic eyebrows, the nose like the thin bridge of a warrior's helmet.

Hargood said, 'You came by way of Mrs Quill's house?'

Grange smiled at the perception. He shook his head. 'Not this evening. I passed it recently on my Christmas rounds.'

'It remains empty?'

'Yes.'

The flames of the fire moved behind Hargood slowly. Sometimes, when the fire settled or murmured, the flames shifted uneasily, like a restless audience of relatives. In the background Grange heard Mrs Simmonds moving dishes in the kitchen.

'Silas, my dear fellow. You continue to rehearse her absence, much as others take religious service. She is gone now.'

Grange nodded, but they both continued to hold their ground, in formal but polite confrontation, while behind Hargood the fire coughed occasionally and uttered, as if by way of comment, a spark or two onto the stone floors.

That evening at the table Hargood drank deeply, as had become his recent custom, raising his eyes slowly while he considered, his thoughts drifting to the upper edges of the room, his eyebrows rising. 'Who?' he asked. 'Who is to know?'

Around him moved the flakes of repetitive, soft silence.

Grange said, 'About Mrs Quill?'

Hargood nodded. 'Concerning her history and her effects upon us.'

'No one but ourselves.'

'Then perhaps that knowledge will die with us.'

Grange was reminded again of the radical difference between them, that Hargood believed she was part of the past, while to Grange she seemed, manifestly and unarguably, a part of the future – a future which, nevertheless, he could not foresee.

The soft flames of the candles flickered and moved the light.

Unusually, a kind of melancholy being upon them both, they passed much of the meal in silence. In normal circumstances Grange relied upon Hargood to provoke and amuse him. And

Hargood, for his part, counted on his younger colleague for the entertainment of being goaded and for a heartfelt response. Yet this night the usual mechanism for their mutual entertainment seemed, temporarily at least, to have been abandoned or lost.

After a certain while Hargood smiled, a brief trace of his former good humour. 'I believe you are alone,' he said suddenly. The smile had left his mouth and his glass was held absent-mindedly as he studied Grange. 'I believe, though your mind is active, you sit in silence.'

Carefully, he poured himself more wine.

'If the mind remains active during solitude,' Grange said, 'that is sometimes enough.'

Hargood drank somnolently. 'You stand still, sir. You pursue your running shadow.'

Grange tilted his face towards Hargood and smiled. Hargood, viewing his calm presence, said, 'I do not know whether to pity you or to be envious.'

'Of what?'

'Of your singleness of character, or perhaps your sense of rest in your own company.'

'Hargood . . .'

'You know, sir.' Hargood was suddenly intense. 'I was asked by some young hell-fire what it is that makes a man into a rake. A rake, I answered, is someone who enjoys the company of women. A great rake, on the other hand, is someone who cannot bear his own company.'

Grange observed the smile on Hargood's face disappear and then the sinking into thoughtfulness that followed it.

Afterwards, still without talking, Hargood nodded towards Grange, and rose from his seat and picked up from the table the five-branched candelabra. Grange smiled, rose too – though a little unsteadily – and followed his host into the passageway.

CHAPTER 77

'Come and see, sir,' Hargood said. 'Come and see.'

He was on his feet and moving, holding the candelabra, sliding like a minotaur down the corridor, his shoulder against the wall for support. There was only one door in the house that was locked and all the silence of the household seemed contained there. Hargood had a key somewhere in one of his pockets and he leaned heavily against the wall as he searched for it. The candle flames wavered in his agitated breath. Grange waited in the nearby darkness while his host fumbled in the right-hand pocket of his breeches. He observed Hargood withdraw a long iron shaft and address the keyhole.

The locks moved. The door was heavy and the hinges complained. Grange was aware of the coolness of air from the room, like that of a vault. Hargood entered, holding the candelabra before him in the attitude of a propitiatory offering. Inside the room's musty atmosphere the flames seemed to flicker and burn low.

There was a heavy oak side table set against one of the walls. Hargood put down the candle holder and leaned for support on the table. Granted a momentary respite from the agitation of movement and the deep currents of Hargood's breath, the flames settled and grew tall. Under their added illumination the paintings which lined the walls emerged into calm, visible life. Hargood turned his heavy head upwards and it seemed to Grange he resembled a priest in his church, admiring the sanctity of the images of Christ and the Virgin upon the walls.

Around Hargood's head the occupants of the paintings appeared to swim in the dark light of the room. The candles, growing in radiance, illuminated creamy flesh, breasts, buttocks. There was not a painting there that did not portray the naked female form in one of its manifestations. The combination of increased radiance from the candle flames and Grange's own adjustment to the dark brought the shadowy, curvacious shapes into stronger focus.

Hargood addressed Grange without turning towards him. 'I believe you have seen before, sir, what I intend to leave behind?'

It seemed to Grange at first that Hargood referred specifically to the paintings. But in the ensuing silence he began to understand his host might perhaps mean something else – not the paintings themselves so much, but what was contained in them – the sensual life which they depicted.

In their present dispositions Hargood was standing sideways on, facing a painting on a wall, a Montmorency, in which a procession of female figures of voluptuous form ascended into the light. It was a strange pattern, a great coil of magnificent flesh reaching upwards into the clouds. To Grange it seemed a sensualist's dream of heaven. According to this variation of the gospel, the day of judgement was not the shriving of flesh and the release of the spirit from the imprisoning body, but its opposite; the precipitation of spirit into magnificent nakedness.

It was true, as Hargood had said, that Grange had seen the painting once before, and it had disturbed him then. He attempted to place some explanation upon his feeling. It seemed to him that the features of the women were deliberately vague or characterless, that the observer's eye – or at least his own – searched in vain for some sign of the deeper human spirit in the swirl of luminescent flesh. In his earlier life, in London, when he had the opportunity to stand before one of the great paintings of the Renaissance masters on the subject of the female nude, his attention had moved naturally between the beautiful tones of the naked form and the human character of the face. There, he had sensed that the predominant expression of female attraction – lassitude, coyness, cupidity – was a mere surface covering for the other, deeper and more mysterious human emotions. In the Montmorency, try as he might, he did not find on a single face any sign of individual character or expression. All the eyes of the women were raised upwards, towards the swirl of flesh above them. Seeking the expressions on their faces had exactly the opposite effect of acting as a frame or counterweight to the flesh. On the contrary, the eyes of each naiad were reflected towards the body of another. Each woman was the witness or voyeur of her neighbour. So the eye of the observer was drawn inexorably into the coil or pattern itself.

Once before, at an earlier viewing of Hargood's private gallery, Grange had been inclined to dismiss the painting as second-rate. But now perhaps he perceived that he had misunderstood the original idea of the painter. This precisely was the artist's intention – not to portray the individual human, but to celebrate sensual longing itself. And it was clear to Grange, too, that the owner of the painting, raising his heavy head to gaze up with a kind of mendicant smile, approved of the design.

Grange was engaged in these thoughts when, almost of its own impulsion, his attention moved to Hargood. He attempted to redirect himself to the painting, then looked again more closely at his colleague. There was something a little odd about the physical state of the great voyeur, which attracted the concern of the physician in Grange. The smile of contemplation upon Hargood's lips did not dissuade Grange from the fact that there was a glaze to his host's eye and an unhealthy film of moisture on his face.

Under Grange's consideration, Hargood swayed slightly and placed the knuckles of his fingers on the table for greater support. It seemed to Grange that he might be about to faint. Without wishing to appear overly concerned, or draw unnecessary attention to his host's condition, Grange made his own private calculations about how quickly and easily he could close the two yards or so separating them before Hargood collapsed.

But he had misinterpreted the momentary loss of countenance. Hargood coughed, cleared his throat and seemed about to speak. There was a moment of waiting, of contemplation, while his host appeared to gather himself. With an odd rumble from his belly and a strange, fervent bending of his back, Hargood was suddenly and copiously sick onto the side table. What followed was – in the eyes of his calm observer, at least – a somewhat torrid scene. If the celestial figures poured upwards into the light, beneath them, more palpable solids were descending towards the table's upper surface. It seemed to Grange that this was not a moment to interfere or offer support. His host seemed too much involved in making the best of the diversion. Hargood, as in all his activities, committed himself with a full heart to the matter in hand, roaring like a lion between salvos, recovering only to throw fresh resources upon the table. To Grange's eye, at least, the supply of his reserves seemed infinite.

At the end of the occasion – for an occasion of a kind it certainly was – Hargood withdrew a large handkerchief and manfully patted the corners of his mouth. He said modestly, 'Forgive me, Silas, an unexpected lapse.'

Having discharged himself, Hargood regarded with a certain satisfaction the heaped table, and perhaps also the fact that only two of the five flames on the candelabra had survived the onslaught, hanging on like the nervous flags of gallant defenders.

In the circumstances, the substantially reduced light had obscured the paintings, so that even had Grange wished to continue his consideration of the Montmorency while his host recovered his equilibrium, physical circumstances rendered further contemplation difficult.

After such expenditure of effort, Hargood required a little time to recover. He was still breathing heavily, though already, to Grange's eye at least, he seemed more cheerful and animated. Although he still leaned forward a little, supporting himself, his knuckles set widely apart on the heaped side table, something of his normal healthy complexion had returned. Grange stood a little way away, discreetly, his hands calmly folded behind his back, his distance a mark of respect.

Among these momentous diversions another thought occurred to Grange, or perhaps not so much a thought as an impression which lurked, uncomprehending, at the back of his mind. Why had Hargood brought him here? To witness the paintings? He had known of Hargood's collection and had seen them at least once before. If so, what had he been summoned to consider on this particular occasion? The impression, slowly gaining upon him, was that he had been brought here precisely to observe, like an expert witness at a trial, Hargood's own bodily revolt against the fleshly life.

At first the thought was too large, or perhaps too portentous, to comprehend or appreciate fully. He knew that the ways of the mind are mysterious, that Hargood had not necessarily planned the occasion – spectacular as it was. But at the same time, perhaps suspecting what was in store, Hargood had felt the implacable summons of his own body to bring Grange to the gallery. As if this were not enough, there was another consideration, moving like a

308

shadow at the back of Grange's mind. When Hargood had asked him to witness the paintings before, Grange had stood by, embarrassed at the largesse of flesh, while his host, in good party, had clearly enjoyed his reticence and attempted by various means to incite Grange to comment favourably on the paintings.

And now Hargood had requested Grange to view the same gallery, though in different circumstances, as a man might ask another to observe the progress of an ailment or disease. There was something that was happening within Hargood, some change or process that seemed both deep and inexorable. And he had obliged his old friend not only to witness it, but perhaps to bring his own mind to bear upon the changes that were implicit in it. Indeed, it seemed to Grange – maintaining his respectful distance from his host – that Hargood had invited his professional opinion on the progress or changing state of Hargood's own soul.

There was little further opportunity for reflection, except perhaps a sense of unease at factors that eluded explanation. By now Hargood seemed to have recovered fully his spirits. The stench, too, was substantial. By unspoken and mutual consent, they left the airless room for the air outside. Locking the door behind him, Hargood said, 'I shall not wake Mr Simmonds from his sleep now, though I dare say he will be impressed in the morning.'

CHAPTER 78

Hargood seemed relieved and lightened. Together, in considerable good humour, given the earlier solemnity of the evening, they walked back down the corridor towards the hallway and the main door. Grange removed his cloak from the hanging hook and put it on his shoulders. He lit his own lantern from the flame of the lamp that hung in the hall. Hargood opened the door and Grange stepped out into the night.

Grange bowed to his host and was about to depart when Hargood said, 'Silas, my dear fellow.'

Grange swung to face him. Hargood was standing in the

doorway, his back to the light. He bulked large, filling the frame, his head forward.

Under Grange's eyes Hargood seemed to gather himself, thickening further in the doorway as though he were swelling to express something. Hargood said, 'I have an odd belief that in due course you will be happy.'

Surprised at this sudden exposition of the philosophical, Grange said, 'I hope you may be right.' He struggled for his own exposition. 'And you, Hargood?' Grange paused. 'What about you?'

'What about me, sir?'

'I detect sometimes, beneath your exuberance, a trace of melancholy.'

'I am no different.'

'Your soul . . .'

'My dear fellow. You are an atheist. You do not believe in the soul.'

'That is true enough,' Grange agreed. 'Yet you seem to be in . . . movement of some kind.'

'Movement.' Hargood seemed to turn the word this way and that. 'Yes, sir, I believe I may be in movement of some kind.'

'Sometimes, there is little that a person might do to help himself.'

'I am aware of that, sir.'

'You know that you have a friend who observes you as closely, perhaps, as you observe him . . .'

'I know that I have a fine companion in you, sir.' As if for emphasis, Hargood nodded.

Their cursory and incomplete exchange of views seemed to have reached an end. Grange inclined his head in salute, turned and walked down the path towards the open roadway. Hargood must have watched him departing, for only when he had passed through the garden and was effectively out of sight, did he hear Hargood swing the door closed behind him and drive home the great bolts against the darkness.

There was cloud and no moon or stars that night, and for his return to his own house he was grateful for a lamp to light his way. It was unusually cold, even for that time of year, the hoarfrost already on exposed surfaces, the glimmer of ice along the wooden railings that ran by the roadway, the white sheets of snow on the fields. Because of the obscurity and the small radius of light, Grange was forced to walk a little more slowly than usual, though the path was now so familiar he could have felt his way home. At the top of Walhampton Hill he paused for a moment. There was a shorter route along a footpath which cut off a corner of the rutted wheel track and reduced his distance by several hundred yards.

The night had become clearer. He could see over the white glimmer of the field towards the darkness of the Lymington river in its Walhampton basin. As a child he had been fearful of the dark, but as he grew older it seemed increasingly familiar to him. It had become, almost, his natural medium. He felt the peculiar richness of the night, as though it were an extension of his skin. He liked the way the frost removed the excess moisture from the air. Everything seemed purified.

A thought seemed to overtake him, which he had reserved to chew afterwards, as a dog might carry off a bone to bury and eat later. There was something else in the gallery of female flesh that had disturbed his mind. Beneath the weight of other more pressing considerations, he had had neither time nor inclination to consider it then, not least because the thought itself was as elusive as the impression of strange movement in Hargood's own soul. Now he found himself approaching it sideways, obliquely, like a man stalking an animal he did not wish to frighten or disturb. Perhaps the clue to it lay in his own disposition after he had observed the great motion of solids onto the oak table and stood in silence while his host recovered from his exertions. As if the display he had just witnessed were not disconcerting enough, what disturbed Grange, as much or more, perhaps, than the insight the occasion had provided into Hargood's own changed state, was that he himself had felt curiously at home among the paintings, no longer either disturbed or embarrassed. More than this, he had begun to suspect, in his own fresh understanding of Montmorency, not so much an intellectual insight as a movement of his own character, a shift of sympathy towards the painter's perspective. He had looked at the sensual swirl and found himself drawn into it, as though into a welcome medium. The more he considered his new insight, the more it seemed an indication, or a hint at least, of his own changing nature, as if there were perhaps odd processes at work inside him too, though in a different direction from his host.

As he opened the side gate and moved along the faintly gravelled bridle-path, a small white flame burst silently from beneath his feet. He was almost upon it before he realised it was the white scut of a rabbit which he had disturbed hiding in the thick grass beside the gravel pathway. It darted beneath the railings, and he observed it flicker and dash in swift bounds across the frozen, snow-covered field. At the same time he sensed there was something else in the dark with them. On the point of crossing the path perhaps twenty yards ahead of him, he glimpsed the shadowy form of a stoat, which perhaps had been hunting the creature. He observed it change direction, cross the path and move in a fast, jerky pursuit. It had not yet achieved its winter whiteness, and it seemed to him like a dark and terrible bolt on the snow. He watched the fervour of its progress across the field, the hiss of their closing trajectories. By now they had moved beyond sight, into a hollow in the vast field. A few seconds later he heard the anguished cry of the rabbit as the stoat bit into its neck, then the quick, rhythmic thrashing of its hind legs, and afterwards silence.

At an earlier time in his life he would have been assailed by the thought that perhaps the hidden creature would have escaped detection if he had not disturbed it, had not set it upon its fluttering path to destruction. He might have regretted his decision to take the diversion down the bridle-path. At such a time, no doubt, he would have meditated, at least briefly, on the ruination that his inadvertent presence could bring to the world. But now he seemed part of the warm blood and darkness, not some detached observer. He was curiously unmoved by the event.

The peace of the night had settled again on the snow-covered landscape. At the other edge of the field he could perceive a faint line of elms in the starlight and behind that the rising sheen of another field.

He brushed off a top-hat of snow from a nearby fence post and set his lantern on it. Then he unbuttoned his breeches and, gazing over the white vastness, he urinated copiously onto the snow-covered grass at the side of the path. A hot, acid smell rose among the splashes of lamp-light. He experienced again the odd sense of being at one with the darkness, as though the night itself were his body. As he emptied his bladder, his imagination was subject to incongruous images of voluptuous women ascending into the sky and he could not fully abandon the strange notion of the movement of souls.

CHAPTER 79

My dear Leman,

Fortified a little by an interval of time, I have recovered somewhat from my strange dream of geese and murdered maidens, and discovered a little more of my equanimity. I have had no further such dreams, and I trust that these imaginings may be behind me. I do believe that what I dreamed was an aberration, though the intensity of it may have caught me off guard in the vulnerable moments of the night. I take pen once more to paper and, trusting again to your patience, do now continue with my account.

In the course of my visits to London, I heard of Mrs Celia Quill occasionally, *sotto voce*, so to speak, as part of the traffic of talk in the capital, but since I now regarded that episode of my life as past, she no longer excited my most immediate attention. Since my meeting with her, in which she had calmly lectured me, I had grown used to her elevation. Yet, despite my other occupations, her example continued to haunt me, and something of her behaviour, some intimation of intent that lay behind her actions, appeared to be directed at me as though it might be a sermon unto my soul.

There were other matters on my mind. I had grown accustomed to my current mistress of six or seven years and, our activities having staled a little, I now sought an opportunity for placing her elsewhere and seeking fresh fields. Still somewhat under the shadow of my previous mistress Celia Quill's abrupt departure and unexpected translation into notoriety, I vowed that this time I would make the transfer easier. I therefore approached the matter with far greater care, taking into account that as much resentment may arise from the contemplation of an abrupt change as the change itself. Over the course of some months I had set about the task of making clear that I could not support her *ad infinitum*, that our sojourn together was temporary, and that I would not become jealous if, our relations having reached their conclusion, she herself chose to look for another protector. The import of these admonitions became increasingly transparent to her, though because they were put forward in the form of general statements, without abruptness and lacking any immediate dimension of compulsion, I believe that her mind became adjusted to her situation. Not unexpectedly, she began to complain a little more querulously once she guessed my intentions were serious. Even so, I had been generous with her during her time with me and, once the girl understood the nature of the provisions which I intended, and that I meant to leave her in good stead, she became calmer and even quite accustomed to the idea of my departure.

I embarked on making other preparations for her longer happiness. I knew a colleague who had devoted much of his time to his practice in London and now found himself sufficiently successful to consider the possibility of establishing, so to speak, a second household. I introduced them as it were by accident and, since he found her attractive, informed him of my own intentions regarding my mistress's future. I recognised in his reception of the news which I had cause to impart a certain predisposition, a concentration of attention, perhaps a calculation or two in his own regard. And so I believed that we had established the beginnings of an understanding between us. My mistress, for her part, found in my colleague's increasing attentions a welcome distraction from the somewhat more distant relations between us. In parallel, therefore, I informed my mistress of my colleague's own situation and his willingness to support her in an establishment of his own, if she so wished. Thus matters proceeded until an agreement among all the parties was finally effected and a satisfactory result obtained.

Between the three of us, we were able to effect as amicable a transfer as I believe is possible in this mortal world. The form of this transaction, civilised in its nature, and based upon the sensibilities and interests of each of the people involved, I do hold as something of a model for such things. If I were reproached by Mrs Celia Quill for my previous behaviour in regard to her own state, I would hold up this equanimity of relations with my then mistress at least in part as an answer to such a reproach.

My dear friend, in the processes of our respective professions, if we wish to examine the nature of the influence of one medicine upon an individual temperament, it is our custom to compare the well-being of that person after the treatment with the person before receiving it. If the person does better after that treatment than before, we may begin to believe the medicine is the cause of his improved health. If worse, then we may think that perhaps the medicine is the cause of his further undermining, and thus we are constrained to consider changing one treatment for another. Comparison is our method. So it was with Celia Quill. For if I may communicate to one mistress the limitations of my commitment to her and find myself abandoned by her peremptorily, and communicate a similar truth to another, so that she came to accept it with equanimity, then I deduce that since my intentions were the same in each case, much of the difference in result can only be due to the specific temperament of Celia Quill. You will forgive me for thus arriving at so laborious a conclusion. This procedure of logic comforted me a little in that, wishing to transfer my attentions in a suitably civilised manner, I had not offended against manners in general, but against a very distinct temperament in particular.

You may say that the circumstances were dissimilar, that in the case of Celia Quill my intentions – to marry a wife and keep her as my mistress – were somewhat different from that of taking another mistress. In my defence, sir, I would respond that in the opinion of most, the former was the happier proposal, for at least it implied a continuity in relations, whereas the latter did not. Whatever the distinctions between them, I cannot escape from the belief that in both cases I sought the well-being of my mistress, and the difference was not one of my goodwill, but lay in the varying natures of the two women thus addressed.

But I consider more closely those different attributes. The most important distinction, it seems to me, was that in the case of Mrs Quill, in addition to earthly gratifications, I sought one who would give some companionship in the domain of learning and reasoning. Now, in the light of subsequent events, I do believe that I should call into question my impulse to further her education, and my attempt to create a companion of the mind and spirit. For perhaps, in so doing, I created not a comfort for my later days, but a monster of independent thought, who used my generosity, not to sustain or support me, but to further her own private ends.

I am reminded of an analogy, and speak of another creature, of no less threatening a nature than my errant former mistress and who lives beyond our immediate controls. I hope that you will forgive me my brief digression. When the wolf howls in the forest, what, in practice, do we fear? Its size and strength? We have arms to match them. Its jaws and teeth? Our own great hounds, sleeping peacefully in our halls, have jaws and teeth of equal voracity. No, sir. The wolf is distinguished from the dog precisely by its independence. It is its independence which we both admire and fear, and from which all remaining dangers flow.

I have walked this ground enough. I mean merely to establish that Mrs Quill was a woman of a certain temperament, whose behaviour was under the guidance of her own specific will, and this was the woman whose subsequent actions I am compelled by circumstances both to fear and to admire. For as I shall recount, she not only disappeared abruptly from my life as my mistress and reappeared again in the form of Mrs Celia Quill, a madam of strangely sober repute, but she continued thereafter to exert an influence upon me by means both direct and indirect.

I am constrained to believe that what happened next was both calculated and wilful. It followed a pattern, which I shall attempt to disinter. The fact is that, having achieved this oddly

316

distinguished and independent position in society, she had accumulated sufficient wealth to retire to the country. But it was not to any part of that country, whose magnificent dimensions and plenitude lay about her, but precisely in my own haunt of Lymington that she preferred to settle. And since she chose to take up residence in an area where the estates are sizeable and the distances between the larger residences of gentlefolk are somewhat ample, is it not stranger still that she set herself down, not only in the same town or borough, but within a few hundred paces of my own house? That development in our relations, sir, which both surprised and perplexed me, shall be the subject of my next missive.

I must return to my responsibilities. In lieu of that account, I shall bid you a temporary farewell.

In the meanwhile, I do most earnestly remain,

    Yours sincerely,

    Hargood

CHAPTER 80

As Grange lay in his single bed, it was the work by Montmorency which, strangely, precipitated his own dream of geese. He was standing at the base of the heavy painting, looking up at the spiral of flesh that rose towards heaven. Under his gaze the female bodies, their eyes upon one another in a perpetual convocation of longing, took on a different aspect. He imagined the rush of beaten air and heard the thunder of wings, wings as thick as ivy leaves. The bucolic landscape beneath the rising figures transmuted itself into the greenness of water.

Water entered his mind, or perhaps he entered water, for he was swimming now, his head above the surface. He sensed their agitation on the sunlit surface. They began to flutter and to move across the floating light; fire-top, flame-light, water-walker. He too was subject to their panic, as though by sympathy, and it seemed entirely natural that he too could fly, could become part of their collective, thunderous rise into the air. Against the sussuration of wings, the report of the fowling piece was like authority, or sanity – a single gunshot upon the orgy of upward movement. Then, like a dream which itself is interrupted, he himself became one of the falling bodies, tumbling back into the water.

In the curious language of dreams, he had suffered no damage from his experience. Hargood had shot him down, together with the geese among which he had flown. Now Hargood leaned down with a helping arm and assisted him with perfect courtesy and amiability from the water. He was seated in a boat. He proceeded to help Hargood raise the bodies of the geese from the water into the bilges of the boat. There was blood on his hands, though not his own. He looked down at the pious red and, far from a sense of guilt or despondency, felt relieved of some curious restraint.

CHAPTER 81

My dear Leman,

Having established the particular nature of her temperament, I hope you may consider the subtlety of mind, and ruthlessness of disposition, of this same woman who was once my mistress.

With her example thus in mind, we may perhaps consider what she did next. For if her explanation of what might be called her *philosophy*, which she offered me in the course of my visit to her, was a response to my enquiry as to her current occupation, her next action seemed to be directly offensive against my interests. It appears that lecturing me upon my previous behaviour, albeit in most formal surroundings, was not sufficient to her purpose. She was like some general who, finding the opposing army a little weaker than expected, gathers his resources to concentrate upon the very headquarters of his enemy.

If my outpost was London, my inner citadel was Lymington, where I had established, through my own good labours, over perhaps some thirty-five years in all, a reasonable and perhaps even a successful practice as a physician. I was, at least in the routine of my daily life, a respectable widower with sufficient reason to visit London regularly to undertake certain offices of the College, in whose ministrations I had achieved, through diligence and hard work, some measure of seniority. I had acted as patron to a younger physician whose collaboration I enjoyed and who I believed would succeed my practice if I should retire. I believed that my castle, though not impregnable, was well constructed against the vicissitudes of life, and I thus continued in my work with a certain faith in the future and security in my position.

It was precisely when I felt most secure that this same Mrs Celia Quill, whose fate is driven by mysterious internal circumstances the nature of which I do not fully understand, should choose to come to Lymington – bearing, as she did, this name out of my past. And so it was that suddenly I found that the particular nature of my existence, which I had set about constructing for myself over the course of my life, was now under subtle and unpronounceable threat.

My dear Leman, in our respective professions, you and I have both known a number of effective and ambitious players upon the stage of life and we have witnessed, with varying degrees of admiration or disapprobation, their movement towards their own goals. Perhaps you will consider the subtlety of Mrs Quill's impressions upon my own life and, in their consideration, you may appreciate the complexity of her motives, her mastery of the details.

Among the most difficult of the forces arranged against her, she knew that I alone was aware of her origins, that I held the knowledge of her past which could jeopardise her settlement – and that if I chose, I could place such a reputation upon her name that she would find no final and satisfactory position in our community. She knew, with a perfect certitude, that I alone held the means by which she could be transformed into an outcast, shunned by the genteel and placed under such passive disapproval by the rest of the populace that her life in this locality would no longer be supportable. And yet she advanced upon her objective with utter confidence, in the assumption that I would not place such a determination upon her name.

Having settled thus in our midst, it seemed she dared me, in my own town and territory, ensconced as I was at the very centre of my life, to react to her presence. She came to Lymington, as we have seen, like a private but living reproach, with her notorious name unchanged, and settled within a few minutes' walking distance of me, as though to challenge me to reveal her true origins and profession. I looked out of my house one day and saw nothing but contentment. I did so on a second day and my entire future appeared clouded, as though under some palpable threat.

I will speak no more of the audaciousness of her choice of residence, or the confidence and assurance with which she settled. I have already written much of the implacable conviction with which she introduced herself into the community, how soon she immersed herself in charitable works. I have mentioned previously (as a result of both these things) the speed with which she consolidated her position and appeared to become indispensable to polite society. Insofar as my own feelings and behaviour were concerned, she calculated correctly. For if I exposed her, I would also bare myself to the same cold winds of gossip to which I subjected her. The fact remained, I could not explain her true presence without revealing my own part in keeping a mistress in London. If I had done so, it would have revived those memories of myself, which lingered below the surface of polite society, as one who had trifled with the affections of the gentle sex and whose behaviour, in the light of such revelations, could easily be construed as returning to his former character.

In addition, as she no doubt surmised, in that calm and expeditious mind, I had other fears of a somewhat different nature, though touching on the same thing. I thought that even here, among the outposts of the rural gentry, there would be sufficient contact and traffic with London that someone would connect the name Quill with the behaviour of an infamous madam. This was my nightmare – that thus, passively, without my active intervention, our two houses would be brought down.

I cannot guess entirely the thoughts in the mind of a woman as subtle as she. But perhaps it amused her that I too hoped so fervently that she would not be identified, so to speak, with that other part of her life – perhaps that I would even conspire with her in some sense to protect her name from such doubts. Thus it was that she achieved in the course of her move to Lymington two objectives which would seem to be mutually exclusive – a threat to my existence, and my silent commitment to her protection.

Meanwhile an uneasy truce held between us. We are, as you know, several days of normal journey from the capital, and few citizens obtain the *Courier* or other such news-sheet. There was a time, in the first year or two of her stay, when she might have been vulnerable to such reports. Yet in the interim she proceeded, by strength of character, to become a byword for charity and good works. I perceive now, with hindsight, the reason for the speed with which she consolidated her position in the community, for I believe she calculated that she could arrive at a stage where her own sober and charitable behaviour was so much at odds with any report of her from London that the latter could be dismissed. Events disposed themselves to follow her plan. Within a year or two of her settling, such was her position in our society that it became almost impossible to believe she could be harmed by such rumours. The very strength of her presence, her manifest beneficence, the extent and nature of her good works, would have provided such a body of evidence as to the true nature of her disposition, that the rumours would have been considered an aberration. She continued to establish herself until that time when, if any had remarked on the similarity of name to that notorious lady, the local society would have merely laughed at the notion, and marvelled at the connection between her own name and that of a notorious madam as being no more than one of those coincidences by which some poor reprobate, say, bearing the same family name as a great Grenville or Spencer, had also drawn from fate's rich bank an inclination to indigence or beggary. Under my own eyes, then, she reached a state of social reputation where I could begin to assume that, even if she were accused of a relation to a former life, she was impregnable.

As her goal was achieved, my own situation was worsened, from impotence to vulnerability. For if she had decided to turn upon me the record of my own contribution in her life, I believe my reputation and practice would have been ruined, while her own would have survived and perhaps prospered. Thus, by the very consistency and determination of her actions, she transformed the weapon that I held against her not only into an ineffective instrument, but one which, if I had been inclined to use it, would have caused myself a mortal wound.

You will begin to understand the effects of these matters upon my character. Each day that passed strengthened her position and weakened my own.

I write to you now in the early hours of the day, with a candle by my page and a fire in the grate against the winter cold. My window is closed against the snow which is heaped along the outer walls.

I must leave here, sir, in order to conduct my habitual dispositions of the day. Rest assured, having taxed your patience for so long, I shall return as soon as possible with my account of her campaign against me.

In the meanwhile, I remain,

Yours most sincerely,

Hargood

CHAPTER 82

During the afternoon Grange and Hargood walked westwards along the foreshore, towards an area in which the land met the incoming light. Hargood said gently, 'Silas, my dear fellow, I have been thinking much of Mrs Quill. What was her motivation, do you think, in coming to Lymington?'

It was the first time that Hargood had raised her name directly, and it seemed to Grange another strange turn in their relations.

'Her motivation?' he asked.

'Let us agree not to raise this question of good and evil to the abstract, when the evidence is that it lies in the particular.'

'Nevertheless,' Grange said, 'you still wish me to confer blame on Mrs Quill?'

'I wish you to make a judgement,' Hargood replied. 'That is all.'

Grange smiled. 'If only that were all.'

'Is it not?'

'We rehearse the same ground. I cannot ascribe evil intentions to her.'

'Even if you do not, can you not at least admit that she caused you harm?'

Grange smiled. The path led towards Oxey. A large barn and house that looked out over the fields. To their left, in the direction of the sea, dozens of small windmills moved in a brisk south-westerly breeze, driving water into the salt-pans. Gusts of wind moved across the marsh grass.

'What is it you search for, Silas?'

'Nothing that is spiritual or abstract, I think.'

'The rest of us believe in a God. Yet I am convinced you pursue this woman as though she offers you redemption.'

'It is true, Hargood. I felt I was close to something when I was with her – something that I have hidden in myself.'

'Some of us pursue the notion of a God who is merciful. You pursue her as though she will reveal you to yourself.'

'We each have our different crosses.'

'What is it that you expect of her?'

'I do not know.'

'You acknowledge at least part of the truth of what I say?'

'Perhaps.'

'Silas, you impugn me in my religion – not mischievously, I grant you. But sometimes you have a way of moving aside when the higher orders are mentioned, as if the question of eternal life is beneath your consideration. You treat me as if to hope for some salvation is a weakness of spirit.'

'That is not my view. I simply do not share your interest in God.'

'I believe our God offers final judgement on what we are,'

323

Hargood said. 'That is why I both thirst for and fear judgement day.'

'As I say, I do not criticise you for that belief. I simply do not share it.'

'No, you do not. Perhaps, then, it is I who impugn you. It seems to me that you search for answers in the character and person of your Mrs Quill. That is the burden of what I have to say. You expect her to offer that final verdict on your own soul.'

'Your God is mysterious and elusive, Hargood. If what you say is true, then mine at least is flesh and blood.'

On their left a rolling gust of wind was moving along the foreshore, turning the marsh grass silver, like hair. A few hundred yards away, at Oxey Barn, a door of one of the salt furnaces swung open, several figures emerged at a conspicuous run, and a flame like an angel's wing issued calmly from the bowels of a furnace house. It flared outwards, curving with the wind. A few seconds later it had gone, folding upon itself, mysteriously jointed. The men, standing apart from the furnace house in a group, appeared too sheepish to return.

Grange said, 'I have learned from Mr Swann that sometimes the fires beneath the pans, fanned by an unexpected breath from the sea, flame briefly out of control.'

'They do? You surprise me, Silas, with your arcane knowledge.'

'The flame scatters the workers and overseer, perhaps causing flash burns on those men not quick enough to leave. I have once or twice had to treat scalded skin from such an incident, even though at the time I did not know its cause.'

'All work has its dangers.'

'But perhaps it is avoidable.'

'How?'

'In the first instance, by refusing to accept that the circumstances cannot be altered.'

'What precisely do you speak of?'

'Swann said they called these flames "God's wings" out of fear and respect, as whalers called the great flukes of a whale's tail "the hand of God". Experienced furnacers can tell by the changed sound of the fire, by an odd silence of a few seconds before it gathers itself and flames outwards.' Grange pointed towards the group of men still standing outside the open furnace-house door, as though gathering their courage to return. 'Strong wind makes the men nervous.'

The two physicians could see no signs of injury in the men, only a kind of embarrassment at having to flee the sudden apparition of flame. They were being cajoled by a foreman and in a body they now returned to the interior of the furnace, where the danger seemed to be diminished. Hargood glanced meaningfully at Grange, as if in emphasis of the view that there was little to be done against the whims of fate.

.

CHAPTER 83

My dear Leman,

If I have tried to account for the behaviour of my former mistress, Mrs Celia Quill, and attempted to demonstrate the subtlety of her mind in laying the foundation of her settlement in Lymington, I must now relate the extension of it into another sphere.

If I had expected some form of truce, albeit an uneasy one, between us, I was mistaken. For just as a general will work to place his troops in an advantageous position before he makes a further assault, so it seemed to me that, having established a stronghold in my homeland, she began to threaten my well-being from another direction. How was I to feel when, within my own sphere, she started to impress her views and character upon the mind of my younger colleague, Dr Grange, who had shown himself so unremittingly rigorous in pursuit of his profession and who one day would inherit my own practice? If it appeared that her interest in him was genuine, you may also perhaps forgive me for believing that, in demonstrating her power over my closest acquaintance, she was, by extension, demonstrating her power over me.

Yet if she had formed a beach-head upon my younger colleague's heart perhaps, in the course of her several years in Lymington, she had also affected mine. I could not easily tell him the truth about her past for another reason, which I hereby record. Though I believe she threatened me, yet my admiration of her had, if anything, grown during the period of her stay in the town. We may be inclined to the belief that a person cannot alter, particularly one as notorious as she, yet she seemed to have changed, not to a new self, but into an earlier self, as though she had discovered her original nature. Her ardour for charity and the good of others resembled her earlier devotion as my mistress and companion. Thus I could not permit myself to sully her reputation, even if the means were at hand. I have never doubted that she is remarkable, and I often told my younger colleague so. Though her presence unsettled me, I bore in mind that, apart from the dubious precedent of settling so near me and unsettling my equanimity, she had never done me any direct or obvious harm.

Instead, I attempted to make my younger colleague consider the wisdom of engaging with so formidable a character. I constantly rehearsed the very strangeness of her unexpected appearance in Lymington, the lack of background, the absence of a husband. I did so not with any malign intent, but to emphasise her independence and to warn him of her power. I attempted to make him sensible that he should perhaps take a little less on trust than was there to be offered. For myself, I would incline to the hope that with time the infatuation might become less intense.

And now, my dear Leman, I must add one final element into our consideration of her. She came here as a widow and established herself. Her increasing circle of friends and acquaintances knew her for herself, but it was also known that she had a daughter. It was widely believed that her daughter lived at Winchester, but (having explained to you her daughter's potential relation to me) this merely added to my discomfort. For a part of me longed to discover the true nature of that same relation.

When she had settled and set up house, her daughter began

to visit her. This increased my sense of powerlessness. I was forced to watch her come and go – this young woman who might have been my own flesh – without so much as the possibility of a meeting. Though she passed beneath my gaze so closely that I could touch her, yet I was excluded by consideration of my own past from her company. This was another of those agonies, which are based in a momentous indecision, but which I could yet place at the door of Mrs Celia Quill. For in the traffic of her daughter's visits there seemed another provocation of me and yet further test of my character.

Leman, you listen to my catalogue of complaints and terrors addressed against this remarkable woman. I sense either your irritation or perhaps indulgence at the absurdity of my life. I could not entirely reject the belief that she had pursued me, carefully and methodically. It was as if she attempted to teach me some form of further lesson about my treatment of her in the past, though the form of the lesson was so carefully and subtly administered I could not react against it until its full nature had become clearer. So it happened that I was forced to endure it, for my own interest and well-being.

This, then, was what I faced and, were it not for an incident in my own life, which I will in due course recall, I might have accepted it in its entirety.

I have tested your benevolence too far already in this missive. Such observation coincides with the fact that these scratchings have absorbed such time as I may devote to them this day. I am called again to my duties, not the least of which is to accompany my patient on his walk. My various bruises and scratches have healed much faster than I hoped, though I was always fortunate in my constitution. I continue to recover in other ways from the fall which my younger colleague occasioned a few weeks ago. My ankle was painful. Now it is merely stiff, but the discomfort that accompanied it has largely disappeared.

I believe and trust there will be no more violent episodes, for on my part at least there will be no attempt at provocation. I bid you adieu and will write again when I may.

In the interim, sir, I remain as ever,

    Yours sincerely,

      Hargood

CHAPTER 84

He no longer read Hume.

There had been a time when Mrs Thompson would rise up the stairs to wake Grange from his bed and instead find him asleep at his desk, a loose gown covering his shoulders, slumped over an open volume. Usually the tremor of her footsteps and the slight sound of placing the shaving bowl on the desk was enough to wake him. He slept as lightly as a bird, as if knowledge were a light meal.

Since Grange had abandoned his favourite reading, he had fallen into a deeper sleep, from which it would require much shaking to disturb him, as if some part of him was nervous or afraid of consciousness. Whatever his mind digested now, it was heavier and more oppressive fare than Hume. Mrs Thompson, her hand on his shoulder, watched him ascend from some unknown depth until he recognised her. An odd sense of relief came to his face, as if she had drawn him up from a river bed.

She did not speak to him, but set aside his shaving things on the wash-stand, while he lay quietly in the dark. She could not see him behind her, but she knew that he stared at the ceiling, that almost out of reticence or good manners he would avoid looking at her. This cogent direction of his thought was a discipline, a constraint upon his own thoughts. Out of some interior sense of proper behaviour, even behind her back he would not direct his attention at her.

She knew that there was much of him that wished to regard her, that wished to turn his attention upon her person, if not with any direct intention, at least as an object of steady grace and implicit fascination. She considered it would have been natural, and understandable, for a man in his circumstances, without wife or constant female companion, to dwell upon her physical attributes, the head dipped in concentration, the fine and assertive back, the voluptuous neck, on the animal warmth and the broad hips of the being who shared his life more closely than any other. She knew, in short, that she represented temptation. And so it was that in the customary and habitual tension between them she found, in the silence of that room, at least a source of solace for her own longings.

After filling his wash-basin and setting down her pitcher, she arranged the shaver and strop and soap beside the bowl, and set down the clean towel brought up from the linen cupboard. Lighting his candle with her own, she drew apart the mated flames. She took up the candle holder and without acknowledging him (since she knew that she had his fullest attention, if only in the negative) she left the room, closing the door softly but firmly, and took herself downstairs.

Descending through the darkness of the stairwell in the early morning, she could feel the coldness in her ankles, the way the gloom settled in quiet pools on the stairs. Passing through the hallway, she moved swiftly to the kitchen. There, even though she set about her work with a certain immediacy, it was clear that she too was compelled to exercise a discipline of mind in relation to her own thoughts. She had temporarily left some part of herself in that small room upstairs, with the alert and silent man. Now it was time to gather herself together before the day, to rearrange her fragmentary thoughts. Sometimes it seemed to her that several minutes were required before she could shake off the final traces of her mental trance.

CHAPTER 85

My dear Leman,

There enters here a certain event, which fate caused to play into my hands. Like many of the young women of London, my present young mistress had heard of Mrs Quill and, though her knowledge was small and based on hearsay, she was of a sufficiently enquiring mind to find out what she could from her limited sources.

Though we may observe the first condition of Mrs Quill's reputation, we should also observe the second, which is the consequence of the first. By some alchemy or fortune she became reputable precisely because of the style and manner in which she maintained herself. Her establishment of means, her independence of the general will, her forthright behaviour, her lack of shame, brought her a grudging acceptance among that very society whose precepts she flouted, but to whose secret and implacable life she was so well attuned. And thus she established an impression among her clients which, though it was not gentility, was similar to that respect or admiration which one man accords another who has made his way in the world. I believe that she had emancipated herself from the society of men, like one of those slaves from the *patria potestas*, so fully that she was no longer touched by it. My mistress notified that certain of her female friends in London had begun to treat Mrs Quill as an example, a kind of paragon of the virtues of feminine independence.

Yet in this report, my mistress had also found some trace and indication of a court case by a young man against a certain Mrs Quill. I had heard something of this previously, though in so vague a form that I had taken no notice of its contents. It seemed merely part of that fame or notoriety which does of itself manufacture rumours and accounts, and which grows from its own mysterious resources.

I found now that the incident fitted my particular case, and would provide me with the means of countering her attack. It appeared that an article upon the subject had been published in the *Courier*. It seemed that some young man, who later was convicted of theft, had accused Mrs Quill of falsely informing him that a certain young woman was her daughter. When he courted that daughter, he claimed that Mrs Quill had withheld her approval of the match against a favour. He claimed that she inveigled him in some manner to be of service to rich ladies of her acquaintance.

Against any other woman the case would have seemed fantastical. But precisely that reputation already established provided an atmosphere in which the case began to assume a certain likelihood. Now it seemed to me that sufficient doubt had been cast upon the case, and the motives of the young man, that the case itself proved dubious. For it was subsequently shown and demonstrated that he was an unsuccessful suitor for her daughter's hand, and had plotted his revenge in like manner, by relying upon her mother's notoriety. But it was one of those particular incidents which feed the generality of a reputation. If it would be believed of anyone, it would be believed of her.

These, sir, were my circumstances. One who considers himself to be the subject of attack is inclined to use the methods which are available. Thus manoeuvre breeds counter-manoeuvre. I had suffered over a course of several years her appearance at Lymington and her gradual incursion upon me through her growing reputation. These I was prepared to withstand with something approaching stoical indifference. But I was determined to draw the line in the conquest of my younger colleague.

Now, it seemed to me, fate had presented me with an opportunity to restore the balance. I decided I would impart the information to my young friend, in the hope that it would check his headlong rush to her defence. In reporting the matter to him, I had no other object than that it would indicate that she had several sides to her character and that, henceforward, though remarkable, she should be considered with a proper caution. In this office I decided to apprise him directly of the full facts of the story, as it had come to me by my mistress. I further resolved that I would present them without embellishment, indeed, with a certain scepticism on my part that such an account could be true of her, and thereafter allow him to make of the matter what he would.

In settling upon the course of recounting the details of her past to my younger colleague I had taken into account certain dangers. It seemed to me now that Mrs Quill was sufficiently well established in Lymington that no mere rumour could harm her. But, more important, I believed I could trust beyond all measure his discretion in not passing on the knowledge to any other person. Thus the benefits of informing him of her past were clear, and the dangers were, by the same token, reduced to a minimum.

I am forced to add to my earlier account, though in the retelling I plunge myself deeper into complicity. But what is true now is true of my previous account. I did not, sir, expect the response from my younger colleague that I subsequently witnessed. I have informed you of how, when he heard the story, he went ashen-white and cried out, as if it confirmed something he had feared in his deepest soul. Those of us who take an extreme position concerning the goodness or otherwise of a particular character may sometimes be blinded by evidence, and thus we may lay at their own door the blame for taking such a view in the first place. But these are superficial considerations, and inadequate to describe the fears that suddenly seized him. I believe that he had taken an extreme position, one of believing Mrs Quill incapable of anything but the most sober and charitable actions. He himself had drawn the string of his faith to its tightest point. In finding that she was not precisely as he had hoped, my colleague had been struck a fearsome blow. He is a man of great control, but I sensed, I felt, that something momentous had happened to his own regard. He did not shout, or rail against me, or even exhibit a sign of his terror. Instead, he now assumed a terrible calm. I knew him well enough to be aware that he strained every nerve to preserve an equable exterior. I offered to accompany him home, but with a great effort of will he thanked me for my efforts and insisted on returning to his own house. In the grip of this control, as we parted he turned towards me and, in the hope of reassuring me, smiled at me. I have never seen a more terrible smile. It was an expression of final despair. When he walked away I experienced a wave of horror at what I had done, and only some measure of my own control prevented me from running after him and begging him to return to my own house rather than face, in the privacy of his own, the full weight of his anguish. I have reported that I learned afterwards that he had entered a fever, after which he seemed to lose the faculties of his mind.

When Mrs Thompson informed me, the following day, of the

course of events during the night and how she had found him insensible in his bed the following morning, I was faced, not with a more cautious and recalcitrant friend, but a soul on the edge of perdition. And thus I decided upon the only remedy I believed might be effective, which was to bleed him heavily and continuously, removing the energy which supported his fever and his ravings, and hope that by doing so I would grant him some small physical respite in which to recover his condition. I was fortunate indeed that in Mrs Thompson, his housekeeper, there could be found no better supervisor of his condition. And thus, sir, I return once more, though by a different route, to the matter of his slow cure and reparation.

You will see that I am not an innocent party, but that even so, in my decision to intervene I did not fully understand the ground on which I stood. And though much of this matter still perplexes me, and certain of its details still haunt me, in reliving my own error I am at least a little advanced towards the explanation.

I have no excuse for thus covering old ground, except in the attempt to clarify, so that we may progress a little further along our course.

These admissions of my guilt and complicity have drawn forth my energy. I rose early this morning, several hours before dawn, in order to compose this letter in the privacy of the dark and the tentative companionship of a single flame. I must now put aside my pen and harness my remaining energies to advance through the day.

With this prospect in view, I bid you a temporary goodbye, and do remain,

Sincerely yours,
Hargood

CHAPTER 86

Fierce gusts of wind struck against the window-pane.

Putting his face to the glass, Grange peered out from his study into the dark. By placing his palms against the glass, shutting out the glare from the candle, he could see the change of shifts from the furnaces by the faint lights which moved from Pennington shortly before midnight. The torch held by an overseer moved slowly down the incline from Pennington towards the Oxey marshes, like lice over a body. On reaching the marshes the shift split into three different parties, heading towards each furnace. When the shifts had been replaced, the process was repeated in reverse. The torches were given to the returning gangs and three separate processions began to converge, until they met at Oxey and once again ascended with tortuous slowness the wind-swept paths on their way to the hovels of Pennington.

Though it was his habit, before settling down to his bed, to watch the midnight change, it could not displace a part of his mind from thinking of Mrs Quill. Until the present, it seemed to him, he had grown used to a rational calculation driving him forward. Now he schooled himself to act upon his deepest feelings, and admonished himself not to hope for anything in particular. Trusting to the emotions, not an objective, was a strange imposition upon his normal processes. Yet he was determined to follow that course and persuade the rest of him to accept the consequences with something approaching equanimity.

CHAPTER 87

My dear Leman,

I have recovered a little from the pain and mortification of admitting to you my part in my younger colleague's downfall. My nerves remain frayed, and it is only in the hope of being able to provide some small recompense to him that I have taken courage to write again. Now that he has made such strides in his recovery, and some of the dust has settled, let us attempt to pick up a few small pieces which have occurred in the aftermath of the catastrophe. Regarding one matter in particular, he begins to cast a seed of doubt in my mind. In his descriptions of Mrs Celia Quill, not least those which have emerged after the event of her leaving, he has painted a picture of her which is both unfamiliar and yet strangely coherent.

Have you looked at a few lines, or a discoloration on a wall, and observed that, as the outlines arrange themselves in your mind into a subject, so you may never view those lines again without being reminded of that subject? When a pattern is formed in the mind, the imagination which envisages it is tenacious and seems to exclude all others.

Among my younger colleague's strangest notions is the view that each of us is good within ourselves, and that evil arises only out of our struggle with the world. I regard the doctrine as absurd and without foundation, as ludicrous as those phantasms we may read into random lines upon a wall. Yet he claims that not only is each of us entirely good but, when the conditions which have caused us to behave in a disreputable manner are themselves removed, we return to the source of our original goodness. When I press him to disclose to me the source of evil, he says there is no need for him to explain it, since he does not recognise its presence. He says, instead, that I confuse evil with destruction. Whereupon I do admonish him that he should explain the prevalence of destruction by some form of motivation. In answer, he states that destruction arises out of

the conflict of opposing goods, just as in the individual evil
arises from the conflicting strains imposed upon us by the
physical world. I was reminded of this absurd generality when I
began to consider another aspect of Mrs Quill.

Through my acquaintance with my colleague, I became
exposed to an entirely different vision of her and of her motives.
Though I may not agree with his version, I may perhaps grant
it the faintest degree of plausibility. It differs from my own view
as much as darkness does from light. I do not know whether it
is true, but like those lines on the wall which seem to fall into
one pattern or another, it has its own coherence.

My younger colleague did not seek to persuade me of the
incorrectness of my views upon her motivations, but to propose
an alternative explanation of her behaviour – more in the
nature of an hypothesis. Recently, on one of our walks, he took
me aside and argued as follows: suppose that Mrs Celia Quill
moved to Lymington not to undermine me but to impress me.
He invited me to consider this hypothesis, as it were, from a
detached perspective. Suppose that having made her way in the
world, and shown herself independent of me, she wished to
demonstrate to me that she was worthy of respect in that very
community in which I lived. Suppose, he continued, she wished
to win by good works precisely that respect which had been
lacking in my treatment of her during her previous life, and
which had caused her to leave my household.

Now, I do not know what you may think of this. I admit
that it was foreign to my thinking, and I was inclined to dismiss
it out of hand. But my colleague insisted that I hear the full
conclusions, if only out of novelty. So, out of condescension to
his insistence, I agreed at least to listen a little further. Imagine,
he suggested, that she wished to demonstrate to me beyond
doubt that she, my former mistress and the mother of my child,
whom I did not consider to be of sufficient reputation to marry
– that she herself was deserving of my consideration. Would this
not explain precisely her movements, and her actions, at least as
well as any other? Was it not at least likely that, far from
holding any malign intentions towards me, she had worked
assiduously to prove, in the community of which I was a part,

that she could establish a place and a name which would be worthy of my respect?

For one who had assumed that she had alighted in Lymington to remind me of my past and to discomfit me, these suggestions seemed strange. I began to prepare a counter-argument, which I believe demonstrated that she had no goodwill towards me. If her motivation was thus to impress me, then why, I asked him did she not allow me to speak to a young woman who might be my own daughter? In answer, he enquired whether Mrs Quill had ever expressly forbidden it.

I admit that I was enraged by this suggestion, for it seemed to place upon me an unwarranted accusation. I answered that she had not forbidden it, but that her own decision not to effect an introduction between myself and her daughter had given rise to the interpretation. It may be, my colleague suggested, she considered that I myself had not deigned to ask her, and that it was her duty to wait upon my own movement in the matter of interesting myself in her daughter. Perhaps, he suggested further, it would seem to her that this apparent lack of interest on my own part was itself evidence of the low regard in which I held both mother and daughter. I believe that in the course of this interpolation I interrupted him several times, but he seemed to have gained some momentum in the expression of these notions and, despite my protestations, continued in the same manner.

And what, I asked him (for we were now facing one another directly and it seemed that both of us were determined not to give way), what of her approach to the person I addressed? I used the word 'seduction' of him, remembering my Latin and reminding him that *seducio* is to lead towards oneself. She had led him towards herself. Did he deny that?

He did not deny it, he said. But why should I assume it were part of a malign design? I answered that, though I did not doubt the genuine nature of her feeling towards him, my suspicion devolved upon the possibility that some part of her initial design was to impress him, as a means of further undermining my position. Thus, the infatuation may have begun with an ulterior aspect, even though I believed that her subsequent affections were increasingly genuine towards him.

At which, sir, he laughed. He laughed outright, in front of me. I felt a perplexity and rage at his response which, had I been younger, might have resulted in some physical display, such as he saw fit to demonstrate to me at an earlier date. When his mirth had subsided, he said the following words, which I do record in their entirety: 'You accused me of interpreting all her actions in my own interests, as her lover, yet now you are doing precisely the same in regard to your own.' Before I could object, he continued with these words, which I do also record: 'I believe she loves you, sir, and has always loved you. And though you may have acted against her, and caused her to leave you, all she does now, and has ever done, is to try to gain your respect.'

I remember a peculiar pause after these words. For several seconds I was speechless. We faced one another in silence for some short while, both breathing heavily, for sometimes emotion costs as much as physical exertion.

My colleague, perhaps sensing my hesitation, added these further words: 'She seeks your admiration, yet everything you have done is aimed to strike her down again.'

I did not know whether to criticise him for his impudence, to laugh myself, or even perhaps to cry for the folly of the world, in which we pursue our own aims in darkness of those of others. For his view of her motives was at such a variance to my own that I hardly believed we had any common ground upon which to communicate.

Instead, we continued our confrontation, directly facing one another, neither willing to give ground. We were both too overwrought to speak further and I felt myself shaking.

Then, as though by mutual accession, we retired from our respective positions, like knights who have jousted through the day, but without resolve. For the remainder of our walk we did not speak of the subject, as though both agreed the matters under consideration were too weighty to resolve by mere discussion. For the time being, each of us exercised a studious avoidance.

Several days have passed since that exchange, and the terms of it continue to exercise my mind and to haunt my dreams.

For I am inclined to see, suddenly, and against my inclinations, the odd outlines of a different perspective, whose view seems to overlay my own. And within this strange perspective I perceive the disturbing lineaments of a figure whose form I now believe I may never know.

Being prey to these conflicting emotions, I am become restless of body as well. Since in private moments I find myself roaming back and forth, like an animal in a cage, I will take the remedial action which is habitual with me and depart to London, where I have the proper excuse of several secretarial duties with the College of Physicians (in addition to the private one of a reunion with my mistress).

Perhaps it is poetic justice that my colleague, who has placed upon me the burden of these thoughts, should take upon himself the responsibility for any small emergencies which may arise in my absence.

In the meanwhile, I remain,

    Yours most sincerely,

      Hargood

CHAPTER 88

The rapping on the door caused Mrs Thompson to move towards it in her rustling skirts, her hair hanging in disarray, grumbling at being disturbed from her work in the kitchen. Some women would not have liked to answer the door at night, but Mrs Thompson was fearless, and would fill the doorway with her peremptory figure. Grange heard a brisk exchange of formalities, a man's voice at first, then Mrs Thompson's own tones in clear interrogation. He heard the slamming of the door, then she returned and stood in front of him, in a state of emotion. 'There has been an accident at the boiler houses.'

'An accident?'

'Burns and suffocation, sir. A whole boiler house has exploded.'

Grange felt himself rising from his chair by the fire, where he had been staring into the flames. It was an instinctive action, as if he had been struck a blow. He experienced, for the first time for many months, that heightened sense of fear or foreboding which is also a kind of exaltation.

'Sir . . .' Mrs·Thompson viewed him with concentrated alarm as he rose and drove past her towards the hall. 'You will catch a chill. I will send a messenger immediately to Dr Hargood for his assistance . . .'

Grange said, 'Dr Hargood is away in London and will not return for several days.'

He sat down in the hall seat and pulled on his boots. Mrs Thompson breathed out a single sigh of frustration and then, having made her protest, insisted on helping him on with his greatcoat. He seemed calm, but as her hands touched his shoulder she felt the fierce, sudden jump of his nervous system. He was impatient of her touch, like a horse. She herself drew back, startled, while he hauled the coat over his shoulders. His face seemed coldly withdrawn. He gripped the handle of the valise, which had stood for so long in the corner of the hallway unattended, and for the briefest of moments felt its weight in his hand. Before he had reached the door, Mrs Thompson, in an agitation of her own, seized the latch and drew it back fully. Following some instinct or perhaps rage, Grange threw himself past her and outwards into the blackness.

If he had not known the precise geography of the two outer stone stairs – the first shorter than the second and with greater camber – he might have stumbled in the street. Outside the door a man stood patiently. Grange halted a few seconds while his eyes accustomed themselves to the darkness. It was sufficiently late for the rush lights that lit the evening streets to have been allowed to go out. Only a single brazier burned at the town hall, perhaps fifty yards away, not close enough to show up the man clearly. His shadow leached sideways, as though another creature stood beside the man. Grange could not see the messenger's face.

'Your name, sir?'

'Marston.'

'Do we need a light, Mr Marston?'

'I know the way.'

Behind Marston, the flame on the brazier was disturbed by a gust of wind, and for a moment hung down like hair.

'You lead, then, Mr Marston.'

Marston nodded, turned and began to walk briskly across the High Street and down the narrow lane past the Hope and Anchor. Grange followed him along the alley, past Flushards and the empty market stalls. He was assailed by the smell of old intestines and gizzards at the lowest end of Flushards, where the waste of the market was washed down by occasional rains and concentrated its effluent in the foul-smelling ditches on the southern quarter.

Marston was walking briskly now, not looking back. Grange followed him towards the marshes, avoiding the low-lying water and reed-beds that spread along the foreshore. Small clusters of trees, bent by the prevailing south-westerlies, dotted the boundaries between marsh and foreshore. To reach the site of the accident more quickly, Marston chose a shorter path across the salt-marsh meadows that was hardly more than a badger's run.

Outside the shelter of the town buildings there was a fierce wind. Marsh grass whipped and sighed against Grange's boots. Ahead of him, Marston's figure kept up a constant speed. He seemed as thin as a scarecrow as he picked his way among the trees.

Passing through the last willows and ashes, Grange beheld a sight. Two large furnaces could be seen at a single viewing, perhaps half a mile apart, their doors open to bring oxygen to the flames. He could hear, in the stillness of the night, the bubble and faint roar of the flames inside them. Beneath that outer limit of noise he could detect the hiss of steam, and the shouts of the men as they stirred the pans and sang and called to one another.

'There, sir,' Marston said.

Marston was pointing. It was not towards another furnace-house fire, but to an absence, a black hole in the night where once a boiler house had stood. To one side, a shower of burning roof timbers still flamed faintly. Grange wondered why the other furnace-house workers showed such cheerful signs of industry, while one of their number had been blasted less than a few hundred yards away. Was it a terrible callousness, the need to continue to burn while the fires were at full blast? Then it occurred to him why the workers would be unaware of the explosion among their number. Its roar would have been consumed by the closer roar of their own fierce fires. They would have sensed the flash and rumble as no more than winter lightning on this disturbed night.

Marston did not speak further, but began to stride faster towards the scene. Grange perceived his thin, hurrying figure in the dark and struggled to keep up. Water lay about them in scattered pools. In their bleak reflections the remaining furnaces, like the mouths of hell, were doubled. As they walked out through the desiccated marsh grass, Grange could hear the cinders crunching underfoot. Marston, peering back with his arm shielding his face, saw Grange glance down in consternation.

'Black frost, sir.' Marston laughed suddenly, out of an extreme nervousness more than humour, showing gapped teeth against the flames of the furnace houses. 'Lymington snow.'

For several moments it seemed as if the furnace had almost magically disappeared. They were in an area of concentrated cinders, slightly higher than the rest of the land, then Marston turned back towards him. 'We are here, sir.'

He could see only by the faint light of the distant flames. The furnace-house roof had been blown off entirely, and lay in scattered beams and shards. It seemed to him that there were animals at the side of the building, before he realised with horror that the blackened shapes were the figures of men, most of them unmoving. Grange saw one of the figures twitch.

'I will need your assistance, Mr Marston.'

'Sir.'

Grange kneeled down at a figure that was almost unrecognisable as a man. The body was black with soot and burns, only the red rims of its eyes showed through. Grange opened the valise, searched in its recesses for a knife and began to cut at the strings holding the man's shirt. 'Hold an arm,' he said to Marston.

He opened a vial, dipped a rag in it and applied vinegar to the wounds. The application of vinegar as astringent caused the man to groan softly, a terrible sound.

He knew there was not remotely enough vinegar to apply to the wounds of all the men. In the light of the other furnaces, Marston's face seemed unnaturally white. Grange sensed his companion was about to be sick. In his experience, some form of activity, however simple, could allay the onset of nausea. He took a battered metal cup from the valise and handed it to Marston. 'Collect brine.' He pointed at the surface of a nearby storage pan. Marston nodded and departed.

Grange had wiped as much soot and dirt from the wounds as he could. When Marston returned he said to the man, 'Brace yourself' and poured the brine onto the torn flesh. There was a fierce hiss of pain, a shudder, the faint sound of a scream. This was what he feared most, in his nightmares, inflicting further pain upon a nervous system already tortured to the final extremity. The man's scream died. After a few more seconds of clenched pain, the first spasms halted. Grange began to bandage the burned and shattered chest as best he could.

For perhaps the next half-hour he and Marston attended to the wounds with a mixture of vinegar, brine and bandages. A number of the bodies were lifeless. As he moved from man to man, making his first dispositions and assessments, a terrible tally began to mount in Grange's head. There were eleven alive, seven dead.

While Grange worked at the cleaning and bandaging, Marston hurried to and from the water's edge, collecting further cups of brine. Concerned to keep him occupied, Grange ordered him to pull the corpses of the identified dead gently to one side, so that he did not stumble over them in his attempts to succour the living. He could hear the scuffle of Marston's feet in the darkness, his sighs and grunts as he dragged the blackened corpses to a small patch of couch grass where they were laid alongside one another, like so many inanimate parcels.

They worked continuously until the first stretcher parties, gathered by Mrs Thompson from the streets, began to arrive. They consisted for the most part of sheepish men somewhat the worse for drink, carrying rudimentary stretchers consisting of two poles crossed with heavy canvas. Grange had a momentary vision of Mrs Thompson hauling bemused, inebriated men out of drinking houses, perhaps slapping their faces to remind them of their civil duties. The canvas for several stretchers was kept in the basement of the house, rolled into a single bundle. Having located it, Mrs Thompson would have hunted for suitable ash poles in the darkness of the garden, where they would be laid up against the wall for use as beanpoles in the spring. She would have chided the men to thread the poles through the heavy canvas loops and then directed them down to the marsh.

Looking around him now, Grange appointed the most sober individual he could find, a foundryman called Charnley, to head the party. He and Marston helped the rest of the crew to raise the wounded onto the stretchers.

'Where shall we take them?' Charnley asked.

'To my house,' Grange replied. He knew Mrs Thompson would have cleared the back room that served as a temporary hospice for patients overnight. 'Tell Mrs Thompson there will be eleven in all.'

Grange watched the group of men depart, two at the front and two at the rear, Charnley taking the rear stretcher, calling out to urge them on.

Marston said, 'Eighteen men, sir. Eighteen men in all.'

Grange struggled to grasp his meaning. Marston was aware of his perplexity. 'Usually only twelve in a winter shift, sir.'

'How do you explain it?'

Marston shrugged. 'A change of shifts?'

It was the first time Grange had drawn breath since leaving his house. His forearms were locked with fatigue from lifting arms, legs and torsos as he wound bandages around them. But he had been surprised by the thinness of the men, as light as birds, some of them, from loss of water. He looked out towards the remaining furnaces, where other crews continued to work, oblivious of the tragedy close by. Several hundred yards away a door opened from one of the other furnaces. Two men emerged, blinded by the heat and light inside, breathing the cold air for a few seconds before returning to the interior.

A second stretcher party was approaching, behind them another group of bemused men.

'Let us prepare for the next party,' Grange said.

He had worked for two hours almost without respite to clean and bandage the wounds, and to provide rudimentary splints for broken bones. He felt a pain in his shoulders from constantly leaning, and stood up briefly to ease them and rub his neck. There was sufficient light from the stars and the other furnaces to see the wounded men laid out randomly on the ground beside the wreckage of the boiler house. On the other side the unmoving bodies were arranged neatly, disciplined by death.

Marston said, 'You should go back to your house, sir. I can arrange their transport myself.'

Perhaps standing up had drained the blood from his head. Grange felt faintness overtake him. He closed his eyes, waiting for the fit to pass. Marston took a step nearer, but Grange gently waved him back. Marston, he realised, must be concerned about the tall, cadaverous physician who himself seemed about to fall.

Grange breathed out, felt his balance return, looked up at the calm night. To the west a low cloud extended like an armature. He heard the occasional muted roar and the faint background hiss from the other furnaces.

Another bubble of men had gathered around them, waiting for instructions.

'You go, sir,' Marston repeated. 'We can carry the rest.'

CHAPTER 89

Throughout the night, Grange and Mrs Thompson tended to the men laid out in the room, bandaging, changing salves, giving out the universal anaesthetic of water and rum, mixed half and half. They needed as much light as possible to see by in order to tend the wounds. They ran out of tallow candles. Grange opened his special box of spermaceti candles, that most expensive of all forms of light which he used only to read by, to provide further illumination for their work.

When the dawn came, Mrs Thompson shook his shoulder gently. He was seated on a chair, where he had taken a brief respite, his head nodding forward. 'You should get some sleep, sir.'

Grange woke from a nightmare of men burned black, their eyes white in terror and accusation.

The majority of the patients were quiet now, either asleep or in that state of shock which is like quiescence. Mrs Thompson's face in the candle-light was drawn.

'I believe you should sleep yourself, Mrs Thompson.'

She shook her head.

He considered her. 'We should begin to operate a system of watches. Four hours on, four off.'

'You take the first one off,' Mrs Thompson said.

Grange looked around at the room, full of the stench of blood and urine, at the restless figures laid out under whatever coverings they could find, with bolsters of rag or straw for pillows. An elbow or knee sometimes jerked. He nodded and stood up.

Exhaustion caught up with him on the stairway. He had to hold the railings for support.

Reaching his bed, he lay down, fully clothed. Mrs Thompson found him a few hours later in the same position.

CHAPTER 90

Attending to the patients of the fire provided a focus. He removed the dressings each day. The burns were treated with salves and herbs. Mrs Thompson was asked to pick fresh Angelica from the woodlands. Grange believed in the daily aeration of the wounds.

Four of the wounded, including Samuel Endicott and Simon Palmer, having been removed to their houses on the first day, followed on the second by Ebenezer Hemmings and Jacob Flear, the five remaining patients had assumed a level of stability.

A few days after the accident, during the course of a morning's work, Mrs Thompson said, 'Dr Hargood is here, sir.'

'Invite him in,' Grange told her.

He continued to administer while, in the background, he heard Mrs Thompson open the door its full width and then the sound of Hargood's footsteps in the hallway.

The burn wounds were black, or sometimes so blue they were

deepest purple. Grange watched Preston flinch and hiss with pain as he applied astringent. As he was doing so, Hargood's heavy shadow fell across him, removing the light, turning the wounds darker.

For several seconds Hargood stood above him, taking in the scene. 'Good-day, Silas.

'Good-day, Hargood,' Grange said, without turning from his duties.

Hargood considered his actions for several moments. 'I heard of the incident only this morning.' He paused, then added for emphasis: 'I have been back from London for fully two days.'

Grange applied the final astringent with a light cloth. Preston's features, tightened against pain, unfolded carefully.

Above him, Grange sensed Hargood's silence deepen into a form of accusation.

'If I had not overheard Mrs Simmonds talking to her husband about the explosion,' Hargood continued, 'I believe I would not have known of it.'

Grange fastened the dressings without looking up.

Behind him, Hargood said, 'I would have hoped, sir, you would have summoned me.'

Grange tied the final bandage and rose carefully to his full height. He smiled at his older colleague, a smile of placid contentment and strange well-being. 'I believe Mrs Thompson sent a messenger to your house, but Mrs Simmonds told him you had written to inform her you were staying in London an extra day. Then, afterwards, matters here seemed stable enough.'

Hargood considered him. It seemed that Grange was impervious to his senior colleague's admonition. Hargood decided against pursuing the matter, and instead said, 'You yourself seem in good health, Silas.'

'Do I? Perhaps I have not had so much time as usual to consider my own state.'

'I would say the crisis suits you, sir.'

Grange wiped the astringent from his hands on a piece of linen cloth. 'May I offer you some refreshment? I believe Mrs Thompson is about to make coffee for all of us.'

'Then please include me, sir.'

They drew into another room. Grange closed the door and now, his attention on his host, turned to face Hargood. 'How was your journey to London?'

'It was a brief visit. I attended to my duties at the College. My mistress is in good health. I cannot complain.'

Yet what did he detect in Hargood's face – a hovering solemnity, some sense of disturbance or perplexity? An internal matter, he surmised. It would have been indelicate to enquire of it after Hargood had just so ostentatiously praised his own appearance of good health.

CHAPTER 91

My dear Leman,

An incident occurred several days ago of which I was unaware, and might still be so now if it were not for overhearing the random remark of my housekeeper to her husband, who referred in passing to 'the tragedy' that had taken place on the marshes.

There was an explosion in a salt furnace at Pennington, which killed some seven men, and left a number of its crew mutilated and wounded. It was utterly unexpected and no one is entirely sure of the cause. My younger colleague, who has a certain reputation among the furnace-men of Pennington, whose ills and ailments he treats, was called out to attend to the accident. Although he is still weakened, he took the responsibility of the matter on his own shoulders. Having tended to the wounded and dying *in situ*, he arranged for the remaining casualties to be carried to his house, where he set up a temporary hospital with the help of Mrs Thompson. This much I know and state as fact.

When I heard of it, by way of my housekeeper, I travelled by horse immediately to his house, in determination to relieve him of his duty, and to take at least part of the burden on his behalf.

Arriving there, I saw that two rooms had been set aside for the purpose of attending to the patients. The temporary hospital was already established, the patients bandaged and well cared for. Mrs Thompson had found beds and pallets for each of them. My colleague seemed preoccupied, but I detected a strange state of calm, if not of peace, which occurs in the aftermath of crisis. I offered my services, but they were courteously and firmly refused, for he means to see the matter through to its end. He looks tired, close to exhaustion, but I know he has a fierce will. And in Mrs Thompson, as his sergeant-at-arms, there is no more formidable second to execute the day-to-day matters and act as factotum. I objected, of course, at his refusal to countenance my contribution, but he seems equally firmly set upon it, as though the responsibility were his own. When pressed, he would only allow me to arrange to order a fresh supply of salves and liniments from Salisbury. I left his house somewhat shaken by his determination, though equally impressed by the organisation which he and Mrs Thompson have imparted to the proceedings.

I visited him again today. Even now, several days after the event, when he has had a little time to sleep, my colleague speaks hardly at all, but goes about his business as though engrossed. He has at least allowed me to provide several pallet beds which I had stored in an outhouse, so that his remaining patients may be borne above the floor. I shall collect the package of salves and liniments from the stage that returns from Salisbury this evening.

It would do my reputation ill, in the light of this terrible incident, to complain about my own state. Yet I do believe it is part of a pattern, a pattern of disaffection from this place. As the older and senior physician in the area, I was not summoned to a major accident. Admittedly I was away in London, but even so, it appears that the first thought of the man Marston, who witnessed the disaster, was to apply to my younger colleague for assistance. So it fell to one who is still my patient

349

to minister to the wounded. I had become so used to looking after his affairs and attempting to return him to health that perhaps I had not allowed him a sufficient degree of liberty or freedom from my regime once again to establish himself. I can have no doubt that at least a part of his insistence in handling these matters entirely without my assistance is due to the impulse to exhibit to me his independence once more.

For several months he has asked me whether he could return to his patients, but I have persistently refused, on the grounds that it is better to obtain a final cure than to re-enter the lists still wounded. I believe I was right to withhold the day of his return as long as possible. I did not plan to see him flung, so to speak, into the deepest water, but I should like to believe that the proper period of recuperation has fitted him at least in part to undertake the strain.

In earlier days I should myself have been wounded at the slight done to me by his ignoring me at a time of crisis. Yet my present circumstances are such that it merely seems that those threads which tie me to this location are being slowly loosened. And the creature which is being released by the changed circumstances emerges slowly, like any beast from his burrow. Yet it is here, it seems to me, where lies my chief terror. I do not know what sort of man or being I would be outside my life and my profession. So, in the manner of a householder who sees a shadow outside his gate and forces himself to investigate it despite his fear, I am drawn towards the resolution of this disquiet by invoking its cause directly.

As regards my younger colleague and myself, what greater proof might there be of the changing circumstances between us than this event, in which my status as protector and adviser to him is changed overnight, so to speak, into one in which he has taken first place in the administration of physic in the local community?

I do not wish to place upon you any further considerations of a morbid nature. Accordingly, I end this letter and, in the meantime, do remain,

Yours most sincerely,
Hargood

350

CHAPTER 92

As Grange had expected, and had often observed to both Hargood and Mrs Thompson, it was in the details of his profession that he lost himself most easily.

Now that the immediate crisis was over, he could address himself to the longer-term care of his patients and attempt to oversee as complete a recovery as he could manage. In the basement of the house were stored numerous medications for jugular, spine, meninges, bile duct, for liver and lights, kidneys and pancreas. Stored on racks and quiet tables were the secret mixing articulations of jars, bottles, metallic cups. He had kept his herbs here and lived among their gravid implications.

Now he found the basement a place of retirement from the conversion of his house into a hospital ward. Taking down the great book of herbs, *De Natura*, he read it carefully before mixing the ingredients, pounding them in pestle and mortar. He brought down jars from the shelves, the components of dried leaves, seeds, powdered roots.

The quietness of his laboratory calmed his mind. There were certain herbs that exercised a beneficial effect on the lungs, blood, heart, nervous system. Having powdered them, the addition of pure rainwater would release their goodness.

He had been subject, in the normal round of treatment of his patients, to the physical distances between them. A prescription might be imbued only irregularly, or not at all, depending upon the shifting inclinations of the patient. In the curious and temporary circumstances of the hospital, however, the remaining patients were directly under his administration, and for once he found an opportunity to supervise their treatment as closely as he would wish.

There was a general tonic he would prepare each day, of sage for the brain, Angelica for the digestion, rosemary for the mental faculties, mixed in quantities prescribed by *De Natura*. He would add a little honey against the bitterness and each day, at the beginning of his watch, he would help the patients drink the concoction.

His attention was focused upon the healing of burns. Daily he combed for such knowledge as he could find and consulted his other works. He had a mechanism – a press made in Edinburgh by MacLehose, finely engineered – for expressing the oil from seeds. There was a school of thought that wheat contained an oil which was particularly effective when applied directly to the surface of wounds. The oil was extracted by hand and the leverage applied was such that it did not tax the muscles. Even so, it accumulated as gradually as teardrops. There were substantial areas of wound to cover, and often he would spend up to two hours in an evening preparing oil and salves for the next day's application. One advantage of the MacLehose press was that its simple nature meant that while he worked the mechanism he could continue to peruse other medical texts, which lay in some profusion across the side bench.

Mrs Thompson, who had her own particular usage of herbs in cooking, was inclined to give him the benefit of the doubt. He imparted a sense of belief in the efficacy of his concoctions, weighted as they were with Latin names and precise methods of extraction. He found, to his curiosity, that she herself had a substantial knowledge of herbs, though her own uses were not wholly medical, but concerned certain forms of folk medicine, love potions and philtres, and various admixtures aimed at generating or healing particular states of mind. When he compared the medical functions of his herbs with the remedies she had absorbed from her own matriarchal line, he was amused to observe the discrepancy. Horseradish, in his universe, was used in the same way as a mustard plaster, to give relief to aching joints. But to Mrs Thompson it was an antidote to freckles and a stimulant to the maintenance of a clear complexion. To Grange, the oil extracted from the flowers of ground-ivy was a counter to colds and kidney complaints, whereas to Mrs Thompson its particular application was to ease the menstruation pains of young women. Grange might view goat's-rue, in the form of a tisane, as helpful for diabetes, particularly in the elderly, but Mrs Thompson considered it an aid in lactation, for both humans and animals. It was perhaps to their advantage that, in their current state of harmony, the strangely dimorphous nature of their two interests was combined under the prevailing requirements. What they held in common was a knowledge of the herbs' habitat, a recognition of their salient parts and the best means of finding them. So it happened that Grange would increasingly rely on Mrs Thompson to gather this or that herb in order that he could process it to his specifications. And if, occasionally and by agreement between them, she held over a certain quantity for her own inscrutable purposes, it seemed to him a just reward for collecting them against the joint purpose of treating their patients.

CHAPTER 93

Dear Leman,

I attended the burial of no fewer than seven men yesterday. The village of Pennington, that small cluster of habitations on the outskirts of Lymington, is usually in a scandalous state of inebriation owing to its dependence upon the salt industry, whose workers replenish their tissues with large quantities of beer and other brews. Yet following the deaths of seven of its inhabitants in the furnace explosion, the village now has uniformly fallen silent. I see there nothing but sober and sombre faces. Even though there are many among the population who do hardly own a suit of clothes, somehow both men and women are all dressed in formal black. The mourning strikes deep into their hearts.

Many or perhaps most of the local populace have contributed in some manner to the burial of the seven, so that the ceremony shall not place an added material burden on their widows and relatives, in addition to heart's grief.

I attended the funeral, though much as a spectator, and in some part of me I believe I was touched unexpectedly, both by the level of organisation and the quiet fervency of those who took part. The coffins, lined up in St Thomas's church, were handsome, made of oak with a lead lining, with brass handles and well-varnished wood. There were families standing side by

side in sober contemplation who are usually riven by the
normal and trivial discords of a small village. We observe, not
for the first time, the great virtues of a universal gentleness and
sobriety emerge in the shadow of death.

The deceased were treated like soldiers, and perhaps that is
what they were, for out on the marshes, feeding the flames,
they conducted themselves like an army of a kind, though more
of a ragtaggle militia than a regiment. And it seems to those of
us who stare to windward over our local industry, and upon
whom the ash and cinders continually descend, that some of
our ragged heroes, whom we have taken for granted, have now
returned to our soil.

At the centre of the proceedings, though oddly detached, was
the isolated and perhaps somewhat intimidating figure of my
younger colleague, who is nevertheless increasingly trusted by
the community he serves. So it is by the oddest circumstances
that we observe, at the centre of a most ancient religious
ceremony, the calm and entrenched figure of a notorious
unbeliever, standing at the right hand of the officiating priest,
apparently at home among the rituals of the burial.

I heard a rumour that St Just, who owns the majority of the
remaining furnaces (having gathered most of those which fell in
bankruptcy) and who has decided against common practice and
knowledge to work certain of them during the winter,
contributed to the coffins out of his own purse. He is not
sociable, and is something of a remote figure in these parts, but
he is capable of being generous when the occasion arises.
Perhaps it will allay something of his own reputation, since it is
not his practice to communicate much with the local populace,
at least regarding matters outside the businesses and ventures
which he owns. The weight of responsibility which he carries on
his shoulders, combined with the utmost seriousness of his
disposition, is not attractive to the more genteel among our
men, or the womenfolk who might otherwise consider the
widower a suitable target for their social attentions.

I believe that he runs, too, a somewhat cold and austere
household. On the few occasions when I have visited, the poor
wretch who attends his gate shuffles at my side to the main

entrance and leaves as quickly as he can, as though he fears his master. The unfortunate creature is no doubt some beggar St Just has taken pity upon, though I understand his master could easily afford servants aplenty in fine frock-coats. Certainly his house lacks all sense of family or relatives. On several occasions his name has come up in certain of the conversations between myself and my younger colleague. For reasons I do not understand, I sense in my companion some strain of feeling, even of resentment, towards the banker, as though, merely by owning the works in which the accident took place, St Just is somehow implicated in the event.

Something of what has occurred – the accident itself, the tending to the wounded – has acted upon my colleague in a manner which appears to have hardened his resolve, and has provided him perhaps with an enhanced sense of his own duty and obligations. There is a calmness or determination about him, and a renewed urgency in his work. I sense also a spirit of zeal, which sometimes seems to me like anger, though whether this is caused by a sense of helplessness in the face of nature's accidents, or even the limitations of his own profession to repair the damage wrought upon others, I do not know. He has attended without reserve to the dying and the few survivors, and now that the funerals are over, he returns to something like his normal self, though perhaps in more sombre frame.

Certainly, whatever cloud has overshadowed him, he has worked like ten men to support the small hospital that his house became after the accident, and has continued resolutely to refuse my assistance when I offered it, as though he were setting down a principle of independence, which he now intends to maintain.

I cite this incident at length only because I suspect that it has tightened the strange mechanism of his emotions, or has woken him from a more pleasant disposition. But I return to another theme, on which I have expended much ink and effort, and to which I once again refer in most careful terms.

There seems to be a rising expectation in him of some outcome in his waiting. I do not know, and cannot express, the foundations upon which he builds his anticipation, but merely observe the result. He has taken upon himself to consider the various disclosures concerning her past with which I have been able to supply him, and has absorbed them and digested them in his own fashion. I do not know the result of his disquisitions, and it is perhaps superfluous to speculate. But he believes that somehow he and Mrs Quill will be united.

These thoughts I commend to you, as always, in the hope that you will not think too badly of me for expressing them, and in the hope that, in the fullness of your kindness towards me, you will not think of replying to them.

I shall write again within the next few days, and continue with the burden of my story.

Meanwhile, I remain, sir,

Yours most sincerely,

Hargood

CHAPTER 94

The day was preternaturally calm, a white sun above bare winter fields. Grange's breath drifted into the empty air.

At St Just's house he drew down the gate-pull and fancied he heard the bell in the gatekeeper's cottage.

A side door opened and Elstead emerged, in a heavy coat but without head covering or gloves. Grange had a brief vision of his emaciated face and the firm, vertical lines rising from his mouth into his cheeks as he slid the bolts on the heavy, wrought-iron gates. Without speaking, he accompanied Grange to the main door. But this time he did not knock and, as was his custom, depart before his master appeared. Instead he withdrew a key, opened the main door and said, 'I believe you will find Mr St Just in his library, at the end of the corridor. He works there at this time of day.'

'Thank you,' Grange said.

Elstead nodded and closed the main door behind him.

Grange found himself alone inside the entrance hall of the great and gloomy house. He began to walk down the main corridor, with its oxblood walls, towards a large doorway at the end. The house was built to a strange and particular design, with a narrow frontage but a large and cavernous interior. On his earlier visit he had been ushered down this same corridor into a side room which served as St Just's private study. Now it seemed he was about to enter the main accommodation.

The door was partly ajar. Grange pressed it and it opened fully on soundless, well-oiled hinges into a great room lined with books. It seemed to him like a church or cathedral. Winter sunlight flooded in from high windows set in its sides. At first the vastness of the room made it seem bare. But opposite him he saw a bulky figure leaning forward over some figures, moving a quill pen carefully and assiduously across the surface. St Just, seated at a desk at the end of the library, reacted to his guest's arrival with a slow raising of his head, an almost imperceptible inclination of recognition. Then he lowered his gaze to the page before him and continued with his work.

Grange moved towards him across what seemed like twenty or thirty yards of carpet. An odd notion took hold of him. This was an English gentleman's deepest lair, his library, the repose of learning and of civilised values. As he walked past the busts of men, the shelves loaded with great works, past further book-filled arbours, he fancied he could hear, like a low hum, the fermentation of knowledge on the shelves: the massed reports of the Geographical Society, the scientific findings of the Royal Society, accounts of histories, wars, revolutions, mass migrations. In an angle between two shelves, the heads of two angels bent silently over as the sunlight poured between them.

Crossing the carpet in the library's thunderous silence, he proceeded down the central aisle of the great room. He passed arbour after arbour, recess after recess filled with the richness of books. In one, a stout female figure was stooping over a fat little baby in a stone basket. In the buzzing light, in the *memento-mori* look of the place, he heard no grunt or cry or moan or mew of life, only the sigh of dead ancestors on the path towards the ossuary.

At the far end of the library Grange halted.

Before him, St Just remained seated at his desk, writing in a ledger. Having acknowledged Grange's initial entrance, he did not look up, but continued at his work while Grange stood in tall proximity, waiting for the courtesy of being asked to be seated. This would be his technique, Grange thought, to treat his visitor like a plaintiff hoping for a loan. These were, after all, his business hours, in which he exercised his formal authority.

St Just continued for a full further minute in his work, while Grange stood calmly opposite him on the other side of the desk, assessing in his own mind his host's intention.

'Sir,' St Just said at last, head firmly down, the quill pen continuing to work, his spare hand indicating the chair opposite. 'You will forgive me if I finish this last entry.'

Grange sat, setting out his long legs, his hands gathered on his cane.

In due course St Just sighed, leaned back, put the quill back in its holder and raised his eyes above Grange to the ceiling in contemplation. Then he lowered his gaze and, for the first time, it seemed, considered his visitor directly. 'I am grateful that you have seen fit to call upon me.'

Grange nodded.

'Perhaps you will permit me to say, sir, that I had been expecting your company. You have come to report on the accident?'

'Now that the funeral is over, I thought it my duty to provide an account.'

'I will call my clerk to finish this work.' St Just rang a bell beside his desk. He rose, with some difficulty and inconvenience, to his feet. 'Let us go to my study, where we can discuss matters in greater privacy.'

There was a panel door behind the desk, which St Just opened. He moved forward into the darkness of the corridor, one leg driving, the other dragging, until they reached his study. Resting there, St Just leaned his shoulder against the door, opened it with a heavy key and stood aside for Grange. He motioned his guest to one of the high leather chairs, closed the door, moved to his desk and sat down, still panting softly with the effort.

'Now sir,' St Just said, 'let us consider what it is that separates us from a combined conclusion.'

From a drawer he withdrew a set of papers, bound together carefully in a single dossier.

'I have received a report of the damage to the furnace from Mr Naylor, one of the foremen of the remaining two working furnaces.

There is no hope, it seems, that the exploded furnace can be repaired. It must be written off our books.' He paused. 'The basic facts, sir, are seven men killed in all, eleven surviving. Do you have anything to add to this summary?'

For several moments Grange did not speak. This 'summary' was what he had dealt with over the past few weeks, attempting to tidy the broken and shattered remains of the men who lived. Eventually, he said, 'Of the eleven survivors, three are maimed for life. Almost all suffer from deafness in varying degrees. I believe the minds and mental faculties of at least two more are precarious following the shock of the blast.'

St Just nodded and closed his eyes briefly.

'Of the eleven, therefore,' Grange continued, 'I believe the likelihood is that only three will be fit to work in gainful labour again.'

Beneath the banker's expression, a number of emotions seemed to move. His eyes closed. The lines of his face and mouth appeared to harden. Grange studied his host with a certain objectivity. When St Just opened his eyes, Grange observed from his expression that he had determined his course of action and would speak his mind.

'You are about to add to your own account, I believe, that the cause of the accident was the same that Mr Swann had identified, and which you had informed me of no more than two months ago.'

An atmosphere of coldness permeated the room. Grange felt his anger fluctuate and grow steady. He was determined to be precise. 'The cause would seem to have been a number of gusts of wind, perhaps in combination with a crew insufficient to take appropriate measures against the danger.'

St Just nodded again. 'You are certain, then, of the cause?'

'Not entirely,' Grange answered. 'I merely propose what seems to me the most likely explanation. As I understand it, the furnace house exploded during a series of strong gusts of wind, while a gale was blowing at its height. The accounts of the men I have treated make independent record of the fact that the furnace was hit by strong winds just prior to the accident. They each confirm the appearance of the type of flame they call the "angel's wing". That being so, the crew seemed powerless to effect a rescue of the situation by the usual means – closing off the doors in sufficient

359

time to prevent a further rush of air from rapidly ventilating the main fires.'

'That is your considered version of events?'

'I believe', Grange answered, 'we are discussing the most likely cause.'

St Just leaned back and nodded, as if allowing the statement to take hold. 'And your observations lead you to believe it might have been averted with greater numbers of men in the crew of the furnace houses?'

'That is my belief.'

St Just shifted in his chair against a seizure of pain that had taken hold of him. He grimaced and closed his eyes. Yet while time continued to stand still, while St Just was subject to his intense and familiar agony, it was Grange who felt uneasy, as if some aspect that he had assumed was unaccounted for. He could not identify the source of his intuition, which added to his sense of discomfort.

When St Just recovered from his seizure, opened his eyes and looked once again at his guest, this sense of unease had not dispersed, but had instead concentrated around the notion of the explosion's real cause. In the ensuing silence St Just seemed to stare through Grange and behind him, into some private universe of invisible feeling or calculation.

'I would offer you a beverage, sir,' St Just said at last, 'but in the circumstances it may not seem appropriate.'

'I do not wish to trouble your hospitality.'

St Just nodded and seemed to turn again to his own thoughts. Grange sensed the fleeting seconds. He gained the impression that St Just was considering some aspect of the subject to which he himself had no formal access.

After a while his host placed his heavy white hands on the table and folded them together. 'These are important matters, I am sure you will agree. We must be rigorous in our procedures. Following our last meeting, and your report to me, I believe I am obliged also to make mine to you. In consideration of your appeal I conducted, as I promised you, an investigation into the possible nature of the danger.'

St Just opened the bound dossier of papers on his desk and for a short while consulted a schedule there. Having appeared to confirm a sequence of events to his satisfaction, he raised his head again. 'Perhaps six weeks ago, after our meeting, I interviewed, separately, each of the three foremen of the main shifts in the winter furnace houses, in order to gather their views independently. Having done so, and after considering their opinions, I decided that the unpredictable nature of the weather and the prevalence of winter gales posed a risk to the furnaces which we should attempt to offset – at least until we could reconsider the matter during the following summer, when the danger would have lessened.' St Just paused, taking a deep breath and shifting his leg beneath the table. 'Taking account of these factors, and at your own suggestion, I decided to increase the number of men in each furnace on the winter shift from twelve to the full summer complement of eighteen men.'

Grange felt a first quickening of alarm, like the shiver of a candle flame before it responds to a breeze.

St Just said, 'You counted the men affected?'

Grange nodded. It was eighteen. He had assumed, blithely, that eighteen was the number of a winter shift, or that perhaps there had been an overlap in the changing of shifts. He observed his error as if from a distance, though his mind started to slide towards the number now, like a man slipping down a slope.

Somewhere, in the background of his fear, St Just was continuing in an even voice: 'Due to the delays in recruiting further men, the first stage in the new manning procedure was instituted on Friday, 7 February – the precise day of the accident, as it happens. The six extra men had been added that very evening to the furnace under discussion.'

Grange sensed a cellar door opening beneath his feet.

St Just was continuing his inexorable progress: 'I had instructed our foreman, on the night in question, to explain to the new men precisely the dangers of gusting wind upon the flames and how they might be counteracted.'

'Forgive me . . .'

'I have no reason to believe', St Just continued, 'anything other than that he carried out my orders faithfully. He was a good man, and his decease has been a terrible loss. In my opinion the accident is most likely to have happened when he was explaining to the new men the procedures for reacting to gusts of wind. The new shift joined the works at eight o'clock in the evening – the usual time for changing shifts. According to our investigations, the explosion occurred between a quarter and twenty-five minutes past eight approximately. If this surmise is justified, I would suggest that during the course of these explanations he had perhaps taken his attention from his immediate surroundings. In such circumstances of reduced awareness, a series of gusts struck the furnace house, causing the tragedy in question.'

Grange felt his mouth dry. 'Are you suggesting . . .?'

'I suggest nothing, sir. I only attempt to deduce the immediate cause of the accident.' St Just showed no signs of emotion. 'It is by no means entirely clear, but we must search, as you say, for the most probable explanation. If our deductions concerning the timing of the matter are correct, it does perhaps explain another set of factors. According to the planned schedule, the increase in crews on the other furnace houses was due to follow on the 9th and 11th, as further men became available.' St Just paused to shift his leg beneath the desk. 'Whatever the precise causes, the accident occurred in the only furnace at the time which had an increased crew of eighteen men. That is the unfortunate fact, to which I believe we must now address our minds.'

Grange could hear the faint pulse of blood in his temples, like a moth attempting to escape. He began to feel faint. At the same time something else started to form in him; he was determined not to let St Just witness his own anguish. They were staring at one another directly now, neither speaking.

Even so, it was St Just who winced, clenched his jaw, moved his discomfited leg restlessly under the desk. A muscle in his face fluttered. The attention to his own pain had caused the banker to remove his eyes temporarily from his guest and to close in upon himself.

In the silence the heavy clock struck its martial rhythm. The sudden unexpected noise seemed to balance the room on a threshold of time. When it halted, both men sat for several moments in perfect silence, as if there were nothing more to time than its mechanism. After a few seconds St Just's spasm appeared to have departed. When he opened his eyes, his own pain having temporarily passed, he studied Grange almost pityingly.

*

362

While St Just waited for his response, Grange, for his part, struggled to hold himself steady. His emotions raged and raced. It seemed to him that his central argument – that the remaining furnaces were in danger of being undermanned by the reduced winter shifts – had been removed from him. St Just, having sharpened the knife, had driven the point home with careful precision. The trap had been set and triggered, and he must now begin to consider the damage to his beliefs and his own self. The first wave of horror having subsided, he turned his eyes to stare directly at those of his host.

Eventually the banker enquired, 'Perhaps you have an alternative explanation?'

'No,' Grange replied. 'I do not.'

St Just nodded, as though confirming a point. 'You are in agreement with me?'

'At first sight,' Grange said, 'it seems an effective explanation.'

St Just nodded in approval. 'I believe you are right, sir, in acknowledging the unfortunate and terrible reality.'

In the ensuing silence Grange glanced around him, as though noticing the details of the room for the first time. The furniture was magnificent and oppressive. There was a large bookcase in classical style, in oak inlaid with walnut. Behind its glass front were a series of leather-bound ledgers holding the mysterious and detailed entries of St Just's empire. On the other side of the room, carefully placed between two casement windows, stood a walnut, slanting-front bureau of older Queen Anne style, rendered imposing by the grandeur of the cabinet fitted on top of it. Set against other walls were several tables on which were further piles of ledgers. Heavy brass paperweights held down mounds of unattached papers, which might otherwise drift away of their own volition.

Roused from silence, St Just asked him, 'May I now, since we have conducted the essential nature of our business, at least offer you some port?'

It would have been discourteous to refuse a second time. But Grange had never accepted hospitality in less auspicious circumstances. When the port was poured, he noted the red shadow in his glass and the way it appeared to leech into the palm of his hands. Suspended in his horror, he drank the unwelcome liquid.

St Just said, 'In this world, in which each of us may attempt to do good, events sometimes move away from us. There are repercussions which we do not understand, and cannot control.'

Grange heard himself say, as if to a third party, 'How may we make moral judgements in such a world?'

'Our motivation must be our internal guide. The rest belongs to fate.'

'Fate is perhaps too abstract a concept,' Grange observed. 'In this matter at least, I believe there are different purposes at work.'

St Just paused, alarmed suddenly. 'But you have agreed, have you not, that what has happened is in no sense due to the use of diminished crews?'

'I have acknowledged, merely, that there was a full crew present at the time of the accident. As to more precise cause, I suspect it was the lack of a full crew which led to the necessity of explaining to a new crew the nature of the danger.'

'I fail to see your inference.'

'According to the witness, Mr Marston, the accident happened precisely at the change of shifts, on the very night on which the first change from twelve to eighteen occurred. I believe the explosion took place at precisely the time the foreman would have been explaining to the new men the requirements of their work.'

'This seems remote,' St Just said.

'His attention would have been distracted by the necessity of explaining the procedures to new arrivals.'

'What precisely do you infer?'

'That the cause of the accident was the placing of a body of new and untrained men upon the work, at a time when a strong gale was blowing.'

'I believe –' St Just's voice was cold '– you are reneging upon our agreement.'

'Which agreement?'

'Our agreement as to the cause of the accident, which I profoundly lament. The single salient fact is that a full crew was present at the time. Therefore a skeleton crew cannot be the cause . . .' St Just smiled, though it was a smile without warmth, but rather of conciliation and perhaps condescension.

Something impelled Grange to draw away, driving his chair backwards with the force of his emotion. Some spiral of anger or outrage moved in him, causing him to stand upright and breathe heavily, almost against his will.

St Just watched him as he struggled to control his emotion and attempted to conciliate again: 'Before you go, sir, I do implore you. You must not blame yourself in any manner for the accident. What you did was entirely justified. It is not our vices which cause us to suffer but our virtues. You were right to express your concern to me as you did. My own response to your plea about safety was, I think, equally appropriate. I believe I was justified in examining the conditions and, after studying them carefully, in increasing the numbers on the shift. The foreman did his duty in warning the men. It is fate which sometimes strikes us, just as it is fate which has placed me in unwelcome authority over my great patron.'

'I must thank you for your hospitality.' Grange half bowed, and turned to leave. He experienced a sense of floundering in darkness. He was still too fiercely immersed in his own thoughts to act directly and decisively. But after a few more seconds of paralysis, the horror of remaining further in that room rose up and seized him. For a brief moment, his hand seemed to drift ineffectually on the handle of the study door. Then the door drew back under his volition and he was able to make his way into the corridor without further delay. He was determined above all to take his leave rather than continue to be the subject of the banker's sympathetic contemplation.

St Just called after him, 'You must not blame yourself, sir. Promise me that you will not. I will summon Elstead. He will let you out.'

In the hallway Grange lifted his coat, drew it on and raised the heavy oak brace of the main door. As it opened, the cold struck him forcibly. Glare from the surface of the snow rose to his eyes, causing a sudden soft pain in the roots of his nerves. He did not look back at St Just, standing now at the other end of the corridor, observing his departure. Stepping out into the snow, Grange swung the door closed behind him.

Outside, he looked around him. There was no sign of the gatekeeper. For the first time since he had entered St Just's household and land, Grange experienced in the middle of his anguish a vague sense of relief. The bell had not been rung for

Elstead and some part of him calculated that if he moved swiftly he would be spared the terrible pantomime of the other's concern.

He strode fast across the paving stones. At the gate, he hauled the bolts across, pulled it open and stepped out. As he was about to swing it back he saw that the door of the main house had been quietly opened. St Just stood in the obscurity, gazing at his departure. A beam of afternoon light from the winter sun fell across the banker's heavy shoulders, but his face was largely obscured by shadow.

The stillness of St Just's stance was unnerving, as though he tried to read Grange's thoughts across the distance separating them. But while Grange paused, the first signs of a shuffle behind the gatekeeper's cottage door indicated at last that Elstead had been alerted, and Grange knew that the mechanism of contrition and human indignity was about to run its course.

Before it began, there was an odd moment of triangular confrontation between the three parties. St Just remained still, utterly unmoving, in the slanted shadow of the great door. Elstead, who had emerged now from the gatehouse, stopped briefly to stare at Grange. Then his eyes followed Grange's gaze to St Just's figure, still half hidden in the obscurity of the hallway. For several moments the three remained there, as though each were arrested and constrained in his own peculiar sense of unease. Then Grange swung the gate closed, turned his back on both figures and walked swiftly away from the banker's house.

CHAPTER 95

Dear Leman,

During the fortnight since the accident at the salt furnace I have noticed an added thoughtfulness in my younger colleague. His small hospital, established so rapidly, has slowly demobilised as his patients have returned to their respective homes. Several other of his patients have been transported, as the condition of each has become more stable, to the care of their own families, where he visits them daily. I do believe it has been the most impressive treatment I could have hoped to see, carried out with great concentration and decision.

He has supervised their transport himself. At least he has accepted the use of my fly, with its springs, as a means of conveyance. The men are nearly all dispersed, except for two patients who remain.

This is the first day for several weeks that we have been out walking. Until now, he has been unwilling, because of duties to his remaining patients, to leave them for more than a few hours. I believe that only one of them is unlikely to survive. He has lost both legs (the second was amputated two days ago, after gangrene had set in) and hangs on by a thread. Yet my colleague is determined to save him, as if he saves himself.

I have myself been unusually fully occupied, for while he tends to the wounded of the salt furnace, I have agreed to tend certain of his patients. And though I am, in effect, acting as his second and his replacement, there are other matters which concern me. For beneath the surface of my formal activities towards my patients, I feel more than ever now that a part of me is emerging which was hidden before, and that what I do is a kind of surface for another process I do not understand. A few weeks ago it was I who walked with my younger colleague, attempting to assist and oversee his recovery. Yet now it is he who walks with me, supervising my condition, as it were, and solicitously observing my state of mind.

In these discussions with him I become aware in increasing degrees of his mind, of its subtle energies, of the curious character that inhabits him. For beneath his exterior of diffidence he has an inner life whose presence is not visible. During the day, when we walk, I observe the trace of interest in his eye when I mention some element related to Mrs Quill and his stillness when he listens.

There is very little that he imparts without my prompting. Yet nothing that he says seems superfluous. I observe him, and afterwards I find myself sifting his words for aspects of meaning as carefully as if they were the auguries of some authority or oracle. In composing these missives to you, kind sir, I have tried

367

to convey some measure or sense of our communication, yet I believe I have left aside, perhaps not wholly unwittingly, something which is essential to our intercourse, a thing which both characterises him and sets him apart.

I used to believe there was some civil virtue in him, some mechanism of restraint or consideration for others which governed his being. It seemed to me that a gentleman is one in whom civilisation has taken hold at some deep level. Yet increasingly I perceive that is not what distinguishes him. For if that were true, what interior force was it which struck a blow at my person of such violence that for several days I was laid low? No, he is not motivated by the detachment of a gentleman. What distinguishes him from others is a separate matter entirely, which I begin to perceive more directly and perhaps more solidly. There is no compromise in him. He knows that which he wants. Perhaps the singular feature of a mystic or saint is not that he is detached, but that his mind and senses are directed to a single aim. Such a concentration of desire may simplify a man's soul, but it renders him dangerous to those around him. Since what we call 'society' occasions in almost all cases some compromise with the desires of others, it is perhaps inevitable that at some stage my younger colleague should find himself in conflict with it. I do not think he knows this himself. Since I am, so to speak, society's representative, at least insofar as I may extend its good offices towards him and assist his return to its favour, I am perhaps more aware of it than he. If he should happen to read what I write to you, I believe he would laugh. But is not the person we know least in this world our own self? It is precisely that unknowing which is his essential grace and the source of his increasing influence over me, who was his physician and guardian in his time of travail.

It seems to me that this lack of self-awareness, which protects him from the consequences of his actions, is that same insensitivity which gives him his strength. In relation to myself, as I become more aware of my own transgressions, not least against my former mistress Mrs Quill, so I grow less comfortable with my own nature.

That we play a role, and that if we are lucky our inner selves may correspond with it – that much perhaps may be agreed between us. Fortunate are those who observe in that role and duty some aspect of themselves by means of which they may find fulfilment. Yet we may err when we think of this inner being as fixed, as static, as stationary. For what may have given satisfaction at one stage may not do so at another. And if by degrees we should become detached, so our soul begins to move within our character as freely as another separate being outside us. It is this mysterious separate being who now starts to loosen and to move inside me, and whose general condition and provenance begins to express itself.

I do not pretend to know of what madness consists, but I believe that inside one being another may fret to be free. The virtue of some small insight, such as I may possess, is that I am at least partially aware of these changes or migrations and, though I may not control them or prevent their advance, yet I perceive their existence sufficiently to alert myself, and place myself on guard against that complacency which persists in perceiving no change or occurrence.

If I am in danger of resolving into two beings, then I shall hope to oversee the process, and see it to its final end. These letters may form some small evidence of the fact that, as I descend into myself, so I may record that descent, as befits a physician who has notified in the past the malaise of others. These missives, however incomplete, shall be my records.

I shall not continue in this vein *ad infinitum*, for it is painful to record, but will write again in due course when I am of a less sombre disposition.

I must return to my duties.

In the meanwhile, I remain, sir,

    Yours sincerely,

        Hargood

CHAPTER 96

They were engaged in one of those light sparring matches which increasingly characterised their walks. It was late afternoon and the day was becoming colder, when Hargood said, 'We return to the matter of profound belief.'

'In what sense?' Grange asked.

'I am religious, you are not.'

'What do you imply?'

'I believe I am sustained by a tradition. You, on the other hand, prefer to live outside that tradition, in a land of your own choosing . . .'

Grange felt a rhetorical blush. 'The English are a pagan race.'

'You think so?'

Grange felt compelled to continue, 'Christianity has never touched us. There is no Christianity in our tradition. There is no great tradition of Christianity in our literature. Look at Shakespeare, not a hair of true religion in his entire works.'

'But our religion lies in our morals,' Hargood said. 'Our religion informs our morals.'

'Yes, it reinforces secular authority. It bolsters tradition. It acts as a means of conservation. Your Christianity suits you, I would say, like a well-fitting shirt. And why should it not? That, above all, is its purpose.'

They came to a rise in the ground and looked out over a long stretch of land towards Sowley, the sunlight golden across the fields, the Solent silent behind.

'Is a comfortable religion such a bad thing?' Hargood asked, taking up the metaphor in order to entice Grange further down this line of discourse. 'I have comfortable boots and, as you say, a well-fitting shirt. Why not a comfortable religion, too?'

'Why not?' Grange said. 'You are as easy in church as you are upon your horse. You have put a saddle on your religion, and a bridle and stirrup upon your faith, and it will carry you wherever you may wish.'

'You speak, sir,' Hargood said approvingly, 'of a very satisfactory state indeed. But there are other strands of religion than my own. What of James Fox? What of the Puritans, the Levellers? What of the Civil War, fomented by the apostles of the low churches and their agents?'

'I admit that there are those among ourselves who use Christianity like a hair shirt. They take the idea of sin and apply it to themselves like a scourge. But perhaps a religion of discomfort is no deeper than one of comfort. It serves a common utility.'

'What, then, is the secular purpose of this discomfort?' Hargood murmured.

'To provide us with a certain energy, I do believe. There are few peoples busier in this world than the English, but our religion hardly appears more than skin deep. That is my point.'

'Surely,' Hargood said, 'a religion of discomfort would suit you well enough? I dare say you might even find it comfortable.'

Grange smiled at his colleague's subtle strike. 'Perhaps I have found in the discipline of science a hair shirt sufficient for my purposes – one that makes religion superfluous.'

'You say that the English are not religious,' Hargood said. 'Yet you believe that there are religious peoples?'

'I believe the Irish are religious in some deeper sense than the English. I believe the Latin countries are religious in some larger manner.'

'How so?'

'Religion permeates their lives, not only their civic laws. The Church occupies a central position in their societies.'

'Catholicism, then, would seem to be your yardstick of religion?'

'Not entirely so. I believe there is a religious tradition of a different kind in Luther's Switzerland, or in the hard Calvinists of Scotland. I believe there is a deep religion in Judaism, and also in Islam. I merely say that religion does not obsess the English soul. It is pragmatic, that is to say, it does not bend before religion, but uses it for its own ends.'

'I notice, sir, you have left out France from our discussions, even though it is our most important neighbour and our greatest rival. You feel there is a religious tradition in France?'

'I dare believe there is a religious tradition in France. But I do not think it is a religious nation.'

371

'You do not?' For the first time Hargood appeared genuinely interested, in spite of himself. 'Yet you say it has a religious tradition.'

'The religion of France is used to suit its civil structures, to support the nobles in their *noblesse oblige*, to give sustenance to the peasants in their hope of an afterlife.'

'You are opaque, sir. Is France a religious nation or not?'

'In my opinion France is neither deeply religious, like the Latins, nor deeply pragmatic, like the English. These two factors make it the prey of ideas.'

'You talk, sir, with the benefit of hindsight,' Hargood said swiftly.

'Do I?' Grange enquired. Having been granted a temporary advantage, he needed to consider his best move. 'Whether by foresight or hindsight, surely the evidence suits the case?'

'I believe that France, before the turbulence, was a very model of good living, and an example of the deepest religion.'

'If that were so,' Grange asked, 'would it have come so easily to its present pass?'

'It is my duty to remind you, sir, that the Revolution was made in the city of Paris. It was fomented by discontented members of the merchant and professional classes, by youthful, indigent lawyers and suchlike. It did not arise in the countryside, and found little support there, except after the contagion had spread. After it had begun, its worst excesses continued to take place in the capital city.'

'Even so,' Grange demurred, 'it seems a society peculiarly fragile to such metropolitan agitation.'

'Does it? Those upstarts, as we rightly call them, have all but consumed themselves. The original leaders have all but disappeared. Soon the Revolution itself will disappear, and all its progeny. That, sir, is my sincerest hope. It will leave behind France as we once knew her, in her deepest traditions, in what certain writers have called *France profonde*. It will return itself to ancient monarchy, and the wisdom of one generation will once more be passed to the next through a stable institution. That is my belief. That is my sustenance.'

'What is a king?' Grange asked suddenly, without warning. 'A cattle thief with a crown.'

The sentence had arisen inside him so swiftly, so disingenuously, that he did not give it thought until it had passed his lips. He had been so deep in concentrated thought that the bubble of expression had surfaced almost without his knowing. It was as if the thought had been spoken to him, not by him. Now it was there, present, between them. But once it had been expressed, he feared that he had gone too far, that to a convinced Tory such as Hargood this would be more than a mere philosophical expression: it would sound treasonous. Following the thought of Hargood's mortification, Grange considered briskly the precedents. Out of a combination of fear and respect he had never attempted to push his senior colleague beyond the pale. There was something of the old warrior in Hargood. Now, in the flare of silence following his sentence, Grange imagined beneath his companion's affability the precipitation of a cold rage, or perhaps even the fierce riposte of violence.

Hargood halted, and the two of them stood side by side for several seconds, staring out towards the sea. Grange waited for the seasoned and terrible explosion. He perceived, out of the corner of his eye, a motion, a slight movement of the head, a sense of the hardening of Hargood's lower jaw, then a calm, imminent shaking, more frightening because Hargood seemed in the grip of some great force of will, or suppression.

Grange was about to cry out an apology for his provocation, for the stupidity and thoughtlessness of his remark, when he perceived that his colleague's shaking was becoming, if anything, more pronounced. Without warning, Hargood let out a great bull's roar of laughter, a single shout of mirth.

Grange witnessed a brief shaking in his companion, after he had given vent to his feelings in this exposition, like the seismic tremors after an earthquake. This was followed by a deep silence.

Having brought himself under control, Hargood said, 'Very droll, sir, I am sure. Now, shall we continue our walk?'

A certain light-headedness affected Grange during the rest of the walk. He did not feel inclined to test his own standing with Hargood again. Instead he said, 'What is your opinion of the method of the Chinese – their so-called acupuncture?'

'I have seen reports of its surprising powers in the relief of pain.'

They continued, somewhat desultorily, to discuss the method, its assumption of certain points in the nervous system, for several minutes. Approaching Hargood's house from the north, they passed by a long field that stretched down towards Hundreds Hill. Behind it, a fold of the river, visible between two patches of trees, glittered softly.

Grange looked at the field and observed a single man moving across it, walking towards the low sun and casting a long shadow behind. It might have been a labourer, returning in the last light of day. The man appeared tiny in the vastness of the field, though his shadow was long behind him. It was as though he walked into light, trailing darkness. To Hargood, watching the same phenomenon, it seemed that he observed a shadow walking towards the sun.

CHAPTER 97

Dear Leman,

I discovered recently the final stone, that key or cornerstone, which allows me to complete the first understanding of my younger colleague's circumstances. It is not definitive, by any means, but what may perhaps be called an insight.

I met by chance – in the house of our vicar of Boldre, the Reverend Gilpin – an extraordinary woman, a Mrs Arabella Pugh, who lives in a fine house in the environs of Salisbury at Downton. She is an heiress, whose husband, as I understand, hardly visits her – a fact about which she is both ruefully honest and refreshingly direct. She even jokes about her predicament, decorously yet without malice, and once or twice in the course of the evening referred to her husband as her 'absent landlord'. I believe he is an owner of mines and forested estates in Durham, though his works keep him at a considerable distance. Yet where other women might be thought to wilt under such inattention, or to pine, there is something in her which seems to thrive upon it – as though she answers her husband's independence with her own. Perhaps, in the pursuit of her life, she has even encouraged his separation from her. Suffice it to say that she seems positively to glow in his neglect.

Enough remains of my earlier existence as a rake to cause me a certain alarm, or perturbation, in the presence of an attractive woman, particularly one so confident as this. I have seen her type once or twice in London, but usually as the wife, or perhaps the acknowledged mistress, of a great peer. I will give a brief physical description of her, but no account of an exterior may yet do easy justice to the spirit which occupies and animates that frame. She is of medium height, with clear features and a fine figure. But her eyes attract the attention, for they appear fearless, and reveal a depth of intelligence which I have only rarely seen. In the midst of my perturbation, I wondered what it is about her that caused me to be reminded, in her type, of another figure in my past. And with some trepidation, my dear Leman – with some odd sense of ancestry and common features of character – I realised that she reminded me of Mrs Celia Quill.

They are not relations, for Mrs Pugh is darker of hair than our former lady of Lymington, and her brown eyes are almost Italianate compared with Mrs Quill's grey eyes and fair complexion. Mrs Pugh is of a lively disposition, where Celia Quill is calmer, more internal in her temperament. No, it is in the broader expanse of the spirit that they are sisters, for both seem to live by their own lights, and govern their lives without reference to others. I had registered these complex reactions to her when the conversation began to be struck in greater earnest, and other things started to emerge that caused me no small consternation.

The Reverend Gilpin, in his gentle (and no doubt well-meaning) pursuit of the truth, had invited Mrs Pugh to his table as an old friend of Mrs Celia Quill, one who had visited Mrs Quill's house on numerous previous occasions. The Reverend and his wife had occasionally met Mrs Pugh there, and had gained sufficient familiarity with her at least to permit an invitation.

I started to appreciate that the good vicar had invited me for perhaps a similar reason – that I was Mrs Quill's physician and had some acquaintance with her. I believe that Mrs Pugh and I both realised the cause of our respective invitations at the same time and that we began to regard one another more closely.

You will understand the conditions of the meal and the somewhat cautious atmosphere attending it. If it seems as though I accuse the Reverend gentleman of a certain calculation (and I do not withdraw that assertion) it was no doubt an enterprise governed by good intentions, to bring together two of Mrs Quill's acquaintances and hope thus to strike a few sparks in the darkness concerning her absence. For myself, I was intrigued by this new guest and, since Mrs Pugh was aware that I was known to Celia Quill in some degree, I believe she may have held similar tentative hopes regarding myself.

So we proceeded through our courses – for the Reverend Gilpin spreads a good table – lightly touching upon this subject and that, and slowly we began to assess one another. There were certain aspects that struck me in relation to her own behaviour, which I regard as worthy of record.

During the evening, the subject of Silas Grange's illness was raised. My host enquired of me how he was progressing and I informed him of my younger colleague's improving health. Mrs Gilpin, who in other respects seemed content to allow her husband to conduct the investigation, asked me if I understood the cause of his malaise. Faced with so direct a question, I believed that my best defence was a proper humility in the face of his decline. I told her, in all honesty, that he was a man of sensitivity and deep feeling, and had been affected by a humour which I did not fully understand.

· I had been expecting some form of enquiry from her husband and had prepared myself for the careful eliciting of information. But there was something both innocent and direct in Mrs Gilpin's occasional questions which, because they lacked guile, were more penetrating than the Reverend's more cautious solicitations. Indeed, her directness upon one or two matters caused a certain embarrassment in him. He attempted to restrain her, as we might prevent a child from asking about matters which he does not fully understand. But her husband had not managed to silence her before she had asked me directly whether Mrs Quill's departure was the cause of my colleague's decline.

Once the question was asked, it could not be rescinded. Leman, you may be amused at my own internal perturbation. I had prepared myself for some elaborate fencing with her husband. This sudden thrust from a toy rapier caused me to fall back upon my defences, and answer with something like directness. I told her that the two events might indeed be connected, but I myself was not entirely sure of the full nature of that connection and, lacking any firm evidence, was not in a position to speculate further. In the meantime I considered it my duty to help my colleague back to his former health.

There was a distinct pause in the conversation while my three companions considered my answer, each from their different perspectives. I do not presume to know their conclusions, but no doubt each made his or her calculations upon it, and so we passed on to another matter. But I should like to add my own commentary, for just as they considered my reaction, so I considered theirs.

If the mention of her husband's absence did not seem to cast Mrs Pugh into any state of sadness or consideration, then the mention of my younger colleague appeared to have a different effect. For it seemed to me, surveying her response, that some emotion in her was touched by his name. Whenever his presence was invoked in regard to the departure of Mrs Quill, she became both more animated in appearance and more cautious in what she might say. I believe I know enough of women to identify a state of mind. I would say, in the case of Mrs Pugh, that in regard to my colleague, what I witnessed was a form of infatuation.

It was perhaps a demonstration of his ability to agitate certain women. His reticence excites or inspires them to this odd devotion. I gained, as I say, the distinct impression that he and Mrs Pugh were more than mere acquaintances, that they were intimates. I rest this assumption on nothing more than intuition, but I have come to trust my senses where women are concerned, and have on more than one occasion profited by them.

Thus, while we spent the meal in polite conversation, taking into account the due proprieties of a vicar's table, the several parties continued to explore the confines of one another's knowledge and, beneath a polite discourse, each began to build his or her understanding of the others' positions. And if the Reverend Gilpin had hoped for some enlightenment on the nature of Mrs Quill's departure, I sought enlightenment on another subject. For whereas Mrs Pugh may have been interested in news of my younger colleague, I was interested in news of Mrs Quill. And this was my second intuition – that Celia Quill had been in communication with Mrs Pugh, and the latter knew more about her current whereabouts than she would openly admit.

Our Reverend host, in order to keep matters on a reasonable course, complained in good heart about the vacuum that Mrs Quill's departure had left in charitable works among the local community, and discussed the arrangements that had been made in her stead. A Mrs Roxburghe had taken over the running of the committee which contributed clothes and other oddments to the Poor House. A Mrs Angela Livingstone, of impeccable reputation, had gracefully acquiesced in the task of teaching the children of unfortunates. Another, Mrs Leigh Peckham, had taken the place of Mrs Quill on the committee of the Poor House itself. Surveying these substitutions, the Reverend Gilpin said that when it was revealed how many replacements were required for her activities, it became yet more obvious how deeply she had committed herself to good works.

Thus two different aspects of Mrs Quill's nature emerged: her charitable energies and her other, social, life which was both more private and mysterious.

Now, Leman, I reach towards that strange conclusion which emerges from these discussions, and combine it with my other speculations. It seemed to me that there were a number of women of independent means who gathered about the figure of Mrs Quill, as though around a leader or a leading light. If they held any one thing in common it was that they were none of them dependent upon a man for their livelihood. In that confederacy of women, of independent spirits, there had been an understanding or mutual agreement between several of them concerning the relations between the sexes. I attempted to set together what I had heard of Mrs Quill's relations with my younger colleague, and with her daughter. So, with the addition of Mrs Pugh, I believe I began to see the shadowy outlines of a possible explanation.

I ask your customary patience, and hope that you will bear with me. What I offer now is constructed from hints, from suggestions, from delicate nuance.

I have mentioned before that it seemed to me that during the course of their relations Mrs Quill was attracted to my younger colleague, while at the same time wishing to preserve her own independence. In her situation, we may perhaps surmise that she did not feel she had the right to seek his exclusive attentions, and therefore seemed willing to share him with others – in the first instance, with her daughter; in the second, I now believe, with Mrs Arabella Pugh.

I admit this was a strange arrangement, but perhaps you will indulge my curiosity and permit me, sir, to press upon the outline, to explore the matter a little further.

We may begin by asking ourselves a question: if an eligible male meets a number of attractive women, why should we not expect a little competition or rivalry between the parties for his attention? Perhaps we do. Yet I do believe it was different in the case of our central character, Mrs Quill, and her friends. I believe she actively encouraged him, out of some generosity or largesse of her heart, to pursue their company in addition to her own. For if she had made up her mind that she desired his company, but was unwilling to forgo her independence, why should she deny him his own independence? And why in turn should she deny to her own good friends the pleasures of his companionship?

And now, Leman, I begin to see how Mrs Quill may have challenged him, this man who she believed had locked himself in his study, whose emotions she thought had dried like pressed flowers. She could not offer herself as a permanent and exclusive object of his attentions, since she was committed to her own continued autonomy. So, I believe, she introduced him tacitly to others, in the hope that he would favour them with his attentions. And these others were not mere acquaintances, offered lightly as diversions, but those closest to her – her daughter and perhaps her great friend, Mrs Pugh. Her offer, if I may express it differently, was genuine and heartfelt. Touching those closest to her, it achieves a strange quality of goodness, or even beneficence. For, in some manner, she introduced him to her deepest fellowship of women.

We have heard of enough strange tales of affection or debauchery among our peers and aristocracy, in which it is common for a man to hold or possess an official mistress as well as a wife, and even for the wife to approve the arrangement – for she herself is free to maintain other obligations, perhaps devote herself to her children, or to the administration of the estate, or even (in reflection of her husband) to a lover of her own choosing. But we are not part of that class, bolstered by privilege and protected by the high walls of their grand estates from the common purview, and so must conduct our affairs with greater discretion, under the eyes of our fellows.

If our world is more confined, more regulated – as I myself have found when I attempted to play the field in the search for a mate – we are compelled towards other arrangements. I found a solution in maintaining a mistress in London. Our womenfolk are even more confined than we are. But such confinement is a challenge to ingenuity.

If Mrs Quill and Mrs Pugh are, for different reasons, independent of the influence of men in the material necessities of their lives, why shall they not attempt to organise their own circumstances as they see fit? And the case is surely strengthened if they are able to do so privately, by civilised and mutual agreement among themselves.

These are odd intuitions and irregular speculations. They are the paths of moonlight rather than broad day. Perhaps we observe in these manoeuvres of the heart the faint glimmers of a strange and novel feminine soul. And even as I put words to paper and attempt to explain my own impressions, the very thoughts seem to glide away from me. Yet there are certain further arguments or points of interest which I wish to impart, for they have a bearing on what follows.

If one inhabits the same room as one of these creatures, who are independent of means, who do not depend upon husbands or fathers either for their livelihood or their tranquillity, it is almost as if one deals with another sex than the feminine one we know. For we can assume nothing that was earlier the case. We cannot count upon their dependence upon us, nor that they seek our protection; nor – since neither of the first conditions applies – are we permitted to take it for granted that they will be submissive to our wishes. They are, on the contrary, concerned only with their own wishes. Since these are odd, new beings, beings we have not met before, we are forced, so to speak, to establish relations between the sexes afresh.

These few thoughts are, I admit, the most peculiar glosses or shines upon the matter. But if I were to attempt to characterise the interest of my younger colleague, it is perhaps the challenge of this new territory – even though he has not once expressed it to me in those terms – which attracted him to their company. I believe I am able to perceive, in shadowy outline, the circumstances which might draw him forth from his study and into the society of these women. These same circumstances, I would suggest, caused him to risk his well-being in certain forms of intimacy to which he had previously closed his mind.

We may discuss the moonlight of the mind, and the depths and shadows of character. Yet all things are open to misunderstanding, particularly in matters of the emotions. I believe my younger colleague entered the circle or fellowship of these formidable women with a certain trepidation, or apprehension. Yet whatever misgivings he may have felt, he was compelled by stronger forces of character than he himself understood. Who among us may fully comprehend his own heart, or may account for his strongest compulsions – not least that of curiosity about the deepest motivations of the opposite sex? And if we wish to attribute cause, shall we not also add that the natural rhythms of the heart shall sometimes seek such beguiling prospects?

What I have offered is no more than an hypothesis. Yet a genuine hypothesis has a duty to explain certain contingent facts or features. To this end, I return to my younger colleague's reaction when I informed him of Mrs Quill's former life. I believe that by my own actions I introduced, into the intense and complex circumstances of his relations with Mrs Quill and her friends, the crude trammels of another world, a world whose influence fell across his own. I do not know what shadows lingered at the edge of his mind regarding her former activities. Perhaps, in that apprehension of her motive, I returned him to his own fears and intimate oppressions. Perhaps he suspected, in a moment of revelation, that her matchmaking was an echo of her former days. Yet we may commit the same action for entirely different motives. This haunts me now, but it does not absolve me from the attempt to alleviate the circumstances which to some extent I may have caused.

I do believe that, as a result of my untimely disclosures, he felt himself manipulated, and the sincerity of his feelings for Mrs Quill placed an unconscionable strain upon him. I believe, further, that he had formed so great an attachment to her that the news of her former life caused in him such a conflict of feelings, that he could not reconcile his emotions. I am come to believe, sir, that the intensity of his dilemma was so great that he entered that fever of the mind and body in which I found him the following day.

Sometimes, when there is cloud or thunderstorm, I discover on the surfaces of metal in my house a strange shine, a bloom of light. These are the thoughts that I find myself pursuing, as though through them I may enter tentatively that strange and delicate realm of quiet illumination. In the course of these thoughts, I find myself in constant wonder at the complexity of my younger colleague.

Perhaps I have explained myself insufficiently, and there are many gaps and infelicities in reaching towards these odd conclusions. In the absence of genius, I commit myself to these jottings in the hope that, if they do not prove to you the ground for my speculations, at least they may serve as an indication of intent.

In the interim, I have expressed and exhausted myself in these speculations, and must now return to my normal existence. I shall confine myself, once again, to the duties and habituations of bright day.

In the meanwhile, sir, I remain,

    Yours sincerely,
      Hargood

CHAPTER 98

Dear Leman,

After resting from my writing for several days, I now enter the final stages of my story. For my account begins to join itself with the present, and the change of tense means that I cannot any longer rely upon hindsight to correct my views and guide my actions. I must examine my conscience and decide upon a course which will serve the best interests of those involved.

There is a time, after the mind has seized upon some new perspective − or is reluctantly forced to consider another purview − when the emotions adjust to the new arrangement, and it seems that one hovers in a strange detachment. Thus, in the process of consideration, I arrive increasingly at the belief that my former mistress, whom I drove from me in my younger years, and whom I have again driven from these parts, was motivated by something approaching goodwill towards me, and that I myself was in error. For I am now inclined to believe that she settled here to impress me with her new-found independence and, attempting to establish her own acquaintances, by degrees fell in love with my younger colleague. It has taken me some little time to reach this conclusion and, having reached it, I must make my deliberations.

But before I do, let us consider her achievement, for what I shall intend depends upon it. In my younger colleague there existed a man of great resolve, who had sown his wild oats in his youth, and had decided thereafter to pursue a course of knowledge with the utmost concentration. He would sacrifice the joys of a wife and family in order to pursue his profession and his studies the more diligently and conscientiously. There is a certain logic, though to my tastes a somewhat ruthless and peremptory one, in his direction. Assume, further, that this dedication met with a certain measure of success for, from humble beginnings, he established a considerable practice, is much admired and, though I would not admit so much in his company, he is perhaps the best practising physician of my acquaintance.

These are the gains and losses. He has settled into his existence. His housekeeper manages his somewhat singular establishment, and provides him with an atmosphere in which he may commit himself to his profession and his studies. This was what Celia Quill faced: a man certain of his aims, clear in his constructions, having achieved a sufficient order of success to confirm and solidify him in his views.

Perhaps I myself did not fully appreciate the degree of this detachment. In order to apprise you of its extent I will provide an example of his strange completeness.

We are most of us born of parents who, for the main part, influence us long beyond our childhood. Although my parents died relatively young, I do admit that I carry within me the seed of my father's ambition and my mother's concern. Yet, in the full course of my association with my younger colleague, I never asked him about his family, for one simple and singular reason. He is such a remarkable individual, so driven by his particular will, that I assumed he sprang fully formed from his background. So independent is he, that the notion of parents appears almost incongruous. He is risen without origin. He is self-created. I have known him for perhaps fourteen years, yet, as I have reported, in that entire period it never occurred to me to enquire about his mother or father. I never met a man who was so complete, and at the same time so isolated in his career and his achievement.

What might be Celia Quill's interest in this solitary and, so to speak, parentless man? Perhaps he supplies her with a challenge to her character. We should not forget that she is used to the consideration of male weakness and, to her view at least, this individual shows none that she can see. This is mere speculation, so let us compound our error and speculate further. Perhaps it was precisely his isolation which attracted her. In his pursuit of his own goals, he matched her own dedication. They are like two animals from the same rare species, though cast in different sexes. I believe she may have seen in him her counterpart. Is it unreasonable to assume that she, too, sympathised with him, not least because she herself had sacrificed the hope of marriage in order to pursue her own ideals? Perhaps in this, too, she had an understanding of his self-imposed isolation, for no other reason than that it matched her own.

If I sensed a natural collusion of interest between them, it appeared to me an intimacy of minds more than emotions. This is how it seemed to have begun, and so it might have remained, except that somehow it was transformed, through the passage of time, until there developed some further sense of intimacy between them.

Though he denies it, my colleague has numerous female admirers among the local population. I have lost no opportunity to chide him, when my purposes suited, about the manner in which he appears to taunt the more eligible local women, not overtly, but by continuing in his ways untrammelled, and by the mere fact of not choosing one for his bride. He affects not to know of their interest, and continues to pursue his course.

He does not lack potential intimates, yet for fourteen years, the time of his residence in Lymington, he has resisted all opportunities to tie himself to another party. This is a resolute man indeed. For one such as myself, who enjoys the warmth of company, this dedication to a singular bachelor existence appeared to offend against nature. Perhaps it seemed so to

Celia Quill too – though, being in her own way similarly independent, she may have possessed the greater insight into his condition.

Before we proceed further, I am aware again, as I have been before, that what I offer is speculation, but speculation which is inaccurate in certain regards is often better than the total darkness which we call ignorance. For if we take a light, however weak, to some obscure area, we may not see the truth, but we may hope to see its shadow.

This is a woman, a most resourceful woman, who observes in her acquaintance a detachment bordering on coldness. He appears immune to the emotions. He is amiable, but retains a certain distance. Perhaps, too, she is aware of the limits of his commitment to her and the border that separates a natural sympathy from true intimacy. Assuming these deductions to be true, how would she cross this bridge into his soul?

I admit that I myself face darkness. For if there were any man who kept a private aspect to himself it was my colleague. It was precisely his loyalty towards her that fuelled my suspicion of the depth of his commitment to her.

I am of the opinion she proposed to him some plan which seized his imagination. I believe I have an intimation of what that proposal may have been. She would have couched it in terms of some ideal, some prospect that would appeal to the rational man within.

Now, Leman, we enter truth's shadow. We cross on the faint bridge of our assumptions. I shall introduce into my evidence something that I learned from another of those strong women who seem to play a part in the life of my younger colleague. I am speaking in this instance of Mrs Thompson, his housekeeper. I admit, in passing, that I have only a few clues upon which to construct my account, but I recall one in particular as follows. During the time of his recuperation, I took the opportunity to question Mrs Thompson on certain aspects of the background to his sudden decline. You will oblige me by remembering the circumstances prevailing at the time of which Mrs Thompson spoke. He was in the middle of his infatuation with Mrs Quill, and visited her and her daughter regularly.

Discussing his few last visits to Mrs Celia Quill's house, Mrs Thompson said that her master returned in thoughtful mood one day and asked her what seemed the oddest of questions: 'Do women's souls sing?' Mrs Thompson imparted it to me, because I believe it haunted her, and she offered it to me out of friendship, as though I might make some sense of it.

We should perhaps consider that strange question. What does it mean? I say the first aspect of it is that it was couched in the plural and thus in the abstract. Mrs Thompson was herself arrested by it. She said she paused, and then enquired what the question might mean. Consider his response, for Mrs Thompson says she reports it accurately. He replied, 'If I knew what it meant, Mrs Thompson, I would not ask you.'

These are words lacking in sense, except perhaps to one who carries a secret. What that secret was I do not know. Yet these matters acquire an importance if only because I am myself subject to the outcome of the relations between them.

I could gain no further idea of its meaning from Mrs Thompson, or of the disposition of the mind which asked it. When I lie awake at night, it sometimes happens that I turn the matter over in my mind, and attempt to consider the conditions in which it might seem reasonable to ask such a question.

Since Mrs Quill's departure, several months have passed without my gaining a purchase on these circumstances. Yet, as I consider certain incidents, and return with a small sense of new perspective to various areas of his behaviour, perhaps there is some fresh meaning to them.

She had formed an acquaintance with him which on her part perhaps threatened to become something deeper. She faced a man who was committed to the life of a bachelor, and had resisted the blandishments of an intimate relationship. How was she to free him from such a singular prison, yet at the same time preserve his essential nature and character?

My dear Leman, we edge towards that shadow, which seems yet vaguer as we approach. Let us keep to our path, as best as we are able, before we become lost in the obscurity. For perhaps, above all, we should remember her infinite resource, and her own determination once set upon a course.

I ask myself, why did she not seduce him to marriage? She is a formidable and most attractive woman. And if I may be permitted to answer, it was that she herself was not inclined to be married. Her life was dedicated to her independence. She had been wounded in her dealings with men, and sought never to place herself in that same position of subservience to them. She was herself free, so that if she wished to liberate him, the problem lay in finding some solution which would hold him to her, and which would yet maintain that very same independence she valued above all else.

What prospect or temptation would she use to attract him from his isolation, if it was not herself, if she herself refused to consider marriage? I consider this, and turn upon my pillow, and gaze at the ceiling. And it seems to me if there were to be some prospect, some temptation, then that lure would be another woman – or indeed, other women. And thus I begin to understand the clearer outline of a possible stratagem. Perhaps she considered that without some form of challenge he would not emerge from his bachelorhood. Perhaps she attempted to construct some scheme that would discharge the hidden man.

Do women's souls sing? I consider the evidence of an association with her daughter, which I shall mention further below, and the possibility of some imbroglio with Mrs Arabella Pugh. The same Dr Grange, who in fourteen years has shown no sign of involvement with the other sex, in the course of a few months exhibits an engagement with no fewer than three different women. This same physician asks an odd, perplexing question of his housekeeper, one he cannot himself answer. I believe, sir, in my heart, that we observe a pattern which, if we may yet untangle its threads, will lead us to an explanation.

On account of the above, I do propose the following – that she made a suggestion to him that certain women, women of a good disposition and reputation, were forced by circumstances to live in life's shadow. Their very virtue protected them from that experience of the world. They are, so to speak, the bachelors of their sex, even though they live in empty marriages or in other staid relations with men. If he would emerge from his study, she would help him free them of their own conditions. And that, too, was how she would release him from the prison of his own emotions, and bring him into the world again.

I sense incredulity even as I set down these phrases. I look at my own words and consider whether I have written them. Since we have already reached a certain point, let us continue in our arguments one final stage and, now that we are fully adrift, attempt to reach the further shore.

We must not forget that Mrs Quill has a past in which she arranged to allay the desires of others. If she had decided upon such a course, there is no one more likely to expedite it than she. And since she is determined, and unswerving, and perhaps even pure in her intentions, I believe there is no one less likely to be deflected from her course.

Once I had deduced this possibility, certain other aspects of her behaviour began to make themselves a little plainer to my view. I believe that at first she suggested her own daughter, who by certain accounts was mired in a loveless marriage, to his kind attentions. And here, sir, I piece together the final aspects of this strange affair. For, viewed from any other perspective, her behaviour was strange indeed.

Before I continue into the final strait I should like to ask you a single question, perhaps of a rhetorical nature. Have you ever conceived a complex hope or plan in relation to a fellow human or to others, which was executed entire – that is to say, without any form of adjustment or change? I have not. In all our social relations, we are subject to the complications of others' wills, and I believe that we respond, not by changing the objective, but by some flexibility towards the unexpected. I mention this merely in passing, before we continue with our surmise, because it does perhaps affect us in our final conclusions.

When he had taken up with her daughter the unexpected happened. He was sufficiently taken with Jane to wish to marry her. Since he is honourable, and honest, he approached Mrs Quill with this prospect in view. Yet, instead of welcoming him, or at least deflecting him with a kind word, she sent her daughter away, and resisted his attempts at persuading with such great coldness and ferocity that he was forced to retire.

We reach the final design of the pattern, the last hurdle, so to speak, in our understanding. How may we begin to explain such behaviour on her part? Had she herself deviated in some point from her own clear intentions and design? I do suggest that she, having attempted to bring him forth from his study, was no longer in a detached position concerning her own affections, and found herself infatuated with him. I do not know whether she was aware of her infatuation, or if she fought against it. We should not assume that so admirably clear-minded a woman is immune from those conflicting passions to which the rest of us are subject.

Whatever may be the case, I believe that her infatuation was such that, when I myself broke crudely in upon this complex and subtle world with certain information of her past, and my younger colleague fell so suddenly from health, it also explains her decision to remove herself from Lymington. She was not afraid of scandal, but was hoping to protect him by her absence. And in the interests of his recovery, she was willing to sacrifice her good name, which she had worked so assiduously to establish in our town, and was prepared to risk any subsequent scandal by association with his fall.

These are the strange circumstances which, I believe, developed between them.

And this, sir, is the end of my missive and the end, I believe, of my speculation upon the matter of the causes of my younger colleague's sudden decline. Other matters press upon me. The consideration of his illness has been a kind of focus for me. Now that I have pressed as far as I am able in the understanding of it, I am increasingly subject to fears and dreams regarding my own state, whose origins I do not know and whose fearful presence forces my attention.

In the meanwhile, sir, I remain,

    Yours most sincerely,

      Hargood

CHAPTER 99

On Lymington quay, after purchasing several fresh halibut and a number of spices from the market stalls, Mrs Thompson turned towards home. As she approached the cobbled walkway on Quay Hill, she made her way carefully through a small throng of customers who had gathered to purchase loaves from a consignment of bread newly delivered from a bakery in Gosport street. The brown loaves were piled on the stall and, drawn by their marvellous odour, she stood at the back of the crowd while a man and a small boy accepted money and handed across full loaves, half-loaves, quarters, and slices. She was standing in the queue, her change ready in her hand, immersed in the pleasant smell of fresh bread, when she noticed a commotion at the lower end of Quay Hill. There was an odd buzz of anticipation or alarm, then several people began to move aside as though to let through an important personage. Whoever was approaching was still hidden from her sight. She was gripped by a small but pleasant expectation of some spectacle – perhaps a horseman, or a sedan chair, or a procession of town burghers. Her first impression, when the personage in question appeared and almost immediately passed through the parted thong – for he seemed to take it as his due that they would stand aside for him, and appeared almost oblivious of their existence – was a recognition of a familiar figure. He was of an immense height, a good six inches above six feet, and he travelled fast and silently, his Malacca-cane swinging from one hand, his valise in the other, leaning forward slightly, his concentration fixed upon something ahead of him. He was a good head taller than anyone in the crowd, clear and vivid and sharp, and he moved through them like a knife, almost unknowing. She could have called out 'Dr Grange,' and attempted to arrest his attention, but he had passed by before she could gather herself and speak to him, and instead she found herself staring in consternation at his rapidly departing back. She knew well enough that he was about his duties that morning, re-asserting his practice, but she had not expected to see him. The throng regathered itself about the market stalls and

Mrs Thompson waited, strangely perturbed, while her thoughts settled once again on the somewhat meagre choice of provisions her master had permitted for his table.

CHAPTER 100

My dear Leman,

I do begin to believe that my sanity is starting to slip. I, who pride myself on my good constitution and the organisation of my faculties, have been visited with a harbinger. I have been afflicted by another dream, but the intensity of it was such that it was almost a vision, albeit experienced in that state called sleep.

This occasion was different not only in extremity, but in its form. I had enjoyed a few weeks' respite from earlier nightmares and had ceased my habit of keeping a candle burning by my bed, so that after waking from such a dream I could compose myself in its cheerful radiance. On this occasion I woke up in the middle of the night and my fear was still around me. And far from clearing from the mind, far from that expected evaporation of spirit, the dream persisted with such intensity that, in order to break its trance, I forced myself to stand up, to go downstairs to the tallow lantern that hangs in the hallway in case I am called out on my duties and, from that flame, light a candle.

I cannot convey to you with what immoderate relief I watched the flame transfer to the wick of my candle, as if it signified the return of real life – one at least that was not imagined. It seemed to me this light in my hand was a small precursor of the daylight hours. I decided to return up the stairs to bed. But even with this flame in my darkness, my equilibrium was not restored. I was haunted by the dream and at my bedside I stood shivering for several moments with its memory. If I could not banish it, I decided I would write it down, perhaps to remind myself of it with a little distance, or even, if it proved in the light of day to be more than mere gibberish, that I might demonstrate its form to you.

With these thoughts in mind, I put on a further cloak against the chill and sat at my writing desk. Still under the influence of that first fear, but with at least the reassurance that writing entails a concentration which might help to dispel my fear, I attempted to set down the lineaments of that dream.

It is in the present tense, as you see, for even as I wrote I seemed to be living through it, and perhaps though I am unable to describe either the full weight and power of its malignity, the present tense, which I naturally adopted, serves at least in some small sense to convey an impression of its immediate force upon my senses. These then, are the words that I wrote down, which I copy without change or comment:

I open my eyes into bright light, into a distinctive landscape. In some curious manner, my mind is different. I know, even as I peer out, that this is a landscape which is as much within myself as outside. The light blinds me at first, making the earth and the sky reel.

I stare downwards at the earth and see the marsh grass flat to the horizon. I hear the faint whistle of the wind. This is an empty place. It is a shore, the land is flat, the sea meets the sky. There are no houses, no trails of smoke, no sign of human habitation.

These are mere physical sensations. But I have others, too, which are of a more spiritual nature. I feel a weight in my heart, as if I can no longer speak, and in myself the living presence of silence.

Sometimes the light grows brighter, like a flame. Sometimes it decreases. I raise my hand against it, so that I may narrow my vision against the burning sensation of my eyes.

In the heated land which I inhabit, there is a movement of this intense light, and at the same time something is emerging slowly to my perception. At first it is a play of light or movement like water. But as it grows, or seems to advance closer, I see that it is animate, something that lives. It appears, on closer sight, to be perhaps a herd of animals. I stand, with the wind blowing, watching the approaching vision. I wait for its advance with a fearful calm, for it strikes me that I am vulnerable here, in these empty spaces, to whatever now approaches. I wait for what seems an eternity to

393

see them, but whatever they may be, individual or collective, they drift forwards and backwards without apparent direction.

Now I see them more clearly. They are graceful creatures though, because there is a collectivity, it is difficult to perceive precisely what they are – horses or gazelles, it seems at first.

They approach me, moving this way and that, and it is only when they are closer that I see what kind of beings they are. They are women, women in a state of grace, but they do not have human voices. Rather, they are like animals or birds. There is something both natural and at the same time agitated about them. They turn their heads this way and that with strange animation. They make sounds like laughter and, if they speak, it is not in any language that I know.

Now I see each one distinctly. Each is similar. Each has the same mask, the mask of beauty.

I feel a terrible longing to be among them, if only for company, for it is as if these were all the women whom I have ever desired; the entire force and regiment of womanhood. They move here and there, in perfect unison yet natural, entirely regardless of me. I want to call out, but when I speak, all I hear is my tongue clacking on the roof of my mouth, and the hiss of my breath, and the faint groan or grumble of my voice. Slowly, as I stare downwards, something unexpected and terrible in my appearance begins to unfold to my perceptions. I perceive that my thighs, legs, calves, even my ankles, are covered in thick hair, or fur. At the extremity of these hirsute limbs, my feet are cloven hoofs, like a goat's.

The creatures begin to leave, they drift away, they become light or water, abandoning me in that alien landscape. I try to speak again, and again my dry tongue turns in my mouth.

I have never felt such pain. As if all sweetness has left me. These creatures, which are sometimes light and water, taunt my soul. My whole mind and body become wracked. I sink to my knees. When I am in the final throes of anguish I hear myself, the sound of my pain, a garbled and terrible sound, a kind of hidden roar, like an animal.

The air around me dissolves. Perhaps it is this which makes them move backwards, like water which is receding. They do not turn and with infinite grace they remove themselves from me, until they no longer hear my incommunicable pain.

At this stage I woke up and thus, with waking, I completed my dream. Then I went downstairs and lit from the tallow lamp a candle, which stood trembling softly on my writing desk.

I scribbled these notes on a piece of paper, put down the pen, and several minutes elapsed before I could take it up again. After the dream, I returned to my bed and lay down, but I could not sleep. For some time, perhaps the best part of an hour, I lay gently shaking. When I had recovered sufficiently, I rose and went to my desk again, and so committed to paper these further brief sentences.

What might I add to this account, except to say that I felt compelled to shout out, to communicate with those souls in order to save my own? And my own physical being prevented me from doing so. I do not pretend to understand my motivations and, since I am myself exhausted from its effects, will spare you any further considerations of my imaginings.

The melancholy will pass. Even as I write, light begins to fill the room, and the single flame of the candle starts to fade into a more general perception of daylight. I believe I will finish here, sir, as the day comes to rescue me from my preoccupations.

I shall write again, sir, when I have recovered more fully.
Until then, I remain,
 Yours sincerely,
 Hargood

CHAPTER 101

Dear Leman,
Several days have gone by since I put pen to paper and I believe I am forgiven much of my past.

This afternoon, while walking, I informed my younger colleague of the bulk of what I know in regard to Mrs Quill. Until recently, I have limited my information to him, insomuch as it suited my purposes. I told him a great deal, if not all, of my own inner thoughts that I have reported to you. I spoke of her background, of her years as my mistress, of the disputation between us and the cause of her departure. On this occasion I spared no detail. Though my heart quaked in the first outline of it, by God's grace I held my nerve and continued my account.

We walked into the afternoon. He listened without speaking, walking beside me. I never saw him in a better light. Out of consideration, though not perhaps respect, for my account he did not interrupt me and, when I reached some hesitation or impasse, he waited patiently for me to continue.

I have spoken sometimes harshly of him, but I do record now that in the shadow of his forbearance I begin to expand my own thoughts. After long prevarication, I was forced to place my trust in him against whom I have sinned, at least by omission. I believe I have not found him wanting in the exercise of his judgement and the generosity which lies behind his tolerance. For I fully expected (since I know that a sometimes savage temper lurks beneath his equanimity) another of those swift and abrupt demonstrations with which I have been previously tested. Indeed, as I talked, I kept a weather eye on his shadow, to establish a moment's forewarning in case I saw the long arm of a singular and personal justice reach out again to chastise a poor sinner.

We walked, my colleague and I, as if into another landscape and with our footsteps we seemed to be falling into time. Sometimes, for several minutes, neither of us spoke, for fear of subsiding further into the silent moments which formed between us.

The eye grows used to flatness, and observes the geometry of horizon and sky with something like detachment. Everything is horizontal except the vertical trails of smoke which rise from the furnace houses. So it is with the story of Mrs Quill. She has left behind her a flat landscape, without any thing against which to compare, except the thin marks of burning against the sky.

What are we, set against implacable nature? The vertical trails of smoke from the few salt furnaces that continue in the winter months seem feeble indeed, incapable of doing justice to the epic scope and barren nature of the earth. Yet it is into this flat landscape that we moved, my younger colleague and I, as we engaged in our discussion, and attempted to resurrect with our imperfect memories some sense of what has passed.

Sometimes, in the course of these perambulations, I feel that I am no longer there, as if some spirit has left me, and it seems to me that my mind – that thinking part of me – becomes as hollow as a shell. We walk until our calves are tired. When the spirit of animation has been temporarily appeased, we halt in the late afternoon, facing into the sun's silence. We lean like scarecrows. So much dust still lies between us, so much distance. Our shadows fall at odd angles. Our voices creak.

I cannot continue in this strange vein, and will spare you further. Suffice it to say that I experience a curious emptiness, even in the fastnesses of my own household. For when I arrive at the door of my hallway I feel a sense of loss, as though it too holds nothing that is mine. It is as if my spirit remains outside, abandoned in the roadway. I hear Mrs Simmonds drift about the outer bounds, rattling cutlery, but she seems to me a planet who rotates in some periphery.

I have delivered myself of my burden of guilt and my relief is great. If there is a small reason for withholding the final condemnation against my own behaviour, it is that I have waited until that time when he is once again sufficiently strong to absorb the singular truth.

I thank the Lord and leave to His notion of irony the fact that he should choose to set upon this earth an unbeliever to be my confessor.

I shall desist for the time being, as promised, from further such ruminations upon this subject.

Until, sir, I have cause to write again, I remain, as always,

Yours sincerely,

Hargood

CHAPTER 102

My dear Silas,

I think you may be surprised by this letter, though I hope
not unduly annoyed or displeased. For I have come to a
decision and all decisions are, in some sense, surprising – even
to their owner.

You know that I have felt a sense of restlessness over the last
months. It is an indisposition, an intimation almost, which I
have failed to disperse with my customary activities. The very
imprecision of my feeling has been my greatest opponent. I
hoped that my malaise was seasonal, some humour of the body,
or perhaps even the onset of age. Whatever its cause, it has
been difficult to allay.

You know, too, that certain events have caused me to begin
the process of considering my past life, not least the part of it
which relates to my previous existence with Mrs Celia Quill.
You must not, I beg you, believe or assume that this is the root
cause of my disability. But it has been, so to speak, one of
several considerations, a part of the larger whole.

Restlessness may take many forms. In some of us it may be a
desire to visit certain parts of the world, of which we have
heard and which we wish to witness directly, before we die. I
myself have little or no curiosity about our European heritage. I
am not tempted to make the Grand Tour. Indeed, I prefer to
say instead that it is precisely this heritage, this civilisation,
which does not interest me and which I seek almost to bypass.

I feel instead that there is some ancient and indefinable sense
of the past, which pursues me and which I will pursue in turn.
I know at last what it is that haunts me. Though I may not be
able to allay it, at least I sense now that I will follow it to its
ancient and barbarian source, and perhaps confront it there.
Strangely, this determination, coming on the heels of my recent
doubts and perturbations, has given me new life and resolution.
When my decision had been made, a few days ago, I woke

again moderately refreshed, in good heart, able to withstand the travails that I know await me. It is as if, in reaching my conclusion, my health and constitution have been returned, as a vouchsafe of my decision, in preparation for the rigours that will face me.

You must not regret my leaving, my dear sir, or blame yourself in any manner for my departure. On the contrary, I would say, if you will forgive me, that you are part of my cure. For I have witnessed the example of your return to health from the obscurity of a malaise that was as much personal as physical. In the process I have observed you with a certain curiosity, extending sometimes to surprise, at the strange and mysterious nature of your recovery. It is as if you have discovered some aspect of yourself which until now has been hidden from you. Each of us is different, and each in turn must face himself.

I have marvelled, for this very reason, that what benefits you is the opposite of what benefits me. For a prospect of a certain lady's return has quickened your impulse, whereas it has driven me to consider my own beginnings.

I am not you, sir. You are not I. That is a strange start on which to find a measure of common ground. But it is precise, and precision is now what we both should seek. It is, I most humbly believe, itself the cause of the great friendship between us, which I shall always hold as a model of good relations between people of opposing views and character. If I have had a certain small success in society, it is a minor achievement, I am convinced, in relation to the larger success of befriending you.

I cannot write of the future except in the vaguest phrases. But rest assured that I treasure your companionship above that of all others. I will continue to correspond with you, if you will permit me.

There is perhaps some strange symmetry in our affairs. When you first arrived, some fourteen years past, I found that you were a wanderer here, that though your practice of physician might prosper over the years, some part of you continued absent. Your soul, if I may use that word to an unbeliever such as you, always seemed to hover at some distance. Yet that absence of soul has now become a veritable presence. I have watched you take charge of a terrible incident, and carry it to a conclusion with a relentless dedication. It is not only my own opinion. Your action in this matter has confirmed and sealed your already considerable reputation here. I believe that now I may leave to you my own practice in perpetuity, until you yourself should seek an assistant or an heir to your work, in the confidence that he too will treat your patients with due respect.

In the interim, I wish you a heartfelt salutation and bid you goodbye.

I trust and hope I shall remain,

Your affectionate friend,

Hargood

CHAPTER 103

Dear Hargood,

I received your letter this morning, and since reading it have fought with the desire to travel to your house and attempt to dissuade you from leaving these parts. Yet if nothing else, I know you sufficiently well by now to understand that my protest is unlikely to deflect you once your mind has settled on a course.

I shall not let you depart, however, without a few inadequate words of gratitude for what you have done on my behalf.

. From the time of my first arrival in Lymington you treated a young physician, whose opinions often have been contrary to yours, with a natural and beguiling courtesy. You helped me establish myself in a practice which is sufficiently close to your own that you could easily have quashed my endeavours at will. Every movement or motion of advice in my direction has been, on your part, an act of open and unstinting generosity. From your elevated position as the finest physician in this county, you have supervised my poor efforts. I never met a more noble soul, or one whom I would better hope to emulate. I cannot continue in this, the expression of my gratitude, without tears, so out of selfish motives I will desist from further expositions of it.

In our walks, you have been kind enough to tell me of your past, and in one instance I rewarded you for your kind efforts by an act of violence against your person, for which I will hereafter continue to pay penance. I cannot apologise to you sufficiently for what I have committed, and so I will not begin. Since there is no mitigation of that act, perhaps you will consider one small aspect of my own circumstances, which may perhaps explain the cause of my behaviour, though it will not begin to excuse or justify it.

I know that my own life has perplexed you. I have lacked your great and generous instincts. My concentration is narrow, and the fervour I have brought to my profession on occasions has caused in you an emotion which is close to surprise or even revulsion. Perhaps, having been brought up in poverty, I attempted to establish some place in the world which was not so easily subject to the whims of fortune as my own poor mother's existence. I sought to impose, by effort of will, my own designs upon my life.

I was raised without a father and my own name, Grange, is that of my mother, who died in straitened circumstances shortly before I came to Lymington, having saved all that she could for my education. My father, insofar as I know anything of him, was a gentleman who set her up in a house as his mistress, and then left her when she was with child. It is a common enough pastime, as you yourself have said, so ordinary that one individual case hardly bears comment. It was my own life, however, which was affected by it, and therefore perhaps I cannot help but carry those circumstances within me.

Perhaps you will take account of this aspect when you consider the effect you made upon me on that occasion when you informed me that your mistress had left you bearing your child. My own conditions of life seemed to rise, and overcome my equanimity, and cause me to behave in the manner in which I did. My mother, I do believe, also entered the larger world carrying nothing but a child from a father she would no longer see. It was the mere outward circumstances which caused my loss of composure. I do not accuse you of the same act, for it was Mrs Celia Quill who left you, rather than you who deserted her. But having lived my own life as the product of such a union, and having never met my father, the notion disturbed me sufficiently for me to lose control.

My act of violence against your person, heinous though it is, is only heightened by the true circumstances of our relations. You have not only been my companion, but a true father to me, who was fatherless, even in my name. It seems that, like those angels who are sent by a God (a God in whom, I do affirm, I most sincerely prefer not to believe), one such arrived in my life, and guided me with the purest of motives.

I wish you well, sir, and my thoughts will be for ever with you. I hope that you will correspond with me whenever you feel able, for I shall be avid of your news for as long as I shall live, wherever you may be, and whatever the circumstances in which you choose to communicate with me.

I remain, sir, eternally in your debt,
    Silas

CHAPTER 104

Dear Silas,
I thank you for your letter for whose words I shall always be grateful.

In the meantime I have dismissed the servants of my house and estate, and made what recompense I am able, except for Mr and Mrs Simmonds, who will act as my representatives while I am away. In addition to their role as housekeepers, they will instruct the remaining maid and the gardener in their part-time duties. I have written to some three dozen of my patients, those who are most influential in the community, to inform them of my imminent departure, and that I commend them into your hands. They will pass the message to their families and acquaintances, and in a few days the town of Lymington will know of my departure, and must make of it what it wishes.

During the time in which I have attempted to oversee your recovery, I have tried also to look after certain of your own patients, and you have kindly taken a number, indeed the majority, into your care since the incident of the salt furnace. I now return the few remaining to you and your radical methods, after they have been reminded (for their own greater good, I feel certain) of the efficacies of the traditional disciplines. I do not think there will be many who are greatly surprised by the transference of responsibilities. During the past few weeks, in one form or another, you have not only taken up the burden of your past work, but much of my own as well, a process which I have both encouraged and admired. I believe, sir, as your physician, that you are now in a position to return fully to your work, and that this is as obvious to you and your patients as it is to me.

Among the things that I leave behind, I shall miss being able to disagree with you on all aspects of life, not least those of religion, women and medicine.

Speaking for myself, I feel as if I am fleeing, a fugitive, yet with a strange sense of liberation. Certain nightmares which I have suffered these past months have not left me, but have become instead my curious familiars. For now that I increasingly perceive the world in so different a fashion, as a frail external casing, my own terrors seem to me its true messengers and harbingers. It is said that when fire burns inwards and consumes the heartwood we observe a purer, more constant flame. But as the fire reaches inside, the world itself becomes subject to a subtle change. For fire seems no longer fire if we are fire ourselves. Now these same dreams, which were the percipient crows and undertakers of my soul, the sources of my dread and discomfiture, are my guides and mentors.

I increasingly perceive that the unease or disease from which I suffered, that malaise of the soul, is the darker circumstance of a confined existence. I believe in the near forty years or so of my active profession I have made my small genuflections to the human good, and perhaps it is in my gift at last to consider my own station and act upon my own condition.

I will take ship southwards, passing wide of France, entering the Mediterranean sea by the straits of Gibraltar. In due course I will reach Alexandria, where I will disembark, and thereafter make my travel into the empty spaces which are no longer crowded with the circumstances of my own life. There, in the deserted lands, I believe I shall seek restitution of a kind.

I remain, sir,

Yours most sincerely,

Hargood

CHAPTER 105

Grange put aside the letter on the breakfast table and felt himself subject to odd commotions. The suddenness and swiftness of Hargood's decision surprised him. It seemed as though, now that Hargood was subject to the discipline of his deepest fears and terrors, he had been blessed with detachment, with lightness, with speed.

He stood up and walked to the window. Between Hurst and the white cliffs of the Island at the western end of the Solent, he could see a line of wind and sunlight move across the surface of the water. As he stood there, he attempted to consider, for several minutes, what Hargood might mean by his statement that he sought 'restitution of a kind'.

Perhaps that was the difference between them: that Hargood had determined to pursue not the answers to his own enquiries, but perhaps the very questions themselves. However closely he considered Hargood's circumstances, he believed he could see no further than this.

CHAPTER 106

My dear Leman,

I took horse two days ago to the port of Greenwich, in London. My luggage will follow by chaise and soon I will embark upon my voyage.

It is curious that in certain aspects of action we begin to recognise our own character.

I suspect that in my heart I am English, sir, by which I would claim that I am pragmatic and largely peaceful. I abominate those authors who recommend in seductive language the illusions of love or the catastrophic trade of war. Yet it is true that when night comes upon me, when I feel the thunder of breath in the ribs of my horse, and swing its bridle towards the north and east, and take sense of myself and the animal beneath me, there is something within me of a cold projectile, aimed towards London. For I have made this journey before, though not to the same ends – towards dissipation rather than flight. And so I travelled through the night beneath the moon's faint halo, under the spur and pain of a new self-government. I observed the blush of snow upon the pale hills and downs. I will not say that I did not feel a calm release in the use of stirrup and spur, or sense that the second mind of de Puysegur may be the true animal beneath me.

On that brisk journey into night I thought of my life, of the life that I leave behind and of that to come. My travelling gave a sense of perspective to it, which I had not felt before.

Sometimes the horse slowed and I allowed him to walk. Once, for an hour or two, I permitted him to feed on good grass at the side of the path. In the early morning, when we had ridden for several hours, I halted, tethered him and dismounted. I lay on my back upon the grass, with a small covert giving protection on one side, and watched my breath cloud above me. I listened to the call of nightjars and the screech of foxes on the bare, cold hills. I slept, I believe fitfully, for an hour or so while my horse continued to forage and drift about me. Then, my animal and I both having rested, I mounted again and we continued our journey, entering the downs. I allowed my horse to have its head in the downward slopes, and we became swift again.

To my right I saw the faint and ghostly accretion of Winchester, with its few early-morning street braziers burning low, the entire place asleep. Once, proceeding to the crest of a down, I perceived the city in something like its fullness, with the silent cathedral at its centre, a black mass of stone. Around it were the shadowy leather works, the deserted markets, the empty slaughterhouses and outside that, the sleeping domiciles of its citizens. The buildings and streets were all dark, and the old city itself seemed like a black stain among the pure white and empty fields which surrounded it. I remember thinking of the city's dark, confining influence and the country's elusive promise of light.

Aside from my occasional duties in London, Winchester forms a kind of periphery in my world, the main city in my county, and the place where I attended assizes and the courts of law in my capacity as physician and witness. I believed, sir, that I could even see the sloped roof of your house, reposing under faint dew, and hoped that you were asleep beside that dark and ancient citadel, and even perhaps that somewhere, in your study, you allowed a few papers, in the form of some incoherent letters from an acquaintance in Lymington, to gather dust and incomprehension. These were my thoughts as we continued on our path, climbing the faint stretch of light on the hill, until the city was left behind.

Sometimes, in the course of my journey, I had to dismount and step forward to release a toll-gate. Once, the gate having been locked with a padlock and no keeper in sight, I approached and showed my horse the fence, so that he was acquainted with it. Then we trotted back and turned, and I do believe, sir, that in the animal's determination, in our breathing, thunderous approach and the fearsome flow upwards into the night, that I left behind something of my final traces. So that when its hoofs struck earth on the other side, and our gait settled after the impact, I rose in my saddle under the moon's light, with the animal in heavy, silent power beneath me, and felt salt tears upon my face, and knew that one part of my life was behind me.

I write to you seated here, at a small keyhole desk in my room at the Carriage Inn at Greenwich, beside a single bed, with my horse housed in a hostelry below, and my saddle-bags my only companions and possessions. When the animal has rested for a few days, I have arranged for a stable-boy to return it to my house, with final payment on agreement that it arrives in good condition. Mr Simmonds will inspect it on my behalf before agreeing the sum. Now I sit over the small desk and write these few words to you, before I take to my single bed and sleep.

I have a full day and a half before I depart. I hope that my trunk shall arrive by chaise on the morrow, and I will be united with it before embarking on the ship – an elderly brigantine called the *Calustra*, which lies now at the wharf, with grain being loaded into its hold for transport to Gibraltar, where we will put in to unload cargo before setting sail again for our final destination of Alexandria.

I feel clean, sir, as if my past is washed away from me. Tiredness from my journey closes heavily upon me, like the honesty of toil.

With this thought, I bring this letter to its end, and in the meanwhile, do remain,

    Yours sincerely,
      Hargood

CHAPTER 107

The market-place at Winchester was already full, pungent with smells of fish and meat. She stood beside a stall that sold partridges, pigeons, woodcock and hanging hares. Grange recognised the slimness of carriage and the sense of something deeper – the extraordinary beauty that stood between them and which seemed, if anything, to separate them. 'Jane?'

She half turned. At first she did not seem to hear his direction in the blur and hubbub of the market. He was aware of being behind her, to her right shoulder, in that area of penumbra in which she could not see him but was aware of his approach. The way she glanced around her, with something of her mother's fearlessness, seeking the sound of his call, struck at his heart.

But she seemed to have recognised his voice, or perhaps his presence in her vicinity, and after a few moments of hesitation now turned deliberately and fully to look at him. Her face, which attention had made pure, appeared entirely still. Her concentration upon him was such that it seemed to freeze her, so that as he approached, her expression almost seemed a mask. As he closed with her she emerged from her trance. 'Silas.'

He saw something in her eyes – some fleeting transition. She placed her arms round him, and he embraced her strongly and kissed her cheek, before she drew away to view him again.

'Mother said she had written to you.'

Grange nodded, but did not speak.

Behind her, a hawker was calling out, 'Eels, elvers, crawfish, trout, gudgeon, crabs.' Carriages moved past on the central track between the stalls, harnesses jingling. He drew her aside from the restless movement of crowds and in a calmer side-street they turned to face one another. There was a signboard placed on the pavement, advertising the name of the adjacent inn, the Three Tuns. There was a handle above the board to carry it more easily in and out of the inn. On this she placed her hands and considered him.

'You are as thin as ever.' She regarded him like a younger sister an older brother, as if she shared his good fortune. 'You seem happy.'

Did he notice a trace of some coolness or hostility? He had long suspected that the emotions of women were purer, and also more savage, than those of men. He became aware of the presence of time. His own chaise was due to leave in less than a few minutes.

He said, 'I hope you will forgive me for asking a direct question.'

'A question?'

'I promised I would do so on behalf of another whenever I met you.'

She considered him without fear, and he paused for several moments, as if to gather himself. Finally he said, 'Did you ever communicate with your father?'

Hesitation, interest, perplexity, then the lifted face, the direct response. 'I never knew my father.'

Grange nodded. 'Or his identity?'

'My mother kept it from me.'

He was less certain now of the ground on which he stood. There were complexities he could only guess at. 'She never mentioned a name . . . ?'

Jane smiled. 'Mother is deliberate. She will not change her mind.'

'She is indeed.'

She swallowed once, as though her mouth were dry, then proceeded carefully, 'You must know that she was determined to make her way on her own, without reliance upon any man. She told me, directly, that if I knew my father, some contact might be established, and a claim might be made over me and so over herself. She has been a fine parent to me. But her feeling was always so calm, so fierce over this matter, that I never pursued it . . .'

She raised her eyes to his. It seemed to him that her anger at her own circumstances showed as a kind of lightness.

'Why, Silas,' she said softly, studying him carefully, 'I do believe you have some idea . . .'

'I have an idea, merely.'

'Then –' she paused briefly, without taking her eyes from his '– I think you are obliged tell me.'

'No,' Grange said. 'I am obliged to do nothing that I do not choose.'

He noticed the look of coolness return to her eyes and also another emotion: curiosity at his stance, perhaps, or equivocation.

Grange said, 'I sympathise too much with your mother. I too have attempted to live outside the influence of my fellow men.'

'You take her side, then?'

'Are there sides in this matter?' Grange asked. 'Perhaps it is time we settled the question. Just as your mother lives by her conscience, so I must live by mine.' He paused, then proceeded, 'If you insist upon it, however, I shall be obliged to give you a name.'

Conflicting emotions moved across her face. 'But a moment ago . . .'

'You must become used to something. I am not inclined to be compelled by any one, to say or not to say anything. Not by you, nor by your mother.'

'But if my mother forbids . . .'

'She has not forbidden any such thing,' Grange said. 'And if she did, I am afraid that on this matter, at least, it would not weigh with me.' He looked directly at her eyes. 'I will ask you, since the identity of your own father is a matter which concerns you directly, independently of any other's wishes – I will ask you whether you wish to know the name of the person in question. If you do, I will inform you of it.'

'Silas . . .'

'I believe I know his name. Do you wish me to impart it?'

She watched his implacable expression, his cold disposition in the face of her mother's wishes. Then, carefully, she nodded.

Grange said, 'The name, then, is Dr James Hargood.'

She gave a startled cry. Her small hands rose to her mouth. She half turned away. 'Why are you telling me this?'

'Because he is about to go abroad.' He looked at her face, at her hands, which had fallen from her face, and now turned white on the handle of the sign. 'Because he is my friend. He has watched you come and go from your mother's house for several years, and such was his respect for your mother's privacy that he would never enquire directly whether you might be his own daughter.'

There was a shout from St Margaret Street, where his chaise was ready to depart, and he withdrew his half-hunter on a chain from an upper coat pocket and glanced at it. He said, 'If you knew the control he exerted over his own feelings, his own natural curiosity, his pride in his single offspring, you would be kind to him. If you wished to grant him the opportunity, he would desire, above everything else, to see you before he departs.'

She was standing facing him directly, her fingers curling and uncurling on the newelled edge of the sign. Carefully, she breathed out. 'Abroad?'

'He is to travel to Africa. It is a plan, an ambition of his. I believe he waits in Greenwich, ready to embark.'

'He says he is my father?'

'He believes so.'

She was silent for several more moments. Now she let out a small laugh of amazement, then was frozen again. 'He is certain he is my father?'

Grange allowed several seconds to pass. 'You wish me to continue?'

She regarded him, seemed to gather herself and nodded.

'He told me', Grange said, 'that your mother was his mistress. Their relations, for some seven years, were close and binding. When he informed her he was due to marry another, she left him, carrying his child.'

He considered her briefly, in one final assessment of whether he should continue. 'Your mother left him and disappeared without trace for many years. He believes that the child she was carrying . . . that child is you.'

He studied again the movement of emotions across her face, the white grip of her fingers.

'You should not . . .'

'Should not?'

'Should not have told me of something which is a mere suspicion.'

'A suspicion?'

'In a man's mind.'

'In the mind of a mere man.' Grange could not prevent the brief, fleeting smile that crossed his face. He was given to wonder at the self-sufficiency of these women. Instead he said, 'What is absolutely certain in this world?'

But she had already turned away, suddenly prey to private thoughts, and he observed something like the final settlement of her neck and shoulders and back, as if she had determined in her own mind what it was that she would do.

Facing away from him, she said, 'What will you do if mother finds out that you have told me?'

411

'She will find out without doubt.'

'Why?'

'Because I intend to tell her. I debated whether I should speak to her first of my intentions before informing you. But in this matter I am of no one's party. You are an adult. I believe I have a duty to inform you directly of your father's identity, irrespective of anyone else's wishes.'

'Is that all?'

'I suppose I also take into account your father's hopes, his fears.'

'His hopes,' she said. 'His fears.'

'Over a matter which is so close to his heart . . .'

'Even though', she said with a certain relentless patience, 'it is a mere suspicion.'

'It is more than a mere suspicion. Your mother left him carrying his child.'

'What if I choose to disregard it?'

'Then that shall be your choice. You also are a free agent. I have done what I consider to be my duty.'

'Your duty.' She half smiled. 'Yes, you have done your duty. Men have a strange notion of duty, sometimes.'

'I cannot argue for men. I believe you are in a state of consternation, and my presence merely aggravates your condition. I am late for my chaise. I must depart.'

He nodded to her and made as if to go, but she turned towards him and carefully touched his arm. 'Why . . . ?'

'You must understand I am not ashamed of any aspect of your mother's past. I will not trumpet it abroad, but I shall not hide it from myself, or from her daughter. We should live differently, now.'

'You forgive her?'

'Forgive?' Grange was surprised. 'There is nothing to forgive.'

Drawing his half-hunter again out of his pocket, he noted that it was already several minutes beyond the time of departure. There were usually delays in boarding, and the driver would hold up the horses a little while if one of the passengers was delayed. But now he was forced to leave her.

'Goodbye, sir.'

She kissed him chastely on the cheek, and watched his tall figure make its way back to the market thoroughfare of St Margaret Street, swing right abruptly, then depart through the jostling crowds.

CHAPTER 108

My dear Leman,

I have had the most strange and perplexing day of my life. I was supervising the stowage of my effects by the steward, a Mr Haldane, in the deeper recesses of the ship that will carry me to Gibraltar and thereafter to Alexandria. My luggage, which included several heavy trunks, had been off-loaded from a stage and placed by the shore alongside. I was supervising its carriage by several tars aboard the waiting vessel. It happened that my accommodation was reached by several narrow passages, and by so many sharp turns, that the largest of the trunks had to be manoeuvred by half a dozen men. I was so engaged, as I say, when, returning to the shore for the remaining packages, I hardly noticed when a fly drew up. Then I saw the girl whom I recognised as Jane, the daughter of Mrs Quill, descend from it.

At first I was so surprised that I thought the gods of chance had played a trick on me. Yet, as I watched her alight, she looked around and seemed to single me out with her eyes from the others at the quayside. Then she began to approach me hesitantly. Yet even as she closed the distance, she stood off from me, as though some terrible gulf separated us. To cover my confusion, and the emotions that had arisen inside me, I dismissed my helpers with several coins for their work and prevailed upon them that they should porter the few remaining pieces to the cabin, telling them that I would see to their final stowage myself. The sailors, having themselves halted to witness the scene, perhaps sensed my emotions and proceeded to carry to my cabin the rest of my luggage, leaving me there to face her.

We stood off, both hesitant, and surveyed one another. When

she observed my emotion and trembling face, she stepped forward, once, twice, three times, as nervous as a deer, and flung her arms around me. I cried such copious tears as I have never cried and believe I would have drowned her, if she were not busy drowning me with her own.

There was a time, after our embrace, when we could not speak, but stood apart, she with a handkerchief, alternately laughing and crying, myself attempting to talk and talk, sir, against my emotion and to hide my pitiable joy. Then, having discomfited one another sufficiently, we turned and walked to my inn, arm in arm and, in the small sitting-room that serves as a place of rendezvous between shipping agents and other such nautical flotsam, we began those discussions that are commonplace between parents and children, but which she and I have never known. I spent several hours with her, and I could not now record much of what we said, except that they were among the happiest of my life, and that what passed between us in those precious moments has lightened my soul.

I understand from her that my younger colleague, hearing of my departure, travelled to Winchester where, not knowing her precise address, he loitered in the market for several hours, hoping to catch sight of her. God granted him a favour, for he espied her a few minutes before he was due to leave. So it happened that Dr Silas Grange, notorious unbeliever and now, I understand, senior physician of Lymington, took it upon himself to send my daughter to me as his final gift. I believe my face betrayed me again, sir, when I heard of it, and she cried with me and, since it would seem that there is nothing we like more, as father and daughter, than to discomfit one another, we embraced again and wept.

As it was, she left me after several hours and I returned to my vessel, which is due to leave at noon, with only a half-hour to spare. I write this letter in strictest haste, before we leave the dock, and will give it to a shore porter to post, in the short time that remains before my departure.

My dear Leman, it remains for me to express my deepest gratitude for your patience in reading my letters and your prescience in not replying. For your wisdom has been my benefit and your silence has been my constant companion.

I thank you for your indulgence, sir, and remain,

Yours most sincerely,

Hargood

CHAPTER 109

Dear Silas,

I am arrived here in Alexandria.

Our vessel docked on the southern side of the harbour at half past twelve, in the early hours, in heat and darkness.

After disembarking, two porters carried my belongings along the waterfront. I slept in an inn there, close to a large tract of derelict land. Through the slats of the window I could hear goats coughing in the mounds of earth and rubble that were once the winter palaces.

I have been here a few days now, making preparations for my journey inland, and I begin to know, and even to like, the place. The warm north wind blows in from the eastern Mediterranean; at night dim candles create pools of yellow lights, the soft wind makes their shadows dance. Outside my windows the muezzin calls and a multitude of crickets quietly scream.

In the evenings you can smell the charcoal fires, the hot, sweet coffee, the cinnamon, incense and sandalwood. Wherever the great braziers burn at the dockside, blizzards of moths turn in their fierce light, like shoals of silver fishes. When you walk in the cooler parts of the night you can hear children laughing among the ruins of old mosques and synagogues and Christian churches, for religion here lies deep as silt.

At my inn this evening I ate a meal of small grilled fish called *lantekou*. The owner, a Hirudati Moslem, brought a brazier of incense on some glowing coals to set down on the table, placed the plate in front of me, then bowed and left.

After my customary seaboard diet of salted pork and biscuit, I ate the freshest of fishes in a room where the cockroaches ran up and down the walls, pursued by small gecko lizards. Afterwards the proprietor brought me sweet tea and enquired politely from whence I came. I informed him I came from England and he nodded, though I believe he had no notion of the place. He did not ask my destination. It is the custom here to make no enquiry of the journey's end, at least of pale foreigners, since the ways of the European are regarded as either absurd or ineffable.

In the mornings, before I set down to arranging my voyage into the interior, it has become my habit to walk along the waterfront. You can smell the disintegrating wood of the old wrecks that lie side by side in the harbour, their main planks rotten from the *toredo* worm, their rigging stripped or decayed, their masts and deck timbers already sawn away and used in the shore buildings and storehouses that line the harbour walls. The ships are those of a dozen different nationalities and civilisations; old brigantines and trading barques, dhows, galleys and even triremes lie roped or chained together, quiet and impassive in their final days. As the water rises slowly in their holds, they lean towards one another, as though more sociable in death.

On the west side of the city is Gabbari, a place of industry: oil, rice and paper mills, cotton, wool, sugar, grain. The houses there have their measure of Greek and Levantine shopkeepers, who trade in dates, in ivory and other riches from the African interior.

It is a fitting place for me to depart inland for the desert, from this great entrepôt of the Eastern Mediterranean, for it seems to me a perfect and promiscuous admixture of European and eastern civilisations. It is a city of many levels; each one is a sign and witness of the impermanence of human habitations. There has been land subsidence in much of the delta, so that on calm days the foundations of ancient buildings may be seen running out to sea near the Pharillon.

I have found an agent, who has led me to another, then to another who knows certain guides belonging to the Ahar tribe, the most feared of desert wanderers. Each little fish demands his take. But the Ahar guides seem fine men, reticent and proud in their bearing. Out of respect for their customs, and with an eye to my own ease and comfort, I will take to wearing the white cloth they habitually use. In the meanwhile I have left certain of my luggage with the British consul and will carry with me only what is necessary to survival.

But before I finish this letter there is another matter which I must address, and which is my main cause of writing to you, before I now commit myself to the desert and the hot sun. Out of deepest gratitude, I extend my thanks to you for your gift to me, which arrived on the quayside at Greenwich a few hours before I left, and which has caused me more happiness than I can express. I know that in seeking her out and informing her of my identity, you ran the risk of incurring her mother's fiercest censure. And yet I believe it is to be expected of you, that you will attempt to do what you believe is right and just, and that nothing will deflect you, irrespective of the consequences to yourself.

I hope, sir, that our gentle English God, whose existence you so disparage, forgives you for being both the victim and the instrument of Scottish universities. I pray that He rains as many tears of joy upon you as He has rained upon me, if only to admonish you for your grievous lack of piety, and to demonstrate the manifest error of your radical beliefs.

With these thoughts I bid you goodbye, and will hope to write again when I reach my inland destination.

In the meanwhile, I remain,

Yours as ever,
Hargood

CHAPTER 110

Grange rose in the grey air, and drew his cotton shirt over his shoulders. Next came his woollen socks, after which he pulled on his breeches and his calfskin boots. He walked to the door where his coat and scarf hung. Raising the scarf from its hook, he wound it around his neck. In the fervent silence he lifted and swung the heavy coat about him, fastened it around his neck like a cloak, and let the sleeves hang empty. Armed against the cold, he eased open the bedroom door and moved down the stairs, avoiding the creak of the oak boards, until he arrived at the lower floor.

It was hardly five in the morning and there was as yet no sign of Mrs Thompson. He drew back the bolts on the front door and, raising the latch, listened once more for signs of his housekeeper stirring. Hearing none, he opened the door carefully with his hand on the cold slide of the metal latch and eased his way out. He closed the latch behind him and stepped out into the dawn, into the faint presence of the moon, the last of the sour stars.

A little further down the high street, he crossed the cobbled road, turned onto the footpath past the Hope and Anchor, and walked down the white slopes, the northern-facing white with frost, across Flushards with only the faint rustle of the meadow-grass against his boots. He followed the mud track towards the shore road and came to the edge of the water.

In the grey of the morning a vast silence of the earth came up to meet him, as if he were standing above his own reflection. He felt no constraint or pressure to speak or express himself on the edge of this unknown. Nothing stirred. He stared out across the still surface to where a faint mist hung above the marsh grass on the Walhampton side.

In a pond in a clearing, fed by a small running stream, he halted and kneeled above the cold, clear surface. He cupped cold water and raised it to his face. His reflection was like some other self, an expression which the movement of the water turned from a strained smile into the clear purpose of his thin lips.

He remained in that position for several minutes, waiting for his private grief to subside. After a while he lowered his hands to the water and again poured its sharp coldness over his face. The image shattered and returned. He observed the water gather and refresh the sutured mouth. For several minutes he was lost in his own thoughts. Then he raised himself and stared out across the water.

A white egret moved with perfect grace in the ponds on the further foreshore, rising to catch large insects on the wing. It was so engrossed, so enclosed in its own actions, that it seemed to hold him.

Hargood had said of Mrs Quill's absence, 'It is like a novel, sir, which should leave some presence with you, some aftertaste, which shall remain widowed away in the soul.' It was, he believed, the first time he had heard Hargood speak of a novel directly, even though it was merely by analogy.

Grange began to walk along the shore towards the two remaining salt furnaces that still burned along the Pennington shore. A low mist touched the surface of the water, which seemed to gather some of the fire's reflection.

It had been several months now since Hargood had left, and he had found his duties the only antidote against the hope that he would receive another written communication from Mrs Quill. He had thrown himself into his work with the intention of drowning himself in it, and his programme had been largely effective. Each day had passed in concentrated and steady activity. Each night he was able to reach sleep through exhaustion. Even so, while he worked, some part of him had waited. He had watched the post arrive with a detached and also covetous eye. So it happened that when a letter finally did arrive, embossed and heavily sealed, somewhat battered by its travels, his mind had been so much on Mrs Quill that he found himself unable to think at first of any other correspondent. Mrs Thompson handed it to him in the hallway. It was in his hands, and he was already walking up the staircase to his study to read it, before he realised it was from Hargood. His feelings changed from hope and terror to relief of a kind, even the beginnings of a pleasant anticipation. This was only his second communication from Hargood in Africa. Indeed, he had begun to wonder whether Hargood would write again, or whether the desert had absorbed him completely. Allowing himself a few seconds to recover from his mixed emotions, Grange split the seal with a paperknife and spread the contents out on his desk. It covered some fifteen sides in a clear and unadorned hand. Leaning over the desk, he started to read the first pages with attention.

CHAPTER 111

Dear Silas,

These notes I transmit from my bed, where I lie in pain and recovery from my journey. Slowly my fever subsides, and my sight clears sufficiently to take up my pen, though my mind rambles.

Over the past few months the desert has been my witness. In its calm wastes I have conducted a self-examination, whose object and purpose is the chastisement of my soul.

In its empty terrain I have found that my mind has cleared, sufficiently at least to consider myself from a point of detachment. For I inhabited a world in which I existed at its centre, a creature of habits, who lived from one moment's pleasure to the next. Thus, it seems to me, we may all exist, trapped in our obligations, moving from one day to another with the simple surety of an animal compelled by instinct.

These past few months I have been driven by a sense of emptiness. It is not explained easily. My state perplexes me. It is my very lack of purpose which, so to speak, propels me. I have attempted to dissect it, using what little I know of the tools of reasoning and philosophy, but it does not yield. I have tried to surprise it, catch it unawares. I have, at times, even attacked it with blind rage in the hope that, by the force of some more powerful emotion I could eliminate it from my thoughts – in the same way, perhaps, that the light of a candle is extinguished by bright sunlight. But such relief has always been temporary.

And so, over the past several months, I have travelled from

one place to another, this way and that, settling briefly in one locality like a fly on a leaf, pausing only enough to accustom myself to my surrounds, before moving on.

There are further aspects of myself which I must record. I will be judged and therefore I confess. Just as I am, for reasons I have never fully understood or comprehended, a traveller in physical form, I realise that in some other sense I am also something of a refugee from the emotions. The two, I suspect, form complementary aspects of a character. But perhaps I am as much the victim of my feelings as I am their perpetrator. Whatever guilt befalls me, I shall attempt to lay before you, in these imperfect words, the essence of my condition.

I write my journal by a thin fire of cedar wood, in a fly-specked room which forms part of a merchant's establishment. In the background I can hear my housekeeper, a woman of the Koré tribe (known for their sullenness, heavy haunches and loyalty) fussing away at preparing my morning meal. I do not know how long I have been here, or how long I may stay. Suffice it to say that in the meantime it offers me a perch on which to write these brief and incomplete notes.

Why did I come to this city? I suppose it began, like most of my wanderings, with that strange unease with which I am afflicted in any threatened condition of permanence. I had heard of it, of course, in the stories of travellers, so indicative in most cases not of the thing seen but of the character of the traveller himself. So I journeyed by horse, donkey, dromedary and, finally, in the stony uplands which lay beneath the plateau, in the company of human guides alone. One day, after the passage of one of those cold desert nights in which the warmth slips away like a ghost into the empty spaces, we emerged from a valley and there, on the other side, behind a grove of what looked like lemon trees, stood the outskirts of the city. It was, at that distance, merely a group of white buildings lost to one side in the harsh glare. There I heard voices from the plateau above, the sound of goat bells. But for the example of ascetic detachment which it is necessary to cultivate with my Ahar guides, I would have run forward, my arms held high.

But I return to the more essential aspects of the journey.

Once I had cast adrift the trappings of civilisation, my guides for the final section to the city were two Ahar tribesmen, from the fiercest of the hill and desert peoples. They were quiet men, thin, with weathered faces and hawk noses, their brown skins made darker by comparison with their loose white garments. It is difficult to describe the character of an Ahar for, in the terms in which we use the word, he lacks one. He shows no emotion, seldom smiles, does not gesticulate or show enthusiasm, and never laughs outright or cries, for to do so would be to lose his dignity. There is a saying in this region which perhaps summarises their character: What is the difference between an Ahar and a scorpion? The scorpion has eight legs. I have said enough. For three weeks of travel my sole companions were two men who were as tough and unyielding as pieces of dried wood. They observed my antics, my washings, my rinsings of the mouth and my insistence on a rudimentary camp-bed, without expression, for in the Ahar tradition it is forbidden even to show contempt. They themselves slept on the cold desert earth, having swept aside a few of the larger stones, with their heads raised a few inches off the earth by hard wooden bolsters against the *ashorga* grub, which otherwise could crawl into the ear and burrow into the brain. With their limbs spread-eagled and their noses sealed by plugs in case the spirit should escape, I was often fooled by their soundless breathing into believing I was accompanied by two dead men.

For my part I gathered whatever solace I could from my knowledge that, while they were with me, I was safe from their kind. I wore their own loose form of white dress. The sun soon burned my skin to berry brown and, but for the fact that I occasionally talked, smiled, or laughed and showed other signs of a human nature, you would have taken me for an Ahar.

If the first part of the journey was difficult, the second elevated those earlier problems to a plane of comfort. For several days we travelled the perimeter of the desert, then, by some unexplained decision on the part of my guides, we turned into the *Waj-Aresh* wilderness. It was as if, like a moth which has flown against a lamp glass on a dark night, we turned into the eye of the flame itself.

Even in desolation there is grandeur. We found ourselves in a place of terrible beauty. The surfaces of the rock appeared to glow with the reds and purples of fire. To one such as myself, used to a gentle, manicured landscape, such harshness seemed to attack the very assumptions which formed my private world. I began to see why, for an Ahar, the concept of a god of flowers, of springtime, of the endless flow of birth and decease, was an absurd aberration. Here the supreme being, if he existed, was an absolute, merciless god, a god of scorpions.

We had, perhaps, four days' supply of water. Yet each day began by seeming to expand into the great, fiery sun which drew us forward. In its path it appeared to burn out everything except that pitifully small force of will which existed within us. The night was merely a time when that pervasive flame ceased for a few hours. We camped on rock or bare sand, preferring open spaces. My guides lay on their sides, as if in a trance, with their heads a vital few inches above the ground. To sleep in that position without falling off the bolster requires absolute stillness, of mind as well as body. Even so, they could spring awake at the slightest stir of a sound, of a pebble being disturbed. On several occasions I woke to find them standing quietly, in the middle of the night, looking into the darkness. On such occasions I did not move, knowing that silence was my best protection. Slowly, some hidden danger having passed, they would return to the earth. Their fleshless limbs would once again take on the aspect of corpses. So the night would pass.

In the morning, before the sun returned to its flaming whiteness, we ate a few shreds of dried goatmeat, drank a little water and moved on.

I shall not describe the desert landscape. It has been remarked on before, by travellers greater than I and writers far more eloquent. I mention only a few things in passing, things which are no more than small asides to the flies, the barren rocks, and the vertical sky. When you live within the blast of the sun, your senses seem to change. You reach the stage where the sun does not burn you, when heat becomes not so much a presence as an absence. It enfolds matter and absorbs it. It is a vacuum which draws out the spirit from the body and loses it.

The process of losing the spirit is a strangely simple one, as natural as, in other circumstances, passing water. No wonder the tribesmen are tight-lipped; even to open the mouth is to risk the spirit escaping. They speak of a man losing his mind as easily as if his sanity were a single word which flew out of his mouth. So, in the desert, one treads carefully in the presence of ineffability.

After a time the senses become hollow, listening to what is not there. When we were walking, every footstep in the sand made a noise like a faint chime. But when we halted, resting at midday for a few minutes, I would kneel and let sand slip through my fingers just to hear the falling crystals jostle each other on the ground. Every sound was refined, a skeleton of sound. When I move finally towards death, I imagine it will be like this empty, musical desert.

All other things except the necessity to continue walking ceased to exist. The only respites from the open spaces, in which even the rocks glow with heat, were the occasional ravines and, sometimes, a single desiccated thorn tree. On one occasion I stood motionless against the staff that I had learned to lean on, one leg raised against the heat of the ground like the Ahar themselves. Perhaps fifty yards away stood one such tree. As I watched, the heat invaded it like an evil, white, swirling dust. I saw half of it disappear and then, my heart dry with fright, the other half also. The heat had consumed it in two mouthfuls. No wonder that this is the land of miracles. A man with his tissues dried is prey to such visions.

My guides were used to this. Or rather, if they were subject to such visions, they did not mention them. They knew, better than I, perhaps, that the dehydrated mind gives off its *djinns* and spirits much as a drying cloth emanates odour. With a minimum of words and actions they proceeded on their way. Curiously, it was only in the evenings that they seemed to lose a little of their sombre sense of survival. Human beings, even Ahars, are prey to anxieties at dusk. I suppose that (remembering those works which I had read on ancient tribes, searching for some glimpse of the human character) in the past the coming of night signalled dangers to their ancestors. The great beasts begin to prowl. They become apprehensive, frightened, morbid. Perhaps it was this anxiety which released my two guides, or at least produced a form of compensating activity. For in the evenings their movements, otherwise so practical and economic, began to assume an almost cheerful aspect. Once or twice I thought I heard one of them give a small dry laugh, a sound not unlike the clash of sand crystals. When they laughed, they showed sharpened teeth. They told stories and waved their hands to illustrate as they fetched scrub for the fire and swept a small area free of stones and scorpions where we would camp for the night. I learned later that they welcomed the night for other than spiritual reasons. Their great enemies, the Wijarra tribe, did not move in the darkness, being in religious fear of shadows. It became clear that they regarded the Wijarra as extensions of their own fears, the products of their imaginations. Still, this left much unexplained. Why did they rise like ghosts in the middle of the night to listen? What fears caused their bodies to stand, crouched like question marks, soundlessly waiting?

At the time, as I say, I could see no reason for their loss of sobriety at sunset. But I had become so used to their guidance, to following them through the burning wastes, that I assumed there would be some good explanation for their actions which they would convey to me in their own good time. In the desert, even speculation is a waste of effort. I knew that they had pared down their actions to barest necessities in order to reserve their minds and bodies for the task of crossing.

On our second day in the wastelands we had seen, far off, a group of figures. Or rather, my guides had seen something which, with a quiet hiss which to them is an exclamation and a warning, they indicated with quick, deft motions of their hands. It seemed to be several tree stumps against the white expanse. My companions did not move. They remained thus several minutes, as though they were frozen. It occurred to me that nevertheless the objects we surveyed could be human, a small group of no more than three or four, standing motionless in the great heat. But the disquiet of my guides began to affect me. We remained still, watching them, until one of my companions dared to speak. It became clear, by his nervous hisses, that these were not men, but *Ach-madi*, half-men, 'ghouls'.

The group was at a distance of about a mile from us, at a slight diagonal, so that our path would have taken us close, almost within a few feet of them. My guides began to make a detour, keeping us at a distance. But I, my inquisitiveness overwhelming my fear and not prey to the superstitions of these men, insisted that we make our way towards them. It was the first time that I observed the true nature of my dependence in the desert. They turned and watched me with a peculiar, fixed intensity. I knew that had I insisted further, they would have left me. Perhaps, to save me from becoming like 'them', they would even have killed me out of mercy. These were the simple facts of my position. From their expressions it was clear that I would not meet these *Ach-madi* or half-men. I shrugged my shoulders and continued with them on a long detour around the group of figures. Several hours later we had left them behind us. I admit that even during that detour I had felt a certain chillness on me, located between the shoulder-blades.

As the days passed we began to see, on the horizon, small clouds as delicate as almond blossom. They dispersed under the heat almost as soon as they appeared. Apart from that, the sky was a deep blue, almost purple. The rocks and trees made hard, spiny shadows. Over this we walked, myself and the Ahars, each in his enclosed silence. Only the soles of my sandals and the horny parts of their feet could be heard, a dry rhythm as we traversed the rocks. An Ahar will never put his foot into a shadow if he can help it, or into a place he cannot see, for there might be snake, spider or scorpion on the same scrap of earth, or one of the three-pronged thorns of the *sibuna* bush, with its poisoned tips. These considerations dictated the erratic nature of their course.

But the fear of putting feet into a shadow was more than a practical reaction to physical circumstance. It exerted, I do believe, the primal authority of ancient practice. I asked one of the guides, the older of the two, Sajim, why this was so. He replied, in a somewhat veiled manner, that a man should make his own shadow, not rely on that of another person or object.

On another occasion he explained that a man was not permitted even to lie in his woman's shadow, except if that woman was his wife. For according to ancient tradition, a man and his wife owned one another, body and soul. And when, for example, a son had usurped the authority of his ageing father, it was said that the father now lived in the son's shadow.

So I pieced together, fragment by fragment, something of the Ahar culture. These lessons confirmed my view that in the next life I should like to be an Ahar, for no other reason than that I believe I should live a life of merciless clarity.

As we traversed the desert, the clouds ahead of us became thicker each day. Finally we confronted, on the edge of a plateau which rose almost sheer from the desert, the city itself. The elder of my two guides began to speak. Their language is no more than a strangely high-pitched guttural stream. To an outsider it seems a congregation of tongue clicks and hoarse sibilants. These alternated with a series of deep notes made by pressing the tongue onto the lower palate and making a sound which is suspiciously like the process of hawking, so much so that I have seen Ahars, having gathered a flock of phlegm in the process of a particularly heated exchange, often follow this by ejecting a long stream of salivary mucus through the filed gap in their top front teeth. If French is the language of romantic courtship, then let it be recorded that Ahar is more suited to chiding an angry, clucking lizard or conversing with a miscreant camel.

However, I have a good ear for phrases and it soon became apparent to me, with the help of some additional sign language, that my guides would leave me at this point, for they were frightened of the city. As agreed, I had already paid them 300 *dahels* for their services and they knew that a further 200 could be obtained from my agent, Selim Abir, when they returned to our last point of departure. If Selim Abir believed his own detailed stories of the terrible revenges of the Ahar against someone who had broken his word, I felt sure he could carry out his instructions and would not, as his soft, fat brethren of the city often did, abscond with the money himself. The two guides said goodbye to me with the characteristic parting of their tribe, tapping the bridges of their noses with their right forefingers, a symbolic allusion to an ancient phrase which means, I do believe, 'Take care where you put your nose.'

My guides had left me my two small packs of belongings, my folded tent bed, and a box containing a few books and medical items. I waved farewell at their disappearing backs and then, shouldering my burdens, I began to walk towards the gaggle of buildings which stood on the side of the hill. I could see, or perhaps only imagine at that distance, people there – men, women, children, the first humans I had seen for many days. I passed through what seemed to be a shrubbery: a clump of trees with small blue flowers. Then my path took me through a grove of huge cedars. The first human I saw, close enough to tell one from a ghoul or a piece of clothing, was a mason repairing the corner stones of a dry fountain. He turned round, saw me and ran off. I realised suddenly that I resembled, in my clothes and bearing – my long white shift and hooded headgear – those Ahars whose company I had just left. I was at a loss for a moment, since I expected him to return with reinforcements. So I lifted off the hood to reveal my European face and neck, and walked, with a mixture of wonder and trepidation, into the city.

Once I had passed the outskirts people no longer seemed frightened, though they pointed and stared. But I, after my long journey, was merely a man at an oasis. I gazed in rapture at the orderly rows of white buildings, the great wooden doors, ornate with brass and copper, which led into courtyards and groves. Water trickled in fountains behind closed doors. Rare scents accosted me, subtle perfumes I did not know. I was thirsty and tired, but I felt like one delirious with joy.

At the corner of an intersection I found a wine seller. Sensing my need, he unstrapped a small metal goblet from leather thongs, removed a large goatskin container from under his arm and poured purest water into the metal receptacle. I drank three cups, unashamed and greedily, but when I held out two *dahels*, ample enough payment for a whole meal in the town from which I had come, the man examined the coins with detachment, closed my hand over them, turned his face aside, and spat carefully into the gutter. Seeing a tired and desiccated stranger, he had offered his service free. He hung his metal cup in a loose thong, returned his goatskin under his arm, and walked slowly away.

That small mercy was the first sign that I had reached my destination. I wandered the streets, as though in a fever. A lively wind sprang up, full of dust. To protect myself I sat down against a wall and drew my cloth over my head. There I fell asleep, or fainted from exhaustion.

I woke later, a little refreshed after my drink and my brief rest. I spent that first evening exploring the streets, the markets, glancing into an occasional courtyard as a door was opened and closed. I followed for a few moments behind swaying, voluptuous women carrying pitchers or bales of cloth. Inside me something stirred, a kind of alarm, for I knew I had found what I was searching for: a place of tranquillity and spells, of secret gardens and unheard conversations, of laughter and bird-song. Even the lean dogs that wandered the streets, moving from offal pile to offal pile at the corners of the street markets, seemed to me sanguine, composed, as if they had their own inner life. I was subject to the fear that my money was worthless, but I had already made provision for a change of currency, having let into my chest a false bottom in which were stored two packets of gemstones, for gold, alas, gives away its presence by its pungent weight.

After walking the streets and bazaars my luggage grew heavier. I pushed aside the tinkling bells of a money changer's offices, placed three small diamonds on the low hardwood table, which separated myself from my host, and signalled with my hands that I was prepared to sell them. Pretending not to understand his terms, I shook my head at every offer until, in a rage, he placed fifteen small gold coins on the table, looked at the ceiling in a gesture of impatience and awaited my decision. I picked up the coins one by one and put them in my strong inside pocket, took up my packages, and began to look for a room for the night. Before doing so, I glanced back through the opening and saw my purchaser sweep the three diamonds into his palm and place them in a small bag.

I have found accommodation here in the house of a merchant, and a place where my belongings will be reasonably safe when I venture further. The Koré woman looks after my washing and cooks my few meals. After some weeks in which to recover my strength, I am once more about to attempt the wilderness. I have found that in the wastes my mind is clearer.

My dear Silas, these are the few notes I have collected on my journey. They are nothing but impressions, with which I hope I have not bored you over-much.

I wish you are well and most fervently hope that in due course the one for whom you wait will be with you.

Please accept, then, the earnest good wishes of your friend.

Sincerely,

Hargood

CHAPTER 112

Early morning spring sunlight fell across the floor.

Mrs Thompson heard Grange walk down the stairs and observed him enter the dining-room. He put down the letter he had been reading in the study on the table and walked towards the window. He slid up the sash and the sounds of the street entered the room.

She cleared the table while he stood watching, immobile in thought. She moved about her business with her usual silent efficiency, until he turned towards her and said, 'I received a letter from Dr Hargood.'

Mrs Thompson halted, several plates gathered in her hands.

'I believe that when you have an opportunity, you should read it, Mrs Thompson. It is a very remarkable document.'

'Is it, sir?'

She asked the question directly and entirely disingenuously, and for a moment he paused to consider her. Assured of her sincerity, he said, 'It is the letter of an exceptional man.'

She continued to regard him without movement. 'I'll read it later, if I may, sir, as you suggest. I trust he is well.'

'He seems so. He lives in somewhat straitened circumstances, but he appears resigned to his conditions.'

She did not cease to regard him. He was no longer pale, nor was he subject to fainting fits. Colour had returned to his cheeks. A curious feature of his recovery was that his adherence to a diet of fish and vegetables had allowed him to fill out somewhat. He was still perhaps too thin, his limbs seemed too long for his body, but he could no longer be called emaciated. Something of his earlier force and energy had risen slowly and was now manifest. The return of his practice had apparently performed its cure upon him. The addition of Dr Hargood's patients had not worn him down but had, on the contrary, summoned up some further reserves of character.

In considering him, she hesitated a little longer. 'When will he return?' she asked.

'I am not sure that he intends to return, Mrs Thompson. I fear he has left us for good.'

They paused there for a moment, both lost in private thoughts. Then it was Grange himself who departed, walking into the hallway, striding upstairs to his study, leaving her standing still in consideration.

When he had gone, she wondered in what subtle manner her master had changed since Mrs Quill had left. Before his involvement with her he had seemed to drift or float through his existence, driven by a remote, almost ascetic detachment. In replenishing himself, he appeared to have gathered indefinable weight, as if some part of the character of his older colleague had fallen upon him, perhaps by inheritance.

She suspected that under the auspices of their friendship, the two men had conducted a fierce contest, although presumably within certain agreed and unspecified rules, and that the older man had lost. It was her surmise that in losing or conceding, Hargood had displayed some special magnanimity, some subtle grandness of disposition and character, which continued to haunt her master. That at least was the impression she had gained after Hargood's departure, and from her own brief exchange of views with her master after he had read Dr Hargood's letter.

She could see something of this effect in Grange's reverence for his older colleague. It seemed to her that this was yet another of those odd occurrences that had taken place, that whereas before he had constantly resisted Hargood's dominance in his own affairs, now that his older colleague was gone, he began openly to acknowledge the older man's influence.

Since her master had become the senior physician in Lymington, the inheritor of Dr Hargood's practice, there had been other changes. His coldness and reticence had been subtly transformed into something else, something closer, perhaps, to authority. She had seen a different relation emerge with his patients, that was difficult to express directly, but to her eye was no less worthy of remarking. Something further was present in his character, that had not been present before. He was no longer the calm exemplar of reason, detached and distant. Increasingly, his patients found a physician who grappled with their complaints, even exhibiting – when the symptoms were chronic and appeared to have been caused by the behaviour of the patient – a measure of emotional commitment and occasional impatience. They recognised, perhaps, a superior force compared with the former Grange, though it brought with it now a peculiar honesty and directness that was sometimes uncomfortable.

He had attempted to explain to her one day that he was less inclined to treat symptoms, more to address himself to causes. A Mr Ruddersley, who had come to him for several years complaining of intermittent chest pains, strains in the joints, breathlessness on the stairs, had not expected a brisk lecture on the necessity for reducing his twenty-two stones of weight. The wealthy invalid Mrs Hartstone, whose niece was both her comfort and her support, had not anticipated that her physician would inform her that there was little physically at fault with her, or compound his statement by asserting that she was one of the healthiest patients of sixty-seven years he had the good fortune to know. But if this was an unwelcome surprise, she had awaited even less his expression that he was more concerned about her niece, who suffered anaemia, bouts of irregular bleeding and who, in his opinion, should be released from her onerous duties for several months, perhaps even a year.

They were nervous enough of his reputation without the collateral – that he was the inheritor of Dr Hargood, or that

Hargood had written to his most influential patients advising them of his whole-hearted support for his successor. They would have been more inclined to argue against his proposed remedies if Dr Hargood had not also written recommending, to their surprise, his own accession to the 'new methods' which his successor practised.

That afternoon, in the respite between washing his clothes and preparing his dinner, Mrs Thompson read Hargood's letter carefully and, later that day, when she had finished it and had had a chance to consider its contents more carefully, she made a point of thanking her master for the privilege of seeing it.

In the two weeks which followed neither of them made any further reference to Hargood's communication. Each seemed inclined to consider it privately. Then another letter followed, briefer than the first, written on paper which was probably torn from the inside cover or endpapers of an old book. Grange, as he had done with the first, showed it to Mrs Thompson, though this time he did not comment upon it directly.

CHAPTER 113

Dear Silas,
I have taken to inhabiting the desert.

Although my guides may fear the onset of evening, there is a time towards midnight when they wake, after four or five hours of sleep, and shake my shoulder. They do not speak, for this is another of their ancient fears about the darkness and their queer doctrine of ghosts. In certain circumstances we may travel at night, but we must enter the dark with the same purity of purpose as its other residents. When we are about to set off, no one looks his companion in the face, since this would be to 'wake' the other person in some deeper sense. Instead, we prepare ourselves, moving about the camp site as if in a dream or trance, gathering our things. Then one of my guides points with his arm and we set off quietly, in single line, drifting towards some indeterminate point on the faint horizon.

For those of us who have lived on an island of cloud and mists, here the sky is so incorrigibly empty of everything that the very world becomes celestial; it seems we are walking in the heavens. And though the indeterminate and distant point may guide us, it does not exist, except as a kind of compass in the mind of my guides.

At night great distances are clear, and the stars glitter like sand. Moving by their cool light across the desert, I do not know what action the mind portends, or what strange reminiscences are suggested by the stillness that reaches into the soul – except that the mind itself becomes empty, contemplative, like the terrain. I think of Our Lord not as a saint or prophet, but as a desert wanderer.

Sometimes we move past silent habitations at night, avoiding barking dogs or nervous herds of goats. We shun all human contact. Sometimes, too, I hear the silent music of those ancient habitations, the wind moving the palms like silver flames. We are never closer to heaven, our very heads are among the celestial bodies. And so we traverse the terrain, like shadows in the firmament.

Yet I love these moments more than life, when it seems there is no one upon the earth except our small company. Sometimes, in the distance, there is the faintest shimmer of movement, perhaps a trick of the light, or the drifting image of a herd of gazelles.

Our only danger is that snakes and scorpions emerge to hunt the sand and boulders at night, and so we observe their faint tracks with caution. On occasion my older guide will make a detour; sometimes with his staff he will push some creature out of the way with hardly a change in stride, and without any sign of hostility except perhaps an emphatic click of his tongue, as though he were gently chiding it for stepping across our path. If I were not present he would ignore such creatures, and would step over them with simple equanimity, but this clearing of the way is a concession to my own clumsiness in following behind.

I have noticed a further strange aspect. We only walk in the night's early hours if our direction is east, into the dawn,

434

towards the prevailing light. It is another of their cautious habits for, with the darkness behind us, we may see others long before they perceive us.

Occasionally at dawn we can notice the sand raised in a pale trajectory on the horizon, indicating wind. At such times it becomes necessary to lie in the lee of a sand-dune or an outcrop of rock, with the wind making its strange singing and howling sounds, while the dust devils advance along the line. If I should suggest to you that the winds which blow around us are those same which have haunted the ancients, and that their breath connects the past with the present, I believe you would consider my construction mystical.

Yet I remember, my dear Silas, how we used to walk into the calm evening, with the light falling on the surface of water in the dykes, and the shadows lying at odd angles, and how the flame of the salt furnaces provided stranger flares to see by than this hot, peremptory sun. The desert absorbs my soul, and cleanses my flesh of its old fears and visions.

I believe I am rendered empty, if not pure, by my travels. I have written this missive in a little haste, because we have stopped temporarily at an oasis to take further water, before we begin again our journey. In the hope of their being transmitted to you, I have left these brief notes with an official of the administration, who was passing through the same oasis, and who has promised to send them on to you when he takes ship for England.

Do not fear for me. I have found what I most desire, which is time to consider my past from a distance, a perspective I never could find in my native land.

My thoughts are perhaps inchoate to any but myself. I hope that you will forgive my ramblings.

I remain, as always,

Sincerely yours,

Hargood

435

CHAPTER 114

Grange received another letter that spring, from Mrs Arabella Pugh, perhaps equally surprising in its contents. He carried it upstairs to his study for privacy and sat down at his desk to consider it.

Dear Silas,

I return to you with news of one who has your best interests at heart, who demands information about your state and health with such constant consideration that I am at a loss to discover why she maintains her detachment.

We are, we women, sisters under the skin. It is a principle to which we may pay a kind of service. Yet it is this to which my dear friend Celia Quill holds so resolutely.

She writes to me and gives no address. She asks me to visit her house in Lymington from time to time and to pass on certain funds to her cook, Mrs Chorley, and her son, Matthew, whose welfare she attempts to oversee in her absence. She requires me to report back to her, which service I am happy to perform. I am to write to her, telling her of their current state, care of an address from which she may collect her mail now and again.

On various occasions I have spoken with Mrs Chorley, who mentioned that you had called by before Christmas and had given her family the unexpected gift of a goose. She is fiercely loyal to Mrs Quill and, suspecting that your interest in her must be related to her mistress, was not inclined to grant you any information on that subject on her own account. But if she remains suspicious of your motive, sir, it seemed that your act of kindness stirred Mrs Chorley sufficiently at least to inform me of your approach to her. I understand she treated your own generosity less than generously, indeed, somewhat rudely and circumspectly, and perhaps she hopes that in some way I may be able to make amends. Because I am her mistress's emissary and it is the habit of country people to treat those who act as their paymasters, even of an intermediary nature, with a certain practical respect, she appears to trust me. She asked my opinion of you and, for my part, I spoke of you in the highest possible terms. So it may be that your approach to her may yet bear some small fruit, though not from a direction you expected.

The address in question – 26 Eastgate Street, Mortlake – is not our mutual friend's current residence, I believe, but I have taken the liberty of enclosing it, in case you may wish to write to her. I do not know entirely why I break faith with her silence in order to inform you of it. It is one of those acts, based perhaps on sentiment, which we cannot easily explain, but which we hope may do a greater good than our small reputation warrants. Perhaps, sir, I too was struck by your gesture of charity towards Mrs Chorley – of tramping through several miles of snow on a frozen evening to deliver a fat goose to a poor family – so that I also begin to take account of the sincerity of your interest in her mistress's well-being.

I hope that you may at least have the chance of communicating with her, and if you do so then she, for her part, will have the opportunity of deciding whether to reply.

If, in the course of time, you should meet with her again, I trust you will give her my fondest regards.

For my part I wish you, sir, my own warmest greetings.

    Yours sincerely,

     Arabella Pugh

Grange placed the letter face down on his writing desk and leaned back in his chair. Arabella Pugh was one of the closest of Mrs Quill's circle and, if her account was substantially correct in its various details – and he believed he would trust her from previous acquaintance – it demonstrated, if nothing else, how closely Celia Quill guarded her current whereabouts from even her nearest friends. He was inclined also to believe his informant that the address, which she had supplied to Mrs Pugh for purposes of occasional communication, was likely to be merely a postal address from which she would collect certain items of mail.

Now that Hargood had gone, it seemed to Grange that he must start again from the beginning, though this time he was determined to distil some understanding from the actions of the past. If he had passed through his crisis of doubt concerning her, perhaps the sacrifices to his health gave him a right, finally, to be true to himself and to his own feelings about her.

He drew a sheaf of paper towards him, picked up a quill pen, dipped it in ink and was about to write when he was struck by a thought which caused him to set down the pen again. For several further minutes he did not move, staring out through the window at the shore line and the Solent, arrested in his thoughts.

CHAPTER 115

'Mrs Thompson!' Grange called.

'Sir?'

'I go to London.'

'But . . .' Mrs Thompson checked herself.

'I would be grateful if you would pack me a meal for the journey.'

Food was far from his mind, but he was determined to give Mrs Thompson a task that would deflect her attention while he packed a few clothes.

'I have examined my diary for the next week. I believe there are no emergencies. In the meantime, perhaps you will be kind enough to send messages informing those I hoped to see that I will be away for seven days and suggest a further time the following week.'

'Sir.'

'Thank you, Mrs Thompson. If there happen to be any emergencies, I have written to Dr Mansell at Milford communicating my intention to be absent for a full week. He will stand in for me if need be.'

Mrs Thompson nodded, though reluctantly, then she turned towards the stairwell and raised her skirt to descend. Grange briefly wondered how, in so simple an attitude, a figure could convey such intense suspicion.

He opened the drawers in his bedroom and put several shirts and two pairs of breeches into his portmanteau. Alongside them he placed some sets of woollen stockings against the cold that seemed to be gathering from the east. The spring air was thin and fine, and the nights still had a touch of frost in them. He would need a second cravat, a shaver, a strop, a hairbrush, some cleaning powder for his teeth. He packed quickly, taking as his motto his older colleague's view that the essence of travel was not to carry your world with you, but to leave as much behind as possible.

The stage took three days to London. There was much mud on the track and, among the woodland and meadows the shine of flood water from early April rains. The driver, approaching occasional toll-gates, blew his trumpet to alert the keeper. By the time they reached the gate there was usually a man in waiting, roused from drowsing in some small nearby cottage or wooden shelter that was often hidden from view.

On the flats leading to Winchester the driver struck his whip and they accelerated. Small stones and gravel had been set down against the slurry of mud. The coach creaked, the wheels thundered and the body swayed biliously.

The ground became steeper and more hilly as they passed Winchester to the south of the city. Sometimes, climbing the outer side of a hill, the coach would lean precariously. The coachman, holding on to the inner side to add his weight to the stability of the whole, attached thaws to his belt so that he could lean inwards without risk of falling over.

In the course of the journey Grange, not given to speaking his innermost thoughts, kept to himself. The interior smelled of carbolic. His fellow passengers, five men and two women, of whom one was a wife of a travelling merchant and the other a governess or companion on her way to take up residence with a family in Russell Square, took notice of the silence that seemed to surround him. After a few tentative exchanges they did not attempt to speak to him further. There followed a number of stilted conversations

439

between the other passengers, on the weather and the prices in London, from which his own contribution was entirely lacking.

His mind was preoccupied, though it was difficult to say by what precisely. It was as if the engine of his private obsession was hidden, though its outward manifestations might show themselves in his sudden wish to make a journey. He might have been inside the hold of a ship, hearing the beams move and the rigging creak, but unaware of the precise destination. As he considered these aspects, withholding himself from the desultory discussions between the other passengers, a commotion outside the coach caused him to glance out of the window. The horses had broken into a trot and the coach swayed. Several half-wild dogs that had followed them started to canter and one or two sprang or feinted at the heads of the horses. The horses, alarmed and inspired, thrust forward; the coachman stood on the board to control the fresh impetus and, in his new position of control, legs splayed for balance, foot against the board, discovered that his confidence exceeded his fear. The whole configuration swept downwards at a great pace, carried forward by its own compulsion, the coach leaping and jumping on its springs, the conversation halted, the women inside holding on to their hats, the men smiling at one another out of embarrassment and that perfunctory courtesy which arises out of situations beyond their immediate control.

It was a long decline, nearly half a mile or so, the great hill leading down past the village of Duncton, within distant sight of Petersfield. Now the coachman was applying the brake, they could hear the thunder of the restless horses, the scream of iron-bound wheels sliding on the stone and gravel, the stray dogs giving cry, the driver calling out to himself as much as to his animals, the heavy coach moving like a barely controlled sled down the decline, sparks flickering from the locked wheels, the cursory snap of saplings, the rumble and crash as the wheels struck larger stones or boulders. In the last part of the decline, their speed having increased until it almost overtook the horses, the body of the coach began to slide sideways towards a group of oaks at the side of the wheel-rutted track. The driver, nervous but calm in the centre of his fear, acted against his deepest impulse and released the brake. A particular oak, singling itself out, seemed to move towards them with a massive and stately intransigence. Stifling his tumult, the coachman eased the brake more, so that the coach increased its speed towards the looming obstacle. The freed wheels gripped, accelerated and straightened slightly; with a sliding rush they seemed almost to bend their shape around the trunk. After that the coachman applied a little more brake, the cabin leaning this way and that, the smell of abrasion rising up bitter until, finally, with a heavy creak and scream of leather, they came to a halt at the bottom of the hill.

The ensuing silence was like the calm after a storm. The coachman locked the brake, tied the reins, sprang down, and approached the door to tell them they were safe and to pacify the women. Grange and the other men were exhilarated, there was courtesy and gallantry to the ladies; the men congratulated the coachman in full masculine pride; the coachman felt obliged, indeed constrained, to take off his great hat and to bow to the passengers, the women especially. The men applauded. The coachman swung back onto the resting board, untied the reins, lifted the brake, called out to the horses, cracked the whip for effect, and then the coach set off again towards Midhurst, the passengers entirely satisfied that everyone had played their part well in the drama, and they could proceed in good spirits on their journey.

That night, Grange left the inn dining-room as soon as was possible within the bounds of politeness, after the women but before sharing port with the men. As he rose from the table and made his goodbyes, he felt or sensed the men's disapproval directed at his back, believing as they did that he owed them some company in return for the hours they had spent attempting to interest him in conversation during the day.

As they approached London he witnessed the outer slums on the periphery of the city, shacks and shallow lean-tos, the sight of women carrying pails of water, occasional ragged horses, barefoot children in the mud between the hovels, pigs and pigeons and other livestock in the bare ground around the shacks. These were the dispossessed, gathered on the rim of the great city, of whom Hargood had said that the men were nearly all scavengers and the women mostly whores.

Many of the hovels had small strips of land, brutally overused, with chickens and other livestock roaming the muddy wastes. He looked out at the starving dogs and the thin, broken horses and pack-mules that were tethered at the sides of the hovels or in deserted fields.

Another thought began to concern him. He had deliberately put Celia Quill from his mind as they drew closer to London, fearing the intrusion of his conscious mind. In the absence of any commitment on her part, he would counsel a careful approach, and strive to find some meeting point of sympathy between them, before advancing the cause he had come to plead. But he had grown to distrust his rational principles. It seemed to him that if such principles had been followed, he would not now be travelling to London in the faint hope of a meeting. For her impact upon his life had changed him in one important degree at least – he must begin to conduct the matters of deepest importance to him as if by instinct, and follow them to their natural conclusion irrespective of the reasons that were thrown in his path.

CHAPTER 116

From Russell Square he took a post to Mortlake, emerging into the calm main street in the late morning.

At Mortlake village a warren of houses lined the road and a gaggle of barefoot urchins, as thin as mosquitos, attempted to carry his valise. The stage-hand struck the side of the chaise with the flat of his hand to signal the new passengers had embarked, the coachman flicked the reins and the horses drew the vehicle away.

At that hour there was the shine of recent rain on the cobbles. A faint, slanted smoke hung above the chimneys.

A voice said, 'Shall someone take your luggage, sir?'

The elderly stage-hand was standing at a slight distance, surveying him with a wall eye.

Grange gripped the handle tighter.

The man indicated the group of urchins. 'One of these will carry it. They are trustworthy, sir.'

Grange gave his valise to the care of one, smaller than the others, who bore it proudly until he reached the Whiteacre Inn. Under the sign of two wrapped snakes he gave the child two pennies. The boy surveyed the coins with professional interest and handed Grange his luggage, as though it were some formal ceremony of exchange. Neither spoke. When Grange turned again the child had gone.

At the Whiteacre an elderly, peripatetic man issued from the interior of the bar. Grange smelled ale on his breath and also something deeper; the strangely sweet combustion of unhealthy lungs. It was an odour he had forgotten, a London scent of confinement in basements where impoverished craftsmen worked in dim light.

He sat for an hour in the small front room, lost in his own thoughts. He decided to take a meal and ate a pie. Afterwards, having allowed his digestion to settle, he took a walk in the cold midday. In the south-west there was low white cloud, lit by the last of the day's sun. A thunderhead was building behind it, as though a number of forces were constructing the weather of the afternoon. The dark mass of the rising cloud seemed to hover above a field of light. Gulls rose and fell, drifting like snowflakes in the almost lucid calm.

He walked by the river. The buildings along the bank were low, the behaviour of the people modest and furtive, so that as he made his way westwards his attention was directed towards the celestial display.

Reaching a lock-gate and a small side stream, he followed a path inland several hundred yards, until he reached a long gravelled street. It extended for perhaps two miles, before it reached a crossroads. He continued over it and then walked for perhaps a further quarter of an hour before he found Eastgate Street.

The house itself was small and set back from the pathway as though out of reticence. He opened the wooden gate and tried the old iron knocker. There was no sound from within. He raised the knocker again, and heard its cough and rattle penetrating the house.

At a loss, he turned away and walked in the direction of Mortlake itself. His path led him through another aggregation of slum houses. Once, in his younger days, he had heard in such a street a single scream. He did not know whether it came from the throat of a man, woman or a child. It was a sound strangely calm, utterly without hope, of a soul in despair.

After perhaps an hour of walking, he returned to Eastgate Street and raised the knocker again, listening to its flat echo like a fall of soot in a chimney. He fancied he heard something, but it might have been a shutter banging in the slowly rising wind.

No one came to the door. Grange stood in the entrance porch for several minutes, at a loss. When he left, he decided to move in a direction away from Mortlake.

He walked the streets for several hours, and returned later that afternoon to the house. He knocked and again there was no answer. He took a supper at the Whiteacre and walked towards Eastgate Street once more in the evening. There was no sign of light in the window from lamp or candle. The house was deserted.

Two further days went by. Each day he passed by the door of the house and raised the knocker. He walked around the side and gazed up at the windows, hoping for a sign of a human presence. He saw now that the upper windows' dark exteriors should have informed him of something earlier – that they were boarded on the inside. The garden was deserted and overgrown. Weeds grew through the pathway, the gate lay askew on its hinges, the upper hinge having rusted through completely.

It occurred to him, suddenly and terribly, that she might be living inside, that her condition might have shrunk to this miserable habitation, without warmth or even light. The sensation was with him for a few moments, but after the intensity of the initial intuition it wore thin against the evidence. As a physician who had visited the houses of the poverty stricken and the dying, he knew that there were usually tell-tale signs of habitation. There was, more often than not, a small path to the door through the weeds, perhaps no more than an animal would make, caused by the occasional visitor. But here there was no trace of such a path; the weeds spread uniformly across the brick. There was usually, in those premises where life flickered within, a smooth unrusted area on the lock of the door that was a sign of a key in occasional use. But the property showed no indication of even these faint marks.

Grange returned to the Whiteacre. It seemed to him that nothing, except a kind of stubbornness, kept him there. He began to grow listless. He tried to read a volume of Seneca's *De Vita Beata* but his concentration faltered. In his room at night he lay on his bed and stared at the ceiling.

As the night deepened he listened to the drunken scufflings below him, the singing and the tears. Sometimes a gang of rowdy men from the local tannery drank beer in the bar; sometimes he heard the screams of women's laughter. The Whiteacre Inn stood at a crossroads of the human thoroughfare that moved along the southern river bank towards and from London. Because there was less chance of being dispersed by the traffic of horses and carts, flocks of sheep and goats were herded along the road at night towards the markets. He could discern the heavy clump of the shepherds' boots, the clicking of the sheep's hoofs, the soft mewling of accompanying lambs, the sound of sheep urinating on the cobbles, the clicks and whistles as the shepherds called to their dogs. Sometimes late night stages swung past and he heard the noise of the horses' hoofs departing like a shower of rain.

When he slept, he seemed to fall into an infinite darkness.

CHAPTER 117

The following day it had turned bright; a cold, sunlit spring morning that had the chill of winter. A silent, permeable wind had risen from the east. It seemed to strike through clothes, though it barely rustled the oak leaves on the ground between the Whiteacre and the river. After breakfast Grange walked out towards the river's edge and stood for several minutes staring down into the dark water. There was a placid pool there, protected by a groin of land, in which flow and flood had deposited their debris – the axle of an old cart, the remnants of a child's carriage, some shards of old plates and pots. In the deepest part of the pool was something pale and vaguely cartilaginous. With a faint sense of shock he thought it might be the skin of a human being, perhaps a small child. But under his concentration he could see what appeared to be the carcass of a dog, perhaps some form of lurcher or greyhound. Long immersion and waterlogging had removed the fur from the skin, and the body itself was obscenely naked. The stomach had burst and the the corpse was infested by eels. Relieved that he had not inadvertently stumbled upon a drowned human being, he observed more closely the silky shimmering of the eels around the carrion.

In due course he returned to the inn. Though he felt restless and preoccupied, he could find no displacement for his energy. Sitting in abstracted stillness in the small front room, he finally raised himself from his chair, put on his coat and walked out.

He made his way down the road, stepping carefully among the fresh piles of sheep droppings. Some curious sense of presence, some odd expectation, seemed to propel him once again towards Eastgate Street. He reached the front of the house and regarded it in silence for several minutes. He had come back to make his farewell to the last traces of Mrs Quill; then he would return to Lymington, his mission having failed.

It was when he was on the point of leaving that he noticed – almost by accident, since he was searching for a quiet place to urinate – that a footpath led along the side of the house, outside the wooden paling fence. On an impulse he decided to walk down it, if only because it might be able to offer a clearer view of the rear of the property.

The path was overgrown with weeds, dock and grass. Pale early flowers of cow parsley covered the gravel. But there were definite faint signs that it had been used; there was a line of reduced vegetation close to the centre of the path. He was considering this when he saw something that he had not noticed before. At the furthest end of the garden, almost overgrown with creepers of ivy, there was a side gate that led from the footpath into the overgrown rear garden. He made his way through the weeds and examined the latch on the gate with an odd sense of hunger. Under his closer consideration it betrayed the grooved, grey areas of iron that indicated the rust had been rubbed clean with occasional use. He looked at the back of the garden and noticed there was the slight trace of an habitual path to the back door. He did not need to enter the garden to guess that the back door would show further traces of clear iron where a key had sometimes made ingress.

Nervous suddenly, his mind running cold, he looked about him. The disused public pathway led to another road set behind Eastgate Street and this in turn gave way to the road following the river bank. He saw that it would be possible to approach the property from another direction entirely, to enter and leave the house without being observed from Eastgate Street at the front.

The weather had grown a little colder. Wind and cloud shadows moved across his path. He followed the footpath away from Eastgate Street to its junction with Cheam Road, perhaps fifty yards behind the house. Whoever visited the property from this direction would need to enter the footpath here. Reaching the entrance, he looked up and down Cheam Road for some innocuous vantage point. There was a small public park at the top of the road, with a wooden bench that he could perceive beyond an oak turnstile gate. He walked perhaps two hundred yards towards the park and sat down. Placing his cane beside him, he picked out the entrance with his eye and set himself to judging the distances between the bench and the footpath. He was engaged in this when rain began to fall, a few single large drops first and then a sudden unexpected downpour which forced him to take temporary shelter beneath one of the park's large oaks.

When the downpour had ceased, the sun emerged almost immediately. He returned to the oak bench. It was still covered in water from the rain. He took from his pocket the large calico handkerchief that Mrs Thompson had given him for the journey and wiped an area smooth of moisture. Then he pocketed the damp kerchief and sat down on the bench in the rising scent of damp grass. In his youth, as an only child, he had had a propensity to day-dream. Now he settled into himself and allowed time to pass.

He waited for several hours, immobile.

He had left the Whiteacre shortly after breakfast and as noon approached he noticed a trace of thirst and a little hunger, but on the whole he felt light-headed and detached. He continued at his outpost through the midday and into the early afternoon. The sun swung through its customary arc. He saw the scaffolding of shadows lift from the east, then fall on the west sides of the nearby buildings.

Towards late afternoon he observed a cloaked figure move calmly down the path and disappear almost immediately behind an adjacent building. For a few moments he wondered if he had seen a ghost. The figure had appeared suddenly, without seeming to approach from any direction. He stood up, disciplining himself to act with deliberation and circumspection, and walked towards the junction of the footpath with Cheam Road. A tall woman in a cloak and bonnet now paused at the side gate, and he saw her hand lift the latch. With his heart beating he followed her up the pathway.

She had seen him approach, he felt certain, out of the corner of her eye, because she froze at the gate, staring ahead, pausing, perhaps, to let him go by before she entered the garden. As he came alongside her he said softly, 'Madam!' and the woman, as though woken from a trance, turned round and stared at him in consternation.

She was elderly, perhaps sixty, with grey hair parted and held back in a bun.

'I beg your pardon.' Grange felt his mind stumble, pick itself up, stumble again.

She continued to gaze at him. He noticed, as if by intuition, the large frame, the plump cheeks, the examining eyes. It was a placid and strong face. Now that her momentary fear of his sudden appearance had passed, he found himself under the scrutiny of a particular intelligence. He felt compelled to reduce the tension between them. 'Do you perhaps know if Mrs Quill lives here?' He felt his mouth go dry and, in the absence of any response, added, 'Mrs Celia Quill?'

She did not reply for several seconds. At last, she said, 'You know her?'

He breathed out softly and attempted to bring his own consternation under control. What was her accent, Grange wondered? Lancastrian? A family retainer, or housekeeper perhaps. He was determined to maintain a conversation and attempted to answer her question as best he could. 'I had the privilege of making her acquaintance during her stay in Lymington.'

Her sharp brown eyes regarded him with something like detachment. He had an impression of shrewdness and kindness. Eventually she said, 'She's not here, sir, not now.'

'She has gone?'

The woman seemed to make a decision as to the nature of his interest. She nodded to him, not out of friendliness or acquiescence, but because she wished to acknowledge his question.

He feared suddenly that she was about to turn and go. By the normal bounds of propriety he would be powerless to detain her. As it was, while they talked she had already partly opened the gate. Now she closed it and let the latch drop carefully.

He attempted one final assertion. 'I believe Mrs Quill has recently visited her daughter.'

She had closed the gate. Now, on the point of going, she paused. 'Her daughter?'

Grange decided upon the final risk. 'Her daughter Jane, who lives in Winchester.'

Hesitantly, almost reluctantly, the woman smiled, as though he had given at least some initial proof of his intimacy, then waited as though for further proof.

Grange said, 'I recently met Jane in Winchester and imparted some information to her.'

The woman nodded. 'I see.'

'If Mrs Quill perhaps writes to you, or you meet with her, would you be so kind as to pass on my regards?'

'From whom shall I say . . . ?'

'From Silas Grange.'

If his name meant anything to her, she gave no indication of it. Instead, she inclined her head, as though against the conversation, turned and moved away down the footpath. Grange watched her walk between the weeds, her cloak brushing the docks and grass stems. She turned right at the junction with Cheam Road, then almost immediately swung right again towards the open park. Without moving, he watched her disappear.

CHAPTER 118

Some impulse drove him, though he would not admit it to himself. Part of him was convinced that if she did not live in the house from which she collected mail, she resided nearby. Why, he asked himself, would she live so far away that it was inconvenient to collect her letters? The disused house would be employed by her as a means of collecting mail without directly jeopardising her own address. He was convinced that her establishment was in the close vicinity.

Even in this he was driven by an obscure sense of propriety, though he could not easily formulate its rules. He did not wish to knock on her door or enter her house – that seemed to him, intuitively, an invasion of her privacy. If he had known her address, he would have made no use of it, but would have departed to Lymington as he intended. It was, rather, that by constantly quartering the ground he hoped that perhaps he could run into her once more, that if they met again – even though he fervently hoped for it – it would be at least partly by chance.

He had learned from her, after all, to live by intuition and, if he knew that she was in the neighbourhood, then it was likely she lived and breathed in these same streets which he walked so restlessly. He was hunting her in the same oblique way, perhaps, as a wolf hunted deer, by hoping for a scent among the other scents, a trail among false trails. So it was that for several days he wandered the neighbourhood of Mortlake, in the hope that she would rise again out of the dark of his thoughts.

He had no reason to stay further, yet he remained for two more days, sitting by himself in the inn, keeping to his room, or taking solitary meals.

Walking in white sunlight by Mortlake, Grange observed the small groups of people out taking the air, the families with their children, the horses and dogs. The leaves were swelling with spring.

Several children were running a ball with sticks along the grass, taking it in turns, observed by their governess. Sunlight glimmered on the water's surface. Staring into the luminous path of water, a perception of the incompleteness of his life touched him, though it did not strike as deeply as another, more pressing, observation.

On the afternoon of his last day he saw, on the other side of the lake on a diagonal path that led among the trees, a woman walking in a heavy blue pelisse. Nervous of too hasty an identification, he watched her emerge from the obscurity of a row of elms and cross a small wooden bridge on the far side of the lake.

He attempted to persuade himself of his detachment, but found his course was already changing of its own accord, like a ship that alters its direction if it is not carefully attended. A part of his mind was calculating how their paths might cross. She disappeared for several moments behind a grey bandstand with a green copper-roofed cupola and reappeared, walking briskly away along a gravelled path. Somewhere beyond a line of lime trees a clock struck the hour of three, in jagged chimes. He began to feel terror take hold of him, and was subject to that unexpected lightness of heart when some unrehearsed but salient truth casually seizes the mind.

The figure was walking briskly now towards a lane that led onto the park. He quickened his pace. He glanced towards her and found she was absent in the place that she had occupied a short while before. With a floating sensation of fear, he searched the nearby spaces. Beside a copse of larches, an open gate swung in the breeze. He changed direction towards it and, passing through it, saw her turn right at the end of a lane and disappear.

He began to quicken his pace, his footsteps echoing oddly. He reached the end of a path and caught sight of the figure crossing the road perhaps fifty yards away. Walking calmly but briskly, she seemed to have gained distance on him, despite his increased pace. There was a flow of traffic down the street, a party of four or five on horses, a mule train of pack animals; a two-horse carriage passing down the road obscured her briefly. He stifled a wish to cry out and, forgetting decorum, ran after her across the grass.

It was only when he had drawn alongside that she turned, almost reluctant, to look at him. He saw the familiar grey eyes, opened in slight alarm, focus on him. He drew deep lungfuls of air, standing in

451

front of her, and heard himself saying, 'Madam, I hope, I trust, you will forgive my trespass.'

For several moments she stood her ground, observing him.

'Madam,' Grange said again, attempting to add to what he had uttered before, but he decided to curtail his plea and so, in the face of her composure, became silent.

'Silas,' she said after several moments. 'I did not expect to see you here.'

It was spoken without emotion, with a flatness of tone which touched some chord of fear in him.

He was standing in front of her now, blocking her way. His nerves seemed to stretch with the notion of some impending catastrophe. He felt overtaken suddenly by a sense that on no account should he appear to threaten her, or apply pressure to her decision – this woman of fiercely independent temperament. Out of this impending sense, as much as courtesy, he deliberately stood aside so that she could pass.

Now they were facing the same space, at right angles to one another, neither moving. His nerves were frozen in apprehension.

She stared ahead of her. 'You sought me out?'

'Yes,' he said, curiously relieved at the directness of the question. 'I travelled from Lymington in the small hope of seeing you.'

'Small?'

'I only knew a forwarding address.'

'I advised you not to attempt to find me.'

He was silent and she seemed to consider. He sensed her determination to maintain control of the conversation. Another mule train passed behind them, the animals' hoofs sounding heavily on the cobbles. A leading one, a small female, halted and brayed loudly; the muleteer slapped her withers with a switch, upbraiding fiercely.

She waited silently until they had passed. 'You are staying in the neighbourhood?'

'Yes,' Grange said.

'How long are you here?'

Such odd, deliberate questions, he thought. Perhaps she was

452

attempting to draw some distinction between his behaviour and her own. 'I have been here a few days. At an inn. The Whiteacre.'

'And you intend to return to Lymington?'

'Immediately I had seen you.'

She glanced around at the surrounding park. 'Well, sir. You have seen me now.' Her tone was without warmth.

He was rendered nervous again, though he managed to control his emotion. The act of standing aside had released something in him. Without understanding himself, he knew that in his heart he was prepared to allow her departure, finally, from his life. He decided to risk one last request. 'Before I return,' he said, 'will you permit me to speak on one brief matter – my colleague Dr Hargood?'

It was an absurd place at which to conduct a conversation. There was continuous traffic on the road and an aggravation of background noise.

'Hargood?'

In the confusion of sound, an event took place then, for which he was afterwards oddly but extremely grateful. A current of horses was moving past, firm flesh on thin legs, a party of gentry. He heard the striking of shod hoofs on the cobbles, then the hesitation of a single horse which seemed to traverse several steps towards them. It was a large roan, surmounted by a fat gentleman in his later years. The animal was mettlesome, prancing and drifting sideways in their direction, despite the application of crop and spur. She could not see the horse or its rider – they were mainly behind her. For a brief moment Grange felt he should act, and only when the horse had halted a few feet away – shaking its head and flicking the reins, still dancing on points – did he set aside the impulse to reach forward and pull her aside. Out of apology at his horse's transgression the gentlemen raised his hat to her, to them both – though she could not see the gesture – and then made to swing his mount once again towards the general stream. But he did not manage to do so before the horse had raised its tail. Though she could not see the rider, the rear end and tail of the horse projected directly into her vision, so that she witnessed at first hand, and under the most directly palpable conditions, the quick accumulation of an inordinately large pile of dung beside the road. The roan and its rider joined the main, milling group and then they heard the laughter of one of the women grow softer as the party departed.

The road had cleared finally and in the ensuing silence there was an opportunity to continue their conversation. He wished to speak to her of Hargood. Turning, he saw, beneath her grave expression, the slow beginnings of a change; he observed how, shyly perhaps, a hint of colour had appeared in her cheeks and then the faint trace of a smile. It rose upwards in her face, quietly, like a fish rising to the surface of a stream. She said, 'An inauspicious beginning to a speech, perhaps.'

'I believe, madam, that we should take advantage of whatever platform we are given.'

She bit her lower lip. 'Even if the platform steams a little.'

He said, 'Even if it steams, madam.'

CHAPTER 119

Later, much later, if he ever had the fortune to meet up again with his senior colleague, Grange believed he would thank Hargood for the manner in which his name, uttered aloud, appeared to exercise such a remarkable laxative effect upon a large and noble quadruped. If Hargood's spirit had been at hand, Grange was certain it would have intervened in precisely such a bold and unorthodox manner. He recalled, fleetingly but vividly, an image of Hargood standing before his collection of erotic paintings, exhibiting a similar exhibitionism in bringing to Grange's attention his own changing circumstances.

As it was, they were at an odd juncture, set in open space like a couple in a room, awkwardly at variance with one another, but neither able to move for fear of making matters worse.

Grange said, 'During my convalescence, when he supervised my recovery, my colleague informed me that in the past you had been his mistress.'

He used the word 'mistress' with trepidation, fearing her response to a term she had fought free of most of her life. But to his

454

surprise she nodded emphatically and almost fiercely, as if she was determined not to avoid the use of the word.

'. . . And that you and he had a disagreement, after which you left the household.'

She did not speak for several seconds. The road behind was empty of traffic now, an odd peace between instalments. Their voices seemed to echo. In the unexpected silence she gathered herself again. 'You were shocked?'

'Yes. But not by the fact itself. Perhaps by the circumstances.'

'You were surprised, then?' she persisted.

'I was surprised only because I did not know of it before.'

'And what do you think now?'

'It explains much to me.'

'That was all you wished to ask?'

'Yes,' he said.

She looked down the empty road and seemed to consider, then make up her mind on a course of action. 'You know what I became afterwards?'

'Yes,' Grange said. 'I believe so.'

She was listening closely, considering his response. 'It was your colleague Dr Hargood who informed you?'

'Under great pressure from my own enquiries,' Grange admitted.

'You asked him specifically?'

'At a certain stage he thought it best to enlighten me.' He attempted to swing the subject onto another path. 'He also informed me how much he admired you . . .'

'Ah yes, admiration . . .' she said, as though it were an unwanted intrusion.

'Admiration, madam,' he repeated.

'From such a quarter, too,' she agreed, compounding her view.

He was surprised at her tone of voice, which was, if not sarcastic, ironic at least. 'Among other things, he told me that when he confronted you, you did not deny your role in my affairs.'

'Did he, now?'

'He said you faced him like a tiger, unafraid.'

'Like a tiger, indeed,' she confirmed.

At another time he might have smiled too, or laughed at her

455

tone, which seemed to chide both Hargood and himself, by repeating what he said.

She stared ahead. 'And what else did Dr Hargood report?'

'That you seemed concerned about my condition.'

He waited again. A single man pushing a handcart went past them, whistling to himself. He had moved on some fifty yards, out of earshot, when at last she said, 'I have always been concerned about your health.'

She turned her glance towards him, as if she were gauging directly the depth of his well-being. 'I see you have recovered well.'

'Yes. I believe I have recovered, madam.'

She was looking at him steadily, with the same calm attention. The intensity of her concentration was unnerving.

Grange continued, 'I believe I have recovered a great deal. That is what I wanted to say to you. You have been concerned at my health. Now that I am well there is nothing lost.'

'Nothing lost?'

'If, out of your kindness towards me in the past, you felt that you owed me some attention, I believe you owe me nothing any more.'

'So,' she said, 'you free me of further concern for you?'

'Precisely, madam.'

He realised suddenly why he had come, even though he had been unaware of it until then. It had been working itself out of him, like a splinter out of the skin. He had been fretting with it during his illness. But this was what he wanted to say to her, that she owed him nothing now that he had recovered from his illness. He knew that this was why he had come to seek her out. Not to plead with her, not to offer or propose to renew their association, but to say farewell. He had to speak it, almost, to hear himself say it.

She hesitated again, for the second time that day. Perhaps it was the simple gesture of returning her freedom that caused her to pause. What did she feel, he wondered, staring ahead, with nothing to prevent her walking away? If she wanted to be independent of him he had presented her with a door to her liberty. He still waited for her to step forward into the offered space and so disappear. He sensed that a part of her struggled to do so.

'And what if that was all there was between us? My concern for your health.'

'Then', Grange said, 'I believe we are both free.'

456

CHAPTER 120

She said, 'Before I go, there is something else I wish to raise with you.'

He waited for her to begin. Several parties had entered the park beside them. An elderly couple strolled a hundred yards away. A governess and two children began to play with a leather ball.

'You spoke with my daughter?'

She was regarding him steadily.

Grange nodded. 'I saw her in Winchester. It seems I meet you both in public places.'

'You took it upon yourself to inform Jane of her father's identity.'

He was determined not to be pressed or panicked by the closeness of her attention. He looked around at the park and the people walking against the wind. 'She is an adult, madam. Her father is my colleague and closest friend.'

She paused for a long time and he waited.

'Indeed.'

Grange said, 'He was about to leave his house and his country, in a kind of personal crisis, perhaps for ever, without certain knowledge of his daughter's identity.'

'Then he was leaving for his own reasons.'

'For other reasons, too. I believe he felt he stood in the way . . .' He was unable to finish the sentence.

She asked quietly, 'In the way of what, sir?'

'Of a possible reconciliation between you and me – of a renewal of our friendship.'

She took in a deep breath, not so much of frustration, but of a deeper emotion. A cloud shadow passed over them and a brisk breeze stirred the leaves.

'It is my observation, sir, that men constantly believe they can arrange the fates of women between themselves.'

He had not expected this implacable opposition. Perhaps because of it, he did not register immediately the calm force with which she spoke. 'Would you have preferred that I did not talk to your daughter?'

'I ask only that you leave our own matters to ourselves.'

'You believe she has no right to know the identity of her father?'

'"Rights", sir, are conferred by men, at their own convenience, for their own satisfaction. We women do not deal so easily with rights.'

'I do not imply anything other than that an adult, of whatever sex, has a right to know her parents.'

'Parents?' She turned towards him directly. 'I was her parent, her only parent. You think that confers no rights? Or are these rights so much a part of male prerogative that they do not apply to women?'

'Madam, your opinion is implacable.'

'And so', she said calmly, 'is yours.'

There was no fierceness or malice in what she said, but a formal directness which seemed, because of its very control, immovable.

Behind the shadows he saw a passage of sunlight move across the park, illuminating the trees in its path. He considered it briefly, distractedly, while waiting for her to speak. The sunlight seemed to retreat, then slowly come forth again.

'Have mercy, madam,' Grange said softly. 'Have mercy upon us all.'

CHAPTER 121

He had found no purchase in her, no hold. They stood side by side, half turned towards one another, each in a private world, apart.

Grange said, 'I believe I should go, now.'

Carefully, she nodded in agreement.

He felt his heart contract. That was how it would feel, he thought, his emotions as thin and desiccated as an insect.

He heard himself say, 'I wish you good-day. I promise you that I will not trouble you further.'

He bowed, turned and walked away through the bright park, feeling the shadows pour in upon him. He reached the grandstand, where the children were playing with the leather ball, and was close by the gate that led out of the park, when he heard a sound against the soughing of the wind.

It was not a cry, though he knew almost immediately that it came from her. She was moving towards him, or at least towards the gate. There was something abstracted in what she did. When she reached him it seemed to him her eyes were blind, and she almost ran into him by accident. He felt the weight of her against him. It was not forgiveness. But whatever it might be, he put his arms round her, held her to him, and waited. Their temples touched, and she closed her eyes, though it was not an embrace. The fine skin of her temple moved against his. Then she withdrew from his arms with a gentle but firm insistence, and stood back to glance once more at him.

He observed her carefully. There was a quality of her thought which he found daunting, as though she lived her decisions in the absolute.

He asked, 'Will you return?'

She had halted at the question, not simply her physical self, but as though her mind were arrested. Something occurred that he could not fathom, though he sensed it was concern for his feelings. Perhaps she was determined not to compromise him again. If she did not answer the question directly, it registered somewhere in her mind. Without raising her voice, she said, 'I have tried that path before.'

Grange was subject to a sudden, violent emotion of his own. She was referring, no doubt, to her former association with Hargood. Yet why should he carry Hargood's cross? Why should he be branded with actions he had not committed? The thoughts moved through him so quickly and with such intensity that he found himself powerless to resist their incursion.

He was about to speak when the decision was taken from him. She said, 'I wish you well, sir. I wish you the happiness that you deserve.'

He wanted to cry out in protest. Instead, he saw her step forward, the dark shawl hiding her expression, a profile followed by a back view, then the strong movement of her walk. He watched her skirt almost trailing the ground, the figure walking through the trees, becoming clothes again, and the clothes receding.

CHAPTER 122

He spent the rest of the day walking aimlessly through the streets, until he grew so tired he was forced to sit on a bench. That evening he showed no interest in the food the landlord placed in front of him. It was as if a watch were missing its spring. Some central purpose had been lost.

The following day he determined to pay one final visit to the Old Deer Park. He sat down in the chair in which she had sat and looked towards the Thames and beyond the rolling grass to where the sleek grandeur of Syon House stood in its curlicue of trees; beyond that, a little guard tower with pointed roof, with its flag of St George hanging in the silent day.

As darkness fell he returned to the inn, brought out his own quill and ink from his valise, and began to write.

Dear Mrs Thompson,
I continue to stay at the Whiteacre Inn, at Mortlake, in London.

I have decided that I will persevere here three days further than I expected. The weather is tolerable and mainly clear, and I have a reasonable room and board. I have failed, however, to complete my intended business here before returning.

When I left Lymington for London, I examined the diary for several days beyond my intended return, in case I wished for some reason to extend my departure. I could not find in that time any singular emergencies in the visits to patients that I had arranged. Accordingly, please be good enough to send notes informing those I had intended visiting, and those who were to see me by appointment, that my return to Lymington is delayed for several further days. I will attempt to see them as soon as I arrive.

Since I put pen to paper, there is another subject upon which I write to you. I hope you will forgive me for raising it now. It is a strange thing, I do believe, that we so seldom realise how much we depend upon those closest to us. Sometimes it seems as if the very proximity of another person induces in us a blindness to their presence. So you may believe that it is an odd and eccentric whim that causes me to express my gratitude for the manner in which you have looked after me during my illness, and for the fact that I have chosen to express this sentiment while I am at some hundred miles distant. The necessity of perspective notwithstanding, I should like to thank you, with a full heart, for your kindness in helping me to effect my recovery and to supervise my well-being.

I believe, in the strange manner of fate, that I am now at the position of my final cure. You who are closest to me may know perhaps the cause of my visit to these parts. I have done what I can, and it now remains for me to recognise what limitations may be placed upon my hopes for the future.

I shall look forward to seeing you shortly, and hope that the weather is fine in Lymington. It is unsettled here, raining when unexpected, and shining fitfully without warning.

In deepest gratitude, I remain,

    Yours sincerely,

      Silas Grange

CHAPTER 123

He walked the entire following day through the boroughs of London, where the countryside coexisted strangely with the peripheral sprawl of the city. His path took him down the long streets of Mortlake, into places of lawlessness. He was, he knew, curiously free from intervention. It was not just his height, though there might have been something ridiculous in his stork-like propensities, but there was present in the concentration of his mind a property which prevented him from falling into harm. People stood aside, as if he carried some weight in front of him.

So he walked for a whole afternoon, past huddled houses and districts of rotting tenements, through streets lined with dilapidated warehouses and old granaries. Sometimes he came across men unloading carts, and felt their hostile eyes upon him as he walked by. The area was notorious for smuggling. Contraband flowed in towards London from the south and east coasts, from landing places all over the country, reaching their final storage place here before being infiltrated into the goods and merchandise which were were sold in the city. The Customs authorities sedulously patrolled the riverside a few hundred yards away for incoming luggers, and would conduct searches of the jolly-boats from the merchantmen anchored in the river. But the goods that reached these warehouses were brought in openly on carts and already accompanied by bills made out to the smugglers' middlemen, and so the process of merging with the economy was in its final stages, and the goods almost untraceable to foreign shores.

In the evening he returned to the smoke-blackened lantern burning faintly at the door of the inn, and pressed on through the slatted leather flaps which hung like butchers' aprons over the front door, into the interior. The air was heavy, the atmosphere close. People seemed to speak in whispers, as though it were an opium den. He passed through the bar room and up the gloomy, strangely intricate iron-balustraded staircase, leaving the customers seated silently below.

When he returned to his room, he found oddly little respite from the noises of the establishment. During his several days of residence he had heard in the neighbouring room the cries of ghosts, of people debating in low fierce tones, yet he had never seen anything more than an old man emerge from the adjacent chamber. He had come to the conclusion that these were the internal fears and expositions of its single occupant, the gallery of disputants and plaintiffs that each of us carries inside, but which perhaps only madness will release.

The following morning he continued to walk. In the course of his obsessive musings he found himself staring into a baker's window, his gaze attracted to a particular confection; the twisted shapes in the bread were like two bodies together. He rose out of his thoughts, smiled ruefully at himself, wrenched himself away and moved on.

His track took him down a long lane, which soon became nothing but a footpath and in turn hardly more than a track. Several men and a woman stood there. Two of the men seemed to be arguing or bargaining and, it was only when he reached them and they halted their conversation that he guessed they were bargaining over the young woman who stood beside them patiently, like merchandise.

He entered an area of allotments, a wilderness lying on the side of the river, with old melon frames and cucumber frames, an empty pen for holding sheep or goats, with the fences worm-eaten and the gate lying back on its rusty hinges. Old tracks led to ancient, dilapidated houses.

Walking through fields by the river he passed by a homestead which seemed set apart. In the centre of it were a pair of great hogs. He smelled the odium of blood and shit, and knew the shallow building for a slaughterhouse. Behind it was a garden with untidy rows of beans and carrots and tomatoes, potatoes and cucumbers. A little further on he came across a group of vagrants gathered about a barrel of tar burning with a pale light in the pale spring sunshine.

That afternoon he returned to the Whiteacre for an odd, snatched meal. He did not remember, could hardly name, a short while afterwards what precisely he had eaten, or if he had eaten anything. He merely wanted to get out of the confinement of its dark rooms again and onto the streets and roads and walkways, pursuing odd bridle tracks and ash-covered paths where, if nothing else, the rhythm of walking brought a sense of equilibrium. Constantly moving, pursuing the narrow intimacies of the streets, he had a compulsion to walk off the rest of the evening. The plan of that poor area seemed to become a part of his mind, a map of his restlessness. The streets were like some grammar which he knew but did not understand, a vast shadowy web which he almost felt that he could conjugate without thinking: the riverside and its ropewalks, the rotting hulks that lay there, the strange hinterland of old houses and warehouses and odd, out-of-the-way homesteads, with their own large barns that seemed always closed and locked, and the strange silent people with their carts and transports moving in and out. He wandered among them unseeing, protected from their suspicions by his own manifest blindness towards their activities, his mind's eye instead focused inwards, on the dark, while he sought to make out the meanings of her actions.

CHAPTER 124

On the second evening of his extended stay he stepped out of the pub with the intention of walking along the river bank to gather his thoughts. It was the height of the flood tide and the water was still. He walked for several miles, keeping to the public paths.

On his return to the inn he found that the landlord, never less than considerate, had taken the trouble to set a lantern on the wall outside the main door to guide his path across the field. He advanced on the flame in the narrow half-light. Having almost reached the dark mass of the inn, with its single light, he noticed a slight movement at the side of the wall, and became aware of a dark shape there in the obscurity. He swung towards it, in order to consider it more precisely, and was almost upon it when he realised it was a woman.

She stood by the lantern, the wind in her hair, darkness streaming out of her. As he approached, he heard her say, 'Silas.'

He felt his heart fill, shudder, fill again, as though he were breathing.

He could see her more closely now. She stood with her back against the building, a few feet away from the wall, facing towards the river. The lantern threw a shadow over her face.

Grange said, 'Would you not care to come inside, madam? There is a fire there.'

But she would not. She made only the slightest shake of her head.

He was at a loss, standing there beside her, waiting in the chill evening. He looked beyond the outline of her profile, over the low roofs of the straggle of poor houses beside the river, towards London, where he could see the spires of the churches, the last fading gold light on the mass of masts upriver in the Thames. She had turned away from the lantern, the light of which fell across her neck and shoulders. Unable to see the expression of her eyes, he could not even tell whether she intended to speak, or perhaps was waiting for him. At length she said, clearly and without warning, 'Were you in love with my daughter?'

Grange paused. The expression 'my daughter' was curiously formal. 'I believed that I was.'

Now she turned to face him directly. She chose her words carefully. 'Why did your attentions shift?'

'Did they?' Grange asked. 'I believe you encouraged me in my interest in her.'

She ignored his remonstration. 'Are you still in love with her?'

'No, madam.'

'Then perhaps', she said carefully, 'you are not constant.'

'Constant?' Grange remembered Hargood's words, that his faith in Celia Quill was so strong and wilful he might as well worship a female deity. He observed her now, considering him with an expression of enquiry. Something seemed to stir in his mind, a perturbation. He experienced a slow movement of mirth inside him, a welling of sensation that seemed to rise into a rictus of amusement.

'You should not smile, sir, on such an occasion.'

'I did not mean to, madam,' Grange said. 'It is simply that our friend Dr Hargood asserted exactly the opposite – that my regard for you was so unshakeable that it was not affected by any evidence to the contrary.'

'And Dr Hargood supported your interest in my daughter?'

He saw that the mention of Hargood had caused a shadow, and hurried to repair a breach. 'I assure you, he has changed a great deal since you last spoke with him. As it was, I never asked his advice concerning your daughter. I had no indication at the time that his interest might have been more . . . personal.'

'Perhaps,' she conceded. 'But you have not answered my question – about inconstancy.'

'It was for you that I felt . . . I persuaded myself otherwise.'

'You told me, sir, that your feelings were towards my daughter, that you wished to marry her.'

He struggled to see her in the fading light. 'I saw Jane as a reflection of you. Perhaps it is natural to love what reminds us of the original.'

'Is that why you were in such turmoil when she left for Winchester? Why were you so aggravated by her absence, sir, when – as you would have us believe – the object of your desire stood in front of you?'

He paused at the force of these combinations. 'I believe my turmoil was caused by your own behaviour.'

'My behaviour?'

'You had encouraged me to take an interest in your daughter. When I declared myself, you became cold, fierce, withdrawn. You sent your daughter away and instructed me not to follow her.'

'It was surely my right to think of her welfare.'

'Were you testing me?'

'In what sense?' she asked.

'You gave me no encouragement concerning yourself. You encouraged me instead to pay attention to your daughter. And then you withdrew her.'

'No encouragement?' she persisted.

'You have never once shown any sign of affection.'

'Indeed?'

'Not once.'

She was facing him, but a little obliquely. Now she turned towards him directly, with a calm expression, and raised eyebrows, and he felt obliged to continue under the closeness of her surveillance.

'If you remember,' Grange said, 'you had suggested that, as a bachelor, I should improve my education in certain matters, that I should emerge from my dry study. You moved so forcefully into my own affairs that I was hardly able to gather myself sufficiently. When I understood that fact, I believed I was an external party to your own deepest considerations. I felt – sensed – that what you planned for me excluded you. I never noticed any sign or hint of natural affection from you and I believed – assumed – that you did not wish for any from me.'

How could he express such complex feelings in language, in its artificial resolutions? Language was a kind of mathematics for the emotions – the word 'affection', for example, assembled behind it a host of feelings which were inexpressible. In earlier days he would have consoled himself for his inadequacy by consulting Hume, and found some apt evocation of the imperfections of verbal communication. Now, however, he wished only for a method by which to demonstrate his feelings. 'I cannot easily express myself. You are right, madam. I am cold and formal.'

She continued to regard him and smiled perhaps for the first time that evening. 'Yes, sir, you are formal.'

For a while she seemed lost in her own thoughts, so much so that he was nervous of interrupting her train. At least, while she was engaged in consideration, she showed no sign of leaving. After a while he decided to risk an intervention, and said softly, 'There were other aspects of your behaviour that perplexed me.'

'Which other aspects?' she asked, though her voice was neutral.

'I had the impression you were attempting a lesson upon me, or that at least you were looking for something you could not find in me.'

'A lesson?' She seemed genuinely surprised. 'I would not be so presumptuous. What could I teach you?' She appeared animated. 'Nothing, I think. Nothing at all. I do not think one person can teach another anything about the heart.'

'Nevertheless,' he said, 'there was a kind of method in what you did. I wondered whether you attempted to press me to understand my own heart, my own feelings. And ever since you departed, the best part of a year now, your actions have inhabited my thoughts.'

'Which actions do you think of?'

It was more sympathetic, at least, and spoken with a certain amount of earnestness and softness.

'All your kindnesses towards me seemed to be led by a persistent goodwill, which only disappeared when I suggested I should like to marry your daughter Jane.'

'I have a view of life, it is true,' she said.

'Which would seem to include the intention that I should not propose marriage to your daughter.'

'It is not the specific which matters. It is more in the nature of an abstract.'

'Perhaps you will permit me to ask, then, what is that view?'

She regarded him directly. 'I think that matters of passion are different from those of the heart.'

'Different in which sense?'

'I believe that they come together only by coincidence. When they do, it is an occasion of great good luck, but that is all.'

'You thought, then, that I should not confuse a passion for Jane with matters of the heart?'

She continued to stare at him, but he could see nothing in those grey eyes which gave him any further clue. On the contrary, it seemed to him that she was considering his own response in the most careful manner.

In the focus of her attention he felt his will waver briefly. But now that some part of the matter had been opened to him, he was determined to proceed towards what appeared to be the final end of their conversation. 'When you sent her away, how could you have known precisely how I felt?'

'I did not,' she said simply.

'But you were certain enough, at least, that we should not see each other again.'

'Yes. I was certain about that.'

He began to see something like a pattern. 'You felt that we should be given a respite . . . from our passions?'

'For a calm consideration of your own feelings.'

'Then, madam, how could you be so certain that I felt nothing?'

She considered him a moment and he saw not amusement but concentration, and a trace of impatience, as if he were a slow learner who must be encouraged.

'Because your heart is mine.'

She had said it with such simple conviction and purity of feeling that he was momentarily taken aback. He fully expected her to qualify it with some further expression, but she let it stand, and continued to watch him and study his response, without the smallest trace of self-consciousness. Even so, he could not remain easy after such a statement, without at least attempting to press her for some explanation. Under these various impulses he smiled and, when he saw the traces of her answering smile, which seemed to be directed at his own, he smiled a little more and started to laugh quietly to himself. His laughter continued for as long as he remained astonished at the pungency of her expression, which seemed to be for some time. In the whole proceeding she continued to watch him, sometimes smiling almost shyly at his laughter, though not apparently at herself or what she had said.

He could not resist enquiring, 'These matters of the heart – they are reciprocal?'

'And what line are you pursuing now?' she asked.

'Whether one person's owning another's heart, if reciprocated, is a pure coincidence . . .'

'Of course,' she said. 'A pure coincidence.'

Then he gained an odd impression of the movement of shadows, her mouth on his. He put his arms round her and held her as tightly as he could, and it seemed all the days of the last year of waiting moved together without effort or separation. He had felt no trace of the old faintness of his illness for some time, but he felt it now, though for different reasons; his mind continued turning while they held together, her body's warmth moving through him.

CHAPTER 125

The Whiteacre had seen better times. There was a hint of grandeur in the weight of its old wallpapers. At least, at that season when winter begins to soften into spring, it was not yet thronged with other travellers. Since the establishment was a common travelling inn, set in a somewhat raffish area, its landlord was not overly concerned with the marital status of his female guests. He was intent, instead, to prevent rowdyism and its extension into violence; that was the limit of the establishment's repute, and there he considered that his responsibilities ended. An extra room was registered for Celia Quill, as a guest under Grange's own name. Not long afterwards, with a civil nod of his head and a 'Good-night', the landlord left them both, with a well-banked fire burning behind a grate in the living-room. He repaired to his own house across the common in the certainty that he had done his duty.

Once the landlord had set out on foot to his small dwelling nearby, they effectively inhabited an empty house and were left to themselves. Both his guests believed he had met his responsibilities admirably and, in the pleasant anonymity of the sitting-room, drew up two chairs and spent much of the evening in talk.

When Grange woke it was into darkness, so close that he pressed down into her, the warmth of her face and cheek on his own.

At some time in the night she called out, as if in nightmare, and woke herself up with her own cry. When her heart had calmed, she rose from her bed, put on a shift and walked to the door. She stood in the stairwell, so still that he was nervous of disturbing her. Moonlight flowed in through the skylight above the carved stair newel. Concerned about her former agitation, he had an impression, standing behind her, that she was surveying something in her mind. For several moments he observed the faint light on her shoulder, the delicate vertebrae in her back. Then, certain that she required no help from him, he moved back to the bedroom and awaited her return.

The inn was so dark that Grange had left a small flame burning on the side table on the further side of the room before he had entered the bed. He picked up the candle holder and returned to the bedside so that she could find her way back without encountering the dark furniture. Sitting on the side of the bed, waiting for her, he leaned forward and watched the flame. Under the impulsion and memory of movement, the flame seemed to crouch, nervous, between his bony hands. Then, with a trustingness that took him by surprise, it rose into the air, giving off fold after fold of light.

He was so absorbed in its unexpected illumination that he did not realise for several seconds that she was standing before him. She looked down at him, her eyes expressionless, but he sensed the meanings harboured within them, the luxurious taciturnity. The light of the candle seemed to reach towards her, lingering softly on breasts, belly, the tuft of dark fur between her legs. He had been turning thoughts over in his mind and could not help smiling again at her notion of the arbitrary nature of reciprocal love. Taken at its own pace, these and other thoughts would yield their riches. By prising them open, and then prising open the meanings harboured within them, he would come at the truth.

Without speaking, she moved silently to her side of the bed and he felt the shake of mattress as she entered the sheets. He blew out the flame and turned towards her in the dark.

There was an event the following morning, which warned him again of what he might expect from her, of the distance that there still remained for him to travel.

They had dressed and eaten a breakfast cooked by the landlord, then gone back to their room. She was turned away from him, staring out of the window at the people on the common, the family groups that walked there in the morning sunlight. At the side of the common a small procession picked its way, the patriarch in front on a large stallion, his wife a little behind him, riding side-saddle. Behind them there followed an open landau holding several children and a governess in attendance.

'Do you see her?' she asked. She looked across the common at the woman in her dark riding skirts. 'Behind her lord and master.'

He was silent.

She spoke, almost as though to herself: 'Would you wish me to be like her?'

Grange said, 'If I may speak for myself, madam, I should not wish to be like him.'

She stood without moving, gazing down on the little group. Did he detect the faint edge of amusement? Her smiles had become more common during the evening and the course of the morning. But now he could see no movement on the line of her cheek.

Yet he knew it was his business to make certain she was aware of his intentions, at the very least so that she could refuse him for good reason. He felt strangely calm in what he was about to do. 'What I propose is simply that you come back and take up lodging in your house. Your homecoming will still the wagging tongues. You will return to your previous existence, unafraid, and take up your life again. That is all I hope for.'

She continued to gaze out at park, at its denizens.

Grange said, 'You will return?'

She turned now and looked at him for several moments. He

raised his courage. 'I would offer you marriage, but I believe you would refuse me.'

He observed her faint smile again, that hardly touched her lips. The air seemed to stand still about her.

'Is that a sufficient reason for not offering?'

'No.' His heart was beating. 'No, it is not. But I am not yet ready to propose marriage.'

'And when might you be ready?'

'When you are settled once more,' Grange answered. 'When you are back in your old life.'

She nodded calmly at him, then turned to look out at the park again. He made up his mind to go back to Lymington the following day, not daring to hope.

CHAPTER 126

Several days after Grange's return, a letter arrived from Hargood, unexpected and unannounced. He recognised it from the address – the clear, bold hand with its forward sweep. The seal was half fulfilled. The writer had been able to find some inferior wax and much of it had fallen away in transit.

He took it upstairs to his study to read in the interval of the few minutes that remained before he met his first patient. He broke the seal with a paper knife, opened it out on his desk and smoothed down the pages. Five sides were covered in all, the words well-spaced, the sentences written with a sense of spareness and clarity. Grange experienced a feeling of nervous hope and a little apprehension – as he did now with many of Hargood's communications.

Before he read it, he noticed that there were several small dark trails on the paper, of gnats or little insects which had been crushed under the writer's fingers in the course of composition, and which gave him an indication of the conditions under which he now wrote.

These circumstances established, he found himself being drawn into it, so that the sound of Mrs Thompson in the kitchen faded into the background, and then his mind floated clear across the surface of the page, suspended there in the robust peculiarities of his older colleague's thoughts.

CHAPTER 127

Dear Silas,

I have established a slender base in this city, no more than a perch – a few rooms to hold my trunks and belongings, and a servant to cook for me. For the most part, having recovered my health, I have taken once again to the desert and allowed myself to wander.

I have written these pages in the evening, when the sun has departed and the worst of the heat is gone and, for a while, the light glows softly.

There is little to impede me now except the examination of my own thoughts. I have learned to live like my guides of the Ahar tribe, who cultivate the emptiness of detachment. In this, my transitory life, I carry only what is necessary – a gourd of water, a few dates and some dried meat, some writing materials – in order that I may live and eat and sleep outside the habitations of my fellow men. Though I am thin, and suffer sometimes from local afflictions, yet my mind seems to hold to its path.

There is little else in the desert but survival, and the prospect of it concentrates the mind. And if one survives, there is not much else to do except contemplate. But contemplation itself is too strong a word for the processes of my mind. I allow my thoughts to drift, and sometimes I am brought up with a start at the regions my mind inhabits, as though it wanders in a landscape of its own.

It is not as if I think continually of my own past life – for in some respects I have never been of a happier or more tranquil disposition – but rather that my mind, allowed to travel in its own direction, sometimes settles upon the events of the past. I think of you, and of Celia Quill, and of my own failures on this earth at any lasting union with a woman. These thoughts are not sad, or morbid, but part of that reflection which is both our privilege and consolation as we move nearer to our end.

Each of us searches for that partner who will fulfil the expectations of our soul. Yet it is precisely into this trap that we fall, a trap of our own making. If we cast so securely upon another the burden of our own expectations, do we permit that same soul the room to live its own life? Do we not, in that very act of expectation, create the conditions by means of which our love will be held and imprisoned?

I know something of this myself, since I hoped for a mistress who reflected my own character, who was sufficiently detached both to enjoy our companionship and to pass on when the affair was finished. This has been, if you like, my ideal. But it is my own ideal, not one which is inherent in any woman, or any that I have met. And to the degree that I understand any woman's preference, if it is not always for perfect constancy in men, it is for the consideration of her own private reserve, for intimacy of heart. Against this belief in the true commingling of souls, a man of my particular character will seem a shadow, a mere dog of his desires.

The truth may be that most of our pain is caused by this subtle crossing of expectations, and the attempted laying of one's own character upon the other. Men may be detached and gallant, and women may be intimate and faithful to their own ideals. But I do not believe in the opposite: that one sex may demonstrate in perfect form the virtues most valued by the other. Yet if we examine our expectations, that is what we drive towards, that is what we base our lives upon. In this spirit of enquiry, then, let us admit a final truth – that neither sex will ever achieve the hopes laid upon it by the other. For to men all women shall always be inferior men, and to women all men shall for ever be inferior women. So it is that we shall always war against one another, caught not so much in conflict with the other sex, but frustrated by the shadow of our expectations.

474

Yet what right have I to frame such arguments? Am I not one of those perpetual sinners who, seeing the gates of death approaching, hastily recants? What have I to offer except emptiness, the emptiness of the desert which I inhabit?

These are mere generalities which may stretch your patience. I would defend myself with more passion, perhaps, if I did not agree with any observer or witness of my life concerning my own manifest failures. Let us instead turn to the specifics. I speak now of Mrs Quill, our most estimable lady. You will forgive me if, with the benefit of years and distance, I unburden my soul as one to another, perhaps even as friend to friend. It may be that I have, despite my failures and mistakes, a small particle of experience that could be of use to you.

Her love for me, if such it was, was rooted in her character, in her very soul, and it is precisely this depth of her commitment which detached herself from me. For it seems to me now, at this perspective, that in her life she was true not to any man but to her own virtue, and her self's ideal. In this demand of hers, for which she is no more to blame than I for mine, I myself was nothing more than her passive object. If I thus display my feelings, you may perhaps deduce from this, in the kindness of your heart, that I was no more responsible for her love than any other object which felt its warmth and weight.

This is not to debase love's authority. We each of us have our own duties. So, having made our obeisance to a personal history, let us not immerse ourselves too much in the past. For the past too is passive, and each of us may read whatsoever he or she wishes from it. I prefer instead to address another aspect.

We were like opposites, she and I, and such intimacy and fellow feeling as we obtained was more an observance of the rule of adversaries than that of friends. I do not criticise or traduce what we had in common, but attempt instead to give it its proper name. We lived as man and mistress, though we were conjoined as opposing principles, united more in confrontation than in love.

Therefore, I most humbly submit, do not either of you blame yourselves for another sacrifice which should not be attributed to you. I should have left on my extended travels without that impulse to provide a little space for you, and for her, to find your own path – except for the admission that it supported my endeavour and gave some extra ballast to my thoughts. My decision to leave having been established on my own account, it seemed to me also that it were better to remove myself from the scene in good order – for a retreat is preferable to a rout – in order to allow that simple latitude to you and to her which would be most enhanced by my absence.

Show this letter to her if you wish, for nothing should separate us from a final truth which lies in our hearts. I do believe that you are suited to one another, not least because you have travelled along your own roads, and suffer fewer illusions. Perhaps you will achieve that greatest of all arrangements, a love based on a true perception of the other's character. At the very least, it would be a union of knowledge and true amity. For myself, I have examined my soul, and from this great distance I pay my honour to you both, and bless your union with my satyr's heart.

I remain, sir,
    Your affectionate friend,
        Hargood

CHAPTER 128

In Lymington in late April the weather seemed to hesitate, then grow decisively cold. In a freakish spring, frost and ice lay upon the landscape. The river froze. Sea-birds stood in small, silent groups on the ice.

In the early morning cold air, lugubrious and solid as a corpse, lay about the house.

Mrs Thompson attacked the cold with brisk ferocity. Grange could hear the wheeze of the bellows in the kitchen. Beginning with the stove, when the pots were starting to simmer above its solid hearth, she carried logs in a hand basket into the sitting-room and there set about constructing a cheerful conflagration. Room by room she advanced, until the creeping warmth, having filled the lower parts of the house, moved upwards. The beams above the chimney-breast groaned with the expansion and, after an hour or so of her ministrations, warmth appeared on the upstairs landing like a welcome guest. Grange opened his study door so that it might enter and slowly infiltrate the room.

Because the water had frozen, Mrs Thompson kept several large pots on the stove overnight, warmed by the dying fire. With these she cooked ham or mutton for his breakfast, for having made his argument in regard to a diet, he seemed content to revert some way at least towards her own preferences and recommendations. She had laid by a supply of hens' eggs and cheese in the basement. If he did not countenance meat, she would insist that he ate something else. When he had finished his breakfast and moved upstairs to his study, she followed (as though by rearguard action) with a tray of tea.

This morning, Grange wiped mist from the window and gazed on the cold, bruised land.

Something in the landscape held him, though he was not able at first to identify the source. He stood for several moments, transfixed. It was only when he surveyed the opposite shore that he observed an extra stream of smoke above Walhampton. It was no thicker than a pencil. But he was sufficiently aware of the placement of Celia Quill's house to know that it came from her chimney and, if it was not her hands which had made the fire, it would be someone who was visiting with her.

He considered for several seconds, alarmed at his own perturbation and the sudden volatility of his hopes. He walked to the door of the study and called out, 'Mrs Thompson!'

'Sir?' Her voice came from the kitchen.

'After Mr Grimshaw, is there any other this morning?'

He heard the sound of a pot being replaced and after a few seconds Mrs Thompson appeared at the foot of the stairs, looking up at him. 'There is Mrs Rennie, sir, but that is at noon.'

'Thank you. I will go out after Mr Grimshaw has left and return before noon.'

Mrs Thompson observed him for a moment. He thought she might be about to express an interest in his change of plans, but if the impulse to enquire rose in her, she clearly thought better of it, nodded perfunctorily, and left the stairwell for the interior of the house.

Grange returned to the window and gazed out. He was still engaged there in contemplation, several minutes later, when Mrs Thompson announced the arrival of Mr Grimshaw.

It seemed to him that the tracking down of Mr Grimshaw's pain, of which he was aware, but could not find a source, was like the locating of unease.

The elderly dyer, one of Hargood's former patients, had felt 'animal spirits' in his gut, a twinge of pain in his left side, beneath the heart, but by the time Grange had examined him there, the source of his unease had migrated to the other side, and had taken up a brief but temporary residence in the region beneath his right lung. Grange listened to him speak about his family and his past.

While he moved his attention from place to place on the elderly dyer's body, he could find no sign of ill health. As he tapped his chest and listened to his breathing, he considered his patient's background, at least as much as he had disclosed in conversation.

Grimshaw had owned the tannery at the bottom of the hill, whose stench sometimes pervaded the Lymington streets when the wind blew easterly. His wife having died several years before, he had retired and had handed the control of the assets to his oldest son, an unusually confident young man who proceeded to make a rapid loss in the first year of his control. It was not the loss so much that concerned Grimshaw, but the sudden lack of communication, either written or spoken, between himself and his first-born. Perhaps Grimshaw had expected to be consulted on the workings, and believed his son had not exhibited elementary courtesy. Perhaps the independence of his son's own family, with his wife and three daughters, was also unexpected. Certainly, Grimshaw felt excluded from the family whose assets he had so carefully accumulated and husbanded. The return to profit of the enterprise in the third year after his retirement had emerged as a further

478

unpleasantness, since now it seemed there was no pressing reason for the son to communicate at all.

Grange, as he pursued the strangely shifting and elusive discomforts, considered these aspects of his patient's background. Grimshaw's face was set in a pained resolve.

Grange raised himself from his inspection. 'I can find no physical symptoms. I believe, on consideration, your pain may be a symptom of your spirit, sir.'

'I beg your pardon.' Grimshaw was shaken.

'Your spirit. I do believe I am following the agitations and torments of your spirit.'

Grimshaw was perplexed. 'It is physical, then, this spirit?'

'The spirit has its physical outlets.'

'I do not think I entirely understand.'

'I suggest that wherever it is located, it will move again, precisely because it has been located. They are elusive – these spirits.'

'But what am I to do? I feel . . .'

'I have no doubt about the genuineness of the pains. I merely give an opinion about their cause.'

'Even so, I do not appreciate . . .'

'A former colleague of mine – for whom I have a great admiration and respect – when he felt such internal pains or agitations, would take himself to London . . .'

'London?'

'. . . And there commit himself to the hands of a woman.'

'A woman physician?' Grimshaw asked. 'Is that entirely decent?'

'I did not speak of a physician.'

'What, then?'

'A woman, sir.'

'You suggest . . .?'

'You ask for a prescription. Very well. I prescribe a whore – a good whore, let it be said.'

Grimshaw rose to his feet, as if he had been touched with fire. 'I will write a note complaining to the College of Physicians.'

'I am not of their body. Perhaps you would be kind enough to address your note of complaint to the Secretary of the Royal College of Physicians of Edinburgh. Here,' Grange suggested, moving determinedly to the desk and reaching towards a quill and paper, 'I will write the address for you.'

'This is an outrage.' Grimshaw backed away from Grange, the table, and the proffered quill.

'The Secretary is a Dr McLachlan,' Grange insisted, 'a most excellent man, who would treat your complaint in the utmost confidence. I hope, though of course I cannot tell, that once he is fully acquainted with the details of your malady, he might endorse my own diagnosis.'

'But not, I trust, your proposed cure.'

Grimshaw fastened his shirt, reached down and drew on his coat. Buttoning it, he moved backwards to the door. 'I believe you are overcome by a strange levity, sir. I shall attempt to forgive you.' He paused in the doorway and seemed to rally there. 'It is you, not I, who are affected by a strange spirit. I also believe I may know the identity of that spirit, sir –' Grimshaw nodded to himself several times '– and I affirm that I can tell you its name directly. Its name is Hargood. It is an interesting spirit, to be sure, somewhat vexatious and agitated, and not without its own virtues. But until now, I had thought it was a spirit that had departed these shores.'

'I thank you for your diagnosis,' Grange said.

But Grimshaw was not mollified by these words, carrying, as they did, a hint of irony. He was determined to have the last word, and now set himself squarely to deliver it. 'Given the nature of your affliction, sir – to be haunted by such a spirit – perhaps I could offer you some advice, and suggest you apply your proposed cure to yourself.'

It was a nice riposte and, when he had finished, Grimshaw nodded again, more out of emphasis at his own words than salutation and, bearing himself stiffly erect, departed across the landing.

Grange heard his footsteps on the stair, and then the slam of the main door. In the silence which followed, he allowed himself the thought, partially satisfying to his own mind at least, that the dyer's pride would heal in due course, and that perhaps he himself would benefit by not hearing from Mr Grimshaw again for a little while regarding his own mysterious maladies.

'Mrs Thompson!'

'Sir.'

'I shall walk out.'

'Now?'

'Now.'

He heard Mrs Thompson ascending the stair. 'It is beginning to rain, sir.'

She blocked his path. Her face was raised towards his in the light of the stairwell. Her bosom rose and fell.

'My overcoat,' Grange said, 'if you would be so kind.'

Mrs Thompson paused and considered him. Then she nodded once, reluctantly, and backed down the stairs to allow him to pass. In the hallway she assisted him with his overcoat in silence, so that he felt, palpably, the weight of her disapproval. He put on a large-brimmed hat that would keep off the rain.

She opened the door for him and stood aside so that he might pass to the exterior. Her eyes were cast down, yet something seemed to gather inside her. As he was about to pass her she said quietly, 'Perhaps you are in need of the same cure as Mr Grimshaw, sir.'

Grange contemplated her. It had been said softly, without any hint of insolence. But he felt the calm strength of her humour. She had weighted her statement with simple force, and now she stood waiting for him to pass, her eyes to the side, without looking up.

He paused for several further moments until her glance rose to his, until he could see there, in her grey eyes, the faint trace of her satisfaction.

'I believe you are right, Mrs Thompson.'

He waited a little longer for her smile, which was slow in coming, but no less worth waiting for – the final smile of a determined woman who has conceded defeat. They stood facing one another in the doorway.

'One day,' Grange said, 'I believe you will forgive me.'

Her expression did not change. She regarded him with her chin up, her eyes equivocal.

He nodded, almost bowed to her out of his respect, and passed through the doorway.

Outside, the soaking drizzle drained the High Street of colour. Pulling his overcoat more tightly about him, Grange began to walk down Lymington Hill.

At the Walhampton causeway and bridge he nodded at the toll-keeper, whose bees seemed subdued by the light shower, hanging in calm suspension above their hives. Turning right along the shore, he walked for hardly more than a hundred yards, then began to ascend the path that led up Walhampton Hill.

Rain stirred the dry dust at the roadside, already turning to mud. At the top of Walhampton Hill he kept to the side of the road, walking with renewed force, swinging his cane, his eye oblivious to everything except the thin trickle of smoke that drifted above the beech trees.